CW00860348

An Engineer in a New World

BEAUTIFUL HORIZON

JOSEPH B· KONRAD

authorHOUSE®

AuthorHouse™ UK
1663 Liberty Drive
Bloomington, IN 47403 USA
www.authorhouse.co.uk
Phone: UK TFN: 0800 0148641 (Toll Free inside the UK)
        UK Local: (02) 0369 56322 (+44 20 3695 6322 from outside the UK)

Published by AuthorHouse 09/28/2022

ISBN: 978-1-7283-7568-7 (sc)
ISBN: 978-1-7283-7569-4 (hc)
ISBN: 978-1-7283-7567-0 (e)

Print information available on the last page.

Any people depicted in stock imagery provided by Getty Images are models,
and such images are being used for illustrative purposes only.
Certain stock imagery © Getty Images.

This book is printed on acid-free paper.

Contents

Preface

This book came to exist because when I played *online fantasy games* back in the day on my father's old, yellowish-white computer. As an eight-year-old sitting in front of the CRT monitor, I was astonished at the way a different world could look. A whole new world awaited for me to discover. I wanted to see every corner of it, even if for just a day I wanted to walk the roads, fight the bandits, drink in the taverns. I wanted to *be* my character, to live in that wonderful and magical world.

I was always intrigued by the sense of wonder and amazement I felt as I looked at something stupendous. Even as I grew up, this childish passion never left my heart! As an engineer, I felt this same amazement whenever I made a technical drawing. That was a ceremony for me.

Whenever I read a book that described a different world in which the protagonist seemed omnipotent—one who knew everything and made drawings in a nanosecond that would take me a whole week—I was not satisfied. I wanted a story in which the world did not orbit around the hero; instead, I wanted to read about a hero who was just a small asteroid among the planets. I wanted to read about a world that reacted to a protagonist who was trying to fit into a perfectly composed chaos. I wanted to see through his eyes what the immaculate horizon would look like for the first time.

Acknowledgements

My good friend Mark helped me to achieve the type of protagonist and the type of world that I had dreamed of. He offered supportive words and pointed out illogical events in the script! Thank you, Mark!

And I cannot forget my mom and my dad, who supported me not only during the writing of this book, but during my entire life! And to tell the truth, if my mother had not encouraged me and forced me to focus on my writing, this book would have remained in the drawer. I love you two! Thank you, Mom, for your supportive words! And, Dad, I hope you will like my story!

Prologue

In the land of Hritandia, magic and magical creatures had always been common, and the largest of the magic-using races was still the human empire, which had a short but rich history and occupied almost the entire main continent.

The kingdoms of the dwarves were relegated to their island, an impregnable fortress surrounded on all sides by a roaring sea. Deep caverns on the island remained unexplored by warlike humanity.

The most ancient race in memory was that of the elves, who dwelled in a dual kingdom. Their northern domain only remained from the once magnificent holy city, hanging in fairy-tale splendour between the crown of jungle trees and the southern continent's hinterland in the midst of the elven wilderness of dazzling and enchanting Nilh'dorey.

The great peace the triumvirate—human, dwarf, and elf–had forged for themselves had been shattered by the fierce attack of the demon king and his horde. They had burrowed deep, biting into the realms of man and elf, and then marched on to increase their fearsome dominion and burn the elven holy city of the north. Kingdoms that remained in the hinterland, as well as the other human city-states, sent aid to the Hritan kingdom trapped in the front line, and with the help of this and the protection of the Bowed Mountain, the exhausted army succeeded in bringing the fierce offensive to a halt, though at a cost that was both enormous and agonising. With the destruction of the holy city and the burning of the gigantic rainforests, the remaining elves were forced to flee to the human kingdoms where their captors either enslaved them or exiled them to crowded slums. Few were able to make it to the friendly republic or the southern forests. The war had reached a stalemate, the mountain walls proved strong and unclimbable, the impeding Rodden River's current swept away anything that relied on the mighty river's power, and so the demonic hordes were held back by natural barriers. However, all it would take was one mistake, one bad strategy. If the evil creatures were to fight their way through the stones, the bloodthirsty war machine that could crush the world would be set in motion once again.

A curious coincidence was unfolding. A simple man—an engineer—was locked in his office and surrounded by his machines unaware of the hell of the bottomless battles that ravaged that other world. Jacob Taylor, a mere engineer inside a mega corporation, spent most of his days doing nothing but servicing the company's machines.

Jacob tightened the locking screw inside the machine's casing with a wrench. Half his body was soaked in grease and oil. A huge sigh escaped his lips. He clambered out of the contraption and pushed back the small door. His face was reflected in the shiny metal surface, and it gleamed back at him.

He was tired, but not in a sleepy sort of way; rather, a kind of inward, cold fatigue filled his head, and with each heartbeat it expanded further and further. He looked at himself, his upper body besmirched with oil and dusty dirt. He wiped his baggy eyes and stroked his untidy face. His stubble had grown into a beard. He glanced at the scar, a raised reddish line that ran along the back of his hand, and he remembered the moment he'd received it. Now he didn't even understand why he thought he had been destined to become a military engineer right before the war. It had not been the wisest choice. But that was in the past. He tried to soothe himself with this thought every night as he lay in his bed and tried to control his racing heart.

He clenched his hands into fists and then shook them out before he gathered together his discarded tools and piled them into his toolbox. As he finished, he heard the long-awaited whistle. The day's work was over; now he could spend some time elsewhere. He stood up and looked down at his clothes. The black cotton glistened with the yellow oil. He sighed heavily as he threw the toolbox onto his trolley and started out of the engine room.

It took him half an hour to leave the factory floor, and he headed to a changing room just beyond a door at the end of the corridor. By then it was empty; none of his colleagues was present. Stumbling, lonely in the dim light, he reached his own locker, opened the biometric lock, took out his change of clothes, and covered his hair with a towel so as not to smear it when he removed his filthy clothes.

As he took off his scruffy, metal-grated shirt, a man came through the door. "Taylor."

"Vincent."

"How come you're still here?"

"I'm always the last to leave." Taylor replied in a monotone tone.

"I know, but I was just about to close up."

"I'll be ready in ten minutes."

"Come on, man. I've got a family waiting for me at home."

Jacob just shot an angry look in the man's direction but didn't say anything.

"I didn't mean …. Just hurry up so we can go." Vincent sighed in frustration.

"Okay." Jacob nodded and stepped into the shower.

The lukewarm water arrived through many tiny holes with great pressure and began slaking the excess grease from the man's skin.

"Are you ready?" Vincent asked. He sounded bored.

"Yes. I'll walk out with my dick in my hand, shall I?" Jacob replied cynically.

"As if anyone would watch." Vincent snorted.

"My wound opened again."

"I told you last time not to use the company soap." He sighed.

"I ran out of mine yesterday." Jacob winced in pain. "I keep forgetting how shitty this stuff is." He hissed again as he scratched his skin.

"It'll be better tomorrow. It's made of one of the fat of one of the creatures—some really cheap and shitty thing." Vincent explained.

"Yes, I know, but I'll be itchy all night."

"Do you want to come—"

"What?"

"Never mind. Get dressed so I can close up," instructed Vincent.

Jacob got dressed and put on a black cloak made of thick plastic. It felt to him as if he'd just wrapped himself in a bag.

"Is it raining again?" asked Jacob.

"Almost every day here."

"Then it's the front again."

"It's better than where I was two years ago. There's nothing but dryness on the other side."

"You call it the other side when it's just the fourth block of the factory."

"Yes, I always forget it." Vincent laughed "I've hardly got any left in my canister." He sighed as he examined his bracelet.

Jacob pulled an identical canister from his own locker. It was a small device that resembled an inhaler. It contained life-giving oxygen for the toxic atmosphere.

"Here. It's half empty." Jacob threw it at Vincent.

"And what will you use?"

"I'm not expected at home," he said in a cynical tone.

"Don't joke, man." Vincent replied angrily.

"I live nearby, and it's less toxic during the rains," said Jacob as he got into the pressure chamber.

"Not a good idea." Vincent sighed.

"I'm not made of sugar."

The thick-walled door of the pressure chamber closed behind them, and the outer door opened with a slight squeeze. A strong draft of foul-smelling air came in. Jacob was used to the smell of filth. He breathed deeply to fill his lungs and get over the sickness quickly. He swayed slightly and then gasped, but he kept his posture straight.

"I can take you—" Vincent offered.

"No need. I'll see you tomorrow."

"I don't even know what time it is." Vincent laughed. "It's always midnight."

Jacob looked up at the darkening clouds from which pitch-black, dirty raindrops fell. He pulled a piece of foil over his head and stepped out into the rain, which fell with loud and heavy thuds on his head. Panting, and with slow, almost lifeless footsteps, he made his way across the car park to the monorail station, a five-minute walk. The train arrived, welcoming him into a bright, dirty world. He looked around at the empty human husks, all as dead as himself. The scene was a mirror to his now meaningless, lonely, and desolate life. He sat down in one of the seats next to a sleeping man and looked out the window opposite as the train glided over the empty factory floors. Ever-rumbling birds rose without stop from the ground as the train sped between the earth-eating, stone-crunching monstrosities of machines, themselves the size of city buildings. He raised his eyes to the small monitors where the fake-smiling slaves in brightly coloured advertisements were writhing, rejecting all human values, sometimes selling drink, sometimes food, sometimes tools that were incomprehensible from their top to bottom.

The empty, machine-infested landscape was replaced, almost in a blink of an eye, with the obscuring gloom of the towering, slender sky-scraping buildings. The train flew past the black, dirty ziggurats that jutted monolithically out of the ground over streets lined with rubbish and sometimes even human bodies.

Jacob got up from his seat, pressed the button, and held on to the door. Finally, the snake came to a stop and opened its doors. The muffled distant sound of the city, the cries of loud sirens, and the smell of used, cheap cooking oil and stale food assaulted his senses.

He tightened the foil on his head and stepped through the door. He looked up at the thick, reddish, intestine-like layer of clouds reflecting the city lights and wondered what it would be like to live on the upper floors where he could see the sun. He was jolted from this thought by a violent push. Some drunk man had bumped into him.

Jacob searched his own pockets to see if he had everything he needed and then set off into the city squalor.

He walked hurriedly on the black stones, looking at the people around him. Turning a corner, he saw something strange. Police androids, wrapped in blue and red lights, patrolled the city. Just now they had marked out the scene of a crime.

Jacob immediately crossed to the other side of the street, but he stopped to watch the events. In the dirty rain, a man knelt with his hands clasped behind his head. The two robots stood on either side of him, one of them pointing a machine gun at the man.

Jacob heard the android's mechanical voice: "QER-201432, Martin Eiser. Crime: double homicide. Time of commission: January third, eight thirty-two. Motive: known. Sentence: final. Sentence to be carried out by JP-321 patrol droid."

The machine repeated this information in a monotone tone. Finally, the second droid pulled the trigger. With a loud but muffled bang, the man's lifeless body collapsed headfirst into the mud on the street.

"Commencing clean-up." The first robot spoke again after a few quiet seconds.

Hm … is it the third already? Jacob thought. Then he turned and walked on. He chose not to watch the burning of the human bodies he had seen it more than he wanted to.

He reached the public house, which was so high it reached the clouds. He took out his card, tapped it on the scanner, and the door opened. Inside, a flickering row of lights awaited him. The place was relatively clean; only the time showed on the structure.

The further inside he walked, the louder the unbearable music became. The lift that took him up to his apartment was in the main hall. To get to it, he had to pass an annoying crowd of people, the source of the noise, which consisted of loud, booming clattering and incomprehensible shouting. The crowd consisted of a bunch of thugs in orange uniforms. One was holding a baseball bat; another was holding a firearm.

"Look who's here!" said baseball bat thug, looking up from his drugged stupor. "This is the little Jacob." He stepped closer.

"Hello," said Jacob, his eyes downcast.

"What's up, engineer? You don't dare to look at me?" The stoned bandit jumped up and down around Jacob.

"I'm just tired," Jacob replied in a shaky voice. A loud commotion sounded in the background, causing the annoying thug to move out of Jacob's way as the mob's boss stepped closer.

"Ervin, leave him be!"

Jacob just nodded and then started walking towards the elevator with hurried steps.

"Jacob!" The deep voice came from the tall man. "The arm you made is great," he continued appreciatively.

"So the dept—"

"Payed." The huge dark-skinned man stood up. "But I can't let such a talent go to waste."

"I service machines in the factory." Jacob sighed. "My job is important. You don't have to stress yourself."

"Be the mechanic of the gang, man." He put his hand on Jacob's shoulder.

"I don't consider myself that—"

"Man, you were able to disable the EMP grenade's effect on the robot arms." He nudged Jacob.

"Sheer luck. It was just sheer luck."

"Think about it. I'll give you some time, but decide wisely, man." He poked Jacob's chest with his robotic arm. Jacob knew he had just been given an offer that he could not refuse.

"I will think about it." He nodded shakily.

"That's the spirit." The half-machine man smiled.

Jacob reached the elevator, removed the foil from his head, and threw his back against the wall with a loud gasp. Then he slid down the wall and sat on the floor in panic. Clutching his chest and coughing, he raised his hand to his mouth. When he looked into his palm, he saw red blood. A strange calm came over him. He smiled, almost glad of the sign. His thoughts were empty and grey. He stood up and slapped the foil under his arm. When the cage reached the top floor and the door opened, he slipped out and hurried to his flat. He fingered the lock code and entered the small, dark, cramped apartment.

The bright light flashed on revealing a rusty interior consisting of a room that was barely the size of a hole and a small, cramped washroom opening off to the right. What a dump. He stripped off his sweat-scented clothes and threw them onto the floor. A small robot emerged from its place against the wall and picked up the clothes. Jacob stumbled into the bathroom. Stepping in front of the mirror, he stared at his sunken, thin, lifeless face, and then he began to cough and choke so violently he almost vomited. Soon, torn bloody globs appeared in his throat mixed with small black chunks—a nasty side effect of the air.

"I would have expected something quicker and more unexpected." Said Jacob lost in his thoughts as he got down on all fours and reached for the sink, which suddenly rang.

"Your health is rapidly deteriorating." A mechanical voice emanated from the sink. "Would you like some painkillers? Only four credits now."

"Give me one." He snorted.

The mirror opened after a slight noise, and the medicine appeared in a bowl.

The mechanical voice said, "Please put the—"

"I know, the bowl," he muttered.

He lay down on the bed and slowly and painfully fell asleep on the uncomfortable mattress.

The next day at work, Jacob waited in his usual corner of the briefing room for the end of the speech. Only then would he be able to leave the other people behind.

"Who wants to be with Jacob?" asked the boss. No one responded; in fact, the room fell dead silent.

I don't understand why they have to ask it every day. Are they just trying to humiliate me?

People whispered softly as they looked at him. He couldn't hear them, but he understood what they were about. No one wanted to work with a man who had served in the old army, especially someone who had been among the elites.

"Nobody?"

"Then I'm off." Jacob smiled.

He went alone to pick up his tools from the storage area as was his wont. He could hear the lies and baseless accusations that were said quietly behind his back. New recruits were always told on the first day whom to fear, and old engineers always pointed to the lone machinists who could do on their own what others could not even accomplish as a team. Jacob knew this. He'd never been a good team player; he preferred to work alone, even though it went against the company's health and safety rules. But before he had finished thinking about it, he arrived at the storage area, picked up his usual tools, and headed back to yesterday's station to start the hamster wheel again. There was always a broken machine, a bad connection, an accident.

He was thinking about the offer he had received the previous night and how little time he might have left to make a decision. Still deep in thought, he stepped around a corner not noticing a loaded forklift coming from the other side. The driverless machine shoved the loaded trolley aside with a huge crash and continued on its path straight towards Jacob. No thought crossed Jacob's mind; he felt that, whatever he did, whatever he wanted to do, the end was inevitable. He just surrendered to the cold sensation that paralysed his spine, closed his eyes, and silently, for the first time in years, felt a sense of dignity as the fork of the forklift pierced his chest and the high speed tore him in half. As his tortured body was crushed under the wheel, he felt nothing but the sweet, cold, and lonely sensation of death, which covered him like sea covering a drowning man.

"Ugh my head! The world is spinning with me."

"Sha Matrios-Satrian!" A muffled voice sounded in Jacob's head.

He opened his eyes and saw an unfamiliar woman leaning over him, looking down with a worried look and teary eyes. A sudden warmth swept across his chest. He directed his gaze to the source of the strange sensation and saw a huge spear protruding from his abdomen. Blood gushed from the wound caused by the weapon, soaking the cloth shirt that protected his body under the armour.

"What the—" His face turned moon pale. He did not cry out. He felt nothing beyond the warmth that was draining from his body.

"Sha Matrios-Satrian!" the woman shouted again, but now she was screaming from the bottom of her throat.

Jacob looked around and saw a human head to his left. It was separated from its body, staring at him with glazed eyes! He was in the thick of a battlefield, stabbed like a pig, helpless. But he felt completely empty inside. He felt no pain, just the warmth of the blood that was gushing out of him slowly. The men around him were dropping like flies, but he had little time to contemplate the horrors he had seen.

The woman—he noticed now that she was elven—pulled the spear from his belly. As if a switch had been switched, his hearing became sharp. An ear-splitting noise vibrated his eardrums. Pain shot through his body with unbearable intensity; indeed, the pain was so intense it paralyzed him. All the muscles in his body were so tight they crunched his bones. He thrust his hands to the ground but could feel only the hilt of his shield and his sword. His face remained still, but his mouth opened wide, and a soundless scream burst from his lungs.

She looked down at the tortured body and wiped the tears from her eyes.

"My lord, you can't fight anymore!" She stood over him and grabbed him by the armpits, pulling him with all her might. Jacob's strength drained from him; he fainted in the bloody heat of the battle.

Chapter 1

When Jacob awoke again, the pain was dull. He opened his eyes and gasped as if he had risen from a nightmare. A loud cry came from him, and at the sound, the woman he had first seen jumped through the tent door. Her dress was blackened with dried blood.

"My lord!" said the elven woman. "It's all right!" She stepped closer to reassure him.

Jacob clutched at his abdomen as a sharp, burning sensation flashed through him. He put his hand over the wound, and after a few moments, he raised his hand to his face and watched as the blood trickle from his hand, down his arm, to his elbow where the blanket had soaked up the red sap.

The elven woman ran out and shouted for a doctor. A few moments later, a man entered. He wore a white robe. The sleeves were bloodied up to the elbows, and the front of the robe was stained red.

"My lord, please don't move," he said softly to Jacob as he stepped closer.

"Get away from me with those hands!" Jacob shouted at him.

"My lord?"

"You want to touch me with those bloody hands?" Jacob shouted again.

"But my grace was fighting with these men before ... I hate nobles," he said irritably.

"What are you talking about?" Jacob looked at him angered in with pain.

"Oh, never mind, it just slipped out."

"I don't care about that. If you touch me with those hands, I'll die of sepsis! Disinfect your hands and use rubber gloves!" Jacob noticed the look of incomprehension on the man's face. Apparently, the man didn't understand many of the words Jacob had spoken.

"Excuse me, sir, but you must have a fever," said the white-robed doctor. "That's why you're talking like that." He stepped towards the bed.

But then the woman drew her sword and pointed it at the doctor. Sparks shot out of her eyes as she stared in the doctor's eyes in anger.

"Ah!" The doctor groaned.

"What are you doing?" Jacob shouted at her.

"I am enforcing the will of Lord Matrios!" she said determined.

Now wait a minute! Who is Matrios? What am I doing here? Ah … the forklift, right! What kind of a man is this Matrios?

"Put down your weapon," said Jacob. "The doctor is respected and honoured!" The doctor sighed as the sharp blade was moved away from his throat.

"Go and wash yourself. You're covered in blood!" Jacob ordered the woman.

"As you wish!" She stepped out of the tent. The physician gave Jacob an angry look, and then he reached for his tools.

"Wait," cautioned Jacob. "Do you have any strong liquor in this camp?"

"I can get it from the master's store."

"Get the strongest you can find!"

The doctor left the tent and returned a few moments later, panting. He was holding an ornately labelled bottle. He looked at the bottle, nodded in acknowledgement, then pulled out the cork and handed it to Jacob, who by this time had more blood on his shirt than in his body.

"Not ... for me ...for you."

"Gift?" asked the doctor surprised.

"Of course not! Wash your hands and tools with this, damn it! Are you crazy?" he shouted loudly and impatiently.

"Why?"

"I'm not going to tell you now ... later. Now, just do it."

Jacob fainted again, and the doctor shrugged. But he poured the liquid into a large bowl. He added the tools, covering them with the liquid. Then he used a bit more to clean the blood from his hands. He left a few sips in the bottom of the bottle, which he kept for his stomach.

"Eh shit! Like poison!" he said appreciatively after he drained the dregs of the bottle. Only then did he start to patch up the wound in Jacob's chest. Fortunately, Jacob had passed out and didn't have to experience the pain of the doctor's ministrations.

It was a few hours before Jacob regained consciousness. He felt weak and listless, his head pounding like a bell. Slowly, he tried to rise up on his elbows and crawl out of the bed, which was still bloody, but the blood was already dry and hardened.

"My lord!" The elven woman jumped up from her chair and ran to him.

"It's all right. It's all right." He looked towards the shelf where the small bowl of instruments was resting in the reddish alcohol. He smiled appreciatively and then leaned against the side of the bed. He tried to get up, but he floundered back onto it. "Can you help?"

"But my Lord Matrios doesn't like it when I touch him," she whispered.

"What?" He looked at her in amazement.

"My lord always said that an elf is not worthy to touch the prince." He could see embarrassment and shame in her eyes.

"Prince?"

"My lord always said. Except when he invited me into his—"

"I think I've heard enough of that!" He shouted, also feeling some embarrassment. *What a worm this guy was! Wait—prince?* "Come and help me. Now it's allowed. In fact, from now on it's allowed."

"I understand, sir," said the woman. She stepped next to the bed and helped him up.

Hm ... thought Jacob. *I seem to be the son of a noble—Lord Matrios. It sounds like that very old doll ... Never mind. Let's sum up. Somehow I'm alive and in another world. I don't know why. First I was on a battlefield, stabbed like a pig. Then here I am in a tent. It must be a camp. Don't tell me I'm in charge of something. No, I'm definitely in charge of something. What a bummer! I'll have to thank the doctor for listening to me. My wound is less likely to get infected. I wonder where I am. How did I get here? No, that's not the point! I have to survive, and that means that everyone here has to survive!*

Jacob would, from this point on, be known as Prince Matrios. He and the woman stepped out of the tent. He saw a flurry of activity and heard a constant din. The sun was low; in the landscape, only the tops of the surrounding hills were illuminated by the golden orb in the sky. But, as they stepped out of the dim light, the last of the sunlight shone in their eyes, causing Matrios's eyes to burn painfully.

"Ah, my eyes!" He raised his hands to his face, and his knees crumbled.

"Are you all right, sir?" asked the woman. "My lord?" She looked at him curiously.

"Don't mind me," he said. "Help me to the medic's tent."

"Are you sure?" She looked frightened now.

"Definitely!" he stated clearly.

"As you command!"

The two stumbled along for long minutes, and finally Matrios faced a scene of horror—the bodies of injured people crammed together. The sick and injured lay huddled on blankets on the grass. Some were wailing, screaming, or thrashing about. Others were lying silent with fever from sepsis. The sight was so horrible that words could not describe it. Blood and dirt were everywhere. Amputated legs and hands lay in a heap nearby.

Jacob felt something move towards his throat from his stomach, but he clutched at his chest and swallowed a huge gulp just in time. He struggled to retain inside him what nature seemed to want outside.

"Gather some soldiers and bring me all the strong liquor you can find in the camp!" he told the woman as he leaned on one of the poles that supported the nearest tent.

"My lord!

"I'll be fine. Go and do as I say!"

"You can count on me!" The woman saluted then ran away.

As Matrios watched the woman disappear into the distance, he was somehow unconsciously able to perceive her magical power.

There seems to be magic here, he thought to himself in wonder and amazement.

Jacob did not remain in one place long. He picked up a lance that was on the ground beside the tent. Leaning on it, he started walking towards the obviously hastily organized hospital. On the way, he picked up a clean-looking piece of cloth and tied it over his nose and mouth.

"My lord? What are you doing here?" asked an older doctor who wore a large moustache.

"Don't talk until you have covered your face with a cloth. The alcohol will be here soon," he announced.

"My lord, this is not the best time to celebrate!" an older man—a priest—said angrily.

"We're not going to celebrate. We're going to disinfect the place!

"What are we doing? Sir, do you have a fever?" The doctor touched Jacob's forehead but found no evidence of fever. "Are you all right?" he asked in disbelief.

"Your colleague washed his instruments with alcohol."

"What did he do?" The doctor looked at him angrily. "Eliott!" he shouted. The middle-aged doctor who had worked on Jacob's wound appeared again, still soaked in blood up to his elbows.

"My lord? Sir?" His face turned pale; his legs were weak. "How can you stand already? The sepsis—"

"No! He does not have sepsis!" said the old doctor with the moustache.

"May the Holy mother have mercy on us! So it is true!" The middle-aged doctor grabbed Jacob's shirt with his bloody hands. "Tell me more about this!"

"Good grief, what has got into you?" The old man pushed his companion away from the prince.

"Father Pelion! Listen to Lord Matrios! His wound was torn open a few hours ago, but he told me to wash my hands and my tools before I touched him, and I washed his wound with a little of the beverage, and he has no sepsis!"

"That's impossible!" the old man snapped.

"I have brought what you asked for, Lord Matrios!" The elf woman arrived with two soldiers who pulled a small cart behind them.

"Ah, just in time!" Jacob turned slowly. "Please use these for disinfection!" He pointed to the cart.

"These?" The priest stepped up to the cart and lifted a bottle from one of the crates therein. "Holy heavens—northern vodka! One of the strongest drinks!" He looked up at the prince in disbelief.

"Pour it out in a bowl," instructed Matrios, "and throw all your tools in it. The strong alcohol will kill all the bacteria and viruses that are on its surface so we can prevent infection."

"Baktremui? Virus. Did you hit your head as well as sustain a chest wound?" asked the older doctor.

"Let's make a deal!" Matrios said to the old medic and to Eliott, who stood a little further away.

"A deal?" asked the doctor.

"Yes. If you do as I tell you, you and Eliott can take all the credit for discovering this new method of sanitisation."

The old doctor thought for a moment and then looked deeply into Matrios's eyes. "Won't it harm people?" he asked suspiciously.

"No!" Matrios said firmly.

"Then what are we waiting for? Eliott, bring that bowl over here right now!"

"Understood!" The young doctor, with the help of several soldiers, quickly rigged up a container into which the doctors could soak their instruments in the alcohol.

Matrios thought for a moment. "I need some help," he muttered.

"What, sir!" The elven woman stepped next to him.

"Get a basin, fill it with wine, and throw in as much garlic as you can."

"Garlic?" The woman blinked curiously.

"Yes! But hurry!"

A few moments later, three bunches of garlic were floating in the vodka soup. Matrios took a leather glove from one of the crates and threw it into the liquor. He began to wash it vigorously.

"What are you doing, sir?" asked the woman.

"Waiting for the glove to soak up the alcohol. Only then will you be able to work in it. I wonder how hard it will be to move your hand while you are wearing it." He seemed completely enchanted. "Oh, by the way," he asked her, "do we have a magician?"

"Some—" the elf woman replied.

"Tauriel," said Matrios.

"Tauriel?" she said. "Sir, my name is Adalanna." She looked at him, astonished.

"It was just a joke." He laughed, puzzled. *At last I know her name!* he thought. "Could you call the magicians for me?" he asked her.

"Of course, sir!"

She ran off in what seemed like a good mood, and soon a number of ill-tempered, grey-eyed people appeared. Matrios's expectations were not met with reality when the magicians arrived. They wore armour and carried swords and shields. Most of them had coal-black eyes. They looked in the prince's direction. Others were just drunk enough to be unable to look at him.

"What do you want?" asked one of the largest magicians as he leaned into Matrios's face.

Calm down, Jacob. You've negotiated with financiers plenty of times. This is going to be easy as pie. "Please tell me how your magic works."

The magicians looked at each other, the inebriated ones sobered by Matrios's question. They looked in unison at the prince. A loud and mocking snort of laughter erupted from their midst. Some slapped their thighs. Some even fell to their knees with laughter. For minutes, the storm of noise around the fire near the hospital continued.

"Now … now … now … prince, sir … don't joke—" said one magician, almost choking on his laughter.

"It's a sure case of sepsis!" said another.

"That ogre must have got it!" said a third.

"I saw him stabbed like a pig!" said a fourth.

Insult after insult followed. Adalanna reached for the hilt of her sword and began to draw the blade out of its scabbard. Her eyes reflected her bloodthirsty intent as her gaze darted from one mage to another as if she were a beast about to exterminate everyone she saw.

"Adalanna, back off!" ordered Matrios.

She lowered her posture and looked questioningly at her lord. "But sir, they're insulting—"

"They've certainly lost a few companions in battle. This must be why some of our men can hardly stand on their feet. The loss of the battle is my fault too!"

"What do you mean, 'too'?" One of the mages stepped forward—a short, little boy. His body was covered by a thin chain mail shirt. An axe and a round iron shield hung at his side. His eyes barely peeped out from under his helmet as he looked up at the prince. "My father was killed in battle!" he shouted at the prince. "He came with me because I was conscripted! He was an old man, but he offered his services to the crown!" The boy's eyes grew watery, his voice became thin as thread, his grip tightened, and there was a look of anger in his eyes as he raised his head again. The sheer hatred in his eyes would have made a bull stop in his tracks. "My father died, and it was your fault!"

The youngster raised his arm. A water ball appeared in his small hand as he walked towards the prince. A burly knight immediately reached for the boy but could not stop him in time. Matrios caught the attack fully in his chest. He was thrown backwards by the great blow. His trajectory was stopped by a tent stake. He groaned loudly as he felt the stopping power of the hardwood along his spine.

Adalanna immediately leapt to the boy. She drew her sword and swung the blade in a twisting motion towards the child's throat. A larger mage tried to get between them in one swift leap, but before he could, Matrios roared as his lungs caught air. "Stop!" His deep and fiery roar bellowed through the ether.

Matrios struggled to his feet, his belly throbbing as if acid had eaten away at his skin, but he managed to get to one knee. He coughed up some blood, and then, with great effort, got to his feet and started to walk towards the child. Even the wounded fell silent. The doctors stopped in their work. Everyone was surprised. Matrios's bandages had become reddened again as his wound reopened and bled through the white fabric. When he reached the terrified child, he dropped to his knees and gently embraced the tiny warrior. The old and burly mage lowered his hand, which had outstretched towards the boy, and the boy began to wipe his eyes, sniffling.

"I'm sorry," Matrios said to the child. "Your father died because of me. What is your name, child."

"I am Picon, sir." The little magician's eyes were soaked with tears again, and he put his arms around the prince's shoulders. Jacob held him tight as a loud cry burst from the boy's little body. The bandage on the prince's shoulders became soaked with tears, while the blood on his belly began to trickle gently down the fabric of his trousers.

"This is my cross from now on," said the prince.

"My lord," Adalanna said, but Matrios ignored her.

"I need your help for the last time," he said to Picon. He pulled away from the boy and clenched his belly as the throbbing pain became worse.

"My help?" the boy looked at him.

"You must help me heal the people here with your magic," Matrios said with a smile.

The magicians fell silent again and looked at the prince questioningly.

"But, sir, there is no magic that can do that," said one of the oldest magicians.

"What do you mean?" asked Matrios.

The old mage held up his mace. After he concentrated for a few short moments, the head of the mace began to emit heat. Finally an aura of intense fire appeared around it in the form of swirling flames. "As you should know," he said to Matrios, "we use magic only to power up our tools, although some people are able to conjure certain spells that affect things besides their bodies and tools."

"I'm sorry, but I hit my head and a lot of things fell out," said Matrios. "Maybe the memories will come back later, but for now I need your help."

"I'm sorry, sir," said the magician. "As you saw, little Picon is a deviant. That one can use magic outside his body, but it tires him out because he has a low magical affinity."

"Is there any way to increase that?"

"It increases with time, or as we use our abilities, but there are some who don't experience any increase beyond a certain point."

"I see, and there are types of magic?"

"Elemental magic, dark magic, and arcane magic," said the magician. "It is all outlined in our grimoire." He held up an ancient-looking book bound in age-worn leather.

"I see," said Matrios. "And what is the definition of dark magic?"

"It's mostly a collective name for harmful or forbidden spells."

"Is there an opposite?"

"I don't know of any. The priests of Aludarne may know more about it, but the teachings of the holy mother are strictly forbidden to anyone who is not in the order."

"So there is a one percent chance!" Matrios stood up but immediately fell back to one knee.

"My lord, are you all right?" The mage helped him to sit on a nearby chair.

"We'll see ..." As he put his hand over the wound, blood trickled from between his fingers.

Let's see, thought Jacob. *How did it go in the online video games? Sacred magic was used in the video game he played called Paladins: Champions of the Realm. The magic was mostly associated with light.*

"Light, heal!" he shouted in a language unknown to the others present.

Nothing happened.

"Holy light!" he tried.

Nothing happened.

"Flash of light!"

Nothing happened.

"Rejuvenation!"

Nothing happened.

"My lord?" Adalanna said to him anxiously as she stepped closer to him.

Matrios raised his hand and then felt his own magic. He focused, feeling that his affinity for magic was very low and was definitely not enough.

How useless this guy is! He sighed. *The elves have always been the best at harnessing the power of nature.*

He looked up at the woman. "Adalanna!"

"Yes?"

"Would you try something?"

"What?"

"Put your hand on my wound and say—"

"Please don't—"

"You'll save my life."

Adalanna hesitated for a few seconds, then knelt next to the chair and put her hand on his stomach. He could see the disgust and revulsion on her face as the blood began to flow between her fingers.

"Repeat after me!" said Matrios.

"Yes, sir."

"Healing touch!"

"Healing touch," said the woman, unable to keep the disgust from her voice.

A huge light materialised. A magic circle began to form under Adalanna's palm, slowly building up and forming strange pictograms of magic. Then the light flickered and disappeared.

"Ah, at last." The prince breathed a sigh of relief. He untied the bandage, slowly and gently, still hissing a little. He removed the cloth from the wound, but there was no longer a hole in his skin. Only a large scar remained. It was tender, but at least it was no longer bleeding. He thought sentimentally, *Thank you online games and BNB campaigns! All those years of role playing didn't go to waste.*

"How's that possible?" The older doctor ran up to Matrios.

"Simple logic!" Matrios replied.

"It's great, sir," said Adalanna. She looked at him with a slightly glazed look, and then weakly staggered to the side, but Matrios caught her and supported her head. He smiled kindly and appreciatively at her, pride in his heart. Even though he had barely known her for only a few hours, he felt as if she had been by his side for years.

"Thank you, Adalanna. I must not forgot to tell you this. Now rest." Matrios found it strange that she had become feverish in the blink of an eye. Also, the clothes on her body were soaked with sweat.

Matrios took the woman back to his tent and laid her down on the freshly made bed. As he glanced on the floor, he felt nothing but heart-breaking shame and deep contempt for himself. There was a blanket on the ground size of a human with a dirty pillow. He found a bucket of fresh water, dipped the small towel he found on the bedside table into it, and washed her face with the cool water. But he couldn't bear to look at her any longer. Even knowing that he was not really the same person, he was disgusted with himself. Matrios stepped out of the tent, looked around, then glanced at his own hands. He remembered everything he had learned about his new self, clenched his hands into fists, and was seized with a sickening disgust. But he had no more time for himself. The old mage and the priest immediately attacked him and began to ask him thousands of questions.

"How is this possible!" asked the priest.

It is a miracle! I tell you, it's a miracle!" said the doctor, grabbing the mage's breastplate.

"How is that possible?" The knight pushed the medic away.

"Very simple," said Matrios.

They both leaned in closer so as not to miss a word.

"I have no idea."

"Huh?" said the priest as the two old men looked at Matrios.

"Let's make a deal," Matrios said with an evil glint in his eyes. "Father Pelior will follow my instructions in the care of the sick, and you—"

"Let's just stick to Verilion. It seems the prince has forgotten my name too."

"I'm sorry," offered Matrios. "There really is a lot left out." He scratched the back of his head. "Verilion will make his mages available to me. I will select some of them, and together we will survive until the end of the offensive when we push back the enemy. Then I will tell you the course of the healing magic, deduced and described. What do you say?"

"You think you have a chance of winning this?" Verilion looked at the prince in disbelief.

"Let's just say I want to bring as many people home as possible."

"If that were true," mused the magician. "I don't think we can hold off their army—"

"I have a plan, but first I need to go to the general's tent and discuss it with the leadership," Matrios said thoughtfully.

"Hmm … I never thought that the vulture would eventually turn into an eagle, even if only for a moment." The magician nodded in acknowledgement. "You have my men, but don't you dare send them to their deaths, or I'll kill you myself." The big mage looked down at him with a serious face.

"My plan is to win this battle with the fewest amount of casualties." He looked back at him with an equally serious face. "What was that vulture thing, anyway?" he asked, letting himself go.

"Don't you even remember?"

"Not really."

"Uh … there's a demon bird-beast out on the battlefield. It has been there for a few days and was given to you by his majesty. His default form is that of a small blackbird, but he can transform into a huge predatory vulture taller than a man." As the big knight described the creature, he seemed lost in his thoughts. "That's how you became the Vulture Prince," he explained with a sigh.

So, I have a bird that's not exactly pleasant to look at. I wonder if there's any way to call it.

"Let's leave that for later," said Jacob. "Time is of the essence! Bring all your magicians to the infirmary."

"I will."

Chapter 2

As night fell, the world became quiet. The tired people hid behind the narrow stone walls and the gates desperately and anxiously awaiting a direct attack from the demon hordes. But deep within the rear camp, a spark of wonder flickered amidst the whirling of the hustle and bustle. Hope arose, and that hope was none other than the prince, who seemed to have undergone a miraculous change. He now treated everyone with intelligence and kindness. He said things no one had ever heard before.

"My lord!" said the old magician Verilion. "I have brought all thirty-six of the remaining knights."

"Marvellous! Thank you, Verilion." Matrios held out his hand to Verilion, who also served as a knight. Verilion reluctantly and in surprise took Matrios's small hand in his huge gauntlet.

"May I know what you are planning?" asked the knight.

Matrios took the measure of all the mages who appeared, each in full gear, helmet in hand, standing before him with firm stances and unwavering pride. Matrios compared their strength and magical affinity to Adalanna's, and with one or two exceptions, they all far outweighed her.

"Wonderful!" He clapped with appreciation. "Strip down," he said with a smile that melted the pride from each knight's face.

But before he could say anything else, Verilion grabbed his shirt. "You think this is a joke!" he snapped in anger.

"Of course not! They'll help at the hospital. They'll do the same thing Adalanna did!"

Then Verilion let go of the prince. Still angry, he remarked, "A knight's shield is his home, his armour his skin, and his sword his life!"

"True, but they cannot concentrate their magic when they are wearing armour."

"What?"

"I can feel the energy radiating from all of them. The magic is constantly evaporating from the armour."

"I forgot to mention that, every moment we wear it, we imbue them with magic. It's so basic to us that I forgot—"

"And we'll have to cool them all with water."

"What does that mean?"

"When I picked Adalanna up, I noticed that her body temperature had risen alarmingly in an instant. It seems that the healing spell requires a lot of energy and works suddenly. This takes a toll on the body, so if we cool the body, we can work more efficiently."

"Hm …" mused Verilion. "Men! Take off your armour!"

One of the female knights spoke up. "But, sir, some of us are women."

Suddenly silence fell over the camp.

"Go and come back in long clothes if you can," he advised, "If none are available, you will have to wear trousers!"

The women followed orders, but both Verilion and Matrios's faces turned red.

"Verilion," said Matrios. "I'm sorry. I didn't think about that."

"Oh, no worries. I wouldn't have thought about you, knowing you."

"What?"

"The Whoremonger."

"What?"

"Nothing! I'm going to take off my armour too!"

"Are you not coming to the commander's tent?"

"All hands are needed, and I'm interested in your theory anyway."

"No, no, no! I need you to help me with the commander."

"No. I didn't say I'd help you with that." He turned back with a smile. "But for certain … things, I'm happy to offer my services."

Matrios had begun to think of himself as Matrios despite his misgivings. He sighed deeply and wearily, then put his hand to his side and spoke slightly angrily. "What do you want?"

"A city!"

"A city? I tell you how to heal and you want a city?"

"It's not certain that we'll survive. If not a city, then at least a village!"

It can be arranged, Matrios thought, but before he knew it, Verilion had already cut the deal and laughed.

"All right, I'll meet you at the tent at the top of the hill. In the meantime, make good use of my men." Verilion waved back as he continued on his way.

Matrios went back to the hospital tent where the magicians were waiting in an unbroken line, the women in skirted dresses that reached the ground. Their backs were arrow straight, but under the fabric, their well-shaped bodies, made so round and desirable by years of training, were still visible. Even Matrios's mind was lost in the vast sea of thoughts, but he shook his head and buried his face in his hands.

"Ladies, you could have kept your leather pants on," he said disappointedly.

The knights looked at each other. One of the female knights stepped forward. With clenched fists, the beautiful woman spoke. "Next time, speak up sooner and give orders clearly."

"Excuse me," said Matrios. "Next time I will." He shook his head.

Hmm ... maybe I should allow myself a little bit of stage presence. It can't go wrong. How was it? He went deep in his thoughts before he spoke. "Honourable knights, I have called you here tonight by the drowsy light of torches to ask your help in saving your comrades. As you have already seen or heard, we have found a way to save those caught in the evil scythe of death." He turned away from the crowd and bowed his head. "Give us your blessed strength to save these soldiers and give them another chance to see the morning after." He turned back with tears in his eyes. "I beg you, knights, save the kingdom's brave warriors!"

Complete silence and stunned faces greeted him as he looked up.

"I fucked this up!" He snorted.

The knights burst out in tears. Sniffling but not letting go of their hold, they raised their hands to their hearts and said one after the other. "For the kingdom, for our comrades!"

"What are we waiting for?" yelled another.

"I will heal as many as I can, as long as I can stand," said one knight.

"As long as my heart beats!" said another.

There were throaty roars, and the soldiers standing in a circle were also caught up in the frenzy. They began cheering and urging the knights on. They made a noise that could have woken the whole forest. The light of hope now shone forth with such power it was as if a new star had been born.

"What must we do?" said one of the knights with a challenging shine in his eyes.

"Bring the buckets!" said Matrios.

At the prince's word, soldiers started filling buckets and barrels with ice-cold water. The magicians were surprised when a pile of water barrels were rolled up behind the prince.

"I will tell you how to use healing magic! I need a volunteer!" shouted Matrios.

Picon, the little boy who had shot the noble man in the stomach earlier in the afternoon, stepped out of line. When Matrios saw the kid, he stepped forward and patted him on the head and thanked Picon for his help. "Your element is water, right Picon?"

"He knows his name! The prince has memorized his name!" someone in the background murmured.

"Yes, sir!" replied the boy, straightening his back.

Hmm ... deviance seems to cause a surplus of extra magic and better magic affinity, thought Matrios to himself.

"You're all right Picon," said Matrios. "I want you to stand next to the doctor with a cloth mask over your mouth. Then I want you to imagine your hand spurting water at the blink of an eye. As you do this, shout 'Healing wave!' at the top of your lungs!"

"Understood, sir. But why do we need the—"

Matrios reached behind him for a bucket and splashed the boy in the face. The boy stood there soaking wet and in shock. "It's cold," he said, shivering.

"Be quick before you catch pneumonia!" Matrios smiled at the boy. "My little hero!" He grinned at the child.

Picon walked over to one of the beds. The doctor Eliott was standing next to the bed, his eyes showing helpless rage as he looked at the man's broken head. The man was only able to grunt and drool. The young boy stepped into an offensive stance and looked at the injured man, staring into his hollow eyes. Feeling his stomach clench, he gathered all his strength into his left palm and swung his hand, screaming at the top of his lungs, "Healing wave!"

Sweetly shimmering waves splashed out from the palms and fingertips, drenching the man's entire body, and then tiny, droplet-like magical circles appeared all over the surface of the man's torso. At the same time, a larger, blue-tinged circle appeared on the top of his head. The cloth dried on Picon's body in the blink of an eye, but what was more interesting was that, when the little circles of light disappeared, the man groaned and gasped for air like a drowning man breaking to the surface. He panted like a beaten dog, gasping. He seemed completely confused. Eliott pinned him to the bed and held him there, and when consciousness returned to his eyes, the twitching subsided and he spoke. "Where am I?" he asked quietly.

The soldiers and the knights were frozen, standing with stunned faces, their feet rooted to the ground. Matrios alone stood with a smug smile and a proud look. Picon shuddered. With tears welling in his eyes, he ran to one of the barrels and threw himself into it. Jacob was taken completely by surprise at this movement. The barrel toppled over and, like a gale of wind, the little child burst out of it and with both hands held out in front of him, shouted even louder at the sick beds.

The patients who were hit by the water spray, which was much stronger and larger in volume than the previous attempt, sat up and recovered one after the other. After the small circles had disappeared, some of them were almost carried away by the fever, but they breathed deeply, filling their lungs. They had recovered from death.

Picon's clothes were completely dry again, but he was panting and weak on his feet.

"Impossible! I cannot believe my own eyes, Prince!" shouted the deputy commander of the knights as she stepped in front of Matrios.

"Eh?" Matrios was startled by the woman's loud roar.

"What must I do?" she asked.

"What is your speciality?" he asked, terrified.

"Fire!" she replied urgently.

"I don't think we can use it," he told her.

"Understood." She let him go, and it was obvious how disappointed she was.

"Wait a minute!"

"Yes!" she looked at the prince, hopeful again.

"Fire is a flame. Maybe it's worth a try!" The prince shrugged. "Point at a man and shout "Holy flames!""

"Certainly!" The knight shoved the now-powerless Picon away from the barrels. She reached for a bucket and soaked her clothes completely. The way the garment fitted her body highlighted every curve that had not been visible under the linen. The soldiers stopped talking and changed the direction of their gaze in an instant. They cheered both the knight and the prince. The woman ignored the scrutinizing gazes. She stepped up to one of the men who held his severed hand was in his lap and pointed at him with her hand.

"Wait, wait, wait!" Matrios ran to her.

"What is it?" The woman asked impatiently.

"Eliott!"

"Yes, sir?"

"Could you sew this man's hand back on?"

"I don't think so, but I can try," said the doctor.

"Just stay there," Matrios said clearly to the injured man.

"I'll try!"

Eliott began his attempt to reattach the man's hand. The man, who had been sitting in silence and grief, cried out loudly as the needle was driven deep into his hand. By the time Eliott had finished the horrendous operation, the man was a writhing, panting lump of flesh.

"Now!" shouted Matrios to the female knight magician.

"Holy flames!" she shouted loudly as she raised her hands in triumph.

A jet of fire started in the injured soldier's direction, and a blinding circle of light appeared in her palm, growing stronger and stronger, and summoning a new sun to the earth. The circle of light suddenly disappeared. The flames did not die down; however, the injured man's scream grew louder and more intense. The woman faltered for a moment, but Matrios caught her hand and held it towards the soldier. When at last the fire died down, the soldier, now fully recovered, sat with his eyes closed in the middle of a burnt-out magic circle. Both his hands were raised to his face, shielding it from the blinding fire. Both the knight and the prince were surprised, but not as surprised as the healed soldier. "My hand! My hand!" he cried as he witnessed the miracle.

"It's witchcraft!" Father Pelion collapsed. "It's-it's not—"

"I did it!" The woman cried out, her body and clothes dry as bone. The right sleeve of her billowing tunic was burned to the elbow.

With a smug grin, Jacob handed guide notes to the knights, at least to the ones who could read. Each of them had different abilities, and if they felt their legs were shaking, they had to stop, however much strength they felt. The water elemental mages were the most helpful, for their magic was able to work in harmony with the healing effect.

"That's it," Matrios ordered everyone. "Carry on, but don't let me hear of anyone overdoing it!"

"Affirmative!" returned the deputy commander as she turned to them. "You heard the prince," she shouted commandingly. "I'll beat the shit out of anyone who thinks he or she can get away with the break!" All the knights responded with loud grumbles.

"Well, I think I have my biggest battle ahead of me," said Matrios. He turned and left the hospital area where the previously desperate and broken people were once again filled with joy and a zest for life.

Matrios walked slowly along the torch-lit grassy path, which was almost as wide as a road. Thoughts of how he was going to convince the generals, who thought they were more sensible than he, were going round in his head. What would he bring against them, for he remembered nothing of the preliminary discussions that had taken place before his arrival. He knew nothing of the terrain or the enemy. But he knew one thing. He must win at any cost! Finally, he arrived at the commander's tent. Two guards were stationed at the entrance with halberds in their hands. They looked at the prince. The sound of the discussion happening inside grew louder.

"Whatever happens, just listen—" began Verilion.

"This bloated blister has caused us to lose a lot of men, at least two thirds of the garrison!" said the angry moustached general.

"I know, sir, I was in the battle!" said the old magician Verilion.

"Then you know what a buffoon we're dealing with! I hope he dies of sepsis and gets on with it—"

The two guards stood aside and allowed Matrios to enter the tent.

"I'm afraid that won't happen!" Matrios stepped into the middle of the heated argument, interrupting the bald general.

"Oh, sir ... I-I don't—" stammered the general.

"Don't apologise." Matrios stepped to the edge of the table. The disputing people was standing on the other side of the table.

"I did not mean—" again began the general.

"Whatever you meant, sir, you are right. When I came to your territory, my inexperienced decisions cost the lives of your people. Please forgive me. From now on, I will listen to you as a more experienced individual." Matrios bowed low. His posture, though not gentlemanly, showed humiliation.

"Please raise your head, Prince. There is no need for that." said the general.

"What I have done, I have done," said Matrios. "And the fates and deaths of many people are on my conscience. I don't know why my father sent me here, but I do know that I need your help to achieve his objective!"

"Mostly they send people here to die." A young man spoke from the background where he had been sitting quietly. His black hair was tied in a bun at the back of his head, and he was wearing green clothes tied at the waist by a black silk sash. He was playing with an arrow and throwing it at the post opposite him as he spoke.

"Keratrin!" The man with the moustache spoke again. He was huge and wiry, but his muscles were well kept despite his age.

"I'm only telling the truth," said Keratrin. "I'm the seventh child of my family. The prince is no more than the fourth heir. We don't stand a chance. You are an outdated knight of the White Lion Order that was disbanded long ago. The mages were also on the verge of disbanding their order. It's no coincidence that there are so few doctors in the garrison." He sounded bored and uninterested.

"But please!" the general said angrily.

Matrios laughed.

"What's so funny about that?" The younger boy looked at him.

"I was just thinking how funny it would be if we called ourselves the army of underdogs," remarked Matrios in a condescending but firm tone. He looked straight at the young man.

"He …. It's ridiculous even as a joke."

"And yet we'd show the kingdom what we're made of," reasoned Matrios.

"What we are made of?" retorted Keratrin. "Didn't you get to experience first-hand what it's like to be stabbed? Wait, how did you come to be on your feet?"

Matrios took off his shirt, untied the bandage from around his body, and showed the scar, now slightly red and tender, almost blending into the white skin of his body.

"Impossible!" Keratrin jumped up in disbelief, but the Old Lion Edalin was able to hold himself and looked at him with a surprised gaze.

"My knights?"

"If they keep going like this and stay so determined, we might be able to close the infirmary in the morning," Matrios said as he put his shirt back on.

"Hehe! That's good to hear!" Verilion laughed.

"What does that mean, Verilion?" the Old Lion shouted at the man.

"Shall I tell you or show you, Old Lion? But maybe your heart can't take surprises anymore." He elbowed the nobleman in the side.

"Show me the way!" The Old Lion pointed towards the exit.

Keratrin and the Old Lion were walking at such a pace that Matrios almost had to run after them. Their destination was unmistakable, a constant flickering of lights and a loud noise marking the spot where they were heading. When they got there, a good number of the thousands of wounded soldiers were still lying on their beds. Ten or fifteen soldiers were on the verge of exhaustion as they carried buckets of water and rolled barrels of water from the well.

Already a full line of men had lined up to help as cooks. Someone had to work to satisfy the hunger and thirst of the knights. It all seemed like orchestrated chaos as the knights urged each other on.

"You can do it!"

"Just one more, you can do it!"

"Hold on, one more this time!"

The words reflected the exhaustion of the soldiers. Those who helped to move the healed, carry the wounded, and help the doctors who were tired but determined. The grass was being trampled to mud, but the constant heat of the magic immediately dried it.

"Father!" The deputy commander ran towards Verilion panting.

"Dana? Report!"

"I … can …barely …stand …but at least ten …people—" The woman collapsed in exhaustion and gasped for breath.

"She's hyperventilating!" Matrios said.

"What's she doing?" said Verilion. He was worried as he fell down and held his daughter in his arms.

"Dana!" said Matrios calmly. "I'll show you how to breathe. Follow me!" Matrios started to breathe slowly and rhythmically, and she followed him. After a few seconds, she managed to imitate him completely and finally came to her senses.

"Excuse me," she said, shaking her head.

"Why are you so wet, girl!" asked her father.

"Lord Edalin—" The deputy commander looked at the old lion. "I apologize for appearing before you in this state," said Dana. "All I know is that it will help me to help more people." She sat up and looked at those in front of her. "If you'll excuse me …" She leaned on her right knee as she tried shakily to get on her feet.

"Take a break. Whoever has this problem, stand back and show them what I have shown you," Matrios said.

"Understood." She turned around and waved kindly.

"What's going on here?" Keratrin looked around.

"The Prince's merit—and mine!"

"Yours?" The Old Lion's eyes zeroed in on Verilion.

"Yes! Healing magic!" He puffed out his chest proudly.

"You're lying!" said Keratrin in disbelief.

27

"Don't call me a liar, sir, or I'll hit you in the head with my mace," the big knight threatened.

"I apologize for my outburst."

"The point is, we've learned that magic can heal," Matrios commented.

After they observed the entire chaotic scene, the leaders headed back to the tent, walking slowly and deliberately. Lord Edalin and Verilion walked in front of them, talking. Matrios thought they had known each other for a long time, but he didn't have much time to think because Keratrin caught up with him and started a conversation.

"Are you sure you're the Matrios I've heard so much about?" he asked, looking at him suspiciously.

"I don't think so. Since I woke up after my injury, I feel different somehow."

"You woke up?"

"After the battle."

"Oh, I see!"

"Honestly, I've lost a lot of my memory. I don't remember much. I don't remember the battle at all. I only remember Adalanna pulling the spear out of my belly. That's it."

"Was it too much for you?"

"Who would like a spear sticking out of his belly?" he asked hesitantly.

"I know what you mean." Keratrin laughed.

Ah, well, he doesn't think I'm strange, Matrios thought to himself.

"But still," continued Keratrin, "you were more into women and wine. How did you find that out?"

"I don't know... maybe the truth is in the wine?"

"I don't think so. Maybe when you stood in front of the Holy mother that made you come to your senses?"

"I don't remember anything like that. I only remember a loud bang and nothing else."

"Bang?"

"Don't worry about that." Matrios dropped the subject. "The most important thing now is to survive."

"The army of underdogs?" Keratrin smiled.

"I see you like that."

"As I like most of your stories, especially the ones about brothels." He smiled.

"Yes, it would be good to remember those, certainly."

They arrived at the tent, entered the lighted interior, and sat around the table that held a map of the garrison and the surrounding terrain. The Old Lion Edalin started to sketch the situation, but then Jacob noticed something. Edalin shared the current situation with him. He had learned that the gorge was a possible crossing point for the demons. They had thought it a natural barrier to keep them at bay. The mountains were impassable, and they towered directly over the demon realm, completely unclimbable from that side. There were more gorges, but they were much harder to get through, so this was the one most likely to be attacked by the demons.

"How long can we defend our lines?"

"Under constant attack, with current morale and equipment, a week at most." Edalin said. "The gate can take the strain because it is reinforced with steel as thick as a palm."

"I'd like you to tell me about the enemy," Matrios said.

"I can help you with that," Keratrin said from the background, and he stepped over to the table. "The enemy camp is not too far away, between the foothills and the forest, and we can't reach them from here. Their numbers vary from about five thousand to eight thousand."

"What's their morale?"

"They're not very cohesive," Keratrin continued. "Many of them are constantly on the run so there's nothing exact. That's why we told you not to ride out against them."

"Yes," said Matrios. "I'm very sorry—"

"This is not the time." Keratrin sighed.

"Yes. Now let's make a plan," said Matrios. "Does the mountain protect their camp?"

"Yes, it leans over them a bit."

"How high is the mountain?"

"Nobody knows. We don't even know why it's shaped the way it is. There are legends that it was made that way by a powerful mage when humans and elves were at war to protect his people, but that is only a myth now."

"Whatever the truth is, it is not important now. The only thing that matters is that this mountain will be the key to our attack."

"Our attack?" asked Keratrin.

"We will climb the mountain!" Matrios said as if it should be obvious.

"That's impossible!" Edalin slapped the table angrily.

"So is healing magic," Matrios retorted.

"What do you mean?" Keratrin asked.

"I suppose you've never climbed a mountain."

"I have, but we can go only on safe paths, and there's a lot of vertical terrain. It would be impossible to move a full team."

"Hmm ... interesting. Do we have any blacksmiths in our camp?"

"All of them are busy repairing weapons and armour."

"No problem. Two should be enough to do what I want."

"What is it?"

"A climbing iron." Matrios said clearly.

"What?"

"It's a metal sole that can be attached to the boot to make climbing easier."

"How does it help?"

"At the beginning on our side, the hill is not so steep and climbing is fairly easy. But after that, it's just too steep for anyone to climb. That's where this tool will help us. Get some paper and pencils."

Edalin handed over his personal writing tools, a rudimentary pencil and a thick piece of parchment. Matrios took the arrow from Keratrin's hand that Keratrin had been playing with. He tore off the feathers and set to work using the shaft as a ruler. He drew for about half an hour. Verilion fell into a deep sleep on the chair, snoring deeply. One of the candles burned out as Matrios worked, but when he was finished, he produced a technical drawing that explained what he wanted the smiths to produce. He had included three points of view and several small explanatory asides.

"It was worth sitting through Mr. Albert's drafting lessons!" said Matrios as he wiped his eyebrows proudly.

"It is wonderful!" Keratrin announced excitedly. "It is finished!" His rowdy response awoke the sleeping magician.

Keratrin took the parchment from Matrios's hand and began to study the drawing. He scratched his head for a few minutes, but Edalin snatched it out of his hand and began to study it himself.

"I don't think anyone could make this." Edalin examined the parchment.

"Your smiths aren't good enough?" said Matrios with a smug smile.

"What?" Edalin snapped with an irritated look.

"You say they aren't good enough to make this." Matrios sighed in disappointment.

"You bastard! My blacksmiths are not village bumpkins! Their leader comes from the king himself and is the half elf named Miraklios! A famous blacksmith far and wide! Give him this technical drawing. At once!" The Old Lion Edalin shouted angrily.

As I thought, Edalin values his men and their skills. No wonder they've held out so long, Jacob thought to himself happily.

Edalin stormed out, his face red and steaming. He carried the rolled-up parchment in his hand, swearing in such a way that a snake could envy his forked tongue. He moved through the camp like camphor, his magic flushing out of his body vigorously. He pushed whoever stood in his way aside, and he did not stop until he reached the forge. He stopped in front of it and sniffed the air, detecting a stale smell and the stench of alcohol coming from the woodshed. The coal had long since gone out as the man lay on a crate beside the anvil. His face was stained with a blush from too much wine.

"Miraklios!" Edalin spoke softly. No response. "Miraklios!" He raised his voice, but again there was not a tremor. Edalin lifted the big hammer with one hand and struck the anvil with it. Sparks shot out as the two metals met and the sound rang out in a way that should have awakened even the dead.

"I'm up … I'm up!" The fat man rolled off the crate.

"Miraklios, I have a job for you." Edalin looked at him with an unresisting expression.

"Are you asking me to hammer out some more armour?" the smith looked up, annoyed.

"No!" Just as Edalin thrust the parchment into the man's hands, Matrios arrived. The dirty smith opened the parchment, and his eyes became teary.

"Ah, what a beauty!" he sounded excited.

"Can you make it?" Matrios asked.

"I've gotten a little rusty over the years, lad, but don't call me Miraklios if I can't create this masterpiece!" The fat blacksmith stood up, and the wine blossom disappeared from his face. His entire face turned red, and steam billowed from his nose as he rose to the challenge. "You may not recognise me as I stand here, but you are looking at the former Miraklios, the half elf who forged your father's armour! I will stop drinking if I can't create this!" he cried.

He turned to face the nearby building "Gertrude! Fire the coals and fetch my hammer, girl!" A huge woman stepped out, her hair red, her face black with soot, her hands the size of a hammer's head, her shoulders like Miraklios's. But her skin was tight, her muscles bulging.

"Coming, Father! What is all this anvil flapping?"

"Look at this!" He handed her the drawing, overwhelmed with joy.

"What complexity!" She said in wonder as she looked at it. "Who made this?"

Edalin and Keratrin both pointed at Matrios, and their faces drained of colour at the question.

"Good sir, I'm so happy to finally not have to do small jobs!" She kept her distance. Matrios didn't understand why; he thought maybe she was bowing down to the noble or something.

But Edalin perked up and looked at the fat blacksmith. "Miraklios!"

"Yes, sir?"

"This is a challenge from the prince."

The blacksmith's face darkened and his eyes brightened. He bared his remaining teeth ominously. "I'll show him what I know!" He accepted the challenge.

Matrios's face turned joyfully serious. "But don't you dare disappoint me!"

Keratrin yawned softly in his weariness and then beckoned to the prince. "I'm going back to my tent."

"I think I will do the same."

So the two younger men started towards the enclosed tents, Keratrin trying to extract information from the prince about what he had seen, where he had obtained his knowledge, and how he could draw plans so well. Matrios, of course, either evaded the answers or tried to put together some explanation that made sense from the little information he had, but the ordeal was interrupted as the prince approached his tent.

As Keratrin stepped up to the prince's tent, through the half-opened entrance he saw the elven woman sleeping on the prince's bed. The noble boy started to chuckle.

"I don't know who you are now, Matrios, but I prefer this side of you." He gave Matrios a mocking grin and turned on his heel to leave.

What's got into him? Matrios looked after Keratrin in the torchlight. He opened the tent and entered, noticing by the light of the mysterious candles that the beautiful woman was snugly dozing on the bed. He paused for a moment, wondering if he should sleep on the floor, but he saw nothing in the dim light of the evening. Most of the candles had long since burned out; only one flickered beside the bed, and that too flickered. Feeling his feet begin to ache and his shoulders grow heavy, he gently pushed her body to one side of the bed and lay down beside her, spreading the blanket over only one leg. The call of sleep was so terrifyingly strong, he didn't even have time to think about the following morning and the consequences of sleeping in the same bed with the elven woman. As soon as the back of his head touched the pillow, all his worries were gone. His body relaxed, and he felt comfortable at last.

Chapter 3

Around noon the next day, Matrios regained consciousness. He had been snoring in his sleep, but he began to feel a strong pressure in his groin. It felt as if the entire world was on top of him, and he could feel the earth spinning around him. He opened his eyes slowly and sleepily, and when his vision finally cleared, he noticed what was happening around him. Adalanna was towering over him. Her face was all red. Soft, erotic moans escaped from her cherry lips. Her breath was as hot as volcanic steam, and her hair was falling in his face. He froze completely, unable to move or utter a word. Only his eyes were wide open. The drops of sweat glistened on her ashen skin in the mysterious light of the candles, and he felt as if he was being embraced by angels. And yet the feeling was so fabulous, he thought he was still dreaming. But soon consciousness came to him and took control of his body. He opened his eyes, grabbed her side with his hand, and gently pushed her away from him.

"My lord, are you awake?" she said, panting.

"What … What are you doing?" he asked in disbelief.

"What you always tell me to do in the morning." she replied, a little puzzled.

"Please. Get off me," he said firmly.

"I did not do it ri—"

"Not because of that!" he interrupted her.

Adalanna cautiously pulled away from him and covered herself with the white duvet.

"Not … That's why—"

"Don't you want me?" she asked, a bit startled.

"I do," he answered firmly and thoughtlessly. "You—do you want me?" he murmured.

"Every morning you comm—"

"But do you want me?" he asked again, impatiently.

Adalanna remained silent and closed her eyes. Her cherry lips tightened in shame, but Matrios was relieved to see her reaction. "I thought so."

"I do, sir," she murmured.

"It's all right, Adalanna. From now on, just do what I ask you to do for me."

"What do you mean?"

"If you would like, I'll give you a handful of gold, and you can go. With that, you'll be able to buy yourself a new life. You won't have to worry, and you can be yourself." He looked at her and gave her a kind smile.

"But, sir I have nowhere to go. After the demons destroyed the elven cities and slaughtered everyone I knew … after …" She started to cry softly.

"I'm sorry," muttered Matrios.

"I have no one. I have nowhere to go. You saved me."

"Hm?" His eyes widened.

"From the merchant—when my lord was young."

Matrios remembered the moment when the man he had now become was perhaps eight years old. A woman who might have been his mother took him to a slave trader and found the little elven girl who even then seemed much older than he was. He chose her as he would have chosen a kitten, and they took the frightened girl to the castle. He remembered the feeling; it was nothing more than what he would feel at being given an animal. Matrios was seized with nausea; he was again disgusted with himself. What meant life to one was to another merely the selection of a pet. His stomach clenched, and his hand clasped over his mouth. He was so angry at the mere recollection of the memory that he could have killed himself in revenge, but he looked again at the woman whose eyes, sad though they were, gleamed gratefully in the dim light of the candles. Matrios understood. This was not his world anymore. These were not his rules or manners. This world was different in everything; not only in the races, but the mentality of the different residents and their lives were different as well.

"I'm sorry. I'm so sorry," Matrios said with sorrowful eyes as he sat on the edge of the bed, not daring to look into her eyes even though he knew it was not him who had done wrong, but someone else. Now he wore this body and with it the crosses born by the person who once inhabited it. He buried his face in his hands and tried to hold back his anger. Adalanna snuggled against him from behind, the touch of hot skin as smooth and pleasant as a sip of cool water in the Sahara. He lifted his gaze from his hands and sighed heavily.

"That's why I was able to endure anything," she said, soothing him.

"But—all of it. I'm so sorry."

"Please, don't ever change back," she whispered.

"I won't. I promise," he reassured her.

Matrios got up from the bed and dressed, never turning back to the bed where Adalanna sat, covering herself with the sheet somewhat nervously and embarrassed.

"And who undressed me?" he blinked.

"I did." She pulled the sheet over her head.

"Aha!" He cleared his throat and continued dressing as if nothing had happened. "Get dressed and meet me at the camp when you've had breakfast!" he told the woman as he stood at the entrance to the tent.

"I'm sorry, sir. I'll be ready in a moment!"

"At ease, Adalanna. Today we'll look for my bird-beast!" Matrios said with determination.

"My lord!"

"Do you know anything about him?" he asked without flinching.

"Um … s-sir, no." Her response was a bit shaky.

"What is wrong?"

"Nothing. It's just that … well, that thing is a little scary," she stammered, confused.

"Do you know where he is?" Matrios asked with a sigh.

"Outside the gate. He's probably still eating."

"Eating?"

"The corpses."

"Oh dear. I guess it's not surprising to hear him referred to as a vulture." He smiled, confused. "Please get a small team together. We need to find him."

Matrios walked away from the tent. He took a deep breath and sighed painfully. *When was the last time I was with a woman?* he thought, and then a smug grin spread across his face. He raised his right hand and slapped his own face. He exhaled, arching his back and hissing in pain. He clenched his reddening palms, and his eyes flashed brightly in the sunlight. "Let the real war begin." The soldiers at his side looked at each other strangely, but Matrios ignored them and started towards the camp.

As Matrios walked across the trampled fields, some people looked at him. Some even bowed their heads, but most didn't pay much attention to his presence.

No wonder, he thought. *We're far from the cities, and the king's hand can't reach here. In the present circumstances, every man is needed, whoever he may be.* With this thought in his heart, he set his feet towards the medical tent. By the time he reached it, the great commotion seemed long gone. Some knights were still suffering on beds made up in a hurry. All of them were exhausted and powerless, moaning and sweating. Eliott and the other doctors were huddled exhausted beside the beds, but still holding their strength. Father Pelion slept with his back against a tent pole, snoring heavily, his clothes muddy and bloody, but his face still flushed from the great fuss.

"Father Pelion." Matrios crouched down beside him.

"Ah, Prince?" the old man slowly awoke. "I beg your pardon. One moment." He tried to get up, but his hands were so tired that he couldn't move a single finger.

"Never mind." Matrios smiled kindly at the old man.

"All these people have been healed. The more seriously injured should be on their feet by now," the old man said with heartfelt pride even though he was consumed by fatigue.

"Yes, I see that only the less seriously injured are lying on their beds now." He looked over the frail patients.

"I apologise, sir. I stopped counting after the hundredth one." Father Pelion leaned wearily towards Matrios and Matrios caught him and held him.

"So doctors in this world are the same as they are in mine as I see it." The prince smiled proudly, then took a quilt from a nearby bed and tucked it around the old man.

Leaving the old man to rest, Matrios moved towards the hissing knights. They were all in bad shape, deeply sleeping but suffering nonetheless.

Coming upon little Picon, Matrios sighed with pride. "I told you not to overdo it," he whispered to the sleeping child. He turned to Eliott, who was working nearby. "Eliott, what's the matter with him?"

"S-sir, they were all dripping with sweat. Their skin became cold, their pulses barely palpable."

"Understood." Matrios started to think. *It's almost the same as my grandfather's symptoms. Let's see, magic costs energy. Energy burns calories. But the energy burned must be replenished by taking in food. That's why all the fires were made up and the cooks arrived. Of course!*

He turned to Eliott. "Go and get a bucket of salt! Give each patient a spoonful and then give them water to drink! If they are weak, hold their noses and feed them the salt with a little water so they can swallow it!"

"Excuse me, sir, but I am very tired." Eliott staggered, but managed to regain his balance just in time.

"Go and rest," said Matrios. "Leave it to me." He patted the doctor on the shoulder and turned on his heel.

"Yes, sir!" and Eliott collapsed and fell asleep immediately.

Matrios ordered two soldiers to get a large quantity of salt. They wearily carried out his order, returning with a sack of salt. Matrios found a spoon in the kit that belonged to one of the cooks. He washed it and then opened the sack. He scooped up cup of the white crystal and thought, *So, salt is not a luxury item. I must keep that in mind.*

He stepped back to little Picon's bedside, propped up the fragile body of the small child with one knee, dipped the spoon into the cup, and lifted it to his mouth. "My little hero, open your eyes and take this little bit of salt."

"I don't want it, Mother," the child whispered, surprising Matrios. Matrios then felt sadness in his chest.

"Open your eyes, Picon." Matrios repeated with a kind smile.

The boy opened his eyes and then spoke, but his words were barely audible and half babble. It was enough for Matrios to cram the spoon into his mouth, and when the child tasted the caustic salt crystals, more strength moved into his body, and he involuntarily began to swallow, clutching his throat and waving his left hand as if he were drowning. Matrios put a glass of well water into the flapping hand, and the boy chugged it down in a flash. He remained just as powerless, but he was now relaxed. Silently, he fell back against the man's leg.

"P-prince, sir?" he said in a hushed voice. Then he fell asleep again.

"Get some blankets and cover him well!" said Matrios, again looking at the exhausted soldiers.

One by one, he administered the salt ration to each knight. Then he wrote down the tasks for the still-awake doctors on a piece of paper. Sweating a little by this time, he headed for the forge.

Smoke billowed from the chimney making the forge look like a dragon slumbering in the hills. The clang of the smith's steel hammer was as loud as any machine. The old blacksmith sang as he pounded the iron. The woman beside him helped him, and she herself sang now and then, but their voices were more tantalizing than pleasing to the ear.

"How are you doing?" said Matrios with his hands over his ears.

"Ah! Good, sir!" The blacksmith Miraklios stopped his work and pointed with his hammer to the top of the big chest beside the prince. Matrios picked up the small tool and then whacked it to the ground.

"What are you doing?" cried Miraklios.

"Hmm ... have you hardened it?" Matrios said thoughtfully.

"Why should I?

"Put it in the coals, heat it until it is bright red, then cool it in water."

41

"I know how to quench!"

"And tempering?"

"I'm not a nipple sucker anymore, lad!" the blacksmith said angrily.

"Well, yes. By the way, do you have any wire?" The prince looked around.

"Of course. How much do you need?"

"All of it!"

"All of it?"

"All of it!"

"I have a roll of it." Miraklios pointed to the corner that was piled high with unusable, filthy, or rusty scrap.

Matrios stepped up and tried to dig out what he was looking for from the sea of rusted armour and blades. "Why is this here among all this stuff?" he asked, holding up a coil of wire.

"That's just spare material."

"I see. Can you make more?"

"I have a wire puller in the back." He pointed at the door of the workshop.

"Great. Great!" the prince said happily. "Get one of your men to start making wire!"

"What for? That coil should be enough for a year!"

"I'll take this coil, and I need more!" Matrios started measuring the coil. Muttered under his breath, he started writing pictograms on the floor with a piece of charcoal. Finally, he stood up and spoke. "I could use a calculator. I need about two more coils like that," he announced to the blacksmith.

"Two?" Miraklios shouted in surprise.

"Do you know where I can find more?" Matrios sounded as if he though such wire grow on trees.

"I think that one is the only full roll in the garrison," Miraklios replied.

"How long would it take to make what I need?"

"A month at least."

"Hm" mused Matrios.

"The problem is we don't have the materials," said Miraklios.

"What do you mean?"

"We don't have enough iron for that much wire. In fact, we're almost out."

Matrios turned around and threw one of the new pieces of armour at the man's feet. "Melt them! And every weapon here until we have enough!"

"Wait, wait, wait!" Gertrude said, stepping out from behind the bellows. "We are blacksmiths, not wire makers."

"I'll give you soldiers if you need them," said Matrios. "Right now these climbing aids and the wire are the most important to get done."

"Then this isn't a joke?" said the woman.

"No. We have to climb the mountain."

The two blacksmiths looked at on another. Then they stopped asking questions and went to work, eyes wide open as they pumped the bellows to liven up the cold coals. They began melting down the rusty, worn equipment. After they had finished the climbing aids, they set up the wire-making equipment.

Matrios returned to the camp and wandered around while he began to put his plans together in his head. He was completely lost in thought and only woke up when he bumped into a chair. As he looked around, slightly flushed, the soldiers stopped laughing. He sighed and, avoiding the chair, he kept walking. Adalanna stood in his way and bowed to greet the prince at the gate. "Is everything ready?" he asked.

"Lord Edalin wishes to speak to you, my lord!" she said, pointing at the gate.

"Not a good idea, my prince!" cried Lord Edalin from the top of the gate.

"I know, but I need my bird-beast." Matrios looked up.

"What do you need that god's plague for?" Lord Edalin shouted back, puzzled.

"I need him for my plans!"

"Don't bring him here again or I'll beat it to death!"

"We need him!"

"I don't!"

"Lord Edalin, please!"

"Even if we do, that creature is worse than an army of demons!"

"He can't be that bad!"

"It ate my clerk's goats!" Lord Edalin shouted angrily.

"I apologize, but we do need him!" Matrios said trying not to laugh.

"Ah … go! But if you don't come back, don't blame me. I've already sent a pigeon to your father with news of your impending death!"

"Thank you," Matrios said, trying to hide his confusion.

"If you want to get yourself killed, I won't stand in your way!" said the general, stepping away from the wall.

Matrios and a small party prepared to leave the garrison and search for the bird-beast. Matrios was mounted on his own horse. Though this way of travel was new to him, it seemed surprisingly easy. However, he found the chain mail and shiny armour very heavy.

Adalanna rode out in battle gear behind him, and behind them both rode a company of more men armed with bows, arrows, and axes. They traversed the hills where the horrendous scene of battle was revealed to them. Only the sounds of crows, ravens, and vultures disturbed the stillness of the dead. Guts and blood were everywhere. A sea of flies greeted them. It was difficult to navigate through the mass of bodies, and the smell was gross and stomach churning.

They heard a loud shout—not a cry, but more like someone trying to pull a violin bow across the edge of a huge pot. The sound was deafening and obnoxious.

"Is that Shrike?" asked Matrios.

"Yes." Adalanna replied in horror.

Matrios dismounted and looked out over the sea of corpses. Leaving his men behind at the bottom of the hill, he set off up the hill on his own. Near the top, he was greeted by a giant beast with a snake's tail and a feathered body. Its hind legs resembled those of a bird. Its wings were covered with feathers, but the creature still used them as forelegs. Two pairs of sharp, flesh-tearing claws flashed bloodily in the sunlight. Its head was snake like but still ended in a beak that was broad and flat, drenched in blood.

Matrios sighed. Disgusted by the smell, he wanted to get this over as quickly as possible. He whistled for the bird-beast. The foul creature noticed him and screamed again as it slowly and gingerly approached him, stomping its feet over the dead, trampling skin and bones with its strong legs. When Shrike got close to Matrios, he jumped up and tried to strike him from above. Matrios was surprised, but he leapt aside and threw himself among the dead. Back on his feet, he drew his sword in surprise and began to swear. "Isn't that my beast?" he said softly through gritted teeth.

He didn't have much time to hesitate, as Shrike swung at him and knocked the sword out of his hand. The blade lodged in the side of one of the corpses. With a twist, the bird-beast struck Matrios with his tail.

Matrios fell to the ground, soaked in blood. He struggled to breathe, but for a few seconds, he could do nothing. He felt his lungs about to collapse. But after spitting out a little blood, he finally managed to take a huge breath. Shrike towered over him and slowly leaned closer, his eyes flashing. Matrios's body became stiff with fear. His legs were weak, and his hands were limp. The bird-beast opened his mouth and licked his blood-soaked beak. Then he turned his head to look Matrios in the eye. "Ah ..." said the beast with a sigh. "The little prince survived!" The words rang in Matrios's head. "What a pity it would be if I were to rip his head off and wash my feathers in his blood!" Shrike licked his beak.

"You can speak?" Matrios cried.

"You understand me?" Shrike pulled his head back in surprise. He stepped back from Matrios, sat down on the ground, and waited for him to get up. Matrios's chest still ached, but he didn't bother with it any more than was necessary. He sighed, finding that he was no longer bothered at all by the smell that surrounded him.

The creature turned its head and looked at him. "So then, little prince. Something is strange about you." The beast leaned closer.

"How well did you know the prince?" Matrios whispered.

"How well did I know him?" Shrike whispered back. "Are you some kind of body snatcher?" His eyes narrowed in foreboding.

"No!" Matrios answered firmly.

"Hmm ... All I know about him is that he was a real prick," announced Shrike with a sigh.

"Really?"

"That douchebag locked me up with his horses! Can you imagine?" Shrike told the story with such determination. "I killed two of them before he realized it was a bad idea." He said this with pride, puffing up his feathers.

"I can imagine. And about the prince?"

"Why don't you ask the delicious elf?" Shrike licked his beak again.

"Delicious?"

"I've bitten her many times. You liked the way she howled." Shrike leaned in close again and looked at Matrios provocatively, but the prince took the insult without flinching.

"You look intelligent," said Matrios provocatively.

"Hmph!" Shrike raised his wings. "Are you trying to insult me?" He stuck out his beak and plucked a slab of flesh from it. "I'll open you up like a fish with one move!" The bird-beast raked Matrios's armour with his dangerous claws. I've had enough of your spoiled brat shit anyway."

"Of what?"

"Of everything! I may be a demon, but even I have good manners. You, little bouncer, sadly lack them." The creature withdrew his claws and sat back down calmly. "I suppose you're trying to tell me you're going to be different," he asked incredulously.

"I'm not!"

"Oh?" Shrike looked at Matrios with deep interest.

"I already am different!" Matrios replied firmly.

"I'll believe it when I see it," said Shrike reluctantly.

"Where I come from, there are no creatures like you. Similar beings are described in stories, but there are none like you."

"There are no more like me!" said the bird-beast firmly.

"What do you mean?"

"The nest where I was born was smashed by monster hunters. My egg was taken as a gift to the king, but only to be pressed into the hands of this half-witted—"

"Why haven't you killed him yet if you hate him so much?"

"He saved my life by accepting me. Although he is a worm so big that even I can't easily bear it. You know, there is gratitude in the world. My world isn't so different from yours, except humans have more intrigues," he replied proudly.

"I understand. Although I find that hard to believe."

"Also hard to accept, I'm not a bloodthirsty beast, right?"

"I'm glad you have disproved that."

"I'm glad you're not the prick I escaped from and swore to kill if he survived!" Shrike looked at Matrios with a teasing look.

"Well, I guess that vow is no longer valid?" Matrios was confused.

"It is. Even though your body smells the same, your magic doesn't have the foul stench it had before." Shrike sniffed the air.

"It's good to hear that."

"What do you say? What do you want us to do?" Shrike looked at Matrios with interest. "Will you let me fly away?"

"I need your help!"

"Oh?" The bird-beast leaned in again. "And what happens if I say no?"

"Then reaching my goals will be harder for me." Matrios scratched his head.

"You wouldn't want revenge if I said no?"

"Why would I?" Matrios looked at the creature questioningly.

"Your kind has a habit of doing that. If they don't get the answer they want, they start killing!"

"Well, I do things differently."

"Poison?" Shrike turned its head sideways.

"Of course not! If you don't help me, I'll have to figure out another way to do the things I have planned."

"And if I say no?"

"You're free to go."

"You're an interesting person, body snatcher." Shrike turned his head. "Let's see what happens if I stay with you. Offer me something better than freedom!"

"I can't."

"Then we're not negotiating," said the bird-beast, and he turned around and spread his wings.

"But I know something more interesting!" said the prince.

"What?"

"Everyone has always thought of you as a monster, and you call yourself one."

"Continue." The creature sat back.

"What do you think would happen if people found out you were free of the king's protection and started killing people and their animals?"

"Most likely, monster hunters would be on my trail again," Shrike mused.

"That's right. I'll make a pact with you, so you and I will both benefit."

"Are you sure? A pact with a demon is usually frowned upon in your world."

"Are you against making a pact with me?"

"You're strange, but so far I like what you say." He nodded appreciatively.

"You can go wherever you want as long as you're near me. You'll help me as long as you think it's acceptable. In return, I will provide you with royal protection. Oh, and you mustn't kill people!" Matrios explained.

"I haven't ... too often. The meat is good, but I can live without it. The horse is heartier, though fewer things are better than a juicy beefsteak!" Shrike licked his beak excitedly. "So you planned for me to give you a foot anyway?"

"A very logical consequence," said Matrios, coughing up a little blood.

"What's the loophole?"

"There is no loophole."

"I'm a demon! Don't try to give me that crap!"

"If you help me, we'll both be better off. You'll stay alive and get limited freedom. And I'll get a simpler life!"

"So my life in exchange for your simpler life? Do you think that's a fair offer?"

"Better than being dead, right?" Matrios smiled at the demon.

"Sure that's all you want? I like the way you think, and the contract is not bad. But is it enough for you?" the creature asked, puzzled.

"As long as I have you by my side, I don't have to fear for my life. What I have planned will be easier, and I will achieve my goals faster."

"I understand. Then let's make the contract as equals, however uncommon that may be. And one more thing!" Shrike held out his foreleg and then pulled it back.

"What is it?"

"You must never hurt little Linary again!" The bird-beast glared at Matrios with deadly seriousness.

"Who?"

"Your daughter! I mean the prince's daughter," Shrike explained, looking at the man with a puzzled expression.

Matrios's face was filled with surprise, and the words caused him to freeze.

"She's the only one who hasn't seen the monster in me. That that little girl can't be more than four years old, and no matter what you've done to her so far, she's strangely attached to you!" The creature glared at him bloodily.

"I wouldn't even write that down if you didn't ask. I'll never touch her with malice. Rip my arm off if I do!"

"Believe me when I say that I'll hold you to that!"

At first Matrios thought Shrike was joking, but his temper never wavered for a moment. "Any more requests?" He swallowed hard.

"For me this is enough!" The creature held out his claws.

Matrios held out his hand, and Shrike made a small and shallow cut on his palm. He then cut his own claw. As they clasped hand to claw, the pact was sealed. Matrios felt triumphant, and Shrike eyed him with a suspicious look. "Well then, Jacob?"

"Let's go back, and I'll outline the plan. Wait, what?"

"There are things I don't need to explain, but what I do know now gives me no reason to doubt." Shrike looked at Matrios in acknowledgement. "I must survive, and so must everyone else!" Shrike repeated Matrios's sentence. "So this is who you are?" the bird-beast looked at the prince with a strange smile on his face.

"Pretty much," Matrios replied, confused.

"Hmm … I wouldn't be lucky to go back like this." Shrike began to shrink! Soon it turned into a snake-headed blackbird. It flew up and landed on Matrios's shoulder. "Boo magic!" the creature said, joking and flapping its wings.

Matrios laughed nervously, revealing his surprise.

Together, they headed back to the group of soldiers and knights who were still standing among the corpses waiting for them. Adalanna ran up to him and looked at him. She stepped back when she noticed the strange creature on Matrios's shoulder. "What happened, sir?"

"We got to know each other," said Matrios proudly.

Adalanna nodded nervously and couldn't take her eyes off the creature. Matrios climbed into the saddle. She followed his example, and the group headed back to the garrison. On the way, they stopped for a moment at the top of a towering hill from which they saw the demons' camp. Adalanna handed the spyglass from her saddlebag to Matrios, and he surveyed the spot from a distance. It was surrounded by black earth, trampled turf, felled trees, and bogs burning with blue flames. He focused the spyglass on the mountain that towered above them. He reached out his hand, stuck out his thumb, and began to count. Adalanna and the soldiers watched in silence, eyebrows raised, as their lord muttered to himself. "It's possible!" he finally said.

"My lord?"

"Oh, nothing," Matrios said. "Never mind." He turned his horse and started again towards the garrison.

"Did you see anything interesting?" asked the creature, who still sat on his shoulder.

"I was just counting," Matrios told him.

"Oh! I didn't know the prince knew numbers."

"I'm not the prince." He sighed.

"I'm still getting used to it." Shrike lowered his eyes.

The small party made it back to the gate and were admitted behind the secure walls. Edalin looked down at the man on the wall and the bird-beast resting on his shoulder. He walked down from his post and greeted the prince. "I see you've brought back that gods' plague. At least keep it away from our animals!"

"Okay, that's fair enough," said the bird. Only Matrios heard him.

"I'll do what I can," Matrios said dejectedly.

"So?" asked Edalin

"Yes?" Matrios looked at Edalin.

"You brought the bird-beast back. What's your plan?"

"Oh, yes! Let's get the others together. I don't like repeating myself. Let me get out of this dirty and dented armour."

When Matrios had changed, he headed towards the commander's tent where he joined Edalin.

Keratrin and Verilion had received the notification of the meeting. They rushed to the tent where Edalin and Matrios were already waiting for them.

A servant brought in a simple meal for the prince, and he started to eat. At his request, it was a mere plate of stew with a bit of bread. *Food will be scarce*, he had thought to himself. *We must conserve for now.*

"How do you like it?" Edalin asked.

"As long as it's edible, I can't complain!" Matrios replied with bread in his mouth.

"What happened to you?" Edalin turned from the window to Matrios.

"What do you mean?"

"You are ... well, you seem completely different." He pointed at the prince.

Oh, that," said Matrios with a smile. "In the grip of death, I reassessed my life so far and I came to realise a lot of things I used to think."

"Used to think?" The great warrior said in disbelief.

"I don't remember much." Matrios finished, breaking the last chunk of bread in half.

"Look," said Eladin, "the reason I sent the letter—"

"Lord Edalin, there is no need to explain," said Matrios. "I'd prefer it if you didn't have to be like that in my presence anymore."

"What?"

"Let's leave aside rank between us."

"What?"

"I respect the way you look after your people, and I've heard many stories about you and your battles with demons."

"Yes, there are some stories." Edalin cleared his throat.

"You have more experience than I do. My only advantage is family, which I have exploited to the fullest," Matrios said with a sad smile.

Edalin was about to say something, but Verilion and Keratrin entered, interrupting the conversation. The eyes of both men were immediately fixed on the creature resting curled up in the middle of the table. Keratrin said nothing, but hatred and disgust were evident in his eyes. Verilion's head was burning red.

Matrios found the behaviour strange and did not know what to make of it. He did not know the history these two men shared with Shrike.

Now that everyone had arrived and taken their seats, even if they refused to look in the prince's direction, he stood to speak.

Before he could get one word out, Verilion spoke: "What is it you have summoned us here to tell us?"

"I would like to explain my plan."

"I am all ears." Keratrin leaned on the table.

The outline of the plan went smoothly and without questions, but when Matrios finally took a deep breath at the end of his speech, Keratrin leaned back in his chair. "I knew we had this thing that could be attached to the feet, that there would be ropes," Keratrin said. "Our men can't climb mountains. Hardly any of them have ever seen a mountain before." He was obviously concerned.

"Keratrin is right about some of the men," agreed Edalin. "They can't learn to climb even if we have a year!"

"Yes, Prince, the lords are right about that," said Verilion. "Your plan is all well and good, but no one knows how to use the new tools. The men will have to practice. It may be impossible." Keratrin sighed.

"I'll prove it's not!" Matrios smiled, confident and firm.

"Of course, if the bird-beast lets him get on its back, it'll be easy," Edalin retorted with a pout.

"I'll climb the mountain myself!" Matrios announced.

"Please!" said Edalin. "It's not even a joke! You're the king's son, I can't let you do something so stupid!" the Old Lion slapped the table.

"It's not stupid!"

"You've never climbed a mountain!" said Verilion.

"Then it'll be an even better example for everyone!" Matrios folded his arms proudly in front of his chest.

"A lot of fuss for nothing!" said Keratrin.

"We have two choices!" The prince pointed his fingers at the others.

"Two?" Verilion asked.

"Yes! Either we do this, or we'll be crushed by the time the legion of demons get here!"

"Yes, that won't be for at least a month," said Edalin.

"We sacrifice a few so the others can live," said Matrios, "or we all die when the demons break through!" He sat down at the table. "We have to make that decision here and now. The four of us!" he continued in a fiery voice.

"Prince—" Keratrin began.

"My father knows I could be dead by now," said Matrios, interrupting. "The situation wouldn't change much if I fell! But we still must give ourselves a chance!"

"The wall is over several hundred meters high!" said Verilion in disbelief.

"Healing magic exists." Matrios shook his head.

The room fell silent. Edalin walked to the window and sighed heavily. "And even if we tried, do you think this pulley, or whatever you called it ... do you think it could take the required weight?"

"If we lift only as much as I prescribe, I'm sure it would!" Matrios replied immediately.

"Even if it doesn't work, we'll lose only one man! But if it works as you say, we'll be able to smash the demons! I've been waiting for this chance for decades!" said the Edalin quietly. Then he looked at Matrios.

"Edalin, calm down!" said Verilion.

"The flame is lit!" He raised his voice.

"Flame?"

"The flame of hope!"

"I see. Well ... no!" Matrios said.

"It's been a long time since the Kingdom of Hritan was in trouble. Then the beacons were lit and the entire kingdom fought as one after the news of the war spread like wildfire," said Verilion. "It is most commonly used in wars against the Kingdom of Midritan."

Matrios looked around the room, his face questioning, but he did not dare to ask any more questions because he had managed to convince them, even if he had to risk his own life to make his plan succeed. He stood up from the table. The stew had long ceased to steam, and the outside of the bread was beginning to dry.

I will hand you all the plans," said Matrios, "everything that must be done with the materials that we have at our disposal here at this moment."

"Do we have enough?" asked Keratrin.

"You should never underestimate an engineer!" Matrios's eyes flashed a mischievous glance at Keratrin.

"An engineer?" Keratrin questioned, sweating slightly.

"Never mind." Matrios sighed.

Edalin, Verilion, and Keratrin again went through the papers they had been reviewing point by point. Matrios needed to make additional drawings of the necessary equipment. A mountain of blank parchments had been placed on the desk from the clerk's office— yellow, fragmented, blank rolls of goatskin, all of shoddy quality and size. Matrios sighed when he saw the pile, but he grabbed a pencil and sharpened the point with his knife. He took the knife apart and used one of the elements as a short but straight ruler.

He looked over the rudimentary tools and sat back, disappointed. "My world for my old drawing tools," he whispered. But he set to work to create artistic renderings on the old pages. The musical crackle of the charcoal once again gave him the euphoric feeling he used to feel in his engineering job. The knife handle element he was using as a ruler slid across the pages like a dream, the black lines slowly giving flesh to the work in progress. What had begun as a tangle of lines now was morphing into a recognisable drawing. He wrote numbers on the goatskin pages, and strange demonic images.

His eyes were dry and so full of otherworldly joy that he would have fooled anyone who looked at him. The candles around him, which lit up the world on the table, burned out one by one, and by the time the last masterpiece was finished, only a few small points of light were left flickering and bending, dancing for their lives in the darkness.

Matrios wiped the sweat from his eyebrow, which only blackened his skin with charcoal. He leaned back in the chair, which made his spine crackle like rotten wood in a gale. He lifted the finished technical drawing and angled it to the poor light source. His mouth curved into a proud smile. The drawing was of a rudimentary crane-like contraption. Two long, thick wooden pillars, with a steel rod with a pulley at the top end connecting the two beams, and a metal hoop underneath connected by wire to a stout peg. In the centre were two metal tubes running between the two buttresses. Beneath this drawing was a drawing of a pulley system representing the rigging, a simple three-gear structure with a simple four-pronged mechanism on the side to prevent the pulley from turning back. "You'll be wonderful!" said Matrios proudly, unconsciously rubbing the purple bags under his eyes.

When he stood up from the table, his mouth was sore, his head was pounding, and he felt dizzy. He picked up the papers and quickly sorted them. Then he walked to the door carrying them under his arm. The doorway creaked softly. Outside Adrianna the elf woman slept with her back against the wall. Matrios felt as if he were about to faint, but he leaned against the door and spoke as sweetly as he could.

She woke to his soft voice, opened her eyes slowly and wearily, and raised her head towards him. Immediately, the dream sprang out of her eyes, and she jumped up in confusion. "My lord!"

"What is it?" he asked sleepily.

"Uh … Lord Edalin just told me to guard the door."

"I see," he mumbled slowly, half asleep. "The plans are ready. All we have to do now is construct the machine. Can you take these to Edalin? I think I'll go to bed." He handed the plans to her, waved softly at her, and headed towards his tent.

"I … yes." She looked after him, confused. *He used to scold me for daring to fall asleep on duty*, she thought. "He really has changed!" she said aloud.

Matrios put his feet slowly and powerlessly, one after the other, and when he reached the middle of the tents, he found shining water in one of the larger barrels, and passing by it, he quickly washed his face and his hands, which were blackened with charcoal. He would have drunk from the barrel too, but the charcoal tainted water did not look appetizing. He stood still, rubbing his face and eyes with his hands. No lullaby was needed; as soon as his head hit the pillow, he was asleep.

Early the next morning, it was not the crowing of the rooster that woke the prince, but the noise of a small crowd waiting outside his tent and the deep thundering voice of Edalin. "Get away, you long-eared bitch!" said the man with the raspy voice. Then Matrios heard a noise what sounded like a sack falling to the ground in front of the tent. He was still half asleep, but at the sound of the rattling he rubbed his eyes and sat up on the bed. "What's going on?" he shouted.

"Prince!" Edalin entered the tent uninvited.

"Edalin, what's going on out there?" Matrios cried out.

"The elf bitch wouldn't let me in, so I let myself in!" he said, making himself clear.

Matrios's eyes turned angry. He threw off the blanket. Still in his clothes from the day before, he walked out of the tent, ignoring anything the old man had to say. The woman lay on the ground in front of the tent entrance holding her face. "Adalanna!" he said worriedly.

"It's nothing, sir. I just fell!" She struggled to get up, but as soon as she dropped her hand from her face, Matrios saw a huge red handprint on her cheek. His mind was a jumble of thoughts and anger. His hands clenched into fists, his teeth gritted in his mouth, and his eyes spewed an angry spark. The mana begin to drain from his body. He looked back towards Edalin, and deadly thoughts ran through his mind.

"What is the meaning of this?" Matrios asked Edalin angrily.

"I told you she wouldn't let me in!" replied Edalin clearly.

"Why was she lying on the ground?"

"The slave wouldn't let me in!" He blinked questioningly.

"Why did you strike her?" He shouted again.

"She's just a warrior slave. No need to make such a fuss," he said, placing his hand on his hip as Adalanna stood behind the prince covering the mark with both hands, her eyes downcast.

Yes thought Matrios. *Here elves, especially slaves, are not considered worth anything.*

"Edalin! Don't do it again or I'll leave you and your men here without a solution." The prince adjusted his shirt.

"But—" Edalin was about to talk back, but just then Verilion appeared in front of the tent. "It won't happen again, sir!" Edalin replied, a little ashamed.

"Ah, Prince!" said Verilion, ignoring the others.

"Yes?"

"They've started to make the structure. Unfortunately, we don't have enough skilled carpenters, but it should be ready in a week." He sounded a little worried.

"What's the problem?"

"How are you going to climb the mountain?" he asked, scratching the back of his head.

"I'll take care of that. Do we have any additional blacksmiths available?"

"Not really."

"No problem! What about the demons?"

"They're not moving yet," Edalin replied. As he stepped out to stand beside the prince, he glanced over at the elf. She looked away, her face reddening. "They attack us every month," Edalin continued. "It's easy to predict when"

"So we have some time."

"Yes. Everything will be ready in a week, so what would you like us to do until then?" Asked Verilion.

"Do we have metal stakes?" asked Matrios.

"Of course!" said Edalin, curiously. "Oh, Prince," he said, "this letter arrived at dawn." He handed over a small letter.

Matrios stretched out his hand, took the envelope, and tucked it into his shirt pocket. He nodded his head but did not read the message, which made Edalin's eyebrows rise on his forehead. But he would not have his satisfaction.

Matrios ordered all the metal stakes in the camp to be brought to him. Then, ignoring the old commander, he yawned and went back to the tent to change.

Everyone departed to continue with daily duties following written instructions. Adalanna, on the other hand, stayed with the prince but dared not even speak while the prince kept singing under his breath in some language unknown to her and to some unfamiliar but pleasant rhythm.

When they stepped out of the tent, the sun was still low, licking the distant plain at an angle, casting long, lingering shadows. A great noise struck the prince's senses, a great whistle pierced the gentle breeze, and then a loud hooting sound emanated from behind him.

"Ah, you found me!" said the prince.

"I brought a rabbit, but I won't give you any," said Shrike proudly.

"I wouldn't really ask," said Matrios, relieved.

When she saw the creature, Adalanna jumped behind the prince in fright. The creature only smiled broadly before busying itself swallowing the rabbit whole. After one gulp, it licked its beak, sated.

"What are we going to do today?" Shrike said, sitting down. "Yesterday was a pretty boring day."

"We're going to fly up the mountain," Matrios announced clearly.

"Great! How are *you* going to get there?" the creature asked.

"With you!" said the prince.

"If you pull out a feather, I'll drop you. Just so you know!" The creature leaned towards the prince smelling of flesh.

"Okay, okay."

"My lord!" Adalanna exclaimed.

"Yes?" He looked at her questioningly.

"Are you *talking* to the creature?" She seemed startled.

Matrios froze, forgetting that only he could hear the bird-beast. His mouth agape at his own clumsiness, he put his hand on his face and looked at her. The creature also looked away, confused.

"Don't tell anyone," he whispered. "But yes, I talk with him." He looked away.

"I thought it was just a beast." She looked more closely Shrike, and he glared at her angrily. Then Adalanna was startled and leaned back nervously. She winced in fright.

"Eh!" said Matrios. "Can't you two get along?"

"I have no problem with the delicious elf," said Shrike.

"I don't think I can trust this thing," Adalanna said.

"*Thing?*" The creature raised its head in annoyance.

"Yes, yes," Matrios said, clapping his hands twice. "Let's go. I need to map the area." He sighed. Matrios grabbed the beast's neck with one hand and jumped up onto his broad back. The feathers were comfortable, and he could feel the beast's muscular body beneath him with his legs. He hugged Shrike's neck as tightly as he could, and then he spoke in a shaky voice. "I already regret this."

The enormous bird-beast spread its wings, staggered onto his hind legs, and then gave a mighty flap with its feathered leather sails. As they slowly lifted itself into the air, Matrios felt the weight of his body pressing down onto the wide back of the creature, but Shrike's supreme energy and strength pulled them through the air. Matrios dared not open his eyes. "I already regret this!" he repeated.

Shrike let out a short scream, proclaiming his existence loud and clear in the sky. The strange feeling in the pit of Matrios's stomach receded, and as the beast continued to rise slowly, he felt the biting cold of the wind through his clothes, chilling him to the bone.

"Open your eyes, little prince!" said Shrike. "I don't think you've ever seen anything like this!" He laughed.

Matrios slowly opened his eyes. The vast Hritandian plain loomed before him in the morning light, and he could see the rushing rivers far away and tiny villages in the distance.

"Beautiful, isn't it?" said Shrike.

"My god!" said Matrios, shedding a tear. "I'd wish I could fly away with you and explore it all!"

"Not a bad idea!" said the bird-beast with a snort.

"But we have to do something important now." He patted the creature's side.

"I know, I know." Shrike sighed, and then began to rise again.

Slowly and leisurely they flew towards the summit of the mighty mountain known as Bowed Mountain, hundreds of metres high, its sides covered with a thick layer of unevenly stacked rocks that formed protruding edges on the surface with cracks opening longitudinally between the stones. Matrios got a better look at the wall as the creature flew closer to it, and then a stronger surge pushed him back onto the birs-beast's back as Shrike leapt and landed on the top of the mountain.

The sudden stop caused Matrios to be catapulted off Shrike's back. He rolled over twice and landed on his side, finally coming to rest on his back on the flat rock surface.

Matrios opened his eyes to see a sea of blue sky silently swirling above him. He stood up and saw Shrike stretch, spreading his wings wide. The wind was strong and blowing from the plains, so he fixed his gaze there and looked across the horizon from the tall mountain. He could see the morning fog swirling across the great plain and around the woods in a mist. As far as the eye could see, fields, woods, and tiny veins of waterways dotted the landscape. A few dirt roads branched off into the distance, just barely visible. With only the faint rustle of the wind to disturb the soundless silence, Matrios stood up and walked to the edge of the mountaintop and knelt before the great scene that opened before him. It was so beautiful that tears welled up in his eyes.

"Why are you crying?" the bird-beast asked.

"Where I come from, there are no more forests. It is no more than vast wasteland. It's just a mass of machines, growing and swelling in the distance. I have never seen anything so beautiful and immaculate. The sky is blue and not grey, the clouds are white and not blackened with poisonous dirt. The light of the sun shines during the day, and there is complete darkness at night—no neon-lit streets of filthy garbage and blood up here. As far as my eye can see, I can find nothing but opportunity—no misery or disease. The horizon is as clear as a sheet of white paper. The world here is like a beautiful snow globe. Was mine like that once?"

Shrike looked at the man but did not speak, letting him sink into the moment life had given him. He could not possibly understand the wonder inspired by his world for he had seen this view every day, so to him it was natural. But to one who had walked only in Matrios's former world, it must have been a wonder in itself. He pulled himself up and felt grateful for the first time in his life that the world had made him the way he was, that it had given him wings and the chance to explore the vast world beyond the clouds, to be free in the sky even if he could never be free on earth. He could soar forever and ever untethered in the sky.

Matrios wiped the tears from his eyes and stood up with a sniffle. He sighed deeply as if for the last time and stretched out his arms as if to swallow the whole world.

Then he turned and stepped to the other side of the mountaintop. What he saw there horrified him. Smoke billowed in the distance. Heavy grey clouds hovered low over the drying forest, which was beginning to give up its green colour and take on the black pall of death. In the distance, the land was also grey and, like a dried pool of oil, disgustingly discoloured and silted. He saw a sly parade of blue flames in the distance. The forest was burning along the horizon, casting a cursed cloud of noxious smoke into the sky. Matrios was assailed by memories of his old world; he remembered how twisted and sickly it was. From one side of the mountain, he had seen the radiant future and the sweetest and most luscious jewel of a beautiful world. Now from the other, he saw the parched wasteland and the monotonous indifferent squalor of desolation, just as he had experienced in his own life.

Anger rose in his heart, and he felt rage burst through his veins. The emotion moved his muscles. His face contorted into a scowl, his teeth clenched in his mouth, and his hands clenched in anger. "I will not let this world be destroyed!" he said.

"What are you talking about, body snatcher?" Shrike stepped up to him.

"I told you," he answered. "My world was exactly like the part of yours that is dying—desolation and torment in all directions."

"Will you fight the demons? Alone?"

"I'm not alone," he said, unclenching his hands.

"Oh?"

"An entire human race is waiting for someone to stand up and follow something bigger, isn't it?" He smiled at Shrike.

"Well, that sounds interesting." The bird-beast grinned.

After Matrios had surveyed the terrain and chosen a place to put the crane that was under construction, he clambered back onto the beast's back and hugged his neck tightly again. "It doesn't bother you that I want to fight your kind?" he asked Shrike.

"They fight you. Everyone and everything fights someone or something. As long as I'm having fun and I'm not starving, I don't care who my enemy is. And we're not going to get anywhere with anyone who can't break free from the whispers."

Matrios would have asked him what he meant, but the creature was in the air in one leap with wings spread wide. Soon they were descending the mountainside. Shrike drew his wings into its chest, and Matrios felt an acceleration that nearly tore his hands off as he clung to the creature. The bird-beast spread his feathered parachutes again when they were frighteningly close to the ground. Suddenly they landed with a force that no meteorite could have done better. Then Shrike soared up with wings spread and flew upside down. The still-clinging man was by this time struggling with nausea. Matrios clung to the back of the upturned animal trying to get his stomach to settle again, and when the nausea ceased to torment him, he looked up powerlessly. He saw that the entire garrison was watching him. Edalin and Verilion were in the lead. When the beast finally landed, Matrios pulled himself up like a gentleman, cleared his throat and spoke to them. "I have good news!"

Verilion began to cheer, and slowly the whole crowd followed him and became overly boisterous. They had never seen anyone ride a demonic beast before; they were amazed he had survived. The soldiers cheered so loud the sound was deafening. Matrios stepped away from the creature and walked over to the men, smiling proudly. Where are my iron stakes?" he asked.

"Here they are!" Verilion pointed to a bundle that lay on the ground behind the prince.

Matrios strapped the sack to Shrike's back and then stepped aside as the creature spread his huge wings and lifted off with a mighty leap. For a full hour, the beast tirelessly transported the things Matrios would need to conquer the mountain. The construction of the crane progressed at a pace commensurate with the great difficulty, but the blacksmiths were slow in making the metalwork because of the lack of sufficient and good-quality materials.

Matrios spent the rest of the day in the camp in the company of the soldiers, directing the operations with Verilion at his side, who often flashed him an inquiring and questioning glance but always remained in confusion when the prince looked back at him. Adalanna, meanwhile, was always on guard at her master's side trying to assist him where she could. At about noon, the prince walked up to the dining tent where only he and the knights and officers were dining. Everyone jumped up as fast as they could and bowed or knelt before him. Matrios just gave an embarrassed nod, at which everyone sat back down and continued to murmur as quietly as they could, the topic of discussion being mostly the prince and his strange behaviour.

Matrios sat down at a corner of the table in the company of Adalanna, and before he could say anything, one of the chefs kicked the door open. In one hand, he carried two full plates of soup and two large loaves of bread, and in his other hand, he carried a tray of smaller soup bowls. Adalanna's stomach began to growl as soon as she smelled the mouth-watering aroma. Some people might not have been excited over such simple food, but to a hungry person, any food looks delicious.

The cook bowed deeply and set the large tray down in front of the prince. He threw the small serving on a tray in front of Adalanna, almost turning the bowl upside down. Matrios grabbed the big man's apron, surprising him. As he pulled the chef closer, Matrios's eyes flashed in anger, his mouth pressed together, and his brow furrowed. Adalanna winced and quickly looked away from the table.

"I apologise, my good sir," the chef said, kneeling.

"I thought you were tripping," Matrios said. "That's why I caught your apron." Matrios's aura was just as much aflame with anger, but his face looked deadly calm.

"Ah … yes. Sorry, my lady, my foot slipped!" The fat man jumped up and rearranged the cutlery that had been knocked out of place on her tray. He placed a loaf of bread beside the bowl of soup and then bowed and left like a beaten dog.

"Please, my lord!" Adalanna said in embarrassment.

"Yes?" he looked up from his soup.

"Please don't do this sort of thing." She crumpled her skirt in her fists in embarrassment.

"What?"

"I'm a mere slave! I don't deserve such fine treatment."

"A slave?" He looked at her, confused.

"Your slave."

"I thought we had discussed this yesterday morning." He leaned back in his chair and put his hand on his forehead. "I really should be more specific."

"What is my lord talking about?" She looked at him, still not understanding what he had said.

"When I offered you the chance to leave with a bag of gold, you chose to stay of your own free will, didn't you?" He looked at her with a kind smile.

"Yes, sir. But—" The woman became speechless, even breathless. She put her hand over her cherry lips, and tears welled up in her eyes.

"Adalanna, you are free now!" Matrios smiled pleasantly and sympathetically.

"Yes." She curled up on the bench and sobbed soundlessly. The fabric of her skirt was drenched in tears as she tried to hold back the surge of emotion. Without speaking, she let her hair fall to hide her face as she gripped the fabric of her dress tight, her upper body trembling as she continued to sob.

Matrios wanted to say something. He reached out to her but pulled his hand back and busied himself with his own food instead as he tried to block out the stares of the knights and soldiers around him. He could still see the glimmer of her tears. Embarrassed, he slowly stirred the thick soup with his wooden spoon. The soup was not very tasty, but it was more than enough to be called nourishing, which was all the more needed for an army. He reached across the table and took a pinch of salt from a bowl, sprinkled it into the soup, watching the salt crystals melt as he stirred them into the pleasantly warm, but not scalding hot, thick broth.

Adalanna, too, grabbed a spoon and with trembling hands dipped it into the broth, which was not nearly as rich as his. She broke off a piece of the bread and ate it slowly, keeping her head bowed. Then she leaned closer to the bowl. Holding her hair back, she took a spoonful of the soup.

Matrios sighed heavily and reached across the table again, but this time he touched her head softly. He stroked the soft, fine hair gently. "Tie your hair up if you don't want to eat it," he suggested.

Adalanna blushed, leaned back in her chair, and secured her hair in a braid that hung down her back. Even after she competed this habitual style, her face remained as red as boiled crab shells. And her eyes were perhaps wetter than the contents of the bowl itself. A tear rolled down her fair cheek.

As Matrios watched her, his thoughts were interrupted by a sentence that he caught with only half an ear: "Look, the prince is playing with the elf again!" Someone in the crowd had spoken quietly, but clearly.

Matrios maliciously turned his gaze over the crowd. All the onlookers looked away or pretended to be busy with their meals. Matrios heaved a sigh and then resumed eating, but a small bird came through the window and landed on the table.

"Oh, are you done?" Matrios said, surprised.

"I see you are not." The prince only smiled. Shrike had transformed to his snake-head blackbird persona. "I thought when we shook hands that I wouldn't have to be a hoarder," said the creature disappointedly. He then sampled a bit of the soup and tore a piece of bread with its foot.

"Very good!"

"I suppose you can give only so much praise in front of everyone here," said the creature. "Well, I'll settle for that." He looked up at the man with the bread still in its beak. "Not that it means anything." He looked away.

The prince laughed at these comments.

"What's so funny, body snatcher?" Shrike grinned at him awkwardly and slurped up some more soup.

Matrios nudged the bird's breast with his spoon and then pushed the bread closer to him.

"You can't buy me with bread," said the bird-beast. "I'm not a bloody pigeon!" He snorted.

"Eat," snarled Matrios a little reluctantly. And he resumed his meal.

"Don't worry, I'll leave you nothing for this humiliating job!" Shrike stepped daintily right into the bowl and began to eat, flapping and slurping loudly as one would expect from a bird-beast.

Matrios blinked. He was completely surprised at the creature's behaviour. He fished the offensive bird-beast out by the back of its neck and set it down next to the bowl. He tapped the bird gently on its head with the wooden spoon and placed the bread next to it. "Eat properly, if you're so hungry!"

"Don't hit me again, if you like your hands!" Shrike warned him. He resumed eating, but not in such a splashy way.

The little comedy was watched by the soldiers, who were left speechless when the creature was hit by the spoon. In their minds, they had already seen the beast slicing the prince into salami, but all that happened was that the beast continued to eat with less fervour, which meant he was obeying the man.

Matrios noticed the crypt-like silence. He looked up and noticed the curious, incredulous looks that fell upon him. He stood up from the table slowly, wiped the edge of his mouth, and then broke off a piece of his bread crust. He began to chew on it as he began to walk out of the tent.

"My lord, where are you going?" Adalanna jumped up, pushing the table, causing the creature to fall headfirst into the bowl. "Oh gods!" She reached out and pulled the creature out of the bowl.

"I see you're getting along well," said Matrios, turning to see what was going on. "Take care of him, Adalanna. I have something important to do."

"Me? But, sir—"

"You can't shapeshift! Do you understand?" he spoke back to Shrike.

"Who are you to tell ... Ah, then tell her to give me a bath!"

"Adalanna, will you take him to my tent and help him wash the oil off his feathers?" Matrios stepped back.

"What?" She looked at the man with a frightened look and dropped the bird.

"This bitch!" cried Shrike as he hit the table. "I'll tear you—" The bird-beast sighed and stepped to the corner of the table. "I'll kill her first, and then I'll kill myself for taking your deal," he grumbled.

Matrios stretched out his arm. The creature hopped on and walked slowly and languidly along. When Matrios raised his arm to her palm, the creature stepped delicately onto it in shame. Adalanna's face showed both surprise and terror. The prince left the two alone and went to supervise the work on the war machines.

Chapter 4

It didn't take long to get the crane and rigging ready. In the meantime, Matrios spent the nights designing a few more useful tools, including a harness to help him survive the climb up the mountain.

When the right amount of wire was finally ready, the prince used Shrike to build a safe line of strong wire system and pegs along a section he thought was passable while everyone else worked as he instructed. The bird-beast's powerful tail thrusts drove the metal into the stones so hard that even the wrath of the gods could not dislodge it. It took hard and tedious work and lengthy reworking, but after a long month, the crane was ready. All that was left was for someone to conquer the mountain.

It was morning, and Matrios was waiting at the foot of the mountain at the beginning of the road. Around him, all the camp's inhabitants, including officers and important people, were waiting for his departure. He adjusted the harness around his waist, checked the ropes and straps, then grabbed the wire.

"If I fall, don't catch me," he said to Shrike.

Everyone who heard him cried out in protest.

"No! But, sir—" Verilion snorted.

"No buts! This must succeed! For Hritandia!" cried Matrios.

The crowd roared, and with a huge cheer, Matrios was on his way. He moved up the huge rock, putting one foot after the other, the climbing aids helping him to grip. His hands clung to the outcroppings, and he secured straps from peg to peg, slowly climbing higher and higher.

By the time he was halfway there, he could feel his hands getting more and more tired. The sun was shining on his back, which made him feel pleasantly warm, but the wind was as cold as death itself and as strong as a horse. He clung to the wire, waiting for a particularly strong gust to subside. He hoped it would soon float on, bored. Meanwhile, his pause gave his hands a bit of rest. Soon he resumed his climb with renewed vigour. He looked up and took a deep breath as he took note of the obstacles rising before him. The long cable ran along the stone wall. Slowly he reached the top, but on the last step he ran out of breath and felt he would not be able to pull himself up to the top of the ledge.

Verilion and the others below raised their hands above their eyes and followed the prince, who had shrunk to a tiny, barely visible dot on the huge surface.

"Why did he stop?" asked a soldier.

"He didn't stop!" said another.

"He won't make it!" cryed someone.

Other words of concern rang out from the gathered crowd. Verilion took a step back as he focused on the tiny dot in the distance that looked like a black tick on a brown cloak.

"Boost!" Verilion casted a spell as he imitated a throw.

A great golden-winged bird appeared in the sky and flew relentlessly towards the prince, tearing the stillness of the air with its wings. When the whistling gust reached Matrios, he felt strength run down his spine. His muscles revived, and there was nothing left of the agonizing cold. It had been replaced by a pleasant warmth and a searing glow of determination that fed his soul. Matrios gripped the ledge as tightly as he could and, throwing his right leg over it, he pulled himself up easily and sprawled across the mountaintop.

Down below, the crowd chanted his name with loud cheers of rapturous joy, and Matrios sat up and looked at the sight before him. He took out of his pack the flag he had prepared— a golden bear and a crown on a blue background. Matrios fastened the textile to a pole and threw it out. It fell quickly to the ground and landed a little away from the camp. The soldiers secured it upright and danced around it.

Matrios made his way down the mountain with the help of Shrike. When he got off the bird-beast's back, the frantic crowd picked him up and carried him around the camp.

◆

A few days later, it was not only Matrios who'd had a taste of the view from the high ridge, but any man who had the will to make the journey and who had the courage to volunteer. Many were strengthened by the prince's actions or his words. They moved slowly, camped on the summit, and then the real work began. With the strenuous efforts of a multitude of men, the crane was hoisted up and adjusted into position. Great wooden stakes were lifted to their intended place. The mighty efforts of a few carpenters built what Matrios had envisioned in his mind. After only a few weeks, the machinery was ready for what it had been destined to do. Four catapults rose out of the summit's soil, and behind them towered huge boulders and barrels.

Matrios stood up on the edge of the peak and raised his arm in the reddish light of the sunset. When he lowered it, a loud whoosh sounded, the machines shuddered, the arms swung, and flying boulders appeared on the horizon, headed to the camp of the demons.

They roared like comets in the sky, riders of death without tails, so swift and so unstoppable that it was almost diabolical. The first to land bore into the ground with a mighty thud, scattering everything around them. Only one hit the camp of the gathered demonic hordes, but it was enough to shatter them.

The catapults were reset, and the prince gave the signal again. The melodious song of a majestic swish rose in the air to be followed by the ominous tune of a whistling wind. This was followed by four loud and murderous bangs, which sounded like an underwater charge.

The demons were trampling each other to escape when three rocks from the second wave smashed several of them to bits and turned their tents into tatters. Then a pile of showering stones appeared above them again, from where, it was impossible to know. The shower plummeted upon them. Their courage left them, and they all took flight.

Matrios and his men heard loud screeching and shouting and a noise of movement. They loaded the barrels into the catapults. When the barrels landed in the enemy camp, their contents spilled out, flooding the camp with oily bits of leather and cloth. Then a small glowing swarm of flaming arrows, like fireflies, appeared in the twilight sky. The arrows, on a low trajectory, landed on the leather and cloth. Soon fire danced a devilish dance among the confused hordes. The flames came to life eagerly and spread with such voraciousness that it was frightening to see their power even from such a distance.

Matrios stepped down from his perch and looked proudly into the distance. The demonic army was crushed. A great cheer went up among the soldiers, but the prince just climbed onto Shrike's back and descended into the camp. Verilion and Adalanna were waiting for him, as was Keratrin. The prince looked at Adalanna and smiled. "Let's go home!" Matrios announced.

Adalanna just nodded happily, but Verilion laughed appreciatively, and Keratrin raised a questioning eyebrow.

A few days later, a small convoy consisting of a fancy chariot with horsemen around it gathered at the rear exit of the camp. Standing beside his chariot, Matrios was bidding farewell to those who would remain behind. "Don't forget to tell the people in the other garrisons about what we achieved here, Edalin!" Matrios said.

"I've already sent messengers! And I included all the plans and methods you put together, my good lord!" The big man bowed.

"Don't get on Edalin's nerves!" he said to Keratrin.

"Actually, my prince," said Keratrin, smiling, "I won't be staying long either."

"Why is that?"

"You made me realise something! I'll see you again, I'm sure of it." Keratrin kissed Matrios's hand and bowed before he stepped back.

"My lord!" Verilion said, sitting on his horse. "Let's go!"

"Yes! Let's not keep my father waiting! He's not a man of patience!"

"My prince!" said Edalin.

"Yes?"

"Are you sure it's better if the king thinks you're dead?"

"But you only wrote that I was wounded!" Matrios laughed. "I understand now, Keratrin. I understand everything. Don't worry, I plan a worthy entrance!" He waved at the man behind Edalin with a serious look.

Matrios and his decorated company left the camp. A long trudge accompanied by wheel and road noise awaited them. They would travel through forests and clearings for days. Every noon they stopped and prepared food. In the villages, the soldiers told people what had happened and what the prince had done. People in each village gave them food and entertainment, so the travellers were able to rest.

Matrios learned about the customs and celebrations of the Hritandian people from the people themselves. He was impressed by the hospitality with which he and his troop were received, even though they were royalty. They met many other travellers on the way, and he gave them all a little money and let them go. Eventually they reached the town of Brenera, through which the mighty waters of the Druga River flowed, bisecting the town. The small company stopped under a small grouping of trees next to the river to rest before they made a grand entrance. Matrios took a bath, brushed the dust of the road off his travelling clothes, and put on the finest clothes he could find in his packing trunks.

"My lord, what are you planning?" Adalanna said as she approached him.

"An unforgettable entry."

"What?" She looked at him questioningly.

He outlined the plan, addressing Verilion. "Get a party inside the city, but send a rider ahead to announce my arrival at the palace. Don't tell them if I'm alive. Just spread the word that 'Prince Matrios's knights have arrived.'"

Verilion sent one of his best horsemen ahead of the troop. Shortly thereafter the rest of the troop set off, this time without the prince.

Matrios watched them disappear behind the hill and then called Shrike, who had been following them surreptitiously all the way. "Ready?"

"I thought you'd be angry with me by now." The bird-beast stretched his wings out as he sat on the prince's shoulder.

"You know I can't talk to you in front of others," Matrios said.

"Of course, of course." Shrike fluttered down from Matrios's shoulder and transformed into its larger form. "What's the plan?"

"We'll wait until the others arrive in the city. Then we'll fly in from above and surprise everyone."

"Great plan. I hope the archers are asleep."

"I don't think they will be, but you'll be flying high."

"Oh, easy for someone to say when he's only riding on the back of another." The creature chuckled and then nipped at Matrios' clothes.

"Don't complain," said Matrios. "You've been living in royal comfort and getting beef every day."

"A little airing out wouldn't hurt my feathers anyway." The creature chuckled a few times.

"It's a good thing Adalanna gave you a few baths." Matrios laughed.

"It's not a bad thing to have someone else scrub the dust off my toes. Maybe someday she can give my bigger form a bath too!"

"I don't think you two are that close," Matrios said, looking away.

"What? I haven't bitten her once during this entire journey." The creature snorted.

"Anyway, don't be ..." began the prince. Then he changed his mind. "Let's go. The preliminary group should have made their announcement by now."

"Yes, Matrios!" Shrike replied.

"I'm getting used to everyone calling me by the prince's name."

"If you're in his body, you should go by his name as you have been." The creature looked away.

"That was pretty good." The prince chuckled.

"I'm more intelligent than you think. We just have different habits."

"And we are of different races." Matrios patted the creature on the back.

"It's obvious. I can fly, you can draw. I don't know who won."

"I think it's a draw."

"I'm not going to get into it," said Shrike, offended. "Well, brace yourself, Lord Matrios!" The creature bowed gentlemanly, overplaying it.

The giant bird spread its wings and flapped them with strong power, which made the whole forest shiver and roar again.

Chapter 5

In the centre of the vast throne room rested the old king, Mathias II Hritan, with his firstborn daughter Elena standing on his right and his youngest child, Elena's half-sister Meri, on his left, sitting in her own chair. Kneeling on the floor of the ornate hall in front of the royal throne was a black-haired woman, holding a little girl hugging her. The child was sobbing, trying to control herself. Her mother also cried as she protected her daughter like a lioness protecting a cub.

"You go back to your father and spend your life with him!" the king ordered, holding the small letter Edalin had sent.

"Please, my lord! Let me take my daughter with me! Have mercy on a mother's heart!" she said tearfully.

"What are you thinking? Maybe Linary is only my third son's daughter, but she carries royal blood in her veins!" Angry, the king rose slightly in his chair.

Hoping for a sympathetic response, the woman looked up at Elena and Meri. Meri averted her eyes. She was too young to speak in the hall, but she was fighting back tears as she watched the mother struggle to protect her child. Elena, the firstborn daughter, was as stubborn as her father.

"Understood, my king." The mother broke down completely and embraced her child as if she wanted to melt the small child back into her own body. Two soldiers stepped up to her and separated her from the girl, who burst into tears and fought with the armoured soldier, as she tried to get back into her mother's arms as her mother screamed and shouted after her.

The commotion was broken by the arrival of a messenger. Panting and dishevelled, he stood in the doorway and paused for a moment to compose himself. At the king's beckoning, the doorkeepers let him in.

"Speak," ordered the king. "What is so important that you should disturb us?" The king motioned for the messenger to come closer, whereupon the knight came forward, bowing continuously. Finally, he knelt down on one knee.

"My lord! The knights of Prince Matrios have returned from the frontier. They will soon enter the city!" said the man loudly.

"Wonderful! Get my carriage!" He referred to the woman and her child. "Let them go! Let them come to mourn on my son's chest!" said the king.

"Linary!" cried the woman, and again she wrapped her arms around the small girl, hugging her so tightly that she could hardly breathe.

Tears streamed down Meri's cheeks. She dared not look at them, but her soft sobs caught her sister's attention, and the lionhearted woman glared in her direction.

The king rose in his chair, leaned on his ornate staff, and beckoned to the soldiers. "Bring our carriage! We're going to the Triumphal Arch to see my son." The king as did his older daughter, who stood beside him. He addressed the distressed woman: "Go, Lady Elizabeth, bring my son's chariot, and follow us, that you may fall on his coffin if you feel the urge to do so. But know that your daughter cannot go back to the Republic with you! Let this be the sweetest and most mournful day of your life," said the king in his rough, strong voice.

Elizabeth looked up at the king like a mother lion while her child sobbed in her arms. Her golden blue eyes hid thoughts so terrible that words cannot describe them. These were the eyes of a mother from whom he would snatch her child. Her rage and bottomless hatred were visible as the tears flowed, just as her soul yearned for the king's blood that flowed in the same way. But he continued to smile, pleased by her unimaginable anger.

When the carriages arrived, the old king took his seat in his with his two daughters beside him. Behind them, in another carriage, rode Elizabeth and the light of her eye. Mother and daughter were filled with mournful and gloomy emotion.

"Mother, is father dead?" said Linary between two sobs.

"Yes. Though I never thought I would say it, it would be better if he were still alive," said the woman softly, almost to herself.

"Daddy's dead!" the small girl repeated between tears.

"Don't worry, my darling. Grandpa will take care of you!" She tried to reassure the child as the carriages moved through the town, but as the wheels went over the cobblestones, she broke down more and more inside herself. With each jolt of the carriage, she collapsed deeper into herself.

Matrios watched from above as the road he had been standing on just a few seconds ago grew smaller and smaller behind him, and the city grew closer and closer. The huge bird-beast flew up and looked down upon the bustling streets, gazing at the beautiful castle towering above them in the heart of the city. He then saw the carriages coming through the gate. He looked at the crowd, so thick that he could see it only as a mass from his vantage point. The only thing visible was the white road with the mob of people on either side of it and the carriages coming from the direction of the town and turning under the arch.

"Do you see anything?" asked the prince, and the creature stopped for a moment in the air.

"I see the king under the arch, his daughters beside him. Ah!"

"What is it?"

"Little Linary!" In the blink of an eye, Shrike changed direction and begin to dive towards the city, his wings tucked into his sides as he streaked through the sky like a meteor. Matrios tugged on the creature's feathers, causing him to snap to attention and adjust his wing position to slow himself down. He squealed across the blue sky, his loud scream thundering through the crowd. All the humans looked up to the sky where the sun already rode high, blinding everyone with its light. The creature spread its full wings and, though powerful, landed gently with the prince on its back. Again the creature shrieked in front of the Triumphal Arch, and Matrios sat on its back as gracefully and as securely as he could, but all he could think of was trying not to vomit.

The crowd fell silent, and the applause died down as startled eyes were fixed on the new arrivals. Matrios hopped off Shrike's back and petted his face, whereupon the big bird-beast shrank to blackbird size and fluttered gently onto his shoulder. Matrios drew his sword and pointed it in the direction of the king. Then he twisted it gently and knelt on the cobblestones in front of the king, gripping the hilt of his sword, the tip of which rested on the ground.

The king did not reply, but merely nodded in surprised acknowledgement, and Matrios and the members of the troop that had been coming up behind him stood up in a line, half-kneeling, and waited until His Majesty had stepped down from the carriage under the Triumphal Arch and walked closer to them. The old king offered his hand to Matrios, and the prince bestowed a kiss on the king's ring. The king took Matrios by the hand and pulled him gently closer.

"What is the meaning of this?" he whispered softly.

"What is it, Father?" mocked Matrios.

"It is nothing," the king replied irritably. Then he pulled Matrios to his side and turned to the people. "My youngest son has returned from his mission that led him to the distant garrison at Bowed Mountain! He has returned home alive, safe, and whole! Let us celebrate!" Then spread his hands.

Matrios felt strange. He had thought he would encounter a thousand eyes piercing and tearing open his body like knives. But that bad thought vanished when he heard the voice of the creature echoing as it flew swiftly over the two men and landed right in little Linary's hands as if compelled by a magnet. The child greeted the creature as an old friend. She embraced Shrike as if he were a teddy bear.

Matrios looked behind him to where those he assumed were his daughter and his wife stood. The woman's face was radiant with shock and disbelieving bitterness oddly mingled with unearthly joy.

After the king released Matrios's hand, the prince turned. As he lifted his gaze to the beautiful woman, she stole his heart in the blink of an eye. He merely stood there staring at her, frozen. She, in turn, looked at him as if she were seeing a ghost.

He shook himself and almost involuntarily took a step in her direction, but she took a stealthy step back, stopping only to raise her hands to her mouth in fear. Matrios looked down at the girl, who was hugging the ferocious bird-beast as if it was a doll. Then looked back at the woman. He put his sword away and, with slow, airy steps, he walked up to the woman. Her eyes were vast and deep like the sea, and her hair was as black as the starless sky on a night when the moon is hidden from prying eyes. For long seconds they stared at each other, her face alternately showing despair and hope and worry.

Matrios was at a loss for words, but he didn't need to search for something to say. She lifted her hand and touched his cheek as if she didn't believe her eyes and was looking at a mirage. Matrios was surprised, but the woman's touch was so pleasant after a lifetime of pain that he closed his eyes of his own accord, holding onto the warm, thin hand that covered his face. He buried his cheek in it and rested as a child resting on his mother's bosom, resting after his ordeal. Her tears flowed again, her lips quivered, and only a few faint words escaped her lips: "You are alive."

Matrios opened his eyes and looked at her. His mind kept replaying all the bad things the old Matrios had done to her, but he couldn't control himself. Slowly he wrapped his arms around her soft body and held her close to him. His heart began to beat abnormally. A tiny, slowly flowing stream of tears began to stream down the beautiful woman's cheeks, and she blinked in disbelief and confusion, as if she couldn't believe what was happening. Matrios clenched his lips and teeth as he clasped his hands over her body; he could feel his legs growing weak and trembling.

"I'm sorry," he whispered. The words were barely audible, but Elizabeth needed no more. She felt, in some way, the way she had felt when they were together for the first time in their lives. Her emotions were high, it felt like he understood the weight of the sins he had committed over the years. She burrowed her face into his black coat and hugged it tightly. She felt it wasn't love for him that compelled her, but the knowledge that she had finally found a shoulder to lean on after so many trials.

"Mom! Daddy's home!" Linary cried as she ran up to them, followed by Shrike. Matrios released his wife and turned to the girl. He wiped his eyes and took a deep breath.

"She's your daughter now, Matrios!" Shrike said. "And Elizabeth is your wife."

"Yes," he replied, fighting back tears. Then he knelt down beside Linary and held out his right arm. But the girl didn't wait a moment; she jumped into his arms, and Matrios put his arm around her. "I am home."

"How does it feel?" the creature asked.

I have a family, said Matrios to himself in disbelief, slipping back to memories of his old life as Jacob.

"Do you still feel that this is not your world?" asked Shrike.

Matrios didn't answer; he just held the child and tried to forget everything he could remember about what the person had done who had lived in his body before he entered it.

As Meri and Elena intently watched the family, a lump formed in the Meri's throat. It was so big she couldn't breathe. She knew that Elizabeth was happy for her brother because he was not going to be separated from her child and not because he had returned, but she found her brother's high emotions strange. However, the idyllic scene was so beautiful that even Matrios's sister did not want to break the moment; she just stood behind Meri and looked at the family, slightly stunned, yet admiringly, her eyes no longer showing the sea of disgust and contemptuousness. The king's servant interrupted the wonderful moment, relating his lord's words to return to the palace.

Matrios let go of Linary, but she did not let go of her father's hand. He looked down at her, whose eyes sparkled like diamonds and whose face was covered with joyful tears. He just smiled as sweetly as no one had ever seen him smile before, and with slow, protective steps he led his daughter to the carriage, occasionally glancing furtively at Elizabeth, who was now his wife. She looked over at him with a startled expression. How kindly he treated his daughter, and how he seemed to have been changed. He seemed so natural, yet so strange to her after all that had happened.

They got into the carriage. Matrios pulled the door shut behind them and took a seat himself.

"My lord, are you still Matrios?" Elizabeth asked, a little frightened.

"Of course," he said clearly, watching her as he caressed her.

"What happened?" She leaned closer to him.

"I'll tell you later. It was a long journey, and I have a lot to tell. I have a feeling you have something to share with me as well," Matrios said.

"I agree, but this is not the time or place. Especially not in front of Linary."

"I don't mind, Mum," said the happy child. "Look! Dad brought Shrike back to me!" She showed the monster to the woman, who looked at it with disgust.

"Shrike?" Matrios said, looking at the creature.

"If you say anything, I'll cut your tongue out!" said the creature, frowning.

"I gave him that name," said Linary, "but you didn't like it."

"I like the name Shrike!" Matrios said, petting the little girl's head softly.

"Really?" Her questioning eyes lit up.

"Yes. I—"

"My lord! I have to tell you—"

"Guess what, Daddy? Grandpa wanted to send Mama away!" She looked at Matrios, and he saw the fear in her eyes.

"What?"

"Yes," she replied, "but then again, you're not dead! Grandpa said you were dead, so grandpa lied?"

"He didn't lie, my dear. He just didn't know the truth."

"But isn't it a lie if he isn't telling the truth?" The little girl looked at him with innocent eyes.

"No. If you don't know the truth, what you say cannot be an untruth!" He turned to Elizabeth. "Why did he want to send you away?" he asked, his voice changing tone.

"He only wanted to send me away," she explained. "Since everyone knew that my husband was dead, it was my duty to return to the Republic." She crumpled her skirt with her hand as she spoke.

Matrios thought about what she had said, and a strong anger burned in his heart at the thought of someone forcibly taking a child away from her mother. The look on his face mirrored the flames of anger that simmered in his heart and his soul. Then he remembered that he was lucky to have returned just in time. He dared not think what would have happened if he had been late and Elizabeth had been sent away. So his anger turned against himself.

"My lord, is everything all right?" Elizabeth asked. She seemed terrified.

"Oh … of course," Matrios said, forcing himself to calm down.

The carriage stopped, the door opened, and they alighted to see huge building before him. The marble stones of the palace wall reflected the sun with gleaming white rays that were almost as glaring white as the midday sun, strong as a yoke of horses. Matrios raised his hand over his eyes to block the glare and stepped down onto the clean stones. He turned and, in a gentlemanly way, offered his hand Elizabeth who waited behind him. She hesitated slightly, then timidly accepted the helping hand. Softly, almost like a feather, she touched his slightly rough but strong hand. Matrios pulled his lips into a soft smile, and his eyes twinkled as he watched the beautiful woman. But he tried to avoid her gaze.

Elizabeth stepped up beside him, and Linary jumped out of the carriage with a wide, playful smile, crying out loudly as she threw herself into her father's arms. Matrios was very surprised and barely caught her, but he finally managed to get a grip on the tiny body. Elizabeth was very scared but didn't say anything. She just waited for his reaction, which was a huge laugh as he sat Linary on his forearm

"Linary! Know your manners," Elizabeth said.

"I've just arrived, and she's only a child," Matrios said. He turned to his daughter. "Today you can do whatever you like," he said, pinching her cheek.

"Really?" she replied while she looked at him with a stunned expression. "Then I'd like to play with Shrike in the garden!"

"Then let's ask Shrike!" He leaned her closer to the bird in the carriage.

"Shrike!" she cried excitedly. "Do you want to play with me?"

The bird-beast tried its wings and then landed on the girl's head and emitted a rudimentary bit of birdsong.

"I'll take that as a yes!" Matrios said, releasing Linary from her perch on his arm. "Look after each other and don't get into trouble! Come up to the room before sunset!" he ordered in a kind voice.

Clutching the bird to her head, the little girl rushed through the huge gate, knocking over anyone who stood in her way. But the king gave him an angry look and said, "You might teach the girl a good lesson! She's behaving like a peasant's child!"

"With all due respect, Father, I prefer to see my daughter's face smiling rather than gloomy and mournful." Matrios bowed like a true noble.

"Come into the hall and tell me everything!" said the king with a scowl.

"Yes, Father." Matrios offered his hand to Elizabeth again, bowing slightly and raising his left hand to his chest, but she declined and started up the marble steps. Matrios didn't understand her gesture; regardless, he followed her and began to put his sentences together in his head.

The doorway opened into a corridor that led to the throne room, where beautiful relics decorated the walls. Portraits of past kings showed the way to the future and reminded each presiding king of the past. Matrios pondered a little on the red satin curtains, the gilded cornices, and silver trimmings. He noted the beauty of the paintings and the artistry of the columns. The old king sat down in his chair, and Matrios and Elizabeth knelt on the soft, thick blue carpet that ran from the doorway to the throne.

"So tell me, my son, what you have seen!" commanded the king.

"Yes, my Father." He raised his head and stood up. "I saw a rabid horde of demons on the other side of Bowed Mountain. I faced the roaring hordes, but there was nothing but death waiting for me, along with several of my men. I fell into battle and almost left my life behind. It was Adalanna who saved my life and called for retreat." Matrios pointed to the woman who had taken a stand in the knight's ranks.

"So you failed and ran back here like a dog with its ears flat and its tail between its legs?" the king slapped the arm of the chair in anger.

"No! If I had acted like that, I would have made it back to the city before the king's soup had gone cold!" Matrios said confidently.

"Would you have failed so soon?"

"I did fail at the beginning, but standing on the porch of death changed a lot of things in me," Matrios said, bowing his head in shame.

"On the porch of death? Has it changed?" asked the king, stroking his beard.

I can't leave the capital so soon, but I can't put myself at risk of an assassin trying to kill me. I'm not welcomed here, and they want to tear my family apart. I need to keep them safe so that Shrike will aid me. I've got it! Matrios thought to himself in a blink of an eye as he looked at Elena and Meri, whose expressions were different.

"I know I've been through a lot in my absence," he continued. "I haven't recovered yet, but it's as if the inspiration of our god has helped me and given me the strength to accomplish all we've achieved there."

"What you have accomplished?" the king wondered aloud.

"We have broken up the demon hordes and driven them back into the forest!"

"What?" the king cried out.

"Liar!" cried Elena, beckoning to the guards who surrounded the prince. "How dare you, in the presence of your king, so blindly—"

"Liar?" Matrios said, and his eyes flashed up to his sister with a blood-freezing glare that made her feel the cold current that rushed through the hall. She faltered slightly from the force of his determination and magical presence.

"Enough!" the king roared. Then he sat back in his chair. Nodding to Matrios, he said, "Continue."

"We have begun to send out the news, and I believe all the garrisons have begun to prepare for the plan I have sent them."

"What plan?"

"We will create a massive fortresses on the top of Bowed Mountain!" He said clearly, spreading his hands.

"My son, the sepsis must have made you mad!" said the king.

Verilion stepped behind the prince, bowing, the mighty warrior now looking half as big in the presence of the old king. He bowed his head and bore himself with respect and gentlemanly manners, bringing no shame to the order of the knights.

"Speak, knight!" said the king.

"My good king! What my lord, your son, says is true!" said the knight, kneeling.

"What do you say?"

"I saw with my own eyes as he mounted the beast, and flew on its back to the top of the mountain. And with my own two eyes I saw him climb the Bowed Mountain by his own might. He made it to the top of the largest mountain in the mystical range. Let my oath be null and throw me into the void if it was not so!" Verilion saluted, whereupon the other knights in the room did likewise, proudly extending themselves.

The king fell silent as did the soldiers and everyone else who had heard the words. Only the knights stood and smiled with a pride that no man alive had ever seen. Elena looked at her brother in disbelief and then the words escaped her mouth. "You are the most useless of us all! How can that be?"

Matrios closed his eyes, spread his right hand out beside him, rested his left hand on his chest and bowed slowly. "The truth is in the wine!" he said.

Meri laughed at the statement and was unable to control herself. The king looked at her in amazement; he had never heard the young princess laugh before.

"How could you?" asked the king.

"I used my wits, my good king, nothing more. And the humble and efficient help of the soldiers of the garrison and their commander. Without them, I would not be standing here before you today."

"Was it not all your doing?" The king cleared his throat.

"You are not mistaken, Father. I have no intention of reaping the glory of the soldiers' sacrifice!"

"I understand everything now."

"But, my lord, I have a request to make of you, as my father and my king."

"Hmm …. Considering your deeds, speak!" the king said wearily.

"I beg you to grant me a village, some land to cultivate, and some serfs. A place where my family can live. From there I can support the kingdom.

"Why should you?"

"I've seen battle. I've seen death with my own eyes. Now I just want peace. I am my father's third son, so my inheritance will be little or nothing. However, tending a plot of land would be more useful to the kingdom than spending my time and energy in the brothels of the city." Matrios spoke respectfully, and the woman beside him was very surprised and looked up at him.

Elizabeth did not understand what was going on. How it was that he, who had once found rest only in the bosom of whores, could return from the front, understand her feelings better than she did herself, and be capable of things she had never seen or imagined before.

The king was about to speak, but then a man in a white robe stepped to his side and began to whisper something to him. The monarch did nothing. Then he nodded and agreed to the mysterious words.

"Very well! Matrios Hritan, go north to the village of Brekan. It will be waiting for you at the foot of Sleeping Mountain!

"The village of Brekan?"

"It is a small village at the foot of the mountain," the old man in the white robes replied. "There is fertile soil and a few small mines. The prince will like it after all the hardships and the crowded city air."

Matrios said nothing. He bowed low and took three steps back.

"Take care of your family and keep your land well," the king said.

"I will not disgrace you, Father," Matrios said, nodding to him and waving to his knights.

Matrios left the throne room, his wife walking swiftly behind him, and the knights bowed to the king one by one, and then followed. When the door closed behind the company, Matrios let out a huge sigh.

"All these NPCs." He held his head as he thought, *Not only did I get what I wanted, but they forgot to ask me how I managed to accomplish everything! Now I have to be quick. If they send someone to investigate the garrison, it'll take some time, and it'll buy me time to make sure there's no trouble. But now—"*

"My lord." Matrios's thoughts were interrupted by Elizabeth's voice.

"At your service." He turned to her.

"How?" She looked at him with disbelief.

"What?"

"No matter." She shook her head. "What do you want to do?" she asked a little shyly, showing a bit of fear.

"Right," he snapped. "Verilion! Prepare my carriage. Adalanna, please gather my soldiers—those I can take with me, not including the knights. Buy food, simple tools, at least two carts, and peasant clothes. Don't forget a chest. I want one of the knights to gather for me all the available information about the village."

Adalanna and Verilion replied in salute, and then all but a few of the knights who were on guard duty with Matrios ran off.

"What are you up to, my Lord?" Elizabeth looked at him in amazement.

"My dear, we're leaving the city tonight!"

"What?"

"Go and pack what you can!"

"But—"

"Don't ask questions, just go! Take three of my knights. They can help you with the packing!" He pointed to three female armoured knights, and she merely nodded and stormed off surrounded by the knights.

"Picon!" Matrios called the little boy to him.

"Yes, my liege!" said the child as he came forward.

"Go to the garden and escort my daughter to my room!" He put his hand on the boy's shoulder.

"Yes, sir!" Picon saluted and ran off, emboldened and glorified, for he had been given a mission of his own by Matrios.

Matrios ordered those who remained to follow him as he made his way towards his room. As they walked, his feet thudded on the polished floor and the knights clattered behind him. When he reached the room, he recalled the memories of his body's first owner as he entered.

A delicate scent of lilies wafted through the room, the bed was tidy, a row of wine bottles sat in a lightless corner on the wall, and opposite it was a huge wardrobe. He stepped over and opened it to see a mass of clothes made of good-quality material. They were of all colours, but he picked out the black ones and put them on the bed. Then a maid entered and bowed respectfully. "What can I do for you?" Matrios said.

"I'm here to help my master!" she replied, sounding a little frightened. "Elena sent me." She stepped closer to him and put her hand on his chest and began unbuttoning his shirt. Matrios grabbed her hand and lifted it away from his body.

"Pack everything, but start with what I have put on the bed," he said, blushing. She, also blushing, stepped away from him and began folding the clothes neatly.

In dead silence, Matrios picked out all the things he liked and then stepped over to the wine rack, which was as tall as he was but twice as wide as his shoulders. He removed a bottle and looked at the fancy label. "If you say what my sister wants to hear," he told the maid, "you may keep this and give it away."

"My lord, what do you think will happen if I am found with these things?" she looked at him questioningly.

Matrios, surprised at his own clumsiness, stepped over to the desk under a large window, pulled out the drawer, and lifted the secret compartment. Then took out three coins from the hidden money and put them in her hand.

"Can we make a deal now?" he asked.

"My lord always spoils me," she said lustfully, hiding the coins between her round breasts before she returned to folding the clothes happily.

Matrios sighed and started sorting the wines. He walked to the door and ordered one of the soldiers to find him a trunk for the wines. When the soldier came back with it, Matrios packed the bottles that seemed most valuable or had interesting-sounding names or that he remembered drinking in another life. He had the trunk loaded in no time, and the maid had finished packing the other trunk with the clothes. Matrios finally selected a few books that he was interested in, and he piled them beside the trunk. They had just been gathering dust on the bookshelf for years.

Picon ran down the stairs and through the corridors. He was so excited that he got lost several times, but he finally reached the garden. He jumped over the stone ledge behind which Shrike and Linary were playing. Shrike hissed at the rushing boy who stood next to the little girl and bowed respectfully. "Miss, please follow me. Your father's orders!" he decreed.

Ignoring him, Linary just kept on playing and chasing the strange little bird around pots and buckets that were bursting with flowers. Picon ran after her and kept calling, but his words fell on deaf ears. He got fed up and grabbed the little girl's skirt. She stopped, and in that second, the bird landed on the ground and stepped closer to the two children.

"Your father's orders!" said the boy impatiently.

But Linary looked up. Then she touched Picon's arm and smiled. "You're the catcher!" she cried. She pulled her skirt from his hand and started running, laughing.

Shrike flew up again and followed Linary. Picon ran after them, and just as he was about to reach her, the bird-beast pinched his hand, slowing him down. Picon became angrier and angrier. He was on the verge of tears when two soldiers stepped in front of Linary.

"Come on, little girl! Your father has ordered it!" The two soldiers snorted at the girl and then one of them reached out for her, but Picon jumped between them and slapped the soldier's arm. "In the name of Lord Matrios, step away!" he shouted, shielding Linary with his body.

"The cheeky brat! What do you think, Marin, should we teach the little bastard to have some respect for his elders?"

"I don't give a shit!" responded Marin. "Just take the girl!" He drew his weapon. "You heard what Lord Matrios said! We get our orders from the prince!"

"So did I!" Picon shouted, looking at them with fury in his eyes. He also drew his weapon, but he was slow, and the soldier kicked him in the stomach, sending the boy flying, the air pushed out of his lungs. Picon landed, staggered twice, and then fell again, landing on his back. But he was a member of the Order of the Rose Knights, so though he was in pain all over, he leapt to his feet, got his breathing under control in a flash, and coughed up a little bloody spit. Then, gripping his sword, he charged at the big man fearlessly.

The evil-faced one easily parried the sword thrust with his dagger. Then he turned around and tried to stab Picon with it. Picon easily rolled out of the way and struck the man in the nose with the hilt of his sword. Meanwhile, the other soldier picked Linary up and tried to slip away. However, Shrike, whom the soldiers had ignored, transformed. As a huge bird-beast, he stood in the way of the terrified man. The soldier threw the sobbing, screaming little girl in terror and drew his sword with a metallic ring, but the creature crushed the man's torso with one powerful blow, throwing him against the wall, splattering his back against the white stone. Then Shrike caught the little girl up gently in his beak and flew up with her before the little one could see what had happened to her would-be captors.

Picon calmed down. He took two deep breaths and focused on the man with the broken nose who was lunging at him to deliver a powerful jab. Picon jumped away from the thrust and cut his attacker's arm with a weak slash. Then he held out his hand and turned to the man. "Cutting wave," he intoned. He waved his hand, and a thin, razor-sharp blue water line moved towards the man. It didn't take a blink of an eye to separate his head from its body. The lifeless torso folded like a house of cards, and Picon rushed back to his master's room.

Elizabeth hurried with the three bodyguards to her own suite, quickly and briskly asked for her maids, and then began to pack as quickly as she had never done before. She filled her trunk with her favourite clothes, packed her most precious trinkets, her favourite books, and her violin. Then she had the soldiers take the loaded trunks to the carts that would transport their worldly goods. She hurried back to her husband's quarters, but Shrike was rushing down the corridor towards her, smashing through everything and smashing the armour stands against the wall. Elizabeth was terrified, and the three soldiers leapt forward to protect her, but the creature stopped in its tracks and released Linary, who ran with a terrified scream into her mother's arms.

"My precious, what happened?"

Linary wiped her tears as best she could, but they were bursting forth in inexhaustible quantities. Elizabeth waited no longer. She picked up the weeping child and cast an angry glance at the creature, which suddenly turned small again and flew towards Matrios's room. The terrified company followed unabated. Elizabeth sent the servants to carry her luggage via the shortcut to the carts. The knights surrounded her, holding their shields as they escorted the woman and the terrified child.

When they reached Matrios's bedroom, they found him sitting on a chair at the table counting his money. The suite was now empty; only the man remained. Elizabeth rushed into the room and disturbed the calmness. "My lord! Something's wrong!"

"What the hell is going on?" Matrios jumped up and swept the money into a bag.

At this moment Picon arrived and pushed his way into the room. "Lord Matrios!"

"What the hell is going on here?" Matrios repeated, looking at the boy.

"Miss Linary was attacked by kidnappers," said Picon, gasping for breath.

Matrios picked up the little girl. This seemed extremely strange to Elizabeth, and she froze for a few moments, but her husband's commanding, unresisting response shook her awake: "We are leaving!"

The knights immediately surrounded the man and his family. Then they all moved swiftly through the corridors. Guards covered every window and kept passers-by from interrupting the journey. The group dashed through the empty corridors, around the corners that the creature had disturbed, and then Matrios addressed Shrike: "Fly forth!"

"Okay!" the creature replied, and with two powerful flaps of its wings he sped up and disappeared around the next corner. The swiftly moving knights pushed all comers, nobles and servants alike, against the wall. It mattered not to them; it was only their task, which they performed without a second thought.

As they ran into the courtyard, Matrios caught a glimpse of the setting sun, its last blood-red streaks just licking the horizon. Verilion was waiting for them with the carriages. He jumped off his horse. From the activity of the knights, he understood in a flash what was going on. He grabbed Matrios, who was still holding Linary, and shoved him into the lead carriage. He shoved Elizabeth in beside them. Then he slammed the door and swung up onto the side of the carriage, which caused the coachman to immediately snap the reins and shout for the horses to run.

The carriage wheels immediately began to spin, pebbles bouncing mercilessly under the spinning wheels. The carriage tore through the beautiful flower-lined stone path as if it was a warship floating on water. Surrounded by horsemen, the great carriage accelerated unchallenged to the gate, and there it roared through with such a power that it almost trampled the striding soldiers.

Adalanna, the elven woman, had gathered a small line of carts that were now lined up in the marketplace near the inner castle wall. When she caught a glimpse of the guarded carriage exiting the castle in a hurry, she shouted out to the drivers in the caravan behind her. The carts stormed after the fleeing carriage from the ring road, following them through the inner city to the outer castle wall. Soldiers tried to stop them, but the drivers spared no horse as they fled under the wall, throwing aside man and animal alike. The horsemen rode in front of the carriage to break their way through the people, so that no one would be trampled by the carts, but they couldn't prevent the terror that struck into the hearts of all.

Matrios was finally able to sit up in the seat. He shielded the little girl from the jolting with his body, and then hugged her to him. He could not help it, for her tiny hand clung to her father's cloak like a little monkey to her mother's fur, and she buried her face deep in the soft cloth. Elizabeth glanced at him and saw him resting his cheek on her daughter's head and stroking her back, trying to calm the frightened child. Matrios looked over at Elizabeth and sighed.

"How did you know?" She looked at him questioningly.

"I was sent to that garrison to die," he said clearly.

"What?"

"I don't know the motive, only that they want me dead in the capital. I don't know and I don't care who. I have a feeling that, sooner or later, I'll find out anyway." Matrios continued to calm the girl as he spoke quietly.

"I understand, I think," said Elizabeth and took Linary gently from Matrios.

Shrike landed on the window frame and looked through the small curtain questioningly, then looked at Matrios. "We can slow down, no one is chase us."

"Get that thing out of here!" she cried. "Wherever it goes there's only trouble."

"Stupid woman!" hissed Shrike angrily. "I saved little Linary!" He spread its wings menacingly.

"Don't worry about him! He is the most reliable one here at the moment," said Matrios.

"How can you say such a thing? The creature is from hell and causes only suffering!" she shouted at him.

"Elizabeth, if it weren't for that creature, I wouldn't be here now, and you'd be on your way back to the Republic!"

She cowered in the corner of the carriage and gave him a murderous look. Matrios merely sighed regretfully. Then he turned to the creature.

"We can slow down now. No one is following us," the bird-beast repeated, preening his wing feathers.

Matrios nodded and opened the carriage door. Verilion rode next to the carriage, his horse snorting loudly. The noise of the road rushed madly in Matrios's ears. The prince beckoned Verilion, who glanced at him and nodded. Then Verilion tapped the bridle three times, which caused the horse to gallop forward. When Verilion reached the head of the hurrying caravan, he raised his hands in a fist, whereupon all the coachmen pulled on their reins, slowing the carriages and carts and finally bringing the caravan to slow down.

The last rays of the sun had left the horizon, and the tiny twinkling stars now formed a shining blanket of light across the countryside. Matrios scrambled up onto one of the carts to inspect the many crates and other luggage. Looked behind the carriage where Adalanna was sitting in the front cart. It was difficult to make her out in the distant darkness. *She must be fast asleep*, he thought to himself as he bolted the carriage door.

"Do we have everything, my lord?" asked Elizabeth.

"We have most everything, but we must have left Linary's things behind," he said with a sigh.

"I brought her a change of clothes, but unfortunately she won't have any play clothes," said the child's mother, looking down at the little girl. "She smiled. "My lord," she said, looking up at him and biting her lip, "what happened to you?" Her voice trembled in fear.

"You must have overheard it in the hall," he said, taking it for granted.

"Yes, but that still doesn't explain—" she said, but quickly choked the words back into her mouth. "Please forgive me … I'm just babbling!"

"I don't know yet, my dear, but I feel much freer, and I've never been so full of wanting to do something!" Matrios raised his hand to his face.

"My lord, why are we going behind God's back then?" asked the woman.

"There's a reason for that. We don't know where we'll end up yet." He smiled.

"But it's not … you—" said the woman with a frightened look.

"Elizabeth, I don't remember everything that happened. I can't explain it to you, but I promise you one thing!"

"What's that?"

"I'll never touch you with malice again, and I'll never touch Linary with malice either!" he said, stroking the cheek of the little girl who was now sleeping on her mother's bosom as sweetly and softly as a falling autumn leaf.

"My lord, allow me to doubt it." She pulled the child and herself away from his touch.

"I know it won't be easy for me to regain your trust as your husband and as your daughter's father, but I'll do my best and I'll move mountains if I have to."

"He always knew how to promise!" said Elizabeth with a wry grin.

"I'll be able to keep my promises now." He laughed softly.

"You do as you please!" She curled up in the corner and yawned.

"Get some sleep. We have a long way to go," he said. He picked up a blanket from the seat and laid it gently over his wife and child.

The mother soon fell asleep with her child in her arms. Matrios watched as the beautiful lady was overcome with fatigue and surrendered her body to the cradle-like sway of the carriage as it rocked as she had rocked her child after she was born. It was not common for a woman of noble birth to raise her child herself, but she had refused to leave her little girl in the care of nannies, and for this reason, many considered her a match for prince Matrios. She had only the deepest feelings of motherly love for her only child. Matrios recalled how he had seen her before him. A mere breathing womb, which was not surprising, for in this world few women are married to more than that, and he could not help but accept the fact. He believed that his former self's evil nature had put her in this position. She had never been liked in the palace, and her only escape was to raise her own child, which had saved her from the screaming madness they tried to cover up with gold and pomp.

Matrios was also overwhelmed by sleep as he delved deeper into his own thoughts and uncovered the riddles of his past life. He slumped slowly in his seat, his head resting on the cushion. Finally, he dreamed with soft sighs. The carriage ran slowly along the cobbled roads, stopping in the middle of the night to let the horses rest.

The knights took turns on guard, all thirty-six of them skilled soldiers and mages, determined and loyal. Only Picon slept soundly through the night. Verilion did not like the boy to be up all night. The old knight believed a good night's sleep helped a young man become a good knight. So the world went quiet around them and stayed that way until the sun came up.

Like robots, the knights, soldiers, and coachmen awoke all at once. The knights cooked and shared breakfast around the fire. The coachmen began to hitch the horses to the carriages and carts.

Still in the carriage, Matrios awoke to the sudden change in noise around him and sat up sleepily from his slightly uncomfortable bed. He stretched his neck, which crackled like a dry twig. "Half my life for a coffee," he said wearily. He glanced at Elizabeth and Linary sitting opposite him. They were slightly spread out although still nestled into each other, resting and breathing softly, almost inhaling each other's air. Matrios pondered the sight of the woman with slightly dishevelled hair, her thin arms wrapped around the child, who was grasping the beaded black crown of hair with one hand and running it across her little fingers. He felt a warm, pleasant sensation in his chest. It ran down his spine. He could do nothing but watch the two of them dreaming so calmly and wonderfully inside the carriage. He felt blessed to be witness to it as he remembered his old life—the constant rush, the roaring sea of machinery, and the overwhelming crossfire of deadlines. He had to stop for a moment and just admire what was before him. He wanted to spend a little time with his family, a little time that had long since fallen apart. He may never have had the chance, but since his resurrection, much had changed, even about himself. He felt that this world was so wonderful that he wanted nothing more than to simply watch and see every corner of it, from the first rock to the last man.

The sound of a knock broke the stillness. Matrios snapped out of the moment and sighed breathlessly. He then opened the door. Verilion was standing beside the carriage holding a large container. The door had been blocking out the noise outside; now that it was open, the two dreamers awoke and quickly sat up behind Matrios.

"Your breakfast, sir! I didn't want to wake you in the morning!" said the big man, handing the small pot over to him.

"Thank you, Verilion!" Matrios took the food and smiled gratefully at the man. "When does everyone else eat breakfast?"

"At sunrise," said Verilion.

"Be sure to wake me next time," said Matrios.

"But sir—"

"I prefer a warm meal," continued Matrios.

Verilion laughed, nodded, and said goodbye. Before taking his leave, he waved sweetly to the little girl, who wiped her eyes and waved back softly to the big man.

Matrios opened the package to find large slices of bread wrapped in white cloth. Next to them were slices of dried meat and some tomatoes.

"Must we eat like peasants?" Elizabeth said.

Matrios's hand stopped just as he was about to take a bite of the dried meat. He looked at her. "What's wrong with the meat?"

"I don't have a problem with meat, just—"

"I thought I was going to have your share." He sighed.

Linary looked up at her mother and smiled. "I'll give you my tomato if you don't like meat, Mom!" She held out the small red sphere to her.

Elizabeth said nothing. She just watched with a smile as the little girl tried to chew the dried meat. Linary looked at her mother with sparkling eyes.

"Lucky us—she has your eyes!" Matrios said, laughing.

"What do you mean?" Elizabeth looked at him.

"Both of you have eyes like the sea," he said, smiling pleasantly, but she caught his glance, blushed, and snatched a half-broken loaf of bread from his hand and began to eat it.

"Careful! Don't choke on it!" he said, laughing.

The journey was long and dusty as the company slowly wound its way from the capital to the foot of Sleeping Mountain in a winding valley far from civilisation. Small villages and farms dotted the quiet and peaceful countryside. Bandits waited for them at the crossroads, but their courage soon wavered when they saw the armed knights riding their powerful battle mounts.

Every morning, the prince sat around the campfire with the knights and listened to their stories.

"And there I was, facing the Brekich, which already had Kreus in its belly! That damned toad was ten feet tall, I tell you, but I'll be damned if it wasn't at least three fathoms long! That bastard looked at me with its big eyes. I bet he thought I'd be as mad as Kreus was and charge at it like our prince would the brothels!" The red-bearded man overplayed the story with every word.

"Do you want me to behead you, Gerald? You are in the presence of Lord Matrios!" Verilion shouted at the man.

"Oh, sir, excuse me!" The knight knelt down, but Matrios only chuckled.

"Where I was?" continued Gerald. "I was standing there facing the worm, and I saw it lift its ass ready to throw itself at me! That brat was going to flatten me with its arse! I grabbed my sword and rushed at the bastard as it was kicking away! And finally, I threw myself away. Then I turned around and slashed the filthy whore from back to front! The guts flowed out of the toad like water from a well, I tell you. And it that stank like a soaked Purtyul. Nasty and pungent!"

"Gerald, you forgot one thing," said one of the knights. "Picon and I watched your epic struggle. When the frog jumped, you threw yourself to the ground screaming, and then your sword got stuck in its spine!" The scarred one laughed.

"It only leaked its insides because, when you finally managed to pull out your sword, you cut its skin," said Picon with a smile.

"The skin of a Brekich is very slippery," Gerald finished. "And what if I embellished some details? The others wouldn't tell it!" the bald man shouted at them.

Matrios had a good laugh at the knights' banter as he protectively watched his child play with Shrike at the edge of the green meadow. Sometimes he even enjoyed Picon's company, though the boy looked at spending time with the princess as a task rather than a game. Matrios had heard the boy emphasise this several times to his companions with a chest filled with pride.

Chapter 6

They travelled for days through rain and dry weather. Finally, in the distance, the mountain was visible, standing alone in the middle of the wilderness. It was quite close to the sea; indeed, they could hear the murmuring sound of the dancing waves. Matrios opened the carriage door and sniffed the air, which was not what he had expected. The salty yet sweet smell of the sea was mixed with the smell of rotten eggs carried on the limp and tired wind. He covered his nose and coughed twice. Then his eyes brightened. "That is sulphur!" he shouted in joy.

Not far from the road, in the thick forest, in a large clearing surrounded by burnt-out turf, was a sulphur mine known locally as the cesspit. It was not large, but it was more than Matrios needed. He sniffed the wind again and hung onto the side of the wagon in a better mood.

He felt strange. His joy was strange to him, and he felt that some unknown force must have brought him to that place. But there was no time to think about it, for they soon reached the village, whose landscape loomed up behind the trees. It was a tiny settlement surrounded by wooden planks with a few houses jutting out beyond the wall. Around it were stables and vast fields. On the hill, high above the village, rose a tiny, dingy grey castle built of stone. It looked quite ancient, unworthy of mention in the royal family. Matrios got back into the carriage after taking in the scenery and turned to his wife. "Do you know anything about the village?" he asked her.

"I thought you asked the knight to find out more about it," she replied questioningly.

"Yes, but I forgot to check the records." He sighed.

"Ah …" She reached down and pulled a book from under the cushioned seat. "I thought, since you're having fun with the knights, I'd find out more about the godforsaken place we're banished to." She opened the book.

"Mom, will you read to me?" Linary asked, cuddling up to her mother.

"No, it's not a storybook!" Elizabeth replied sweetly.

"If you read it, then all stories are fairy tales!" the little girl snapped and lay down on her lap.

"Oh, so be it."

Elizabeth read: "The village of Brekan is one of the villages in the Sleeping Mountain area. The name comes from an ancient word meaning 'work'. There are mines of high-quality ore, but the 'stinking death' made them inaccessible from the year 3000 when a fatal mine collapse occurred. All thirty miners lost their lives, and the deaths of another fifty people are linked to the site. Many crops survive on the topsoil, but the more sensitive crops do not survive. Until 3254, the village was loyal to the town of Egerton, but the Duchy of Berolt destroyed and burned the town after their second campaign, leaving the area without a stronghold. Only after the demonic threat did the duchy's territorial claim stop, presumably with no intention of getting any closer to the threat. The village includes a stenchstone deposit and a salt deposit that cannot be reached due to the stinking death. Number of souls: 210. Noble: Matarion nobleman (died without heir). The village is a militia village." She paused. "This is what the book says," she announced.

"Mom, that was a boring story!"

"Okay, I'll read you something else." Elizabeth gently pecked the girl on the cheek.

"Hmm ... stinking death?" Matrios asked.

"I don't know what it is. It's the first time I've heard of it," said his wife.

"Sounds interesting," said Matrios. "Do you know what happened to the town of Egerton?"

"I only know it's a den of bandits, and all the merchants avoid it like the plague," she told him. "It was a great castle, because it was besieged by the Berolt army for six months," she said, and she pulled another book from under the seat.

"Six months?"

"Yes! After that, the kingdom made an agreement with the duchy, and a truce was concluded. But why am I telling you this? You should know it already! I'm sorry to prattle on," she excused herself.

"Come now, I like to hear your voice," he said sweetly.

There was a knock on the door, and the carriage stopped. Matrios jumped up, dusted off his black clothes, cleared his throat, and leaned on the door handle. Slowly, he opened it to see the people of the village staring at him with strange, scrutinizing eyes. He stepped down to the ground, adjusted his attire, and looked out again at the welcoming crowd. Across from him stood a small old man leaning on his cane, his beard white with yellowish patches around his mouth, his face wrinkled and dusty, his clothes patchy and plain. The old man gave a bow, which was really only a nod, and then spoke from under his great beard. "Welcome, good sir, to the village of Brekan where no bird goes." The old man laughed, and soon the laughing turned to coughing. "Never mind the serfs, I beg you, and go up to the castle at once with your family. We are neither interesting nor curious. We are only simple folk," said the old man, pointing to the castle, which only about a quarter of an hour's walk away.

"May I know your name?" asked the prince kindly.

"My name is Marabas, and I am known as the old man of the village. I may be old and feeble, but I am in charge of the village and its problems," said the old man a little reluctantly in his gravelly voice.

"My pleasure, Marabas. My name is Matrios Hritan!"

"Hritan, is it? Isn't he just some nobleman who came along?" asked Marabas, stroking his beard.

At this, Verilion's eyes flashed, and he stepped forward, but Matrios gave a barely visible hand signal, and the man got back in line.

"Yes, as of today, I am the empowered lord of the village."

"Eh, just what I needed," said Marabas reluctantly. "Please forgive my rudeness. I will soon prepare everything the lord may ask. We have received no letter announcing that anyone was coming. But if we had received a letter, it wouldn't have mattered since only the young priest can read. Damn that one too!" grumbled the old man.

"Don't worry, old man!" said Matrios, laughing. He turned in the direction of the caravan and shouted, "Adalanna, bring me the tool cart and three barrels from our supply wagon!"

"Yes, sir!" the woman answered from a distance.

On Matrios' orders, the backmost cart was brought to the centre of the village. Matrios instructed his knights to distribute among everyone as many tools as they needed. They also collected those that were worn out or of poor quality. People could not believe their eyes when they saw the shiny, freshly forged tools. However, they tried to hide their surprise and did not burst out in great enthusiasm.

Then the knights rolled in three barrels filled with good things of the earth—salted meat, preserved fish, and pickled cabbage. Soon the queue snaked up to the village border, and the wilting people were so happy to receive the food for their tables. Everyone was counted, and Matrios quickly divided the rations among them. The distribution and the gifting of hoes and shovels and picks as well as food lasted for two hours. As soon as the knights and soldiers had finished, the people scattered to take home all they had received, but Matrios was a little disappointed. He felt that it was not enough for them, but he could not give them any more presents at that time.

"Old man!" said Matrios.

"What can I do for you, my good sir!" said Marabas in a much softer voice.

"There are two trunks of new clothes in the cart. Distribute them to all who need them, but equally and well!" he pointed to the cart.

"Yes, sir, but we are just simple peasants here. I believe we don't deserve all this!" Marabas excused himself.

"How can farmers dig and miners pick when they have nothing to eat and no tools to work with?" Matrios asked, putting his hands on his hips.

"Ah, you're right, my lord. I'm just a stupid old man! The Holy Mother bless you for his kindness," said Marabas, nodding his head again.

"Please come with us and tell us all you know about the village," invited Matrios.

"No offence, Your Grace, but I'm no longer cut out for the journey. I can barely walk. I'm old and weak." He bowed his head.

"Raise your head." Matrios smiled and put his hand on the old man's shoulder. "Then take me to your humble home so that we can talk indoors and not out here in the cold wind."

"Do not delay us, old pa! Our horses are tired, and the bed calls for a child in the carriage!" said Verilion from behind.

"Ah I see, good knight. Please follow me to my house."

"Go ahead to the castle," Matrios said to Adalanna. "I will follow you shortly. And bring my horse!" he said, pointing at the black stallion. "Go all of you. Verilion, stay with me!"

"Understood, my lord!" said the great knight, and he sent the knights away.

Marabas walked with tiny but nimble steps along the path, stirring up the dust with his shuffling gait. Matrios smiled at the old man's hurried steps and thought about how much he had changed. He felt that, if his presence hadn't grown much in the eyes of the people, it had grown much more in the eyes of the old man. They reached the old, tiny, wooden house on the corner, which had seen better days. Beside it was a small sign post, but Matrios did not pat it any attention. When they went into the musty house, Marabas lit a candle and pulled a sizable sausage from the smoker. He broke some sourdough bread for the prince and poured him some old lager. Matrios thanked the elder for his hospitality but did not touch the food; he only looked at the old man who sat down opposite him.

"What would you like to know, my good sir?" asked Marabas.

"Tell me, my old man, how much does the village pay?"

"Well, my good sir, all the families pay their tithes, and the church tax is used to maintain the church in the centre of the village. The adventurers who come by sometimes pick up our errands for the monsters, but more pass through than stay. We pay the nobleman a war tax per porch. Besides, the smoke tax for the coal mine and the blacksmith is not free in the village as well. Though Old Lazar was kind-hearted and strong handed, his son is a little clumsier, but he too has a heart of gold. I think that's all there is," said the old man.

"That's all?"

"That is more than we should have, my good sir. The countryside is swarming with muggers, the mines are worse than bedbugs, and the ground is rotten to the core! Only grass grows in the fields. We can hardly even mow it! Worse than corn!"

"Worse?

"I'm telling you! Tiny, sticky grains. I don't know what that weed grows! If you taste it, you'll fall into bed! But it's as sweet as honey! There is nowhere else where this crop grows but here!"

Hmm … interesting," Matrios said quietly. *If something is sweet, it must be glucose, and that means nothing but sugar,* he thought in himself. "Do you have sugar?" he asked Marabas.

"Do I look like a king? Not even the nobleman next door can afford a spoonful, let alone me. Since the Berolt army trampled and burnt and salted Egerton Castle, there has been no sugar. Only the plainest food. Nothing but ruins and refugees everywhere!" complained Marabas, shivering. "If my good prince wants to live, he will turn his back now. There is nothing but hardship and torment awaiting you here!" said he, troubled.

"Don't worry, old man! I'm not going anywhere! Our luck will soon change for the better!" Matrios touched the old man's hand.

"I'm not saying this as a peasant, sir, for I've eaten my share of bread, but I've heard many sweet words. Don't feed this old soul with hopes," said the old father, almost in tears, but he gave only a reluctant smile. "I have seen more than you could imagine, and I don't mean to be bad, but the elders are here to tell stories, if I can't lift a pick, am I right?" said Marabas, but he turned away from the young prince.

"Don't be discouraged! Hard work can build the world!" Matrios smiled kindly.

"I've never heard that from a man who born with a sliver spoon in his mouth!" said Marabas, snorting.

"I'm different from the rest."

"Aye! They'd have cut off my gourd by now, but what could they do? I'm over sixty winters old, and they'd only help me, I tell you!" He laughed, and Matrios laughed with him.

For the first time, Matrios had spoken to someone freely, someone who didn't just see his rank or his name, but just complained to him, saw a smile that had life behind it and not fear or ambition. It was a simple man who sat opposite him, and Matrios felt he had met something simple that wanted nothing from him but his ears to listen to quiet explanations without counter explanations. Matrios sipped his drink and then passed it to the old man. "It will be a pleasure to work with you, Marabas."

"But don't work me to death, sir! Or you know what? Do it!" The elderly man laughed and took a sip from the cup.

Matrios got up from the table, said a polite goodbye to the greybeard, and left. He mounted his horse and rode off with Verilion towards the castle. As they rode, they talked. "How do you like the scorch on the devil's arse?" said Verilion.

"I'm positively disappointed, I must say."

"Really? I thought you were going to take a look at it and then we could go home!" said Verilion, laughing.

"I have nowhere to go home to," said the prince, a little wryly.

"I didn't say anything," said the knight, ashamed.

"Don't worry about it. We're going to be busy I heard."

"What are your plans?" he looked at the prince.

"First I have to see for myself the plant Marabas told me about. Then I have to talk to the blacksmith, visit the priest, and settle the village taxes."

"It seems like a lot."

"One thing leads to another. You just have to get the order right, but I'd prefer to find someone to handle the bureaucracy. I don't want that on my back."

"My lord is good at it," replied Verilion.

"I'm getting tired of it really fast, Verilion." The prince sighed.

"Why don't you ask your lady?" The big man wondered.

"What do you mean?"

"Lady Elizabeth is the daughter of the best merchant of the Republic, a noble daughter if you can describe her that way, and I heard she is skilled in trade as well as in bureaucracy.

"So you say?" mused Matrios.

"Do you not even know your own wife's talents, my good sir? Did my lord get a hit on the head as well?" he looked at the prince, a little disgusted. "You know there is a saying in the villages. The man gets the wealth and the woman protects it." Verilion's tone was instructive.

You're saying something! thought Matrios.

Eventually, Matrios and Verilion reached the castle and were let in through the gate which creaked as the soldiers opened it. They galloped to the stables and dismounted. Matrios entered the castle and trudged wearily up the dark and chilly corridors to his room, having received directions from a servant. He had taken a torch from its holder and held it in front of him as he went. The route was winding and dark, so he soon lost his way despite the instructions. He wandered halfway around the castle, but in the end, he found his quarters.

A faint ray of light filtered into the hallway, and the musty smell was broken by the sweet scent of lilacs. Matrios stepped close to the door and pushed it gently in. Inside, Elizabeth sat at a table, a bowl and a flickering candle beside her and a candelabra glowing on the wall. The wind shook the shutters, and she had not heard the door creak. She dipped a cloth into the bowl and then twisted it and rubbed it on a bar of soap. Then she touched it to her delicate, soft skin. Slowly, gently, she washed her shoulders. Again she dipped the cloth into the water, rinsed the soap from it and wiped the foam from her skin. Sitting in the cool room in front of the steaming bowl, she wiped the steam off the mirror with her hand and then noticed the man standing in the doorway. She turned around and shyly covered her glistening ash-white skin with her hands.

Matrios merely gulped and felt his mouth slightly hang open at the sight. In the dim light of the candles, the outline of her gorgeous body played in the darkness. She averted her eyes as if regretting covering the curves of her body. At this very moment, he came to his senses and lowered his eyes then closed his lips, pressing them together in shame. He stepped deeper into the room, the air between them as cool as autumn. He stood at the corner of the bed and threw off his cloak, keeping his back to her, trying to avoid any questions. When he had removed his shirt and thrown it into a nearby basket, the scar on his back, carved into his body by the demon's spear, was revealed in the mysterious dance of light. She sighed as if the last gasp of a cry had escaped her lungs. Matrios turned slowly and looked at her in horror as if his eyes were searching for danger around her.

"What?" he asked, and the sight of the wound what stretched wide across the man's abdomen revealed itself before her eyes.

She removed her cloak from the back of the chair and draped it over her shoulders. Its weave was fine and slightly translucent, but the black cotton threads allowed only a hint of mystery. Slowly she stepped up to him and smoothed the scar. The man felt the soft touch and took a step back, throwing his back against the cold wooden panel of the closet. She jumped up and threw herself on the bed as she stepped back among her shyness.

"Excuse me, my lord! I've never seen a battle wound before!" she said, confused.

"It was just so sudden!" He excused himself, and then pulled his back away from the cold oak wooden board.

"What caused it?" she asked.

"My own foolishness." He smiled.

"What are you talking about?"

"A demon's spear did it. The damned monster stabbed me from the front. I remember nothing but the pain that tightened my body and

Adalanna leaning over me screaming for help," said the man, putting on his nightgown.

"How many died there?

"Too many." The prince sighed as he closed the open door of the old wardrobe. "Let's rest. It's been a long journey, and we're in for even longer days." He stretched out facing her.

"Yes, my lord." She pulled herself smaller, climbed onto the bed, and crawled under the covers with her back to him, her hands folded across her chest as if to protect her body.

Matrios looked at her and sighed heavily, not from contempt, but from a strong sorry aching and burning his heart. He extinguished the candles at the table, put a little more wood on the fire that burned opposite the bed, and then nestled himself into the wide nest, tucking himself into his side. At first the sheet was cold, but then it warmed up more and more. It felt so pleasant to his weary body that sleep rushed over him like a wild boar.

The beckoning call of the night was drowned out, the lutes of weariness played slowly and quietly, and only she remained awake in the room. Softly and subdued, she shed her tears on the cover of the feather-filled pillow, which slowly drank up the salty liquid. She dreaded the evenings she had to spend with her husband in their bed, but when she heard his soft snores, her breath was soothed, her fear vanished, and soon the soothing voice of sleep called to her as well, and she joined her bedfellow, bitterly but without a bitter cry, in the endless sea of dreams.

Chapter 7

The loud banging of shutters and the light filtering through the wooden planks woke the prince as he turned over onto his other side in the morning. Tired and dazed, he opened his eyes, quickly squinted, and noticed the sun's blatantly intrusive beam. He raised his hand to his eyes, and his elbow caught on something on the bed. It was Elizabeth's head he had touched.

He looked down and saw her slowly panting, a little away from him, but closer than she had been at the beginning of the dream. Matrios only smiled and pulled the thick blanket up over her. The thought of stealing a sweet kiss from her ran through his mind, but it was soon interrupted by the rhythmic sound of knocking. He turned over on the bed and lay on his back, pulling the blanket higher and covering his upper body. She, too, awoke to the muffled noise, and, realising that she had changed places with Matrios during the night, immediately blushed and crawled under the covers.

"Come in," said Matrios sleepily.

At the sound of his voice a servant entered, an old man, his moustache spread like a grey brush over his lips. He paused at the open door and bowed in a gentlemanly manner. "My lord, the breakfast is served," he announced in a monotone voice.

"I see," replied Matrios, yawning. "We'll be down soon."

"Tradition has it that the lady and child will have breakfast later, and the master will eat breakfast while he discusses the day's business with the castle authorities," the servant explained respectfully.

"My wife is the head of the house, and my child will have no trouble in learning and getting used to the way of the meetings," he explained.

"In that case, I will immediately tell the maids to help Lady Elizabeth prepare for her day as soon as possible."

"I should like to go to the village during the day along with my wife, and I ask you to choose the proper clothes for it."

"I'll do my best, my lord!"

"Why do you want me to go there?" she said angrily from under the covers.

"You're awake! If you remember, I told you it is going to be a long day," Matrios reminded her with a grin on his face.

"But to go among peasants!" she said indignantly.

"You don't need to go among them. You should just see the village. I wonder how a merchant's daughter would see our situation," he said, determined and encouraging, but mostly provocatively.

"I am only my father's first daughter. I know nothing, my lord. Beyond childbirth," she said sadly.

"I wonder what your father has taught you. He must have taught you something because my father agreed to our marriage." Matrios smiled.

"I helped to manage the warehouses and wrote delivery letters and took part in negotiations, but—"

"I think that's enough for a letter of recommendation!" He clapped his hands together and sat up on the bed. "Isn't it?" he looked at the servant.

"I believe so, sir." he answered respectfully.

118

"But—" said Elizabeth.

"Believe in yourself!" Matrios said in a reassuring tone.

She didn't answer. She just lowered her eyes and wondered why the heavens were beating her with such a husband. Matrios got out of bed, stretching his limbs, which were not used to a comfortable bed. He creaked like an old oak in a gale. The prince stepped to the wardrobe and took out a suit of black clothes that was just to his taste. He looked over the garment, touched the fine woven silk, but the servant stepped closer and took it from his hand.

"My lord, this is for special occasions."

"It is a black suit, and I prefer this colour."

"But it's the colour of mourning!" The old man snorted slightly.

"Then I mourn my life in the city!" He took the clothes from the old man's hand with a smile.

"If the lord so wishes." He sighed.

Three maids entered the bedroom. Elizabeth sat up on the bed, clutching her blanket to her chest and sighing loudly while Matrios slowly got ready.

Tibald the servant was surprised at the prince's pace as got himself dressed. The servant was used to dressing high-ranking men as they lay on the bed! He couldn't imagine what had come over the lord, but he felt that he was finally not needed to take care of a grown man as he would a toddler, although had not forgotten his ordeal so far, and so he didn't say anything, as if he didn't want Matrios to wake up and fall back on the bed like a child.

Matrios buttoned the cufflinks, adjusted the pretty coat on his upper body, and then turned around where his lady was already sitting on the edge of the bed, enjoying the servants braiding and combing her hair.

"How do I look?" he asked with high hopes in his eyes as she looked at him.

"Like someone coming from a funeral," she said carelessly.

"Perfect!" said Matrios, smiling.

She had a questioning look on her face, but she turned back and listened to the girls chattering, occasionally saying something to them. The prince walked through the doorway as the old servant held the door for him. The great hinges creaked as the door shut behind him.

"Why is my lady up so early?" asked one of the servants.

"I was woken up by them," replied Elizabeth.

"But my lady always got up later in the day and had breakfast in the courtyard."

"Ask my husband, if you dare." Elizabeth sighed.

"Of course." The servant smiled in puzzlement. "My lady has a very good-looking master," said one the maids sleepily.

"Better on the outside than the inside." Elizabeth sighed sadly, whereupon the three girls stopped their chatter, but a few moments later, though puzzled, they went on, as if they had heard nothing.

Elizabeth adjusted her clothes after being fitted into a white-and-red top over a wide skirt. Her face was sad and buried deep in thoughts. One of the women tugged at her corset. "Careful, you!" cried Elizabeth.

"Excuse me, my lady!" the girl excused herself.

"Oh, I must go downstairs." Elizabeth sighed and started towards the door.

Matrios walked through corridors that now seemed more spacious and brighter than they had the night before. Still they were chilly even though the sun was shining brightly. The entire west wing was as cool as a pantry. He staggered as he picked his feet, glancing over at the old man, who, covering himself, was already wiping his own nose but trying to keep his gentility as much as he could.

Matrios wondered to himself what a hotbed this castle was for pneumonia even in the middle of summer, and then his mind raced as he thought about what he was going to do and how. He wondered about the plant the peasants had spoken about, the mine, and the mountain that emitted such a high volume of boiling steam. But always the cold pulled him back to the ground and would not let him contemplate calmly.

He saw that the windows were covered only with wooden shutters; he saw no glass anywhere beyond his own room. This was unlike the castle in the royal capital. He paused for a moment to think about that too but didn't linger on it any longer lest the servant notice.

Matrios hurried downstairs to a room situated beneath his own where little Linary slept. The door creaked softly and slowly as the metal hinges turned on themselves, and he stepped inside cautiously. The shutters moved gently, playing a soft lullaby in the morning breeze. The whispering wind playfully disturbed the dust in the room; it was difficult to see in the dimness. He walked through a scattering of rudimentary and battered toys and sat down on the edge of the bed watching the tiny girl sleep in her nest of bedding.

Her fine hair fell across her face, her right hand moved under her head now and then, and she kicked sometimes with her little feet. Her left hand poked her cheek, and then she stretched it out and rolled over onto her back. Matrios just sat there and couldn't believe his eyes. Strangely, he felt as if he had just realised that the tiny person he watched sleeping the sleep of the just on the bed was his own little girl. In his eyes, she was the most beautiful pearly flower.

He felt an otherworldly, indescribable, yet pleasant, counter-intuitive, and irrefutable love he had hitherto only felt for his own machines. He did not understand this feeling, for the child did not belong to him. He was not, in fact, Matrios here, but Jacob, although he felt his soul beginning to merge with the former prince more than he would have liked. Yet he was unable to resist the prince's repressed emotions.

He touched the small, soft hand that protruded from under the blanket, and it immediately, almost reflexively, her fingers tightened around his fingers. He looked down at her hand with an even wider and happier smile, stroking her forearm a few times with his ring finger. The little girl woke up tired and groggy. She sat up on the bed, her tousled hair standing out like a haystack. She yawned and rubbed her sea-blue eyes, washing the sleep from them. He withdrew his hand and leaned back on the mattress. He looked at the child who looked up at him with tired eyes.

"Mum?" asked Linary, almost as if in a dream with her eyes barely open.

"No, my darling!" Matrios said softly.

"Father?" She opened her eyes, and as the world cleared before her, the mirrors of her sea-blue soul shone. "Where is Mom?" She looked around the room.

"I think she's waiting for us in the dining room."

"In the dining room?" She looked at him questioningly.

"It's breakfast time, my darling." He stroked the little child's head.

"But I want to sleep!" She snuggled back under the blanket, her back to him.

"Now, now! Come on. It's time to get up."

"No!" the child said clearly and cheekily.

"Hmm …," said Matrios, "I thought Shrike could have breakfast with you today."

"Will Shrike be there?" she asked, slowly turning to face him.

"Well, he's waiting for you I think." Matrios pretended to think about it.

"Oh, I can't keep him waiting!" Throwing the covers from the bed, she burst out of bed.

"Didn't you want to stay in bed?"

"A lady can't keep anyone waiting," she explained to her father as if she were talking to a fool. "Why, how would it look if the prince couldn't find the princess in the castle because the princess was in the outhouse?" she cried as if it was obvious.

"I can't follow your logic."

"Grandpa always told Meri to always be in the right place at the right time. When I asked Meri what that meant, she told me this! Then I didn't go to pee for a week so I wouldn't miss the prince!" she said angrily.

"And what happened?"

"Mom told me that's not how it works because I'd have to be kidnapped by a dragon, but she said that wouldn't happen because she's here with me!"

"But it's better to be with Mummy than with a prince, isn't it?" He smiled.

"Mummy gives me strawberry doughnuts every day. Not even one fairy tale says the kidnapped princesses get strawberry doughnuts while they wait for their princes," she pointed out.

"Then it's time to get dressed!" He laughed at her childish fantasies.

"True. Let's not keep Shrike waiting. I don't want to make him sad!"

Linary ran across the cold stone floor in her bare feet and started throwing her clothes from the trunk. She put on a pretty, but not fancy, dress with simple fringes, but it reached to the floor. Her hands were free in it, and she stepped into her little green clogs, which made her shiver a little, for they were cold.

Matrios stood in front of her giggling as he watched the performance, and then he held out his hand to her, and she touched it gently and softly. The touch felt so wonderful that, for a moment, Matrios was awakened by the wonder and felt his eyes well up. He took the little hand gently, as if he held a broken-winged bird, and with his other hand he wiped his eyes. He looked down at the little girl who was smiling joyfully with a wide smile as beautiful as the moon itself shining.

The prince smiled gently and kindly, and then Linary looked at the door and, with happy long strides, went out, leading her father as if she held a leash in her little palm.

Matrios laughed to himself as he watched the purposeful little girl's steps. He followed her, matching her stride. He had lost all sense of time just watching Linary leading him, disbelieving his own luck that he could experience such a miracle even if it meant losing his old life. *It was worth it*, he thought to himself, lost in a sea of memories of his past.

"Good sir!" The rough voice of Verilion pulled the prince out of his nest of thoughts.

"Are we here already?" Matrios asked in surprise.

"My lord!" Elizabeth greeted him from a distant end of the table. She was still standing behind the chair as Hritandian etiquette dictated.

"My lord!" The servant pulled out a chair at the head of the table. Then Linary let go of her father's hand and ran to her mother, oblivious to the rules of etiquette.

"Behave yourself!" said her mother.

"Excuse me, Mom!" said the girl, who was trying to hold back her bubbling joy.

Matrios just smiled and took a seat at the table, but before the servant could push his chair in, he pulled it in himself, surprising the old servant, whose eyes went wide. Tibald looked at Verilion who just gave him a barely visible smile. Then the knight ignored the old man and coughed loudly.

"So, I guess let's eat and talk!" said Verilion.

"All right!" Matrios clapped his palms together, and two servants leapt away from their stations along the wall and began their morning routine around the table, dancing with dishes, glasses, and freshly heated meat and bread from the sideboard as if they were carrying out a rehearsed choreography. Their actions were almost precise and ballet-like, and soon the food was in front of everyone—whatever they craved in the morning. Red liquid sloshed in the pitcher as the servant spun with it. Matrios pushed his glass to the edge of the table, and one of the servants filled it. Elizabeth looked at her husband with disgust on her face, then rolled her eyes. The prince looked into his cup, then stated. "This is not water!" At his unequivocal statement, the symphonic chaos stopped.

"My lord has always enjoyed his morning meal with a good cup of wine," Tibald said, wringing his hands.

"And what about the water?" Matrios asked at the old man.

"Does the master want dysentery?" asked the maid shile she filled Verilion's cup.

"Why would I?"

"Well, we might be able to draw water from the little stream, which wouldn't be bad, but I don't think the master should drink the water from our well."

"What's wrong with the well?"

"We don't know. For a year, any water from that well has made the servants fall into bed with dysentery," the servant said nervously.

"Bring me a bucket of that water!" the prince said imperiously.

"But, my lord!" the old man exclaimed. Then he realised he must just carry out the prince's order. "Certainly, sir." The servant ordered one of the guards, and the soldier opened the big door and went out to get a bucket of water.

"You, maid!" Matrios pointed to one of the girls, who was holding the wine jug.

"What can I do for you, sir?" Her eyes flashed up.

"Had anything strange happened when the castle staff started to fall ill?" he asked her.

"I'm not sure, my lord. I don't remember anything that was strange."

"It was a year ago that the previous lord had the latrines deepened," answered the older servant.

"What happened after that?"

"All the staff began to fall ill, and then the lord himself, who, because of his old age, passed away on his deathbed," she said, making a triangle with her right hand.

"The guy from the hermitage was here too, but even he himself could not help the lord. The plague doctor examined him, but he could only recommend leeches and bloodletting.

"Did you not come from the capital?" asked the prince.

"Aye, my lord. I came with Tibald last night, as did most of the servants."

Matrios sighed thoughtfully.

The conversation was interrupted when the soldier opened the door carrying a large bucket of water. He struggled to carry to the table and set down as gently as he could in front of Matrios. He bowed and hurried back to his seat as Matrios gave him a sign—not a soft one, but a thanking one that surprised the soldier.

Matrios rose from his chair and looked into the bucket. It looked like clean water, but there was something strange about it. He leaned close to the bucket and took a few tiny, sniffs. He could smell it at first, but it wasn't the smell of stale water; it was as if there was something else in the water, something entirely stinky, something unknown even to him. He seized the bucket, turned it round, and lifted it from the table.

Tibald called after him, "Good sir, what are you doing?"

"Get a cauldron large enough to hold this water!" he said, his eyes sparkling.

"What for?"

"We must boil it!"

"Does my lord want soup?" asked Tibald.

"No, just water to drink, and this water is not clean!" He turned and held up the bucket in the direction of the maid. "Just smell it!" he commanded.

Tibald, a little afraid, leaned close to the water and sniffed it, and soon she turned her nose away from the water.

"What is it?" she asked.

"This is not clean water!" he said clearly.

"My lord, what do you know about it?" Elizabeth asked.

"Water should be odourless and colourless, but this water smells bad," he said, pointing to the bucket.

"If you say so." She sighed and turned to her daughter, ignoring him.

"Is the fire still burning in the kitchen?" Matrios asked the servant.

"Of course!" Tibald replied. Then he opened the kitchen door and motioned the soldier to take the bucket into the kitchen.

Matrios followed him. An elderly but tall, strong, and burly bald cook, toothless and unhandsome, was waiting for him

"How can I help you, my good sir?" the cook asked.

"Boil the water." Matrios pointed to the bucket.

"Would you like to take a bath?" The cook looked at the soldier over the prince's shoulder.

"No. I want to drink this water."

"Well water?" said the cook loudly and bluntly. "If you don't want to shit blood, sir, I humbly beg you not to think such nonsense!"

"Put it over the flame until it comes to a boil and then take it off the fire."

"My lord, you don't have to tell me how to boil water!" The man snorted and wiped his nose with his forearm in a show of resentment.

"Then let's see how well you remember the basics!" Matrios clapped his palms together.

"How well I remember? What kind of question is that? Well, who do you think put that meal on the table, my lord! I made the dough for the bread myself this morning!" He took the bucket from the soldier and poured the contents into cauldron. He hung the cauldron on an iron hook over the fire. "Come back when I shout, my lord, and I'll give you water so clean that even wine won't taste good afterwards!" He wiped his hands on his apron.

"I will!" Matrios smiled and returned to his seat in the dining room. He ate his breakfast as if nothing had happened while the others at the table looked at him with strange looks and glances.

"What do you want to discuss today, my lord?" Verilion broke the awkward silence.

"Thank you for asking!" The prince put down the bread he'd been eating and wiped the crumbs from his palms. "The financial situation that currently exists here must be resolved. I will talk about this with my dear wife later."

Elizabeth felt a shiver run down her spine as she heard the words and looked at her husband in fear.

"Since she is the only one with experience in trade, I will ask her to take a look at the paperwork to find out what is happening in our financial sector."

"Sector?" Verilion asked.

"It means in the area that belongs to us."

"I don't understand either way, but it's the lady's business anyway!" The knight laughed.

"Yes! Then I must go and see that plant called a 'weed'. The village elder Marabas said it was sweet but dangerous."

"Excuse me, sir," the elder maid said, bowing again. "I know I'm only a servant, but I know a thing or two about that plant."

"Hush, girl!" Tibald ordered.

"Let her speak!" said Matrios. "All information may be necessary, even if it seems trivial!"

"Triv ... what?" The older man scratched his head.

"Last night my sister and I accidentally dropped a potted plant into her bathwater. It was a bulbous plant with a pretty purple flower. We noticed that the bulbs were hardened and prickly when we fished them out of the water. And the next day, some of them had turned to stone because we had left them on the table." She talked as she poured wine from a jug for Verilion.

"Do you still have them?" asked Matrios.

"We threw away the plants—the flowers and the small pebbles—because the flowers wilted in the morning."

"Interesting!" Matrios put his hand to his mouth. "Thank you. This information will probably come in handy."

The servant girl bowed deeply, blushing slightly, then looked at her sister and smiled. Finally, they returned to their work.

Matrios returned to the table to hear a conversation between Verilion and Elizabeth. "I guess that wasn't the only thing," Verilion was saying, feigning fatigue. "Like after he woke up in the camp, there was no stopping him!"

"After he woke up?" asked Elizabeth.

"After they stitched the prince together. He had a wound in his belly so big it would have killed a boar!"

I had died, thought the prince.

"And what did he do after that?" Elizabeth asked.

"I didn't understand half of it, and I didn't even want to understand the other half!" he said, slapping his knee. "I thought you would have discussed what happened at Bowed Mountain on the journey here," he grumbled.

"We didn't really have time to talk." She sighed.

"It doesn't matter!" Matrios interrupted. "The next thing I'd like to learn is the state of the mineral mines, especially the sulphur mine. What happened there? And how is the work going now?"

Is that all?" the knight asked.

"We also need to talk to the blacksmith," Matrios said. "And we must reorganize the patrols, train the soldiers, help the agriculture to flourish, curb the warlords and muggers, secure our borders, maintain good relations with the neighbouring lords, increase trade, solve the famine, and improve the living conditions of the people." The prince spoke without taking a breath. Then he took a deep breath at the end of his list.

"But isn't that a bit much?" Verilion looked at the prince."

"We just have to get it in the right order." Matrios smiled; he was deep in thought. "We must look at the mysterious plant first because trade and the eradication of famine may depend on it since it is infesting the land. Then there is the problem of sulphur and the mines. We might use it to boost trade. The blacksmith should be able to help me with the land and the mines, and also with the equipment for the soldiers. The schedule for training the soldiers depends on the condition of the farmland, but until we have a proper strike force for defence, we will not be able to start trading. Our efforts will be in vain if our cargoes are looted on the way. The knights can also help with that. Raising the living standards of the people will boost our morale and efficiency and our relations with the villagers. A good relationship with the surrounding lords is good because we can't fight the bandits on our own."

"Hmm … it's complex." Verilion sighed. "I didn't know running a village was such a hassle."

"If you want to be a good ruler of your people, there is no such thing as an easy day." Matrios smiled.

"How do you know all this?" Elizabeth looked at him with disbelief.

"A divine suggestion, I think."

"But you—" She bit off the sentence before she could say it and then sighed. "What do I have to do then?" she asked.

"Let's leave the diplomacy for later so you can get used to it slowly. Right now, the most important thing is to take inventory and assess our trading power."

"Me take inventory?"

"Knights can count, I believe." Matrios looked at Verilion.

"Yes! I'll assign ten knights to help you, my lady!" he said, patting his chest.

"That was not the problem." She sighed nervously.

"We're not in a castle anymore," explained Matrios. "We're nobles of a land. Maybe this is not how you imagined it when we married, but it is the way it is now." He frowned. "I need your help to provide a better living situation and later a better life for Linary."

"For Linary?" She looked at him again.

"Who do you think I'm doing all this for?" he asked. "The more and better things we can do, the more and better things there will be for our little girl."

"Then I'll help," she murmured as she watched her daughter, who was eating beside her.

"Thank you, Elizabeth!" Matrios smiled gently.

"What will I do then?" asked Verilion as he folded his arms across his bull chest.

"You will be needed to help us set up our patrol methodology and to train the soldiers later on."

"Train soldiers?"

"If you can train knights, what's wrong with training soldiers?"

"I'd say it's beneath my rank, but I know what needs to be done and I'll do it!" the great knight said with closed eyes.

"Then there's nothing for it but to go forward!" Matrios announced with determination.

"Good sir!" the cook called out from the kitchen. "Your water is ready!"

Matrios got up from the table. It struck the old servant as strange that his master should stand up at the word of a nobody, but there was so much that was new to him that he could not cope with it all. They went into the kitchen where the sweating man stood by the bubbling pot. When they arrived, he lifted the cauldron from the fire and set it on the butcher's table. Matrios stepped over to the steaming liquid and lifted a pint cup from the counter. He dipped the cup into the water.

But the cook stopped him. "My good sir, I am so concerned for you. Let me show you what I invented not long ago!" He took out a slightly worn little bag that appeared to be filled with spices, and he dipped it into Matrios' cup and left it there for a while.

"Tea?" Matrios was surprised.

"Have you ever seen anything like this in town?" The big man was surprised.

"No! I haven't."

"I thought, if they make soup taste good, why should you have a problem with plain water?" he laughed. "But please tell me—am I more skilful than the cooks in town, or am I imitating them as a bum?" The man knelt in front of Matrios.

"Not a bum!" Matrios put his hand on the man's shoulder. "You surprised me with this drink, which I assume is not the first you've served. Few people can surprise me, and yet you've succeeded."

The man received the prince's words happily, and, taking off his chef's cap from his bald head and crumpling it with both hands, he rose to his feet.

"Thank you for wasting your words on such an old fool, my good lord."

"The real victory would be if you could make me some homemade strawberry jam," Matrios mused.

"Strawberry jam? That's very expensive, my good sir. It's not customary to waste a woman's fruit on jam!" The man apologised. "So be it! If you get me some strawberries, I'll make you a jam. I'll make it from my grandmother's recipe, just with strawberries!"

Matrios smiled, then took the small bag out of the glass, twisted it slightly and took a deep breath. *It's now or never!* he thought, a little worried. He sipped the tea and tasted the fresh red burst of rosehip mingling with the intoxicating golden and soothing breath of chamomile. There was even the slightly tart greenish aroma of rosemary on the back of his tongue as he swallowed. Then he was greeted with a slightly sugary aftertaste. Matrios downed the entire hot mug of tea and sighed in satisfaction. "That was great!" He put the mug down on the table and sighed heavily.

Verilion watched from the doorway and then stepped closer. He grabbed another cup off the stool and put it under the big man's nose. "Give me one too!" he said firmly and impatiently.

The cook looked at the knight who was the same height. He then took the cup from the big man's hand and, with childlike enthusiasm, plunged it into the steaming water. He placed another small bag into the water and handed it back to Verilion, nodding his head forward knowing he was talking to a knight.

Verilion raised the glass close to his nose and took a long sniff of the drink, then took a small sip. Immediately his eyes lit up, and he drank the entire glass. When the glass was empty, he sighed in relief and reached back commandingly, asking for another serving.

Matrios tried to hold back his laughter and instead left the kitchen. In the dining room, he was met by a curious look from Elizabeth. He turned on his heel, returned to the kitchen, and prepared another cup of the lovely tea. He returned to the dining room and placed the drink on the table in front of her and took a seat himself.

"What do you want with this, sir?" she asked curiously.

"Just take a drink and you'll understand." He smiled with curious eyes.

"Is that from the stinky water?" She pointed to the glass with disgust.

"It won't taste of anything like that, and it won't do you any harm," he reassured him.

"I'm not going to try it until I've seen you hours from now." She pushed the glass away and turned back to Linary.

"It won't—" he insisted, but the lioness drowned any further words from him with a death glare.

Matrios quickly finished his breakfast and wrote down in a book the tasks he had asked the servant to do. He stretched and yawned and then sat back in his seat and looked at Verilion. The knight yawned as well and jumped up from his chair. He walked to the cabinet behind him and strapped his weapons to his side. "Dana!" shouted the knight in his husky voice. His second in command, his daughter, came through the door.

She quickly wiped the stewed juices from her mouth with a small handkerchief and then hid it between the slits of her armour. "Yes!"

"Order at least ten knights to work today with the lady. Choose those who are best at writing and reading and counting."

"As you command. Picon should continue his training?" she asked.

"He's brave, but he's only a boy. Order him to protect the little princess for the day." He laughed.

"Understood! The usual escort for the prince?" Looking at Matrios at the head of the table, she bowed low and respectfully.

"Yes! I have a feeling we won't be bored." Verilion sighed.

"We've never been bored since Lord Matrios revived!" She smiled, looking at her father.

Verilion looked back at the prince with an appreciative look. Then he dismissed the woman.

Matrios just sighed. *What have I got myself into now?* he thought. Matrios stepped over to the little girl, whose face was again smeared with the butter even though her mother had just painstakingly wiped her face. He crouched down beside her and bit playfully into one end of the small piece of bread she held in her hand. Linary was surprised, but then she laughed and clung to the bread herself. Matrios growled and began to play gently with the bread as if he were a dog. The servant's face whitened, and he almost collapsed where he stood. Elizabeth looked at her spouse as if he had gone mental. The piece of bread finally broke in half as the two played, and then Linary ate her half, laughing as she chewed it. Matrios straightened up and looked at her. "Are you coming to see the little village with Daddy?"

"Yes, yes!" She jumped down from the chair, scattering all the food.

"Then wipe your face first, like a lady does." He tweaked her nose, and she clapped her hands and giggled playfully. Then she turned back to her mother and snatched the napkin from the woman's hand. With determined strokes, she set to work to remove the butter from her face. Elizabeth scolded the child and then held her chin gently and wiped her shining cheeks clean. "You look like a lady girl now!" She smiled, and Linary turned and immediately rubbed her face into her father's legs. Then she stretched and looked up at him with pleading eyes.

Matrios didn't understand at first, but as soon as he looked into those pleading blue eyes, he reached down and picked her up and sat her on his forearm. She grabbed his hair at the nape of his neck and, as if on horseback, started her father with a flick of her bridle, pointing in the direction of the door.

Matrios just laughed to himself and moved to obey the little girl's will, stepping out the door and closing it after he and Verilion had left.

Elizabeth watched the scene in astonishment, not understanding the sweetness that surrounded the aura of the girl and the man.

Tibald broke the silence that had fallen over the dining room. "My lady! I think you should be going soon, too." The old man stepped up behind her.

"Tell me, Tibald," she said, looking at her own hands, deep in thought, "Did I go mad in the courtyard?"

"What are you talking about?" he asked, puzzled.

"You have seen him. He's not himself!" She looked at him between tears.

"Indeed!" Tibald looked at the door. "But now I like him better, even if he is the complete opposite of his old self."

"That's all very well. I am grateful that he won't climb into bed drenched in wine, but still I find my husband's existence unnatural!" said the woman, breaking into sobs.

"Do not weep, my dear lady, but rather praise the two gods that our lord has recovered." Tibald held out his handkerchief.

"Thank you, Tibald, you have always stood by my side and Linary's. I know I can always count on you." Elizabeth accepted the small piece of cloth and wiped her eyes with it. "But it is still strange to me."

"Our Lord Matrios has returned from the battlefield," said Tibald, "and he is completely changed, but don't forget what happened in the past, if only to be hopeful for the future, Lady Elizabeth." He spoke kindly and bowed.

Unable to reply, as the knights she had asked for arrived and saluted her with a loud clatter, Elizabeth took a deep breath and spoke to the newcomers. "Thank you, for coming!"

<hr />

Matrios put Linary on his horse and then climbed on behind her. He held the reins with both hands while Linary nestled between his arms and played with the horse's mane. A small contingent of knights followed behind them.

Matrios clicked the reins, and the animal advanced into a slow gallop. Linary shrieked in delight, which, though it hurt his ears, only made Matrios laugh. Soon afterwards, at the sound of the squealing, Shrike fell from a vast height and landed gently on her head.

"Shrike!" she cried.

"Where have you been?" Matrios asked.

"I had breakfast! The border is full of fat rabbits! You hardly see any game around here, so it took me a while.

"Where have you been?" Linary grabbed the bird. "I thought we were having breakfast together!" she said disappointedly, to which the bird only made a few low squawks. "In that case, I forgive you!" she said, only a little offended.

Matrios ignored the game the child and the bird-beast played. He just thought to himself and felt a small joy that he didn't have to suffer with animal husbandry and fear of predators.

The loud murmur of the rhythmic trickling of the stream drowned out the waking morning songs of the surrounding forest. The small party soon reached the village they had visited in the late hours of the previous day. The fresh sunshine bathed the tiny settlement, painting a very different picture than the one he had seen in the darkness. Dusty, wide streets cut easily through the multitude of houses. A loud animal noise greeting the prince and his knights, who had also recently ridden into the village. People walked slowly but purposefully along the road. Many others had long since gone to work in the fields, but there were a few who wanted to get the day's chores done first.

Just before the main crossroads, Matrios noticed a small shrine that consisted of two statues. Old grandmas sat beside them, chatting, and a fresh arrival knelt and prayed. There they spun wool by hand, gossiped, and laughed. In front of them, young girls were sitting on the grass as they learned the craft from their elders. But the only boys in the village were toddlers.

Matrios looked around the horizon into the still life and turned to Verilion. "I see no boys!" he said.

"They are all out helping in the fields, my lord! Verilion replied naturally.

"Hmm ..." said the prince as he continued to scan the village. Slowly, the armoured army appeared to the serfs. Looking in the direction of the prince, they bowed low and then went about their business as if nothing had happened. Matrios was somehow impressed by this attitude, for it suggested that he was not going to be treated like some messiah come down from heaven, and he liked that.

Linary continued to play with the bird-beast as she sat in her father's saddle. She was oblivious to what was going on around her. So the prince spurred the horse on and rode into the centre of the village. There he stopped beside an elderly old man who was loading hay onto a cart. "Good morning!" said the prince.

"May the Holy Mother give you good life, my lord," said the old man.

"Do you know where I can find the blacksmith?" asked the prince.

"Go on along the main road and turn right. You'll find it easily from there!" he explained as he pointed the way.

"Thank you!"

The prince set off again with the escort behind him, and soon they reached the hut that was the blacksmith's workshop. It was a small, basic little tool shed with a forge that was not very large, but just big enough for the work he had to do for the village. Black smoke billowed from the fire. Beside the forge sat a dirty, battered-looking but well-muscled young man who was pumping the bellows to enliven the fire. His face was expressionless and bored, his pipe had long since gone out, but he would not let the fire go out in the forge. His leather apron concealed a belly, but it was not as gross as that of Miraklios.

Matrios dismounted, lifted Linary off the horse, and sat her on his forearm. *Let's see how long she can tolerate people around her*, Matrios thought to himself.

Shrike flew up and landed on Matrios's left shoulder so he and Linary could continue their somewhat nerve-racking game behind his back. The prince opened the gate and stepped through. The blacksmith startled at the noise and looked up, took the pipe from his mouth, and jumped down from the bench. He knelt and raised his right hand to his heart. "Good sir, what have I done to deserve your presence?" said he respectfully.

"Lift up your head and stand up straight," said the prince. "I do not wish to speak to you without seeing your eyes. What are you called?"

"I apologize for my rudeness! My mother, if she were alive, would be whacking my ass now! My name is Eric. It is a pleasure to meet you, my good sir." He bowed again. What can I do for you?" He bowed slightly.

Your workshop has seen better days," said the prince, surveying the equipment.

"Since my father died—the holy mother rest his soul—the workshop has been getting worse and worse! It's as if my old father had put a curse on me," complained the blacksmith.

"Don't say that about your father."

"It is true, my lord, but I respect my father's knowledge," he said firmly.

"I've got it." Matrios continued to examine the room.

"How can I help you today with my shabby workshop?"

"I need to melt down that big bag of tools." Matrios pointed in the direction of the knights who had driven a cart filled with worn metal tools through the gate.

"What's all this stuff?" Eric looked picked through the mess of metal in the cart.

"These are the old tools that belonged to the villagers," the prince replied, picking up a hammer.

"What would you like to make of this? I don't think it would make a good material for any trinket. I wouldn't even call it good for a torch holder." Eric sighed. "And I'm not much of a craftsman myself."

"Can you forge iron?" Matrios looked at the blacksmith and put down the heavy tool.

"Of course I can forge," defended Eric. "I'm not a good blacksmith, but—"

"Then I'll need your services."

"Well, sir, you could find a much better blacksmith two villages away."

"I have no desire to go two villages away and pay taxes for a blacksmith who won't see a penny of it," the prince explained, somewhat bored.

"What does that mean?" Eric scratched his head.

"My name is Matrios Hritan, third prince of the House of Hritan, and as of yesterday, I am the lord of this village and its lands." He adjusted Linary's position on his arm. She was fiddling with the blacksmith's chains that were hanging above her head.

"Dad, what's this?" The child reached towards one of the tools.

"That's the blacksmith's pliers." Matrios smiled at her. "Do you think you can be quiet a little longer?"

The blacksmith knelt again. "I apologize for my rudeness, my lord. I heard from my wife that a nobleman had arrived in the empty castle, but she did not tell me that the prince himself had become our new lord! Long live the—"

"There's no need!" Matrios interrupted. "I told you I wanted to speak to you if I see your eyes." He looked at the man.

"Yes. Excuse me, my lord." Eric rose and dusted his knees.

"How much for a job?" asked the prince, examining the anvil in the middle of the small shop.

"It varies. I usually work for the people in the village in exchange for favours or goods. Mostly only passing through adventurers bring money."

"And the nobles?"

"I'm happy to do what they want. It's the only way to keep my head on my shoulders." He chuckled with suppressed anger.

"Great." Matrios said, a little disappointed. "I need you to make something for me."

"I can melt these tools down for you. Don't worry," replied Eric a little forlornly.

"I was thinking of something a little more challenging."

"Challenging?"

"Have you heard of a heavy plough?"

"What's a plough, Daddy?" said the girl.

"A plough is a large hoe that is pulled through the fields by a cow," he explained clearly.

"With a cow?" whispered the girl.

Matrios turned to Eric. "I need you to make this plough for me!"

"I'm sorry, sir, but we already have ploughs."

"The one I want is much bigger and more complex. If I bring you a drawing of the machine, will you be able to make it for me?"

"It's worth a try." Eric wiped his nose. "I've had enough petty small jobs, and I admit a little money wouldn't go amiss." The blacksmith sighed. "Little Tim needs new shoes," complained the man bitterly.

"If you make the plough for me the way I think it should be made, your little Tim won't have any more trouble!"

"You don't have to go that far, my lord. I don't deserve it, but I'll take the job and do what I can."

"What happened to your parents, Eric? You look very young."

"I am not young. I have seen twenty winters! My parents died four years ago because of the plague. My mother died first, and my father could not bear to be without her, so he followed her to the grave a few months later. Since then, I have owned the workshop and all the problems with it," the man complained briefly.

"I am sorry for your family."

"I am sure they would be proud now that their boy can talk to a prince." The man laughed at last in good taste, but soon stopped. "Thank you for honouring me with your presence, my good sir."

"My pleasure! I must go now. I have much to do. I will send a knight this evening with a technical drawing of my heavy plough."

"You may trust me, my lord. I will do what I can!" Eric responded, finally displaying a bit of cheer.

"I hope so!"

"Why is he so dirty, Daddy?" asked the little girl, barely audibly.

"Because he's doing important work. Very important work!"

"So you don't do anything important?" asked the girl innocently. Matrios just grinned, and the blacksmith could hardly keep from laughing.

"I think it's time to go," said Matrios, embarrassed.

With the little child in his arms, who resisted the temptation of curiosity with a tolerance that was acceptable, the prince left the forge and closed the small garden gate behind him. Outside, Marabas, the elder of the village, was waiting for him, leaning on his cane and greeting the little one with a broad smile. He then looked at the prince and nodded deeply. Matrios greeted the old man politely, and then got down to business without hesitation. "Show me the damned plant!" he said, smiling.

"Good lord! This way!" Marabas pointed to the village road that led straight out of the settlement.

Slowly, the old man stumbled along while Matrios walked behind him, leading his horse, on the back of which Linary played with Shrike and rewarded the creature's every performance with loud screams and laughter. The horse, however, was less appreciative of the noise and gave a conspicuous snort, as if disturbed by the good game going on behind his ears.

"Is the horse angry, Daddy?" said Linary.

"I guess he doesn't like being left out of the game." He winked at the little girl.

Linary lay down on the horse's neck and hugged it, rubbing her face in the coarse fur. That gave her an idea: she began to braid the thick mane. The animal soon calmed down and stretched its body out contentedly as it walked along. Matrios was surprised, but only smiled at the animal's reaction. The big stallion seemed to him much smarter now than he had first thought. He looked over the body of the big animal. In his former life, he had only ever seen horses in books. His knowledge of horses was very narrow, even though he had heard of quite a few breeds. But this thought was interrupted by Marabas when he stopped in front of a large, flat field and pointed ahead. Matrios stepped closer and examined the plant that grew there.

From the ground, thick and fleshy leaves encircled the trunk of each plant, which was brown at the base and maintained a shade of green at the tip. The flowers bloomed at the height of the prince's hips, full with beautiful, decorative purple petals. Beneath the flowers, tiny globular spheres—a globule—coated with a sticky sap awaited the insects that would foolishly touch it. Matrios drew his sword and poked one of the small globules. It popped open, and the liquid ran down the stem of the plant to the ground. He looked around him and saw a large twig in the grass. He shook a slug off the twig, interrupting its siesta. Using the twig, he gently touched another globule. Slowly, the slimy material stretched. It stuck to the stick, but this time the gluey membrane was not damaged, and the entire globule stuck to the wood. He lifted the small ball close to his nose and sniffed. It did not give off any sweet smell; rather, he detected a slight herbal scent. It was not an unpleasant spicy scent. He attached some additional sticky globules to the stick and turned to the knight who stood behind Verilion. "Bring me a cauldron," he ordered.

"What is it for, my lord?" asked Marabas.

"One of the maids has drawn my attention to something," said the prince thoughtfully.

"What is it?"

"If you put the little globules in a bit hot water, they will harden," explained Matrios.

"It is true, but then it will attract flies and bees even more," explained Marabas.

"Attract bees?"

"Yes! The beekeeper often uses it," Marabas stated clearly.

"And how?"

"As you said!" Marabas stated clearly.

"Great." Matrios sighed, relieved.

Matrios went back to the horse. Linary had braided the horse's entire mane in the mean time. He lifted her from the animal's back and put the stick in her hand. "Linary!" he said. "Interested in a race?"

"Yes! Yes!" she said immediately.

"All right. Take this stick into the field and collect as many of these little globules as you can! Don't poke them open. If you do, then I win!"

She giggled. "Doesn't my father know that I'm the best butterfly hunter in the yard?" The child cheered herself up as she approached the plants that grew closest to the road. First, she bashed at the globules using great force, but she only succeeded in popping them open. She examined the sticky stick. Next, she tried to remove the globules from the plant with a delicate motion. She succeeded and had her first small globule on the stick. Her eyes lit up, and with a big laugh she darted over to the other plant and gathered more globules. After a few minutes, the stick was full, and she returned to her companions, balancing the packed twig.

"Look, Father! Did I win?" She thrust the stick under Matrios's nose.

"Oh, yes, you did!" he applauded with a sweet smile.

"What did I win?"

"I'll tell you later." He took the stick.

"Oh, that's not funny! I've just won, and I want my prize now!" she snapped angrily.

"All right, you can go back to the castle and do whatever you want until I get home!"

"At least I can have my noble ball at noon! " the child said happily.

The prince turned and called little Picon to him. "Go home with my daughter and take care of her in the courtyard. Take Shrike with you."

"As you wish, my lord! I will guard her carefully!" The little knight bowed.

Matrios watched as the noisy children together with Picon disappear over the hill. The knights of the little company, in their all their gear, were roasting uncomfortably in the summer sun, but all of them bore the morning heat without a sound as they stood beside their prince.

It was not long before the silhouette of the man Matrios had sent to fetch a cauldron appeared against the distant undulating landscape. As he drew nearer, the cauldron glistened at his side in the sunlight. Soon he was back, leaping down from the saddle and placing the metal container on the ground. As Matrios looked at it, it occurred to him that he had not brought water, but before he could speak, the knight took a canteen from his saddlebag and poured water into the cauldron.

Matrios was very surprised. He looked at the man, put his hand on his shoulder, and said, "Well done!"

"I heard you'd need water, so I filled my canteen while I was in the village," he said, bowing.

"Well done."

The prince ordered the knights to gather some twigs and light fire under the cauldron by the road. In a few moments, the fire was blazing. Matrios sat down on a small collapsed fence and watched the beautiful landscape play before his eyes. There were golden wheat fields at the edge of the forest, and the great woodland went on to the horizon. He turned and saw Sleeping Mountain towering above. He ran his eyes over the black rocks that broke into grassed fields at the foot of the mountain. He sniffed the air, noticing the faint and barely perceptible smell of the sulphur mine, which was overpowered by the youthful summer scent of the countryside.

Verilion walked up next to Matrios, sighed heavily, and sat down beside the prince. He stretched and turned to him. "What do you want with this flower business?" he asked sleepily.

"If my idea is accurate, we can make sugar out of these plants," he said, pulling a small grimoire from his pocket.

"What?" the big man snapped.

"What do you mean, 'what'? Sugar!" said Matrios, puzzled.

"Sugar?" Verilion leaned closer.

"Yes." Matrios looked at the man in confusion. "Do you know how much sugar is worth?"

The knight was puzzled. "Not exactly, but I know it's a luxury." He shook his head.

"Well, that's all I know as well," said the prince. "Do you know why?"

"I know that it is very difficult and time consuming to produce, but I know nothing else about it other than the fact that the largest producers are among the Bretburgs.

They're west of here," the prince mused.

Well, since diplomatic relations broke down, we have been unable to trade for Bretburg sugar."

"What happened?" asked Matrios.

"There have been recent grievances about helping the Duchy of Berolt during their war for independence, and then there's the matter of the border wars with the demons. It is a long story."

"We have time while the water boils." Matrios smiled.

"But you should know that history." The knight sighed. "Don't tell me you have forgotten." He raised his hand to prevent the prince from making that excuse. "It so happened that, during the reign of the seventeenth king of the Hritandian throne, when the whole continent was still united, the Bretburgs and many other noble houses, who called themselves the West Wanderers, rebelled and took a large chunk of the kingdom for themselves."

"Are the Bretburg and the Western Travellers one and the same?"

"Aye!"

"How big is their kingdom now?"

"They occupied the entire territory of the western cliffs up to the Rodden, but they couldn't build a strong political system so the Bretburg civil war broke out, which inspired the Hritandian continent war."

"The war gave birth to another war?" Matrios asked.

"Yes, because all political groups wanted to redraw their borders. So many nobles supported one side or the other. Hritandia and the Republic supported the monarchists and wanted a Hritandian noble to be a puppet on the throne of the kingdom. However, the Western Wanderers, the Bretburg side, would not let this happen. They were embraced by the Pentrupuni and Midritan powers. At that time, those were much smaller states than they are today. Hritan's kingdom was centred in Centrinia until the Midritan legions took it. The monarchists were wiped out, Hritan's legions were destroyed in the offensive, and the kingdom took a huge toll on the republic.

"I understand now."

"I'll tell you this—about twenty years ago, a civil war broke out in Bretburg, and the country was split in two, but if I remember well, the small state only lasted five years and surrendered to the kingdom. Our king's relations with the Republic then broke down because of the heavy taxes.

"How did the Republic come to life?"

"After the fifteenth king, the Hritan throne fell into war with the principality, which broke the Hritan empire in two after ten years, and the Hritandian Principality was formed. It then became a Republic after the death of the prince. Since then, their state has been largely impartial in military affairs.

"It's an interesting story."

"To me, it's just boring. I had to learn this instead of training because a knight should know his history."

"You can see it's come in handy now." The prince laughed.

Verilion snorted mockingly.

"How was the kingdom of Hritan able to withstand threats from within and out?" asked the prince.

"I don't know." Verilion scratched his head. "Ask a chronicler about it."

"My lord!" A knight came up to them and interrupted their chatter. "The water is boiling!"

"I'm coming!" The prince stood up and stepped to the boiling cauldron. He tried to shake the little globules off the twig, but they were stuck fast to the wood. Finally, he gave up and threw the entire twig into the water. After a few minutes, the globules came away from the twig, and the glue-like substance floated into the water in tiny shreds. Everyone watched in amazement as the globules floating on top of the boiling water became more and more misty and foggy. Suddenly, with tiny thumps, the little globules settled to the bottom of the water while the threads continued to play and dance among the bubbles.

Matrios noticed this strange phenomenon and touched one of the threads on the top of the water with a new twig. Nothing stuck to the twig, but as soon as he touched another thread with the twig, the threads twisted together. So he stirred the liquid until a ball the size of a quarter of a palm had formed. He fished it out of the water, placed it in his hand, and felt the heat of it, which was gone in moments. The ball was transparent but fibrous. He pressed it with his finger. It was flexible and reminded him of rubber. He put the stick down and began to examine the little ball with both hands. He tried to split it in two, but it wouldn't separate. It just stretched a little and then returned to its original spherical shape. He rubbed its surface, and it resisted the impact solidly. Then he raised it to his face and bit it.

Everyone else watched the prince's scientific experiments in amazement, but then Marabas spoke up when Matrios put the ball to his lips. "My lord! This plant is poisonous!"

"We don't know if it still is after it has been boiled," Matrios said nonchalantly.

As he bit, the ball seemed to have the consistency of rubber. He wondered what he could do with it. What else could it contain? Then he had an idea. He began to twist it. After a few twists, it began to tear. Slowly the strings became visible and slowly, with great force, they pulled apart. The prince struggled and struggled, and finally he was left with a large pile of thin strands, still knotted in some places. He smiled and slipped these thin white strands into a small bag that hung at his side.

"What is this?" Verilion asked, picking up a thread from the ground.

"This is natural rubber!" said the prince, laughing.

"Rubber?" Verilion looked at him questioningly.

"A material without which we would get nowhere!" Matrios snapped, drunk with joy, as he grabbed Verilion's shoulders.

"I understand." Verilion was shocked by Matrios' reaction.

"I can do almost anything I want to do with this! If it turns out to be resistant to electricity, then even—" In his joyful moment, Matrios forgot himself and gave in to the thrill of success, but he looked up at the faces of the knights, who were looking at him as if he was crazy. He sighed, straightened up, cleared his throat, and pointed to the pot. "I think the little globules should be ready by now." He stepped up to the cauldron.

The little tiny globules were really done. The membrane that had protected them had become prickly and hard; their translucent bodies were now a greyish white. With the aid of a forked stick, the prince fished out a steaming ball and placed it on the grass. He waited for it to cool and then picked it up. He felt the sharp little spikes pricking the skin of his hand, so he put it down and pulled his glove from his saddlebag. Wearing the glove, he took hold of the little pebble-like globule again and looked at it more closely.

"Do any of you have a hammer?" asked the prince, looking up.

"I have, my good sir!" said a one-eyed knight, a member of the entourage, holding an ornate war hammer.

"Very well! Bring it here and strike this ball!"

"What?"

"Strike it!" repeated the prince.

"Are you sure, my lord?"

"Well, not as hard as you'd hit a demon," he added, and then he moved away.

"If you say so." The knight raised the hammer and inflicted a small blow upon the globule, which resisted, bouncing the hammer back towards the knight. The knight was startled, and behind him, the others began to chuckle amongst themselves. The man once again raised the hammer and inflicted a harder blow. This time, the globule fell apart in three pieces.

"Ha!" The knight laughed and moved away.

Matrios picked up one of the pieces in his hand. Inside the piece was what looked like fine-grained sand. He touched his tongue to it and experienced a nice sweetness spreading in his mouth. There was also a slight herbal flavour, and the intensity of the powder was strong. The prince pursed his lips and spat out the sugary substance. "It's sugar!" he said appreciatively.

The knights rushed forward and plucked at the remaining pieces, even grabbing from each other's hands as each attempted to get a piece of the little ball for himself. Some reached into the hot water with their armoured gloves and cracked open the globules with a stone to get the sugar. Matrios and Verilion watched the men fighting with surprise and frustration.

"Enough!" cried Verilion, and the knights stopped. They looked at their leader in shame. "I apologise for the behaviour of my men." Verilion said to Matrios as he knelt. Then the other knights fell to their knees, their faces bowed with shame.

"No—" Matrios said quietly.

But Verilion immediately interrupted him and spoke loudly to the soldiers. "It could be gold or opium. I don't care!"

Opium? Matrios thought.

"It does not matter!" Verilion continued. "Now then!" Verilion clapped his hands together. "What if someone were the first to test whether this substance is poisonous!"

The blood drained from the knights' faces. They had forgotten that the old man Marabas had warned that the plant was poisonous. Several of the men tried to reach down their throats and induce vomiting, but the prince stopped them. "Marabas," he said, "what are the symptoms when one has ingested this plant?"

"Fever, nausea, and vomiting are the most common!"

"Death?"

"It hasn't happened often, as far as I know," he reassured the knights.

"If nothing happens in the next two days to anyone who has eaten it, we can go on from there." Matrios outlined the situation to Verilion, who was still kneeling in front of the prince.

"I cannot rise until the prince gives me permission and forgives my men," he explained in a shamed tone that only made the knights look more devastated. "Their behaviour has brought shame on the knights of the Order of the Rose, and moreover it has happened in the presence of royalty! I have only two choices as their commander—either execute them or beg for my lord's mercy, which I will do now!" said the knight, squeezing the words out of himself in shame.

"I forgive the knights this time." Matrios put his hand on the man's shoulder.

"Thank you, my lord, and I am deeply sorry." The big knight bowed even deeper.

"I beg your pardon, my good prince!" said one of the knights.

"I was carried away by the excitement!" said another.

"Don't let it happen again!" cried their commander. "You are knights, not the rabble of some village!" He stood up and slapped one of the knights on the cheek. "Don't let me see you disgrace me again!" he told them, his temper steaming.

"Forgive us, Lord Verilion!" said the knights at once.

"Then, when we're done," said Matrios with a sigh, "we might as well get on with our business for the day."

After a short wait, the group gathered and headed towards the sulphur mine without Marabas as a guide. It wasn't hard to find; they just had to follow the smell as it grew stronger. By the time they were close to their destination, the knights were already feeling nauseated, but Matrios looked ahead with gleaming eyes, unafraid, and watched for an opening in the foliage that would reveal the mine. It was not long before he saw the mine. Matrios jumped off his horse, though Verilion chalked it up to more of a fall. The prince held a thick cloth to his face and stepped closer to the shaft. Along its wall ran a long yellowish vein that led down into the depths as it broke into many other veins on the wall. Matrios's excitement grew. He cried out, pulled another rag from his pocket, and picked up a palmful of crystal-clear sulphur stone. The yellowish hue seemed to mesmerize the man for a moment, but suddenly he broke into a fit of coughing and ran back to his horse.

"Did you take a good look at this cesspit?" Verilion asked. "Would you stay?"

"No, we'd better hurry before the knights vomit up all that sugar." Matrios mounted his horse and started to ride out of the clearing.

The company quickened its pace, leaving the place almost in a flash and hurrying back to the village. On the way, Matrios's mind raced with thoughts of how to create what he had planned and what else they would need to do to achieve his goal. But his long contemplation was interrupted by Verilion's voice. "What's next on the list?" Verilion pulled his horse closer to the prince. "Perhaps we should go and see the other mines!" he said thoughtfully.

"I think we'd better go and see Lady Elizabeth," said Matrios. "It's almost lunchtime anyway."

"Yes, it is already so late!" said the knight aloud.

"My gods! Let's hurry then. We mustn't be late!" said the prince, laughing, and then he spurred his horse.

The great gallop sent a great cloud of dust over the road. The people didn't know what was approaching the village in such a torrent. But they soon saw the prince leading the entourage with the knights in shining armour behind him. When they reached the village, Matrios drew in his reins, and the beast slowed to a trot. The prince patted the horse's neck, and the horse gave a proud prancing neigh. Marabas, who had already returned to the village and was talking to the people, stepped forward. "Good sir, the honourable lady is waiting for you at the storehouse!" The old man fumbled with his right hand, nervously.

"Thank you," said Matrios, still mounted on the horse's back. "Is everything all right?"

"I ... yes, of course." Marabas looked at the prince in confusion. "You'd better go there at once!" he said.

"Right!" Matrios urged his horse forward, his mind playing out worst-case scenarios at the old man's words. He jumped off his horse when they reached the old shabby warehouse, as did the knights who accompanied him, and he quickly burst through the door, looking around nervously. The knights who had been working on the inventory inside the room immediately leapt forward with swords drawn, hiding the woman who held her child in her arms behind their shields. Their eyes showed that they were ready to do the unspeakable, which terrified the prince as he looked into the ten pairs of eyes and the gleaming edges of the weapons that each pointed at him. However, those inside recognised who had surprised them, and they put their weapons away, but their image remained etched in Matrios's mind. He may have had grand plans, but these guards could have blown all his calculations right here and now if he had made a wrong move after storming in. He felt his hands grow cold, his feet turn to jelly, and the blood drain from his face. He took a deep breath as the knights dispersed to continue their work. They made no apologies, said nothing, though they looked angry. The prince didn't press the heated situation. He just sighed and stepped closer to the beautiful woman.

Elizabeth slowly raised her eyes to him. Matrios smiled and felt her soft hand caress his cheek. She suddenly slapped him harshly across his cheek, the sound echoing loudly through the warehouse. Linary was so surprised that she didn't dare speak, but she wept silently in her mother's arms, cuddled against her mother's bosom.

Matrios raised his hand to his flushed cheek, which throbbed with a deep and sharp pain. He tried to speak but could only gape in his astonishment. The knights stopped working. Verilion could not breathe. They remembered that the last time she had struck the prince, he had angrily rebuked her. And so all the men waited with blood frozen in their veins to see what the prince would do.

The hall, which reeked of stale smells and the earthy aroma of harvested crops, suddenly stopped in time, and not even the flies dared to take wing in the air. The knights clenched their hands into fists, and the guard closest to the frail woman stood ready to leap in front of her if Matrios threw himself at her.

Matrios closed his eyes in shame and covered his face with his hands. The great silence was broken by Elizabeth who was furious but still remembered how he had treated her the last time something like this had happened. She was afraid of the man. "How dare you send my daughter back to the castle with only Picon to guard her! It is just luck we met on the road!" she shouted at him, and she was burning with a fire so intense the prince could feel her narrow magic seeping from her body.

Matrios did not speak.

"It's not been even a week since they tried to kidnap her from the courtyard!" she recalled with tears in her eyes, perhaps from fear, fear that he might attack her again. "It seems I misjudged you. You haven't changed a bit! You're the same selfish, spineless man you were before, Matrios Hritan!"

Matrios's mind replayed all the things his old self had done, and he felt his heart breaking bitterly. He saw in his mind how the belt had slashed across her back and how she had cried out for forgiveness, drenched in painful tears. He saw in his memory the face of the knight commander as he pulled him from her. Now he turned around and looked over his shoulder at the burly knight, who was also waiting, ready to pounce, if the prince moved towards the woman. Matrios then understood. All that he had seen so far was merely a mask to his rank and to the empty words that he had said. He uncovered his face and turned back to her, but he dared not look her in the eye because of all the things he had seen in his flashbacks. The prince had been worse than he thought. Elizabeth had been so excited on her wedding knowing she would become a princess, but the reality was that she wed a man who looked at her only as an item. Elizabeth looked at Matrios quizzically, not believing what she saw, but her anger would not allow her to change her mind. "Don't touch my daughter again! You have already made her childhood miserable enough!" she snapped.

Matrios felt his own legs grow weak as he felt the demons of helplessness and shame rise within him. He felt abandoned and alone, just as he had in his previous life when he had fled to look for company surrounded with machines for what had happened to him. He had learned how to behave with people. He had learned when to wear a "mask" to show the face that helped to make things happen as he wanted them to. But this new world had given him little human experience, and he did not know all its rules. Dizziness gripped him. His body began to lurch from side to side, but he pinched his thigh with his fingers, which drew him back from his deep thoughts and also stemmed the watery torrent of his emotions. Then a sharp, thin sound cut through the overcast clouds in his mind.

"Don't hurt Daddy!" Elizabeth reached for her daughter, but to no avail. The tiny girl leapt out of her mother's arms, fell to her hands and knees, and quickly sprang up to run to her father.

"Don't hurt Daddy!" she repeated.

Everyone froze as Linary sided with her father. Verilion stood up and signalled the knights to stand down. Matrios looked at the little guardian, who, with her tiny arms and frail dove's body, now as brave as a thousand warriors, wedged herself between himself and her mother. Her black hair was like the darkness that devoured Matrios from within, and he could feel the innocent, sweet magic from her tiny body, soft as if she were a feather, but swirling like the storming sea.

"My father has changed!" the child shouted as she turned to the man, who caught his gaze. "He came into my room and woke me up! He let me play with Shrike! He brushed my hair!" She sniffled. "Daddy's different now, and I love him like this!" she screamed, clinging to his legs.

Matrios could feel the emotions mixed with magic light up in his heart like the flames of a torch thrown on oil. The dark emotions burned to white ash in an instant by the child's golden fire. Matrios knelt on the stone floor and slowly, almost pleadingly, locked the tiny girl in his arms. Closing his eyes, he lifted the child with the elegance of a man of his rank, and then, covering his face with his own forearm, pinched his shoulder in an attempt to control his wildly racing emotions.

Elizabeth felt ashamed and sighed nervously. "That is all beautiful, but that's not what we're talking about, Linary!" She rubbed her eyes

157

angrily. "This is grown-up business. Don't interfere!" she told the child angrily. Then she turned to the knights. "Get out!" she ordered.

"But, my lady!" said Verilion.

"If he does something, you'll be able to hear it," she said to him in a nonchalant manner.

"As you wish," said the big knight unenthusiastically. He waved to the guards, and they all left the warehouse.

The child continued to cuddle into his father's shoulder, trying to get over her emotions, while Matrios struggled with the old demons of his own past as Jacob and the past life of the prince. He felt his entire magic consumed by this struggle. His memories stirred and rose again as a huge raging beast, an amorphous and hideous monster.

Matrios remembered the last time he had cried. He saw himself as Jacob at his mother's funeral, alone in the crowd, clutching a white bouquet in his hand. His brothers and sisters were huddled together in the distance, and he stood forlornly at the edge of the grave, watching the dirt slowly cover the coffin. He felt nothing but a painful emptiness. By then, everyone who would have cared for him had left. He had long since grown estranged from his brothers and sisters because of old grievances, and he looked in their direction in vain, only to find in them empty strangers. His ex-wife had left him because of all the work he had to do. She had long since run off with another man, and all he had left were the machines that, even if they killed his world, were his last refuge in a world where he could hide from prying eyes, where only he and no one else could be, where he would not be disturbed or spoken to. He remembered kneeling at the grave and placing the flower inside, a final farewell to his last loved one and perhaps the only remaining link he had to that world. He felt a lifelong chain snap in his soul, and at the same time a storm of bitterness washed over him like a raging, galloping wave. The very edge of loneliness beat its way into his already aching soul, piercing through it, cracking his heart, which was frozen so hard. Still, he had tried to control his tears, but they were unrelenting and uncontainable. Quietly, dully, abandoned, and yet embraced by the eyes of the world, and in defiance of its condemning disgust, he had cried out his grief in silence into the silent meadow, covering his eyes, covering himself from the world and everything that lived and denied him. The tomb was full, as was his bleeding soul of gloomy anguish. He had risen to his feet, smoothed the pile of earth, and left the funeral with an emotionless, unruffled face.

The same man now clung to a tiny girl, perhaps the first soul capable of loving him, the first soul who saw in him not rank, free labour, or knowledge. But that broken soul had been split from the slap like a dry, fire-eaten stump split by an axe. So he lived the pain that belonged to two men at once, and yet he had to bear it alone.

Elizabeth did not know what to do or how to feel. She was angry with him, but she also felt sorry for him. She had heard from the servant what his life had been like, what had been done to him and why he had become the worm the prince had once been, but a person who had lived the horrors herself could only pity the other. But it was different now. As if there was no pity in her heart for the prince as she watched him crush in the arms of the child. She felt the greasy knot of inexpressible emotion in her throat, and tears gathered in her eyes.

Elizabeth had never seen Matrios so vulnerable or so emotional. He had always been irresponsible and ostentatious, but now, for the first time, the monster in human skin seemed to be truly different. The way he gently, yet tightly, held the small body in a protective hug erased all doubt from her mind. However, she could not wash away the memories of the old life; neither could she forgive him.

Linary pushed away from her father and roughly wiped, her huge sea-blue eyes that were full tears. She pulled her beautiful cherry lips into a soft smile full of love. "I love you!" she said in a wonderfully happy tone.

Matrios closed his eyes and felt all the memories that had been weighing on his heart suddenly recede like powerless spiders into the deepest darkness of his soul. He wiped his eyes, took her hands in his, and said with a sigh, "I love you too. Thank you." He spoke with a happy face, as if the world had cleared up, but more likely his soul had been bleached white again.

Elizabeth couldn't keep her emotions to herself. At the sight of the closeness between her husband and daughter, tears streamed down her cheeks. She caught them, one by one, with her hands. Linary saw this, so she ran to her and wiped her now happy tears on her mother's skirt. Elizabeth bent down and picked up the child. Then she clasped the small body to her breast and stroked the child's back. Linary rested her head on her mother's shoulder. Elizabeth looked at Matrios, but he was still unable to look her in the eye.

Matrios got up from the floor and dusted himself off. With slow, lifeless steps he stepped out the door without a word. There the knights were waiting for him, looking at him, puzzled and demanding an explanation. But he only straightened his coat and spoke imperiously. "Back to your posts! Commander, I'm going back to the castle. I want to be left alone!"

"Understood, my lord!" The mighty knight bowed his head. "Are you certain—"

"I am! I'll be fine on my own!" said Matrios. He walked to his horse, unhitched the bridle from the fence, and mounted the tall animal. With a quick gallop, he headed back to the castle.

Verilion spoke with bowed head. "Did you not hear our lord? Back to your posts!" he shouted at the knights.

Matrios slowed down when he came out of the village and saw that there were no people around him. He heard a loud flapping of wings behind him, but he didn't attribute much significance to it. Shrike landed on his shoulder and looked at his tear-stained face. "What's happened to you?"

"Nothing," he replied in denial.

"Nothing doesn't look like that, body snatcher," he said, bored. "But I'm not your friend to care."

"Right. You're just another familiar who's with me to—"

"And?" asked the bird-beast indifferently.

"And you even admit it," sputtered the prince angrily.

"I'm not a person to lie to your face," said the creature casually.

"Hm … you're right," said the prince. "Thank you."

"You're welcome!" Shrike spread his wings. "So, are you feeling better? Shall we start the secluded life you were been living before all this?"

"I haven't been secluded," he said curiously.

"We both know which life I'm thinking of." The bird-beast sighed.

"No! But it would be nice if the noise of my thoughts could be drowned out by some machines." The prince smiled.

"Why? Isn't the point of the problems? To solve them?"

"Yes, but it's a bit more problematic." He made excuses.

"I don't know, and I don't care. The truth is, I swore I'd help you, but I didn't say I'd be your friend."

"You don't need to remind me."

"I'll let you know before you forget it! I don't want to end up with your tears on my feathers." The creature shuddered.

"You're not funny."

"I'm a demon. What do you expect? If you want tenderness, go see a succubus!"

"That's a good one." The prince smiled.

"What are you planning to do now?"

"I have some ideas! You'll like them!" said the prince with determination.

"Well, that sounds good!" Shrike spread his wings again.

When they arrived at the castle, the gate was lowered and waiting for them to enter. As they crossed over the deep dry trench that surrounded the castle, Matrios looked down and saw the carcasses of some dead animals. He didn't like the sight, but he chose to ignore it. He rode into the courtyard, dismounted from his horse, handed it off to a groom, and turned his steps towards the door of the great hall. The events of the last half hour continued to swirl in his mind. The sun was an hour past its highest point. The high walls broke the mild summer wind, and it weakened as it tumbled over the stones. He looked up at the ramparts and saw the patrolling guards, some pacing, some looking down, some just talking to one other. Sighing, he opened the large oak iron door and stepped through. The area was cool and dark, a little gloomy, mostly damp. The prince did not like the atmosphere of the place, even though it mirrored his own mood. In the flickering torchlight, a man approached him. It was Tibald, the old servant, who bowed with dignity before the man. Tibald looked up at the young man. "May the gods bless you, good sir. How can I help you?"

"Get a pencil, a ruler, and as much paper as you can find!" said Matrios in a rude, careless manner.

"Excuse me, sir, but what is a ruler?" Tibald bowed again.

"Hmm ... Get me some sort of stick or rod that is straight and has one side that is perfectly flat." Tibald pondered, then snapped his fingers. After another bow, he disappeared into the corridors.

Matrios sighed again and started up the wide staircase leading up the centre of the building. He walked with slow, heavy steps, almost oblivious to where he was. His mind was on nothing but the tool he was about to draw.

"What are you planning?" asked the bird-beast, who had flown through an upper window to join the prince.

"I will draw a heavy plough," he answered clearly.

"What?"

"A machine that will revolutionise agriculture," he explained, exhibiting a slightly better humour.

"I see. And what is it?"

"A large hoe driven by animal power."

"What is a hoe?"

Matrios sighed. "Never mind. My machine will help the peasants to work the land."

"Weren't you an engineer or something?" asked Shrike.

"I didn't have many friends left after the war, but I had lots of friends at the academy. Some of them were agricultural engineers. One day we sat down for a drink in our favourite pub, and some history students arrived. They started discussing—after around six beers—what was the one thing that had reformed human life." He experienced bittersweet memories as he spoke.

"And that's the dirt digger thing?" the bird-beast said, sounding doubtful.

"Let's say it now takes a team of men an entire month to plough the fields around here. With this tool, powered by a cow, one man can plough a field in one day!" He spoke with sparkling eyes.

"Ah, I see! That would really be a big help!" Shrike replied inexcitedly. "What are you going to do about the people who lose their jobs because of this?"

"Well, I haven't thought about that, but I could use a helping hand in every direction." The prince said as they continued on to his workroom. He pushed through the door. Inside, Tibald had already prepared everything for the young prince and was waiting in the corner in front of the table.

"Great!" Matrios stepped over and looked at the tools. "What is this?" He picked up an iron object.

"I couldn't find anything that matched my Lord's description, so I brought a piece from a broken torch holder."

"Perfect!" Matrios snapped.

"Really?" Tibald had doubted his own decision.

"Yes! The surface is just straight and smooth enough. It could do with a bit of polishing, but I won't bother with that now, even though it's dirty."

"Oh, I beg your pardon!" Tibald said. Quickly he wiped the piece of metal with a damp cloth.

"Thank you, although it lacks the engravings, it will still be usable.

"My prince?" said Tibald.

"Yes?"

"You are no longer Prince Matrios, are you?" Tibald's voice was low and reflected his fear.

Matrios was very surprised to hear the question, and at first, he did not know how to answer. He knew that he had known the servant Tibald since he was a baby. This made him worry about what was happening to the prince. He realised that he had handled the situation badly till now and that the former prince had ceased being Matrios Hritan and had, instead, become Jacob Taylor. He put down the ruler and turned to face the old man. "In some ways, yes. In some ways, no," he replied calmly."

"What does that mean?" Tibald looked up, startled.

"I'm not the same man I was, Tibald! I no longer want to be the same man I was." His emotions were again bubbling to the surface. "Everything I did—" The prince bit his words back as he struggled to prevent a tear from falling. "I am no longer Matrios Hritan, at least not the Matrios Hritan you knew."

"Then who are you?" Tibald took a step back with a frightened look on his face.

"I am nothing more than a purified Matrios, who, at death's door, has realised that the way he lived and the things he did were all wrong and there is no absolution for me." The prince gave the servant a bittersweet smile.

"My lord—" whispered the servant, his words barely audible.

"Thank you, Tibald, for staying by my side and looking after my family all this time." The prince smiled.

"It's only natural, sir!" Tibald knelt.

"This is not necessary," said Matrios. "I owe you my gratitude, and I should kneel at your devotion!" The prince put his hand on the man's shoulder.

"Sir!"

"I have changed, Tibald, and I think that is good!" The prince smiled again.

Tibald straightened up and bowed to the prince. He said nothing, simply nodded in acknowledgement as he left the room. One last time, he looked back from the doorway at the man whose entire life he had watched, and then he closed the great door.

The bird-beast looked up at the man. "You're a good liar," he said approvingly.

"I'm not. I've changed a lot since I came here."

"What do you mean?"

"I used to look down on the people here because they have little knowledge. I could probably teach them more in a sleepy morning than the greatest sages ever known to them. But I underestimated their spirit, Shrike!" He sounded soulless and disappointed.

"Underestimated their spirit?

"Where I come from, all forms of togetherness and family devotion have been almost completely eradicated. Families are organised on the basis of efficiency, and spouses have taken each other's biology as their priority.

But you loved your mother, didn't you?" said the creature, interested.

"That's … that's true." The prince sighed. "I never understood how people could put up with each other like that."

"Could it be that you were the only one who didn't see the love between them?" The creature looked up at him again.

"I thought you didn't care." He smiled, sitting down at the table."

"I don't, but until you solve this, I'll never know what this plough looks like," he said casually.

"You're right." Matrios took a deep breath and looked out the window. "This world is strange to me."

"With what I saw in your memories, I don't wonder. I could never fly in such clouds." The bird-beast shook himself.

"Don't tell me!" Matrios laughed softly. "The machines provided the last bulwark in my world. They provided a place where I could retreat and be myself."

"Maybe, but those metal monsters will never talk to you," Shrike pointed out. "I've seen your past. Why are you so good with humans now?"

"It's a long story." Matrios stretched. "I'll tell you about it another time, maybe, but I have to get started now. I have to finish my drawing tonight."

"At long last!" snapped the bird-beast. He flopped down on the bed. "Wake me when you're finished!"

Matrios felt a pleasant warmth in his chest. Strangely enough, even if Shrike was always uninterested, Matrios felt that the bird-beast was the only one who could understand him. And that was because the bird-beast was the only one who knew his secret. Matrios was finding it difficult to live another man's life while he had to remain himself in his soul. He sighed and grabbed the pencil—a solid, well-crafted little metal instrument with a screw on the side that held a thin piece of carbon. He placed a piece of paper in the middle of the table and touched the writing instrument to it. He felt the worries that had been weighing him down vanish in a blink of an eye, and all the demons that had been sitting on his shoulders crumbled to dust in the smouldering emptiness of the yellow sheet before him.

He drew the first line, appreciating how the black carbon sizzled across the scroll with a familiar, protective sound. The gloom and darkness vanished, and all that remained was the sharp pleasure the contoured drawing gave him. He took out his "ruler" and placed it on the page. It landed with a metallic ring. He drew a new line and joined to the previous one. It was a very important, irreplaceable line.

Matrios smiled, his soul at ease, his surging emotions becoming as clear and calm as his lines on the paper. He closed his eyes and imagined what he wanted to create. He saw the metal edges curving upwards into each other, the wooden framework that would connect and support the edges, the nails that would hold the machine together and keep it intact, and the strong and sturdy traction rings that would have to withstand the force of the animal.

He opened the mirrors of his soul and set to work to carve reality from his imagination. He drew three figures on the page, all masterpieces of their kind. He drew the contours in thick, strong lines and then reinforced them with ink, making them indelible. On another sheet, he painted each little part of the tool and numbered them. Finally, he began to draw the completed miracle itself.

He exhaled, leaning back in his chair, which gave a loud, but gentlemanly and appreciative whine. It was not the whine of some ill-assembled chair. He wiped his brow; thick drops of sweat were absorbed into his sleeve. He looked out of the window and saw the beautiful landscape, now clothed in the white, mournful veil of moonglow instead of the sun's magical rays.

Beside him, on a wooden platter, he noticed a tidy meal and a cup of wine. He was surprised, for, as time passed imperceptibly, he had not noticed how it had arrived. He yawned, raising his hand to his mouth. He took a thin slice of bread from the tray and bit into it slowly. He heard a sweet, delicate sniff behind his ear. He looked at the bed and saw Elizabeth turning towards him, breathing softly as she slept. Long had she slept the dream of the just, her face relaxed and calm. He had not noticed her arrival.

He rose from the table, stepped to her side, and crouched down as unhurriedly as a cat. For long moments, he watched the beautiful face as it swayed in a sea of dreams. Then he reached down and, with a careful movement, pulled up her blanket to make her more comfortable.

He sat back down in front of the papers, took a deep breath, and settled back into his own peace. The moon was high when he finished the last of the illustrations. His eyes were heavy, his hands cold and tired, his face weary. But he felt happy. He lay down his drawing instruments and raised the paper shield before his eyes. He gazed at it and felt the overwhelming force of fatigue pulling him like an irrepressible force towards the bed.

He leaned back. Only one candle remained burning, the light dim in the room. Even that could not repel the horde of darkness. The flame's spirit went out, leaving a thin trail of white smoke. With the room half in gloom, Matrios fell asleep slumped on the table, his mind guiding him to a new place. So clear were his dreams! And they were the ones he had always longed for. His body relaxed after a long ordeal. He sighed softly over the wood-scented papers.

Chapter 8

The next morning, the unrelenting rays of the sun broke through the window, perhaps the only one in the castle to be glazed, and illuminated the man. He woke wearily and languidly to the morning song of the offending rays of light. He raised his hands in front of him and looked out into the world, into the flames of the reddish sparks of the sleepy sun, over the hills that were painted in a blood-soaked colour. The prince sat up in his chair, wiped the sleepiness from his eyes, and stretched long and painfully. His back was numb from his night sleeping in the chair. Slowly and wearily, he clambered up, and it was then that Tibald opened the door. The old man bowed low to the man and then stepped closer. "My lord, may I suggest you take a hot bath in the morning?"

"Good idea," he said. He rolled up the papers, tied them with a thin thread, and pressed them into the old man's hand. "Would you mind handing this to a knight and asking him to take this to Eric the blacksmith?"

"Of course, my good sir!" Tibald bowed again. "I'll have your bath ready soon." And with that the servant left the room.

Matrios turned his gaze back to Elizabeth, who was still asleep on the far side of the bed. He could see only the back of her head. He lay down on the floor on the large rug at the foot of the bed and stretched his back as he worked through various exercises. When he was finished, he jumped up and took a sip from his cup. The wine was cold, but pleasant, slightly bitter with a fruity aroma. The two loaves of bread had dried up a bit as they lay on the table overnight, and the tomatoes had seen better days, but that didn't matter to a hungry man. He tore off a nice piece of dried meat with his teeth and took a bite of the tomato. It was sweet inside yet green tasting. As he ate, he watched the sun slowly and gently rise on the horizon as his mind turned to the day's tasks.

Tibald entered again. He bowed and addressed the man humbly. "My lord, the bath water is ready."

"Thank you."

Matrios walked through a door opposite the bed. In the tiny adjoining room, a metal tub stood in the centre of the floor. Beneath the tub was a deep metal box decorated with carved runes. A fire inside this box kept the steaming water from going cold. The familiar scents of lavender and aloe vera mingled in the room. A languid blanket of foam rested on the surface of the water, a white shroud that undulated gently. He dipped his hand into the water. It was hot but pleasant. As he stripped off his clothes, which stank of the dirt and sweat, he felt the fabric clinging to his body. He thought to himself that it was time for a good bath.

A maid entered the room. One of them picked up the clothes he had discarded so far. Matrios thought hard, as he knew they were watching him. Tibald stood by the door. The maid impatiently waited for his underwear, her face flushed red. Matrios shyly covered himself as he spoke. "Tibald, please bring me a cup of wine."

"Yes, sir, at once!" he said. He bowed and left the room.

Matrios turned to the maid. "You, girl, find me a razor. My face is covered with stubble!"

"Certainly!" the maid said, holding the laundry in her hand.

When the room emptied, Matrios quickly threw off his underwear and jumped into the water. He sank into the warm depths with a satisfied smile and a sigh. He dipped his hands into the liquid blanket, then clung to the edge of the cold tub and tilted his head back. He was almost asleep when the maid returned. He instinctively jumped at the creak of the door, and the woman looked away immediately.

"Yes?" Matrios asked, surprised.

"I have brought the razor the lord asked for." She held up the sharp, curved blade.

"What's that?" The word slipped out of his mouth.

"This is the razor! Does my lord use anything else in the royal court?" she said, looking at him questioningly.

"No!" he replied a little nervously.

"Lay your head back, please, and put yourself in my care!" she ordered meekly.

Matrios didn't object. He just closed his eyes and did as the woman ordered. She took a strange bottle from under her apron, which smelled of strong alcohol. When she put some of the contents onto her hand, it foamed it up. She applied it to Matrios's face. He was terribly nervous, and his breathing became irregular.

"Don't be nervous, sir, or my hand might slip!" She smiled down.

"Not funny," he said nervously.

"I'm sorry. I thought the joke might relax my lord a little. Perhaps something else?" She slid her hand down his body.

"A joke is enough," he said firmly, at which she jerked her hand back in surprise.

"Don't men do the shaving usually?" Matrios asked.

"Most of the men are either at war or working in the fields, so it fell to me to do the shaving for the previous lord," the woman explained as she drew the blade across a thick leather strap.

"I understand now." He sighed.

"Don't move, it's been nearly two years since I last did this!" she said, and Matrios' desperation was only deepened. "How is it that my

Lord has wandered into this cursed land behind the back of the gods?" she asked, but got no answer. "I will not continue if the lord wants to speak, I will not cut you," said the woman as she sat back.

"Ah, I see! Well, ask Tibald," said the man, startled.

"I'm sorry, sir, I didn't mean to bore you. My previous master used to talk to me while I was shaving his beard," the maid said, a little despondently.

"Really?"

"We had a good lord! It's a pity he died." She sighed. "Not that I'm not happy for my Lord Matrios. Don't misunderstand me, Your Grace!" she excused herself.

"Why would I do that?" He looked up.

"Don't mind me! I'm babbling on here!" She laughed nervously.

"As a new lord, I have to get to know the customs of the land and the people," he explained, once again submerging in the water.

"It's really good to hear that!" She dragged the razor along the thin chin, then wiped the foam off on the towel on her arm. The blade cleaned a wide, straight strip. Where it passed, the foam and the stubble magically disappeared. With small strokes, she adjusted the blade to capture the surviving hairs, and after each stroke, she meticulously wiped off the residue and got a new grip on the blade. Matrios closed his eyes and immersed himself in the water. She knelt at his head, and he now and then felt her bosom teasing his hair, but he thought nothing of it. He only enjoyed the touch of cool hands on his chin and the constant glide of the blade as it ran down his throat with a crackling sound. With an almost unearthly contradiction, it soothed his nerves.

"There we go." She drew a sharp line at the sideburns, then cleaned the shiny blade in the towel one last time and jumped up from her knees.

Matrios leaned his head forward languidly and ran his hands over his neck and face. He was pleased with his now smooth and soft skin, which he had never had before. His pores had always been filled with machine grease and oil. His face had remained dirty and unwashed and unshaven in his previous life.

"Is there a mirror?" he called after her.

"Excuse me. Certainly, my good sir!" The servant came back from the door and with hurried steps, opened a cupboard in the small room, lifted out an ornate silver hand mirror, and handed it to him.

"Excellent!" he said upon viewing his reflection.

"Thank you for your kind words!" She bowed.

The maid left the room, her face a little flushed. As the prince slipped back under the water, he noticed that the white shroud of foam which had covered his body was now floating in fragments like tiny, fading islands. He tilted his head back and cursed himself for his inattention, and now he understood the meaning of her face. He pulled up one leg and reached for the soap, which was resting on the chair. The facilities were rudimentary, but he had the better of it. After rinsing his body, he stepped with his spindly feet out onto the mat beside the tub. He shook himself, for despite the steam, the room was cool, not pleasantly so, more like dreadfully so. Quickly he reached for the towel, which was only a face-wiping scrap of cloth. Sighing in disappointment, he wiped himself with the rapidly dampening cloth. He put on the dark cloak that had been lying over the arm of the chair, and then he heard the creak of the large door. He spun round, so fast that the fabric of the cloak did not follow him, but his eyes saw only the familiar face that had stood by him through many trouble and hardship. Adalanna bowed low and humbly, her hands raised before her to her heart, her clothes soiled, her boots muddy, her shoulder covered with a tattered cloth soaked with blood that did not hide the arrow sticking from the wound. There were other wounds, other arrows as well. Matrios was taken aback by the sight of her. "What's happened to you?" He stepped closer, pulling the cloth over his body.

"I came back, sir, as you ordered!" she breathed.

"Ordered?" He looked surprised.

"You sent me out into the forest, through Lady Elizabeth's words, to survey the bandits, didn't you?" She raised her head, puzzled.

"I did no—" Matrios choked on the word, and a great anger suddenly flared in his heart. "What?" He stepped up beside her and then supported her with a gentle touch. The power in her was but a flicker.

"Lady Elizabeth ordered me," she said. "She told me we need to protect the village and the castle, so it fell to me alone." The elven woman smiled naively.

"Stay here!" He sat her down at the foot of the wall. "I'll fetch a doctor!"

Matrios tore open the big door and ran barefoot through the corridors, shouting for the knights. Panting, he reached the kitchen, kicked the door open, and saw his men, who were eating heartily. They immediately jumped to their feet at the noise.

"Anyone who can heal, follow me at once!" he ordered urgently and exhausted.

"Understood." The deputy commander, Dana, jumped out of the crowd. Without hesitation or a word, she turned on her heel and hurried towards the bathing room behind Matrios, where the battered-looking woman was already panting, having slumped onto her side. Matrios sat her up and immediately ordered Dana to heal the elf. "Heal her immediately!"

"But she's only an elf." Dana sighed. "This is what caused the big—"

"Don't talk back!" he shouted at her.

Dana's eyes narrowed in anger, but she turned to the elven woman reluctantly, and in a bored voice, recited the incantation he had heard at Bowed Mountain. A great flare of light shot from her palm, and dazzling rings of magic swirled around the flames, which were pleasantly soft. The smouldering light died away, the room was once more enveloped in a mysterious vapour, and she lowered her hand a little wearily. Adalanna opened her eyes slowly and with difficulty, and then turned her face towards Matrios. The protruding, broken arrow still stuck out of her shoulder, but the pain seemed beyond earth; the sensation of pain did not show so obviously on her face.

The prince turned to the knight and said his words. "If I tell you to heal, you heal!" he said. "If I tell you to fight, you may run, but as long as the lives of others are at stake, you must follow my orders!" His eyes nearly pierced the skull of the beautiful knight with the flame-red hair. She could feel the faint energy that was released from his body in his anger. The knight was not frightened; she simply bowed as she had been taught and left the small room with calm steps, wiping the sweat from her brow.

"My lord!" Adalanna tried to get up from the floor.

"Don't speak!" He ordered her. "I'll get dressed and we'll find a real doctor to take the arrows out."

"My lord—"

"Stop!" he grabbed the door handle and raised the volume of his without looking back.

"Thank you." She lowered her eyes.

Matrios rushed into the bedroom where the servant was waking the lady, and at the noise, the awakening woman was suddenly startled. The servant Tibald, frightened, clutched at his heart, but the prince paid them no heed. He took up all the clothes he could find and thought it simple enough to put on him. He cast an angry, furious glance in Elizabeth's direction. With a frightened face and dishevelled hair, she looked on him in horror at his haste, and then, as quickly as he had come, he went away.

"What has got into him?" she asked.

"The elf has returned," said Tibald with some disgust.

"The slut!" cried Elizabeth.

175

Back in the bathing room, the prince helped Adalanna up, supporting her wounded body under her arm, and with slow, marching steps they made their way through the cold corridors, down the stairs, and across the great hall where the knights were dining. Matrios paid them no heed, but something strange happened. Little Picon dropped whatever he was doing and, standing beside the woman, took the weight of her on himself and helped them.

"Where are we taking her?" asked the child.

"To the temple!" said the prince, surprised.

"You heard the prince, boys!" said Verilion. "Let's take the elf to the priest!" He wiped his moustache.

The prince was surprised and somewhat relieved when the commander took her weight from him, but he did not remain in that state. He immediately opened the door to the little party and called out the horses. They mounted the wounded elven woman on the prince's horse and set off.

Adalanna fought back tears as the knights helped her, though her wounds ached and her muscles were cut by the many wounds on her body, including some other arrows, but she had probably never received any help in her life till today. She felt in her soul that a storm was raging as strong as the taut nerve on the bow and as destructive as the broken arrowhead.

Matrios snapped the reins, and the horse took off at a fast pace with the knights behind him urging their horses on, but not catching up with the prince, who was already hurrying his animal in the distance. Soon they came to the edge of the village, and Matrios shouted in advance to keep the people out of the way of the horse, which was now panting and running at a fast pace. "Get out of the way!" the prince shouted vigorously.

When he reached the temple, long streaks of reddish blood were already oozing from her wounds, running down her ashen grey skin. He helped her off the horse, who was now acting like a sack, and taking her in his arms, slowly struggled to carry her up the temple steps. He banged on the huge door, which was opened a few moments later by a young boy, barely two decades old.

"What do you want?" He snorted.

"Are you the priest?"

"Yeah."

"Then help me."

The youth looked at the elf, who was panting. "She's just an elf." He sighed.

"And I am Matrios Hritan, third heir of the Hritan dynasty, noble of the village and castle of Brekan! So let me in or I'll have your head!" he shouted at him.

"Okay, don't get so upset!" He sighed again, opened the door wider, and let the man carrying the wounded woman inside.

"What happened to her?" He grabbed her under the arm.

"There are some arrows in her," Matrios said hurriedly.

"Let's put her down there and I'll help you!" The young priest pointed to one of the marble stands.

They laid Adalanna on the table. She was already suffering from gangrene. Her body was covered with cold, sticky sweat. Her face was red with suffering and burning with pain. The priest ran off in the direction of the cellar and descended the spiral staircase with loud clattering footsteps. When he returned, he brought with him a small bowl filled to the brim with a transparent liquid. There were metal utensils inside. Matrios was very surprised when he smelled the alcoholic odour in the air.

"Is that—" he said, curiously.

"I must pull out the arrows!" the priest said hurriedly. "This is going to hurt. Make her bite this piece of wood!" He handed the prince a cylindrical piece of wood.

Matrios took it and lifted it to her panting mouth. He pushed aside the delicate cherry lips that were dry but soft as clouds. He wedged the small stick between her white teeth and then, with both hands, he clasped her wrists.

"Holy Mother, who protects us in the darkness, I pray to you in this hour, help your child in his difficulty, grant her with your hands to shield her." He examined the arrowhead in prayer and then, with a strong movement and a cleaned hand, he began to slowly and gently push the half-broken piece of wood into her thigh. Her body stiffened. Her screams quickly turned to tears as the skin on the back of her thigh was torn open and the metal arrowhead appeared, glistening bloody in the candlelight. She started to leap up from the cold stone, but just then Verilion arrived and put all his strength on her shoulders. He looked into the green, tear-soaked eyes that begged for the pain to cease and the old knights soul, as hard as obsidian, crumbled like a rock broken by the waves of the sea. The priest pulled out the entire broken stick and looked at it. He knew the workmanship and knew well that it meant no good.

Adalanna calmed down, her mind not so foggy at this point. She perked up for a few moments and then fell back into a blur of unconsciousness. The other knights held her legs one by one, and Verilion stroked her soft locks and spoke in a soothing tone. "Good, just a little longer," Verilion soothed her in a fatherly, pious tone.

Matrios looked at the big paladin in amazement but said nothing, concentrating only on keeping her hands down.

The priest positioned himself again, eyeing the soft part of the rod that had pierced the woman's abdomen. The blood flowed out in a red stream with every one of her breaths.

"Deep breath!" the priest said. He pressed the foreign body and the sharp object in her back made the muscle bundles in her body strengthen again and the shock of the stimulus ran through every part of her body. She closed her eyes and sobbed soundlessly against the knight's hands, now gasping for air without resistance in a mournful dance of pain. When the priest passed the metal across her back, the agony subsided. The blood acted as a slick lubricant to protect the rest of her body, and so the wood quickly was pulled out from her flesh. She opened her eyes again, snorting like a bull, her gaze haggard, her hearing dull, but she sought the kind knight's eyes, which now proved to be her only warm shelter. Her emerald-green eyes moved upwards, her eyelids grew heavy, and her breathing became dull. Tears glided slowly and gently down her reddening cheeks. The elf, steaming with agony, fainted, her limbs going limp and heavy.

Matrios immediately fell onto her chest and listened for a few moments to make sure her heart was beating. Then he sighed heavily. "She's just fainted!" he said to the others, to which Verilion nodded resolutely.

The priest was now sweating, but he more easily and confidently pulled the remaining shaft from her shoulder and threw it to the ground. Everyone relaxed. Little Picon immediately set about healing the woman's wounds with his own magic, which the young priest watched with a deadpan expression. "What in the—"

"Healing magic," said the boy, concentrating on the wounded woman.

"It can't be," the priest said powerlessly.

"Get the priest!" said the prince, who sat exhausted beside the marble bench.

The two knights looked at each other, then sighed and grabbed the young man by the scabbard. He tried to resist, but the two warriors locked him in the cellar, the hatch of which was next to the priest's quarters.

"Sir, we shouldn't—" said Verilion, who stood up straight above the elf.

"I can't deal with this now," said the prince.

"My lord, I understand that—"

"I don't care what retribution the Church takes for this," he said. "I need some time." He looked at his hand, which was covered with Adalanna' blood.

"I understand." The great knight pulled up a chair and sat down opposite the prince. Dana, the second in command, stepped up behind him and gently clung to her father's shoulder. Then she motioned with her head for the other knights to leave the hermitage. Without a word, they all stepped out the door, and little Picon pulled it shut behind them. "I had two daughters," said Verilion. "Dana is the older one; Lana was the younger."

"Verilion, I—"

"I lost Lana in a battle three years ago," continued Verilion as if Matrios hadn't spoken. "During a border battle against the Kingdom of Pentrupun." The great knight wrung his hands.

"I'm sorry, Verilion," said the prince.

"An arrow pierced her breastplate on the left side of her heart. Then she was hit in the leg and finally in her right upper arm," he continued, full of emotion but calm. "I immediately crossed the battlefield to help my daughter, throwing away everything that mattered. I immediately fought my way through the battle and carried her to the hospital tent." He showed his hands to Matrios. "My daughter's blood was all over my armour." The giant man broke inside.

"I'm sorry, Verilion," Matrios repeated.

"My daughter breathed her last in the same agony the elf has now suffered. I watched her gasp for breath, and her eyes ..." The great knight put his hand to his face. "It was the way she looked up at me as I stood there helpless." Tears ran down Dana's cheeks, and she began to sob. She knelt behind her father, so that his great body would cover the broken-hearted girl. The prince remembered the woman who at first had refused to help, and now, as a child, sobbed behind him as if she were a different person. "Two days later, the sepsis took my little girl, and I sobbed in my tent for three days, begging the goddess of light to give me back my child." The knight looked empty as he told the story. He did not cry now as his grief was deeper than tears could tell. "Thank you, my good lord, that at last no more fathers have to go through this." The knight knelt.

"What are you doing?" The prince looked up.

"The bowl with the instruments in it smells of alcohol, just like you told the doctors in the camp." He pointed to the small white bowl.

"Yes." Matrios smiled.

"Thanks to you, the elf will live. If I had known about the healing magic then, my daughter might have lived." The great knight sighed bitterly. "But perhaps this will be the cross I bear for the rest of my life—for my own obsessive thinking."

"Don't blame yourself." Matrios reassured him. "Your daughter's death was never your fault, Verilion. Neither will Adalanna's fate be my lady's fault."

"What?" The great knight snapped his head up.

"My wife sent her out alone into the woods to scout the bandits' location. I think we don't have much time before they smell the blood and attack us in revenge," explained the prince.

"Sound the alarm at once!" the knight shouted back to Dana.

"It is unnecessary," said Matrios. "Let's not arouse suspicion. It will only make them wary."

"What shall we do then?"

"We'll trap the bastards!" Matrios rolled his eyes in anger. "From now on, the clock is ticking, the plan is in motion, the machine is turning." The prince smiled maniacally.

"What do you mean?" asked Verilion, rising.

"I don't have time to put together a musket," said the prince half to himself. He looked up at the man opposite him.

"A what?"

"Get me a bow and a hoe handle! We're going back to the castle!" The prince jumped up from the ground.

"What are those things for?" the great knight asked.

"I'm making a bow that will shoot through steel, cut through bone, and knock the urge to fight out of bandits!" The prince looked ahead of him with a smile. "Let's go! Bring Adalanna. We'll have her put to bed in one of the guest rooms!" he explained, pointing at her.

"But, sir, she's just a slave," Dana said.

"I have freed her, and she serves me willingly!" Matrios explained with an ashen face.

"What did you do?" Verilion came closer and looked at Matrios accusingly.

"I freed her!"

"Is that so?" The knights looked at each other.

"We don't have time for this!" snapped Matrios

"But, my lord, the priest!" said Verilion after him.

"Ah ... bring him with you. I have things to discuss with him too!" He stepped back and looked at the six warriors waiting outside. "Bring the carpenter to the castle at once! Give the priest a meal and tell the village chief that the bandits are coming."

"Understood!" The knights saluted, immediately mounted their horses, and rode off.

Matrios also jumped into the saddle and rode back to the castle where he swept his desk clean and immediately set to work on making a drawing of a crossbow. With only a minimum of time and materials at his disposal, all he needed was a machine cobbled together in haste, suitable for a single shot. Just as he finished a quick sketch, there was a loud knock on his door.

"The carpenter has been brought, my lord!" said a knight.

A sturdy bearded peasant entered the room and bowed. "Long live the holy mother, my lord!"

"Yeah, yeah!" said Matrios, preoccupied. "Please, can you make this? As quickly as possible. And do you have a hoe handle at your disposal?" The prince pressed the drawing against the man's chest.

The peasant, who had taken Matrios's half-hearted greeting amiss, looked at the drawing and said, "Does the lord want to pierce a wild boar lengthwise?"

"No," answered Matrios, "I want to pierce shields and breastplates!"

"Give me two hours and a short bow!" The craftsman wiped his nose.

"Not a minute more!" The prince held out his hand.

"I cannot touch royalty as a peasant, my lord," said the man, bowing.

Matrios ignored the formality and said goodbye immediately. The knight led the craftsman to the armoury to choose from the many bows.

The prince suddenly had a lot of things to do, which he had to quickly organize in his head. He stopped in the corridor for a moment, and his stomach churned. The sun was high in the sky. He figured it was about noon when he ran down to the kitchen.

"Gods bless you, my dear sir!" the cook greeted him.

"Yes, yes …" Matrios, again, was preoccupied with his thoughts.

"Can I help you?"

"Give me a loaf of bread to take away my hunger." Matrios looked up at the cook, who was already handing him a small basket. Matrios took one of the many loaves and headed for the door. The cook just scowled at the prince's lack of manners.

Matrios took a bite of the warm bread and sat down at the table with his papers. "Now I just have to wait for the garrison to get their act together." He sighed.

"My lord!" Verilion entered the room. "The scouts have arrived." He sighed and sat down beside Matrios.

"And?" Matrios looked up from his plans.

"A large group of bandits have set off for the castle."

We've only just arrived, and we're already facing a siege?" He shook his head.

"What's wrong?" Elizabeth stepped out of the darkness of the corner.

"You sent Adalanna to assess the bandits' strength, and now a larger group of them are coming to take our heads!" Matrios explained irritably.

"That bitch!" Elizabeth hissed.

Matrios jumped up from his chair in anger. The chair was thrown backwards, causing a loud echoing noise in the cavernous room. "That 'bitch', as you call her, saved my life! She stood by my side the entire time, alone, with no ulterior motive!" He slapped the table. "I demand that you stop this senseless hatred!" His angry gaze flickered in the candlelight.

"Senseless hatred?" mused Verilion.

"Yes, the hatred towards the elves."

"But they won't treat us any differently." Elizabeth folded her arms in front of her chest.

"So we have to sink to their level?" Matrios righted his chair and resumed his seat.

"Why should I treat them any differently?" Elizabeth argued. "Slaves don't deserve to be treated well anyway."

"But Adalanna is not a slave," Matrios said.

"What?" Elizabeth looked at her husband.

"I freed her for what she did at Bowed Mountain, and she has served me ever since—faithfully and without question." The prince spoke in a calm voice. "You saw it too, Verilion. There is no difference between human and elf."

"What do you mean?" Verilion looked up at Matrios.

"She felt the pain just as your daughter did. She looked as desperate and as terrified as Lana did," said the prince in a kind voice."

"Do not mention my daughter in the same breath you use to refer to an elf!" The knight stepped closer Matrios and then fell silent for a long moment, as if he had changed his mind. "It's true, they both feel the pain, but you can't erase a millennium of struggle." He sighed.

"Just because an elf—" began Elisabeth.

"Because humans aren't vile?" suggested Matrios.

"Yes, but—" she became confused.

"We're not facing a huge and bloodthirsty threat that only nature's barrier could stop, are we?" he asked her. "We're not facing anything but fathers losing their daughters in border wars. And demons slaughtering our sons." He pointed to Verilion.

"Yes, sir," the knight said bitterly. "The doctrines of the Lord of Darkness also state it. He who forgives holds more than he who holds grudges," he said.

"But still …" Elizabeth objected.

"Shouldn't the Republic accept elves?" asked Matrios.

"Tolerate them."

"Tolerate them?" Matrios looked at her.

"They are only tolerated as long as they are in transit or are rich," she explained. "The Hritandian continent has no place for long-eared people," she stated clearly.

How petty and silly, Matrios thought to himself, but his face only broke into a pleasant smile as if he had been listening to a child's argument. He leaned back in his chair, his face pulled into a superior smile and said, "And why is that?"

"Because this is the continent of men!" Elizabeth said firmly.

"Whose was it before?" He crossed his fingers in front of his chest.

"The ... elves," said the woman timidly.

"Then why should a handful of land be ours or theirs?" He looked puzzled.

"Because we fought—"

"They fought, too, but lost the war," Matrios interrupted her. "It's true that the strongest survive, but it's still spineless to retaliate against someone who has lost everything, don't you think?" he asked inquiringly. "Imagine what would happen if one of the kingdoms attacked the Republic and didn't stop until everyone who lived there was slaughtered. What sense does that make?" He leaned forward in his chair.

"But they're the people of another nation!" She threw her hands on the table.

"If you take the nation, they're your people, aren't they?"

"All men are equal in the eyes of the Holy Mother." Verilion highlighted the belief.

"And who do the elves pray to?"

"Aludarne, the goddess of the moon," said Verilion, looking at the prince in contemplation.

"And who is she?"

"The child of the Holy Mother and the Lord of Darkness." Verilion became speechless.

"You see?" asked the prince, smugly.

"But—"

"With this, faith is no reason for war, and there is no reason to oppress them any longer. We are no different except for the ear—"

"They have longer lives and are better at magic," Elizabeth exclaimed as if she had found a sound difference.

"Good for them." He smiled and continued. "They're just like us, only a little different. They get better at magic with practice, but they make mistakes like us, they cry like us, and love like us."

"You are right, my prince." Verilion nodded shyly.

"Verilion!" Elizabeth scolded him from across the table.

"I am too old to argue, Lady Elizabeth, but I will never be too old to recognize the truth if it is in front of my eyes." He laughed. "I will never be able to atone for what I have done, and if what the prince says is true, then I am a terrible man." He sighed.

"We all make mistakes—humans, dwarves, and elves." Matrios smiled sweetly.

"Yes, my Lord, though I do not deserve to be a knight," he said, disappointed.

"If you strive for better, then you may yet earn it. Set a good example and do what you think is best in your life," explained the prince.

"I will." The great knight knelt by the table. "Allow me to raise my sword to your cause, my lord."

"I would be pleased if you would protect me and add your sword to my ranks." The prince rose from his chair and placed his hand on the old warrior's blade.

Elizabeth just looked at her husband, who had accepted the knight again. Her mind refused to accept all that the older man, who had seen so much, had so easily accepted. She stubbornly defended the ideas she still believed in. She wanted to speak, but she had had enough of Matrios's condescending tone, and she refused to listen to his reasoning. She stood up from the table and left in a huff, but Matrios called after her. "Don't ever put my men in unnecessary danger again!" He looked at her with an angry look that made her flinch. With a downcast look, she nodded and disappeared around the corner with quick, timid steps.

Matrios sat back in his chair, sighed heavily, and looked across the long table in front of him. He didn't need to ask, the cook had already brought out a large jug, placed it on the table, and looked at the prince. "Are you feeling well, sir?" he asked, surprised.

"Why, of course!" Matrios looked up at the man, surprised.

"You know—the water," the cook said, wringing his toque in his hands.

"I told you it was all right after we boiled it," he answered with a poker face.

The cook looked surprised. "But everyone else—"

"Everyone else has fallen into bed with illness before!" finished Matrios. "I must add to my list of things to do to bury the toilet and make a new one in a new location."

"Why, my good sir?" asked the prince.

"Because the waste from the toilet makes its way into the water. Don't give anyone a bucket from the well until we've sorted it out." He propped his head on his fingertips as he rested his elbows on the table.

"I'm sorry. Now, if you'll excuse me, my lord, I'll go back to the kitchen. Enjoy your tea, and if you want anything, just shout." The big man bowed.

Suddenly a great noise filtered in through the door, and a few moments later, the carpenter kicked the gate open with a thud. "Good day to you, my good sir!" he bowed, a little spitefully.

"What's the matter with him?" the prince pointed to the man as he directed his question to Verilion.

"You, peasant, don't you know your place?" cried Verilion, jumping up.

"Shut up and look at this!" The peasant pointed at the harnessed weapon, which was huge and seemed heavy; indeed, the man's hands trembled under the weight.

"Ah!" Matrios said, and he jumped up from the chair and ran to the carpenter. "Wow, this is beautiful!"

"Isn't it?" the peasant snapped.

Taking the crossbow in his hand, Matrios looked over the wooden structure, which had been crafted together in a haste. He examined the small bow at the end, which the carpenter had reinforced with a metal plate, and the nerve, as taut as young skin. He gripped it expertly, felt the weight of the structure against his back as it pulled him forward, looked into the sights, and released the trigger. It snagged at one point, just where the prince wanted it to. So, he just pulled the nerve back with both hands, his foot braced in the metal triangle at the front of the mechanism. The nerve was strong, the wood bowed slowly, resisting, but he finally hooked it into the firing mechanism and took a smaller arrow from the quiver provided by the carpenter.

"Small and massive, as you requested! But I've carved arrowheads into it so there's a chance of breaking the tip," explained the craftsman, smelling of alcohol but coming out of his stupor.

They went out of the castle in the courtyard where, in the distance, the archery targets were lined up against the wall. The prince took a deep breath and lifted the heavy weapon. He took aim at the centre point, which was painted red. He pulled the small lever at the bottom, and the nerve ran off the tree with a loud snap, swinging the structure, which resisted the impact with a tremendous vibration. The prince's shoulder jumped back violently as the stock pressed to it. And with invisible speed, the massive arrow, snapping off its nerve, slammed into its target slightly off the middle, but smashing through the straw and wood-backed board and shattering against the stone wall of the castle like a toothpick.

The carpenter took his hat off and fell to his knees, his words soundless but a prayer on his breath. Satisfied, Matrios leaned the structure against the pole and went to survey the damage. The head of the arrow had broken off, and the wooden section was split in two lengthwise, tiny splinters all around it."

"Get me a suit of armour!" Matrios called, holding the remnant of the arrow in his hand.

"What?" Verilion asked, exasperated.

"Give me a suit of armour to shoot at!" he snapped, delighted.

Verilion called to two soldiers who had watched the prince's stunt. They ran off and, after a short while, appeared with an old, rusty breastplate, which they placed on a table in front of the target. Matrios once again raised the crossbow. Now it felt heavier than before. He could feel his hands tiring from the first firing, but he kept his aim and again unleashed the wrath of the weapon. It whizzed through the ether and pierced the breastplate, then was stopped by the backside. Matrios threw the crossbow and leapt for joy. "Yes!" he shouted. "I did it!" he shouted again.

"My lord!" Verilion seemed to have lost his breath.

Matrios turned to the carpenter. "Make more arrows for this one, and make as many more of this weapon as you can. Get people to help you!" he shouted with joy.

"I will!" the carpenter said with a cheer. Then he stumbled off towards the armoury.

Matrios relaxed and noticed a strange noise. Soldiers and knights alike applauded the happy man. He adjusted his shirt on his body and bowed.

"With this weapon!" he said, raising the crossbow with his hand. "There is no need to train anyone! Come and try it!" he handed it to Verilion.

The great knight took over the weapon. He was a little wary of it, but he respected its solid proportions. With one hand, he reloaded the weapon, and then, under the prince's guidance, prepared to fire. He stood to one side, resting his left hand on the bottom of the crossbow, resting the stock of it on his shoulder, as if it were not the first time he had used the weapon. Matrios thought it might be because Verilion had used a bow before. He let go of the man's hands and stepped back from him, then smiled broadly.

The arrow now pierced the air with perhaps even greater speed and penetrated both sides of the armour, bouncing off the wall. Matrios held his head in excitement, and Verilion shuddered at the incredible power he had unleashed.

One of the soldiers on the wall snapped up.

"Unbelievable!" celebrated the other.

"Let me try it!" Dana jumped in behind them.

She snatched the crossbow from Verilion's hand, and he stood to her side so the prince would not have access to her, to explain it to her himself. He showed the young woman everything the prince had shown him. She took the bow. The nerve tightened again, but this time she cheated. She touched the arrow and sent magic flowing into it; it began to glow. She fired the weapon. The arrow flew with a whistling sound. Upon impact, a huge explosion blew the pierced armour apart.

Both Verilion and Matrios stared dumbfounded at the woman, who was also stunned by the power she had unleashed.

"What was that?" the great knight cried.

"I just put a little magic into it, that's all." She set the weapon down with trembling hands. "I don't think this weapon is for me." She sighed, showing a little fear.

"Wonderful!" The prince snapped. "Better than I had hoped! If you put magic into the arrow, even if it is destroyed, it will have certain abilities."

"Do you understand what he is saying?" Verilion whispered to his daughter as Matrios continued his complex theory in the background.

"I have no idea, Father," she whispered back, barely audible.

"What an unexpected turn of events!" cried the prince in ecstasy. "We need more! Ah, indeed." He sighed and calmed down, adjusting his clothes. "Verilion!" he cried out.

"Yes, my lord!" The knight came to attention.

"Today, if the enemy leader shows himself, I want you to shoot him with this." The prince pointed to the crossbow.

"But, sir, in battle—"

"These men are robbing peasants and pillaging the hinterland, helping the demons to gain power. Do you think they deserve any mercy?" the prince asked with folded arms.

"No, sir," Verilion replied with a determined face.

"You are right," said the prince, "however ..."

"What?"

"Let us not sink to their level." Matrios thought for a moment. "I will offer them the chance to surrender and join us in building another village."

"I don't think—"

"If their leader rejects my offer, I want you to shoot him in the shoulder." The prince smiled approvingly.

"But sir, what if I miss?" Verilion expressed a lack of confidence.

"If you were able to hit me with unpractised magic skills from hundreds of meters away back at the garrison, then hitting a target a few meters away will not be a challenge." The prince smiled.

Verilion thought, then looked at his daughter. He lifted the weapon from the pole and once again flicked the nerve. He took an arrow from the quiver and nocked it. Then he ran two fingers along its side and murmured something. He aimed at the sun and loosed the arrow. In the sky, the highly aimed piece of wood whizzed quickly. The knight averted his gaze, and the arrow veered off its trajectory. It was moving fast, so it couldn't quite change direction, but it was visible in the distance. Finally, the great knight looked at the ground in front of him, and when gravity pulled the arrow back, it fell and drilled into the ground exactly where the great knight was looking. "It can be done!" The huge man clenched his fist and his eyes burned with fire.

Matrios said nothing but was shocked by what he had seen. The huge man surprised the prince with his action, not just that he could do it, but that he had put the idea together in his mind. A smile of satisfaction and pride settled on his face, and he went back to the castle to supervise the knights and prepare for the attack.

A few hours passed. The scouts continued to report the enemy's position until the village elder Marabas appeared at the gate and asked the guards for admittance. Matrios thought it unusual that the old man should appear under the wall, as he did not like to go on such long walks. He thought it must be important to the man to say something, so he went to the gate himself to speak to him.

The village chief, Marabas, was sitting on a bench in the cool shade, waiting for the prince, his hands resting on his staff, his eyes scanning the hurrying soldiers as he sighed heavily.

"What can I do for you?" Matrios asked.

"Sir, please don't kill the bandits!" said Marabas.

"This is a strange request. Should I let them come in and raid my castle?" He folded his hands in front of his chest.

"I didn't say such a stupid thing." He shook his head.

"I'm not obsessed with fighting, old man, but if someone spits on my porch, I can't tolerate that," he explained.

"Yes, my lord. Is the elf all right?" Marabas looked up.

"Thank God she's staying with us." He sighed in relief. "Why do you ask?"

"I could see by the lord's face that he cared for her fate." Marabas smiled.

"If I didn't, people wouldn't follow me." He returned the father's kind smile. "Don't you think?"

"I've never lived under a bad ruler," he said thoughtfully. "But none of them brought food to our tables and put tools in our hands as you did."

"A mere gesture of friendship." He smiled a little shyly.

"People are tough on the outside here in the North, but inside they appreciate being looked after. Believe me, my lord," the old man confessed.

"Well, who would want to work for a vile man do you think?" Matrios laughed.

"Yes, that's true, my prince." Marabas smiled, lost in thought. "I'd better go before the bandits find me on the road."

"By the way, when will the villagers arrive? We'll have to hide them in the cellar so they don't get killed." The prince spoke urgently.

"You don't have to worry about us."

"Why shouldn't I?"

"You know, whoever leads the bandits wouldn't hurt the villagers," he explained.

"How do you know that?" the prince wondered.

"Because it's my nephew, Gelborg." Marabas sighed.

"What?"

"The poor foolish boy." Marabas shook his head. "He's just a lost child, that's all. I am too old to restrain him. You can try to talk to him and see if he will listen to you, but don't kill him, my lord, I beg you. There's no one else but me to look after that foolish wretch. It started when they marched against the neighbouring lord and the leader got killed. The evil man in command forced my nephew and his men to do the terrible things they did. Ever since that worm has been gone, they've been hiding in the woods among the trees!" said the old man, obviously in anguish.

"I'm not promising anything, but I'd rather solve this simply."

The conversation was interrupted by the arrival of a scout on horseback. He stopped under the gate, a long arrow sticking out of his chest. He turned from the saddle and fell dead to the ground. Matrios ran past the old man to help the soldier, but it was too late. As the gatekeepers lifted the boy's head, it moved lifelessly on his neck. The prince immediately ordered the gate closed. The large wooden gate began to descend between the stone channels. With a great dust and clatter, the metal spikes on the bottom of the gate were driven into the ground by the weight of the gate, and the men inside began to raise the bridge.

Gelborg and the roving party cut through the thicket to the castle while scouts kept moving ahead and behind them. The bandit army paid no heed to uninvited guests, for they fired no arrows at them, and he who does not seek a fight will not be found. However, as the bandits slowly reached the castle a young boy, feeling brave, shot an arrow at the feet of one of the veteran soldiers from the group, whereupon several of the bandits also took up arms and returned the kindness with their second-hand bows.

A man marched along the centre line of attackers. Beside him walked a woman who carried little baggage. She had a small rounded belly, and she wore a forced but sparkling smile on her face. On her other side walked a stallion that was more of a haggard beast of burden than a proud trotter. Behind its saddle hung a rucksack tied in a sturdy knot so it would not fall off. The woman looked at her lover and spoke anxiously. "Are you sure, my dear?" she said uncertainly.

"Do I have a choice?"

"To attack the castle with so few men?" she cried, looking back.

"We lost Faradh's cause when one of the squire's archers shot him in the chest, but Brekan Castle will give us shelter over the winter."

"But we're talking about the prince." She was worried.

"I know, but as prisoners we can keep the lord at bay and be safer from the mercenaries," he replied wearily.

"Are you doing this because you hate the nobles so much?" she asked in a serious tone. Then she stopped.

"I want to keep you and the baby safe, no matter what it costs!" he snarled.

"I don't want safety at the cost of people's lives."

"But we can't stay in the forest either!" He was running out of patience. "Over a hundred people have died in the camp, Melanie, and winter has hardly begun! They're broken and hopeless. Faradh's death has broken us all, but we can't just give up." He took the woman's hand and held it softly. "This is all we have left."

"Let's run away!" she said with tears in her eyes. "Let's leave the country if we have to, but I don't want to go through this again." She clung to his chest. "I had to grow up fatherless, but my child shouldn't have to." She sobbed inconsolably.

"I know what happened in the countryside, Melanie, but that's the last thing that holds us all together still." He lifted her head and kissed her forehead.

"Let's stop this, please!" She kissed him.

"If I leave now, people will take all their anger out on me, and I'll want to pay the crown for everything they've done to us." He walked away.

"Gelborg!" she called after him.

"Stay back and wait for me! You worry too much!" he said with a smile.

The ragged warriors appeared at the base of the trees, bows in their hands, their bodies draped in worn armour, swords or axes flashing at their sides.

The prince ran up to the top of the wall as he ordered the old man into the castle. Verilion waited for him above the gate. Beside him rested the weapon and two others. He glanced at the people as they came. Those who could be seen in the trees must have numbered about two hundred, and who knew how many were left in the cover of the foliage? We must be heavily outnumbered," said Verilion.

"Yes. We have seventy warriors at most," said the prince.

"But most of them are trained knights."

"Do not feel overconfident! One axe is enough to kill a man," said Verilion with a serious look.

A bearded man with long hair and a blue cloak rode out of the trees on a brown steed. Matrios took a good look as he strode along in front of his men, no doubt explaining something to them. Then, when he had finished and had drawn his sword, the motley company broke into a cheer that was not triumphant, but rather tired and scattered like the army itself. Then the man rode closer to the castle. When he was within earshot he began to speak. "The lord of the castle, who moved into this land without permission! Show yourself, coward!" he cried.

"Gods be good! The sun seems to be on your side for vigilantism." Matrios leaned over the castle gate.

"What?" The horseman looked up, puzzled.

"Are you the leader of this band?"

"We are not a band! We are the true army!" Gelborg puffed out his chest.

"And why did you disturb the people of my castle today, dear ..." The prince spread his arms.

"My name is Gelborg! Commander of the true army."

"Hail, Gelborg, the commander! I am—"

"I know who you are, Whoremonger! Matrios Hritan, third heir to the crown, usurper of the village and castle of Brekan." He continued his invective.

"I do not usurp the castle and the village," explained the prince. "My father gave me the right to rule as I see fit."

"We have long sought to seize the castle, but if we only take it empty, it will mean nothing! Rejoice, prince! You'll be the reason the true army will be taken seriously!" He raised his sword.

"Certainly you've thought it over well?" Matrios said condescendingly.

"Why?" Gelborg looked up in wonder.

"What do you think will happen to your little army, which at best consists of a thousand men storms my castle?

"Explain yourself!"

"Here we are at the foot of Bowed Mountain," said Matrios, "where the bulk of the Hritan armies are camped. How long do you think it will take them to find you and exterminate you after you've taken my head?" He pointed at Gelborg dismissively.

"The Hritan army must not move from the passes or the demons will break in!" said Gelborg, laughing.

"We're talking because I want to offer you a deal," said Matrios.

"A deal?"

"If you lay down your weapons, I won't confiscate your goods, and I'll give you amnesty while you trample my land. However, you must stop plundering and harassing the people and instead build your own village not far from the village of Brekan, and you can be the chief!" The prince outlined his plans.

"I don't want your stinking mercy!" Gelborg retorted.

"But listen, Gelborg! Here is your uncle, who has come to me to plead for your life, and I am not in the mood to take a life."

"That will be a problem because I came for yours!" shouted Gelborg. "I will avenge my ten warriors, hunted down by the nightingale!" he cried angrily.

"The what?" Matrios looked at Verilion.

"The elf."

"Ah, I see!" Matrios said. "I'm sorry for the loss of your companions," the prince shouted.

"Shut your pity! You noblemen never know what it is to be destitute, suffering, and live in misery."

You are talking to the wrong man, idiot, Matrios thought to himself. "Listen to reason," he pleaded with Gelborg.

"I listen to it, and it demands your head!" Gelborg drew his sword.

"Verilion," Matrios spoke softly to the knight.

"Yes?" The great knight immediately readied his three crossbows and took the first in his hand.

"When I give the signal, shoot him in the shoulder. If he falls from the horse, shoot him through the leg. If he signals with his sword, put an arrow through his butt. He'll learn from that."

But, sir—"

"The people need a parable, but I don't want to make a martyr of him. If you hit him on the side of his ass, you won't hit anything vital, but it will hurt him terribly," he said callously.

"I got it."

"What can we offer for our deal?" Matrios shouted at Gelborg.

"Your head!" the attacker replied.

"Be serious!" said Matrios, rubbing his eyebrows.

"Even with that you are insulting me and not taking me seriously! I'll have your head for that!" Gelborg reined in his nervous horse.

"Is it because you're offended?" Matrios snapped.

"I'll hear no more of this!" Gelborg snapped back.

"Now!" said the prince with a deadly calm.

Verilion raised the crossbow and took aim. He dragged his hand along the rod, which glowed golden, then released the force that had been raging in its nerves. The arrow whizzed through the air like death and pierced Gelborg's shoulder armour. The man tumbled backwards from his horse and landed on the ground with great force. He cried out in pain, his hand showing by its unnatural grip that his shoulder had been broken by the great force. Then he began to crawl on the ground, gritting his teeth and burning with agony.

"Second!" said Matrios.

Verilion dropped the crossbow and fired again with the other. It hit Gelborg at the bend of the knee, and he gave a yelp as the piece of wood wedged between his bones, separating them.

"Good shot, as I see you pierced him through the middle of the joint so it didn't hit the artery!" Matrios applauded the knight.

"Soldiers of the true army!" shouted Matrios, standing on the castle wall. "I offer you forgiveness! Your leader wanted to reject the new, pure life! If you decide to accept my offer, I will exempt you from paying taxes for a year, and you can build your own village not far from here! No one will persecute you anymore. You will not have to fear for your women and children, and you will not have to throw your lives away in unnecessary fighting!"

The people in the trees were shaken. The battlefield, which had not yet opened, fell into a profound silence. In the distance, the clatter of weapons broke the silence of the world. Gelborg raised his head and cried out at once. "Don't believe him! He'll make fools of you. As soon as you give yourselves up, he'll slaughter you all. Just look what he's done to me now!"

"Indeed! My knight shot you," said the prince with a snort.

"If you were a man, you would have done it!" Gelborg rolled over on the ground and struggled to his feet.

"If I had shot you, one of the arrows would have landed between your eyes." informed Matrios. "Better to live with grave injuries than to die!"

"You have crippled me!"

"I have not crippled you! I would rather prevent the battle at the cost of one man's life than see thousands perish!" said the prince angrily.

Gelborg didn't answer. He only clenched his teeth and drew his sword from its sheath.

"I will not be some noble's toy!"

"Lay down your weapon," instructed Matrios. "Your men are already broken."

"No chance!" Gelborg staggered towards the castle.

"He must truly hate me!" Matrios said to Verilion.

"My lord, you just turned him into a pincushion."

"Right." Matrios thought for a moment "Picon!" He leaned out over the courtyard as the boy in arms ran up the stairs to the prince. "Can you make me healing water?" he asked the boy kindly.

"Of course, my lord!" The child bowed.

"Then please turn this canteen of water into healing water!" the prince smiled at him.

Picon touched the leather container and chanted the spell. A great light appeared, visible to all outside the castle, strong and blue, shining around the stones in the red of the sunset. When the spell was finished, Matrios handed the canteen to Verilion. "Throw this at the fool!" he ordered.

"Are you sure?" Verilion asked.

"We have nothing to lose, but it might convince him."

Verilion dropped the crossbow from his hand and took a step back. He focused on the man who limped painfully in their direction, and then threw the small flask.

As the little leather container fell towards the man, he was trying to parry it with his sword. He managed to slice through the edge of the container, but its contents burst out and flowed onto the man. Frightened, he fell on his back and cried out in pain. And then he felt the agonizing pain in his body fade and become numb. He raised his hand and looked at his leg, which had a rod sticking out of each side. He shuddered, and then looked up at the prince.

"What was that?"

"It is healing water, which one of my knights can create! If you accept my offer, all your men who are sick or wounded will receive it!" Matrios said.

"Gelborg!" A woman ran to him across the battlefield.

"We have won." Matrios sighed.

"What do you mean?" The knight looked at the prince.

"She'll beat some sense into this fool." Matrios told his trusted knight.

"I see."

"Yes. Actually, we've won." He wiped his face with his hands.

As soon as the woman got to Gelborg, she dropped down beside him and looked him over. She was horrified at what the unfamiliar weapon had done to him.

"Get away from here, Melanie! You'll get yourself shot!" Gelborg pushed the worried woman away.

"I accept your offer! But I won't kiss your feet!" Gelborg shouted up at Matrios, protecting Melanie with his arm.

"I never asked you to!" replied Matrios with a kind smile. Matrios turned to Verilion. "Bring him in and have the priest treat his wounds. Find them a comfortable room to use during the healing."

Verilion hurried down the stairs. As soon as the gate was raised and the bridge was lowered, the knights immediately went out to get the leader, but by then his men were already surrounding and protecting the broken man, who was breathing weakly in the woman' arms. The priest was called out of the castle to attend to the wounded man on the spot. He sawed off the dangling ends of the arrows at the entry sites and then pulled them out with meticulous skill. Finally, little Picon helped the unconscious man and healed the wounds with his magic.

The ragged bandits standing in the circle were all amazed at the sight of the miraculous magic circles and the brilliance they produced. The priest knelt down beside the man and began to pray to the Holy Mother, joined by several others. Thus the evening began. The sun coloured the clouds of the horizon in deep red hues and then sank drowsily in the distance. Matrios yawned loudly as he ate his dinner inside the castle.

Chapter 9

Gelborg stood in the crossfire of the torchlight, his hair and beard dishevelled, his clothes ragged, and his blue cloak caked in red dried blood. His hands were secured by handcuffed that glittered silver in the flickering light. He looked up from his humiliated position at the man sitting at the table, visibly grinding his teeth. He returned his gaze to the gleaming restraints that held him at bay, moved his hands, causing the cuffs to clink loudly, and heard the sharp grinding of the blades emerging from their sheaths as the waiting knights prepared to act. He ran his eyes around, and as soon as he was accustomed to the light of the interior, he saw the shining armour of the knights in the shadows, waiting for him to act foolishly. He knew they would immediately leap at a chance to take his head. He smiled in defeat and would have accepted his fate, but then he looked behind him to where a woman stood. Melanie was extremely nervous, and a flame of terror played in her eyes, reflected in the darkness. She looked up pleadingly and into the man's eyes, but he only smiled reassuringly. Her face took on a different emotion, becoming hopeful, and she herself parted her lips into a smile, but a tear escaped her eye, surprising Gelborg. He turned back and sighed heavily. He forced himself to look again at the man sitting opposite him, waiting, on the other side of the table. "What are we waiting for?" Gelborg finally said impatiently.

"Oh, right!" Matrios sighed. "Sorry. I got a bit caught up in the paperwork."

"What?"

"I was just going over some notes to determine the amount of supplies you might need, and I realized that there is a strong possibility that, if we can't come up with a solution, we all will be suffering from food shortages very soon." He chewed his nails in nervousness.

"What?" asked Gelborg.

"Well, you know, accommodating five hundred people is not so easy. We weren't expecting to be managing and supporting so many." Matrios sighed.

"I know that." Gelborg shook his head.

"But that's okay! Where there's a problem, there's a solution!" Matrios said with hope in his voice.

"What do you mean?" Gelborg looked at the man.

"The blacksmith made me a heavy plough that would have freed people from the fields, but now I have about half a thousand men doing nothing. If I use up all my remaining gold, we may, with great difficulty, get a crop in and harvested before winter sets in."

"I don't understand," said Gelborg.

"How many men did you lose last winter?" Matrios asked, looking up from his papers.

"About a hundred people died during the winter," he said, a little crushed.

"That would be too great a loss."

"What? What the hell is going on here?" Gelborg raised his voice.

"Ah, right!" Matrios clapped his hands together. "I'm sorry, Gelborg, I've been a bit busy since yesterday!"

"Since yesterday?"

"You and your men have accepted the amnesty, so now I must find a way to keep you all busy. And I need to manage your housing." He explained, rambling.

"Housing?" Gelborg was stubborn, but, from behind, he felt Melanie's hand touch his shoulder. He shivered slightly against the cold of her skin, but he turned and glanced at her beautiful face. It was full of hope as she gave him a gentle smile to soothe his troubled soul.

"Melanie." He sighed.

"It's all right, my dear."

He turned back to Matrios. "What do you want from me?"

"But we've already discussed it." He looked at the bandit leader with a startled expression.

"What?"

"I said you'd have a village and lead your men as their chief. Your uncle, Marabas, will help you." He pointed to the old man at the table.

"Gelborg." The old man sighed.

"I will not be a puppet of the nobles!" Gelborg stated.

"This lord is at least as merciful as Lord Matarion was." Marabas said confidently.

"You always bowed to their will!"

"Because that was the only way we could survive!" the old man retorted.

"Of course! Did the nobility protect us when the demonic raiders came over the wall? Or when the Egerton City bandits looted and burned the villages?" he snapped.

"What did they do?" Matrios looked at the elder, astonished.

"They looted and burned the surrounding villages, raped the women, and slit the children's throats to make an example for the area!" explained Gelborg angrily. "Did we have any protection when the nobles started human trade with the Duchy of Berolt?" Gelborg continued to insinuate himself, but Melanie squeezed his hand, and he fell silent in shame.

"Did the crown know about this?" The prince looked angrily at Elizabeth, who had been sitting silently next to him observing.

"I didn't know about it," she said quietly.

"Nobility is worth this much!" Gelborg spat onto the floor.

Verilion drew his sword and stepped in front of him. "Watch your mouth, you stupid bull!" he snarled.

"Because what will happen? You're going to cut my head off?" Gelborg said threateningly.

"Verilion!" The prince rose from his chair. "Leave him alone." He stepped towards the big knight. "Well, though my father has not taken any steps to crush the marauders on our borders, I am here, and I promise that, before winter comes, I will wash the filth of Egerton with their blood and avenge all those who have been corrupted and slaughtered." Matrios looked Gelborg in the eye angrily.

"Big words. The castle is almost impregnable!" Gelborg snarled.

"They took it somehow, didn't they?" The prince smiled.

"From the inside."

"What would you think about attack from above?" Matrios replied.

"From above? Are the knights grasshopper-legged nowadays?" Gelborg laughed.

"Shrike!" called the Prince. A blackbird-like creature flew to the table, hopped onto the floor, and transformed into a monster. Its body grew larger, and its wings spread out, darkening the room. Perhaps the creature was even more terrifying than it would have been by default. Elizabeth jumped from her chair and stepped back in horror, and the elder Marabas nearly lost his mind as the beast towered over him. The servant against the wall began to sweat as he felt his limbs go numb. Only Linary, having escaped from her mother's arms, was exalting in ecstasy. Even Verilion experienced a bead of sweat running down his forehead, and his eyes were open wide in terror.

JOSEPH B. KONRAD

Gelborg hit the floor as soon as he saw the monstrous creature, his eyes dilated, his pupils constricted, and his mouth open in a soundless scream. Behind him, Melanie curled up hiding behind his back.

Matrios stood silent and unmoving, and then the creature screamed. The loud, guttural howl echoed through the great interior, reverberating off the walls. Gelborg fell on his back and howled in terror as he looked at the creature, terrified and fearful of death.

"This is Shrike!" The price introduced the creature as the bird-beast licked his beak while standing behind the man.

"What is this abomination?" Gelborg burst out as soon as he could speak.

"He is my familiar and my family's protector. A demonic beast." Matrios stood at the bird-beast's side.

"What the hell is it doing here?" Gelborg sat up.

"Oh, don't worry!" Matrios reassured him. "Because we're all on the same side, Shrike won't hurt you." He chuckled. "We *are* on the same side, aren't we?" he asked, holding his hand out in front of the creature and putting himself between Shrike and Gelborg.

Gelborg glanced back at Melanie, who was frightened out of her wits and praying with tears streaming down her cheeks. Then he glanced at the great knight, who was staring into space, and his face, even if he tried to hide it, showed fear. He then he looked into the bird-beast's eyes. It looked as if it was looking at the deity from the wrong side of the sword of the goddess of light herself.

"I like that!" thundered Shrike." Did you see how he pissed himself?" The bird-beast laughed, but Matrios did not answer.

"You want to keep me at bay?" Gelborg laughed.

"Did I threaten you?" The prince looked at him, puzzled. "I was just introducing you to my family pet." He touched the bird-beast's head and ran his hand over its feathers, stroking the hideous creature.

Gelborg reached back for Melanie's hand, and turning his back to the prince, pulled her back to the ground and lifted her head so he could see her eyes. Her face was wet with tears and full of fear. He clasped her to him and felt the fear run down her spine as she shivered from its coldness.

"As you wish!" Gelborg snapped. "I will accept your terms as long as you do not lay a hand on us! Deal with us, but not against us!" He looked up at the prince with an angry expression.

"I accept that," Matrios snapped, and in a flash, Shrike enveloped himself in a cloud of black smoke and turned back into a raven and settled on Matrios's shoulder. "I, Matrios Hritan, swear to be a good and honourable lord, whom you shall look up to with pride. You shall want for nothing so long as my strength permits."

Gelborg waited a little, his fear and distrust showing, but he made his final decision and reached for the hand that came from above. Matrios helped the man up and nodded with a kind smile. Then he sat back down at the table.

Gelborg's heart was beating so fast he thought it would jump out of his chest, but with his woman in his arms, he bravely endured the ordeal. The silence was broken by the breathing of the others in the room. Everyone heaved a huge sigh as the questions were clarified and the bird-beast retreated.

"Oh, that reminds me, Elizabeth!"

"Yes?"

"Please give them a cart and a horse to take with them. And load the cart with tools that might help during a building project."

"We're not building anything at the moment, so there are some tools in the storerooms," she replied.

"I've already picked out the right location for their village!" Matrios clapped his hands together. "Gelborg, go and get some rest for today. I think we've had enough going on." He waved at the knight who stood at the wall. The knight walked to Gelborg and released his hands.

"You're just going to let me go?" snarled Gelborg.

"Shall I put you in a dungeon?" Matrios suggested. "I don't need good-for-nothings, only hard-working men! You must be out among the people!"

"But I attacked you!"

"A good leader knows when to show mercy. No one died on either side. However, I want you to never forget the pain we have caused you and the desperate terror you experienced. They don't call me Vulture Prince in vain. Never forget that!" he warned him.

"I will. Then I will return tomorrow for further discussion, Prince Vulture." He bowed.

"Matrios will do." He laughed.

"Oh, I see."

"One more thing!" Matrios said in an angry, demanding voice, "I cannot change the past. But I can change our fate if you help me. I want the names of all the nobles who have trafficked in human beings. Don't leave anyone out!"

"Why?"

"For those who trade in humankind must hang until they pay for the suffering they have caused!" Matrios said, in a serious voice and a firm tone.

"You can start with the neighbouring landlord Toyne," said Gelborg, with a puffed-up voice. "The woman who stands beside me was sold by that worm, and he has done far more terrible deeds."

"I plan to cleanse the kingdom of these men."

"But you are nicknamed the Whoremonger."

"And I will never wash away the shame of that, or the pain I have caused to my loving and faithful wife." He looked over at a surprised Elizabeth. "We all make mistakes, but I have been given the chance to make up for my irreparable mistakes, though I will never be able to erase them, for history is carved in marble," explained Matrios in a bitter voice.

"My lord," said Elizabeth, barely audible.

"Prince." Gelborg nodded goodbye.

As Gelborg and his wife left the castle, a group of knights rolled a cart out through the gate, the contents covered by an old tarpaulin. The crowd immediately stormed the cart and removed the cloth to expose a mass of hammers, saws, spades, and other tools, their metal surfaces flickering in the sunlight. The prince looked down from the ramparts at the crowd and watched as they, still broken but in better spirits, plundered the tool cart. Gelborg had disappeared into a distant tent with his wife and might not come out again until evening.

"Melanie, I—" he sat down on the edge of the quickly made bed and buried his face in his hands. "I have betrayed Faradh's cause!" he said.

"You don't have to say anything, Gelborg!" She sat down beside him and put her arms around him protectively. "You have betrayed no one, Gelborg!" She pulled one hand away from his face and placed a loving kiss on his cheek. "Faradh put you in charge because he saw in you that you could make the right decisions!" she persuaded him.

"But he would never have surrendered!"

"Like the Toyne Castle, we could not have taken this castle. Faradh put you in charge because he saw that you could make good decisions," she persuaded him.

"But he would never have surrendered!"

"He could have sent people to their deaths! I remember what the Toyne family did to us, but at least we have each other, and I'll be here for you whatever happens!" She hugged him tighter.

Gelborg wiped the tears from his eyes. He embraced her fragile body as if he was saying goodbye to his love at the end of the world. "Whatever happens!" he repeated.

"It is better that we can finally settle down in peace. I'm tired of sleeping on lumpy roots and eating tough, tasteless boar meat." She smiled, wiping her face.

"I thought you liked boar meat."

"Do I look like someone who wants to eat nothing but wild boar?" said the woman cynically.

"I never know what you think." He smiled.

"After all these years, I won't have to go to sleep dreading tomorrow."

"Who knows if they'll break out of the castle and slaughter everyone? You saw that monster! Who commands such a thing?"

"It's better not to play with him!" she interrupted him in a serious tone.

"Melanie!" he snapped.

"For the sake of our family, listen to me! I don't care about anyone else in the camp—just you! I've lost everyone but you!" She touched his cheek and leaned in, their foreheads touching, while her eyes welled up with an unrelenting stream of tears.

"I haven't forgotten that."

"Don't throw your life away in vain and leave me to die alone," she begged.

"I won't." He kissed his lover.

The entrance flap of the tent swung open, and the elder, Marabas, entered. Gelborg's face turned angry as soon as he saw his uncle. "What are you doing here?" he asked with unpleasant anger.

"I just wanted to talk to my nephew." He stepped in.

"Well, you've done it. Now get out!" Gelborg pointed towards the open flap.

"Gelborg." Marabas sighed. "The lord is not a bad man!" He leaned on his stick.

"Indeed. It would have taken but one more shot to kill me!"

"But he didn't give the order!" Marabas raised his voice. "Who is that pretty lady?" He looked across at her with kindness.

"None of your business!" Gelborg put his hand between her and the old man.

"You know, your father would have been proud of you."

"What do you mean?"

"I am reminded of Geldor, seeing you now." The old man pressed his lips together, and a bitter tear ran down the hollows of his old, wrinkled skin.

"What?"

"Your father was just like you—stubborn and stumpy—but his heart was always in the right place." Marabas blew his nose into his little handkerchief and wiped his eyes.

"My name is Melanie," the woman said in a nice voice.

"She's a beautiful lady." The old man smiled at Gelborg, his eyes red with tears. "Thank you for looking after this stump!" he said to Melanie gratefully.

"He looked after me!" She stroked Gelborg' arm, reassuring him. "A human trafficker from Egerton castle bought me and wanted to take me east to stand as a whore in one of the brothels there," she said shyly.

"Tragic." Marabas shook his head in horror.

"It was Gelborg who saved me and cut the merchant down."

"He was always a good boy!" The old man laughed, obviously steeped in nostalgia.

"What do you want?" demanded Gelborg.

"Lord Matrios first arrived maybe two, maybe three days ago. He brought with him equipment and food."

"I imagine he had a long journey."

"That's right, but he didn't take the barrels of food to the castle."

"What?" Gelborg asked.

"He parked the cart in the middle of the village and distributed it to the villagers," the old man said proudly.

"It must be a ruse." Gelborg snorted.

"I thought so at first, but then he sat down at the table with me," he continued. "A prince was sitting opposite me, and yet I felt as if I was talking to a normal person, not a prince," he said in amazement.

"You've become a senile old man." Gelborg laughed, but Melanie pulled his hair.

"He drank with me and asked how he could help the village," continued Marabas. "I thought I was crazy when it happened. I didn't want to believe it myself."

"Neither do I," replied Gelborg cynically.

"I know what has happened in the past, but he's different! I can feel it in my bones." He shook his hands. "Even if you can't trust or believe in him, give him a chance to prove himself." The old man rubbed at his fingers. "He told me when I was begging for your life that he didn't want to kill anyone, and he didn't! He's a good man, whatever filth the people say about him!" said Marabas, standing up for Matrios.

"You don't have to defend him, Uncle!" Gelborg sighed "I have no other choice. My men lost their morale a long time ago."

"Gelborg!" said the woman calmly.

"I knew that if someone told my men that, if they put down their arms, they could go home, they would have done it anyway. But this way!" He laughed bitterly. "So they'll have somewhere to go home to and a clean slate after what happened to them." He shrugged. "I never had a chance to get as far as the castle with them. They were tired and dishevelled. The vulture knew exactly what he had to say to make them put down their weapons."

"Gelborg." She leaned against his back.

"I don't need your wise talk, old man," continued Gelborg. "I've already decided to give up and concentrate on my family, which I have now even if I've lost the first one!" He looked at Melanie, who only smiled gently.

"You mean—" Marabas seemed surprised.

"Yes!" said the man proudly.

The old man's legs went limp, his mouth trembled, his cane slipped from the weakened grip of his hand, and deep and loving smiles appeared on his face. His eyes shed tears incessantly, and he stumbled forward. Then, clinging to the last living member of his family, the little man sobbed like a baby for joy.

At first, Gelborg wanted to push him away, but his uncle's emotion overcame him and, though he hesitated, he finally embraced the old body.

<hr />

Matrios stretched his hands high into the sky and looked at Verilion, who was leaning against the castle wall, yawning as he watched the crowd below him.

"Good sir," said the knight, "how did you know they would surrender?"

"I just hoped." The prince smiled even in his confusion.

"But why did we have to do this to the poor boy?"

"He was their leader. If a leader dies, the cause may die with him. True, there were more of them, but no one would want to fight a castle full of soldiers armed to the teeth and ready to fight. Am I wrong?" the prince said confidently.

"It's true. The sieges can drag on for a very long time," the knight agreed.

"And the fact that Adalanna was able to kill ten of their men singlehandedly while wounded means that we are not talking about a well-prepared and cohesive army." He leaned against the castle wall.

"A lot of them are angry serfs, and a few are deserted soldiers," the great knight concluded.

"When you put a weapon in the hands of a man who has never seen battle but has seen many horrors, he is easier to break than a loaf of bread." The prince smiled sadly.

"I underestimated you!" Verilion bowed.

"I didn't know I could do it either. It's as simple as that," he apologised.

Verilion did not question the man further. He sighed heavily as if something was bothering him, but the prince did not ask. He looked across the small camp, which was very quickly taking up the small clearing near the castle. He walked back into the fortress, walked up the steps, and headed towards the west wing. When he arrived, he pushed open the door, and behind it was none other than the elf. She was looking out the window into the expanse that surrounded the castle. Clutching a hot cup of tea, recently brought to her by one of the servants, she turned her gaze to the other side of the room, where the prince greeted her. She lowered her eyes and greeted him. "My Lord Matrios, what brings you here?"

"I thought I'd see how you are!" He entered the room.

"Well, thanks to you! And thanks to Picon and the priest." She nodded, embarrassed.

"The cup?" he looked at the cup.

"Oh, one of the servants brought it. It's still awfully hot, so I couldn't drink it." She smiled thoughtfully.

"One of the servants?"

"I had a little talk with her. She told me there's a stoner half-elf on the outskirts of the village," explained Adalanna happily.

"I didn't know that." Matrios was surprised.

"I guess it wasn't very important to the elder."

"Probably! There's been a lot of things going on lately as it is." He wiped his face as he stepped to the window.

"I heard the news that Lord Matrios has triumphed without killing a single man!" she said proudly.

"Verilion deserves the credit!" he replied with a laugh. "He was the one who held the crossbow."

"Crossbow?"

"Imagine a very powerful bow with a projectile twice or three times more powerful than that of a longbow."

"The truth is, I'm not a very good archer," she explained, confused.

"It even goes through a knight's armour," he explained briefly.

"I see," she said. "Can I do something for you?"

"If you want to leave—perhaps to the Elven Forest—I won't stop you," Matrios said bitterly.

"My lord."

"I wouldn't be surprised if, after this and all that has happened to you, you wanted to leave. I'll give you a small bag of gold and a horse."

"Please stop it!" she shouted. "I told you, there's no one for me to go to, no place for me to go." She squeezed the hot mug. "So please don't send me away from you!" She winced and felt the salty drops of tears soaking her cheeks.

"I didn't mean that I want to send you away." He sighed regretfully.

"I'm sorry if I'm not good enough at anything, my good sir! But don't send me away from you!" she pleaded. "I have nowhere to go, I have no one left."

"I'm sorry, Adalanna." He looked out the window again. "I don't want to send you away. I just thought you'd rather be somewhere else."

"Indeed, after this, I'm reluctant to enter the battlefield again." She sighed painfully. "But if you command me to, I will!" She looked up at him.

He turned back just then and saw the determination in her eyes. "From tomorrow you will help Verilion organise the patrol and train the soldiers!" he said, and he started for the door.

"Thank you, my lord!" the woman said gratefully.

Matrios threw his back against the wall after closing the door, buried his face in his hands, and sighed heavily. It was then that he noticed the maid clutching the tray, her face flushed and her breathing almost soundlessly, startled. Matrios straightened up, smiled at the young girl, and went on to solve the problems that had arisen and were still to be solved.

Chapter 10

Several weeks had passed since the attack, which had gone down in the history of the area as a bloodless victory. The days flew by like eagles on the unbroken sky, each day with an obstacle to overcome. In the camp, the atmosphere became more and more difficult as people had to pitch tents in the rain and in the heat. Matrios discussed the details of the new village with Gelborg. Many people had signed up to build and were already taking down their tents to make the abandoned half-ruined village their own. Some were carpenters and some were simple folks, but finally the gigantic and heavy structure that the man had envisioned was up and running.

By the end of the week, the heavy plough was ready. Although it was very rudimentary and crude in construction, it seemed suitable for testing. The prince watched with his family and the knights as one of the serfs hooked the new plough harness onto the cows and used the bridle to encourage the animals to move. The prince kept telling the peasant what to do and how to do it, but after a few minutes the whole village was bustling around them, watching in amazement as the metal ploughshare dug its way into the earth and dug up swath of a colour they had never seen before. The structure went deep, the huge wedges of the ploughshare at the front opening the soil to bring the lower layer to the surface. Behind the plough a container made of metal by the blacksmith spilled seeds into the row of disturbed earth. Then two small but strong ploughs beside the big one turned the earth back into the open row. Finally, a large container arrived with manure and the odd salt. It stank to the knights, but not so to the peasants. They threw the stinking dung on top of the seeded earth and mixed it in.

Matrios said nothing, but this industriousness proved to him once again that the people here were not ignorant chance survivors, but clever villagers. The women were singing songs of joy, and the men were tipping their hats and patting each other on the back to get behind the plough and try out the not-so-new but more modern invention for themselves, or to just throw manure at it. The prince was satisfied. The remaining unplanted acres of desolate land had already been cultivated using his invention. He showed them the rotary, which he divided into five stages, but he could not explain this sufficiently to the serfs, so he offered the one with the largest plot land to skip one stage and just divide it into four. The prince heaved a sigh of relief, and the villagers were delighted to be able to contribute to their own livelihood.

Many had lost their day jobs because of the heavy plough, so they complained to the prince. They were angry and frustrated, but the prince embraced them and started his own programme, which he had been planning for a long time. He resumed the mining effort outside the village. They avoided the places where the stinking death had taken its victims, but there were still at least three long pits left of the seven. The men carefully lit the shafts with torches, and the prince placed supporting dikes every five yards to prevent any cave-ins.

The bandits scattered, and those who did not ask for the prince's mercy quickly became victims of the surrounding adventurers or the guards' constabulary as they had lost their leaders. This inflated the reputation and security of the area. The prince was not very popular with the raiders. After brief negotiations, he gave the prisoners only two choices. They could either do hard labour or hang on the gallows until the birds devoured the flesh from their bones. This became the nickname of the lord—the Just Vulture—in the surrounding villages, which then spread to the neighbouring nobles, who, one after the other, requested an audience with the royal heir. But the prince always refused these requests on the grounds of illness or occupation.

And Matrios's last big surprise was to reveal to the people the gold mine they had been sitting on. The sugar plants bloomed until late autumn, and when winter came, the seeds retracted into the ground but did not die. A good number of villagers were then given the task of collecting sticky sugar globules as their new job. A bag of sugar a day. This was the amount that could be produced by a few people in a factory no bigger than a fishing hut, but the news spread so quickly and suddenly that uninvited guests began to besiege the castle. Nobles emerged from under every stone, demanding to see the new and interesting crystal for themselves. Some even ventured to dig up a plant and plant it in their own fields to make sugar, but the plant died very quickly in other soil, and the method of producing sugar was never known, as the villagers refused to spill the beans. Competitors gave up after a few attempts and opted for barter. Word of the high-quality sugar quickly spread through the market, angering the prince. At present, a prince was arguing with a weary merchant.

"Look, my good prince," said the merchant, "I know that your sugar production is operating at low capacity. If you could just tell me how to do it—"

"I'm sorry, but I have no intention of doing that, and the plant can survive only on this piece of land," retorted the prince.

"But it is the highest value commodity on the market at the moment," said the merchant impatiently. "Its value is slowly rivalling the value of gold!"

"You are right about that," Matrios agreed. "And as a nobleman with such a fine commodity, I will name the price of the offer myself." He smiled at the man.

"Of course, my good sir. I only want to know how you are able to produce the sugar. Of course, I will pay you a fair price for your procedure!" He rubbed his hands together.

"Alas, I have iron and sugar to trade, but there is no more valuable commodity than information, and even my good father himself cannot afford it at present!" the prince snapped.

"What impudence!" the merchant said with a snarl.

Matrios turned to his trusted knight. "Verilion, please show the gentleman out. The area can be dangerous in the evening. I'd take it very much to heart if anything untoward should happen to him during the night." The prince smiled coolly, instilling fear in the merchant's mind.

"Certainly, my lord!" The great knight grabbed the man's shoulder.

"Ten thousand gold coins for a sack!" the merchant shouted back, but Matrios made no reply.

Matrios sprinted up the stairs, swept down the corridor, and turned through the door of his room. Then he went to the bed and threw himself onto the covers with a huge sigh. On the other side of the bed, Elizabeth sat in a chair reading her book while Linary played with small wooden blocks on the floor. "Oh, my goodness! Are you all right, my husband?" she gasped and jumped out of her rocking chair with a great thump.

"Everything's fantastic," he murmured dully.

"Shall we go out now?" she put the book down.

"No, you don't have to." He turned over onto his back. "I'd just like a little company with people who don't want to slit my throat or lick my buttocks."

Elizabeth sighed, reassured.

"What's a buttocks, Mama?" The child looked up questioningly.

"Don't say those words in front of Linary!" Elizabeth hit his head with the spine of the book.

"Excuse me."

"Have you reached an agreement?" she asked.

"Of course not," he sputtered.

"How much did he offer?"

"Ten thousand thalers for a sack."

"And you refused?"

"We can sell a small bag of sugar for about two hundred and seventy thalers. And we can fill a sack with fifty or sixty kilos of sugar," he pointed out.

"I still don't understand your system of measurement," said Elizabeth wearily.

"It's called a system of units of measurement," he corrected her. "It's to make the world more understandable by greater precision and coherence." He yawned.

"I'll never understand it." She ran her fingers through his hair.

Matrios was very surprised when she touched him. He looked up, astonished. Elizabeth immediately sat back on the edge of the bed, blushing.

"Anyway, why doesn't we make more?" she asked. "There are barely ten people working in the hut, and there are plenty of crops in the fields."

"It's a simple political question," Matrios replied. He seemed bored.

"Political?"

"If we produced more, we could flood the market with our perfect sugar, right?"

"Yes, but that wouldn't be looked on too kindly by the other sugar producers."

"Yes, that's right, so I'll save myself the headache," he said.

"But why don't we produce a little more?" she asked.

"On the one hand," he explained, "We have enough to buy everything we need, and on the other hand, everyone thinks it's crazy hard to produce sugar, and we won't fill up the warehouse so quickly."

"Why would they think that?"

"The Bretburgs are the biggest suppliers, and they can produce about thirty-five tons of sugar a year, I believe."

"They don't share their numbers, but yes, one of the traders said something like that," she said.

"If we produce about eighteen tons of sugar a year, our price will stay well above theirs, and there will be plenty of potential customers every year, so the price will remain stable." He smiled.

"Is that your reasoning behind the small production runs?" she asked.

"It's to spread the word faster and generate revenue from more places, so there will be more repeat customers," he explained.

"I never thought you would ever teach me about economics." She smiled sensually.

Matrios was very surprised and turned his eyes away in confusion as his face turned red.

Elizabeth noticed his reaction and immediately wanted to change the subject. "What have you been drawing lately?" She pushed her hair back in confusion.

"A new type of cannon," he said, turning his head away in childish embarrassment.

"A cannon?" She leaned over to the table and picked up one of the papers.

"I haven't had much time to finish it, but I'm not in a hurry." He turned to the end of the bed and looked down at the girl playing with the wooden blocks.

"I don't know how to look at this," said Elizabeth, turning the page this way and that.

"This is the base," he said, pointing to a portion of the drawing. "It's a fixed structure designed to absorb the kinetic forces of the shot so the cannon doesn't tip over or slip." He traced the lines of the drawing it thoughtfully.

"Kineptic?" she looked at him, stunned.

Matrios got up on all fours, threw himself on his hands and knees next to her, and spread out the drawing. "See these two longer parts?"

"Yes."

"They will be backwards because, when the cannon fires, a force equal to the force of the bullet that flies out of the barrel of the gun will occur, but in the opposite direction. It will act—" Matrios could see from the look on her face that she was trying to understand, but she was not succeeding, and she seemed to be becoming desperate. "The important thing," he finished, "is that it don't move."

"Oh, I get it!" she snapped, looking at him with delight.

Matrios laughed to himself, but his face only smiled gently, and he thought of the childlike joy on the beautiful woman's face when she "understood".

He got up, stretched his hands to the sky, and yawned. Then he adjusted his white shirt, which had slipped up his body, and stepped to the desk. He glanced through the technical drawings, all of which were highly ordinary but terribly complicated. His mind wandered, but she asked the question he hadn't wanted to ask himself. "And who is going to build this for you?" She waved the paper.

"Good question." He sighed, admitting his worry.

"I've only seen a device like this in the hands of the dwarves," she said.

"What?" he snapped, jerking his head up.

"We've had dwarves in the Republic a few times. They trade goods with us because—"

"Have you seen such a device with the dwarves?" He interrupted her in his eagerness for information.

"Well, not exactly like this, but something similar," she said, startled.

"I need a dwarf mechanic!" Matrios said.

"But, sir, they don't work—"

"I don't care about the price! I want a dwarf mechanic!" the man snapped.

"My lord, please calm down! The dwarves work at extremely high prices! We wouldn't have enough money to pay one!" she said slowly.

"Damn!" he cursed. "What could be valuable to them?"

"What is more valuable than gold?" she asked, almost laughing.

"Damn it!" grumbled the prince.

"Sir, you know the dwarves, don't you?" she asked.

"My memory is still not complete." He shook his head.

"There is a great deal of competition among the dwarves to see which house can produce more or more complex gadgets. Even things that are worthless to them can be vital inventions for humans, and they just throw them away," she explained.

"I have a plan!" The prince jumped up and immediately started looking for something on the table.

"What are you looking for?"

"This!" He showed her a drawing of a gyroscope stand, but all she could see was a jumble of lines on the paper. Her eyes darted around as she tried to find the beginning of the drawing, which would help her understand the rest of it. "What's that for?" she asked, pointing to the drawing.

"I don't think you'd understand."

"I really don't. But, my lord, how can you draw something like that?" she asked, looking into his eyes.

"Strangely enough, when I died—and I think I told you about it—I felt as if I had been enlightened," he explained, examining the paper.

"I still don't believe it's true." She sighed dismissively.

"It is."

"So much has changed in you, and it's so strange." She pointed at him. "It's not you anymore."

"But it's better this way, isn't it?" he asked in a thin and timid voice.

"Nevertheless, I'll help you where I can! I can arrange a meeting with one of the dwarves." She looked at him again and smiled sweetly.

"Really?"

"Of course." She smiled curiously.

"Thank you, Elizabeth." He took her hand and kissed it gently, looking into her eyes.

"By all means." She cleared her throat in embarrassment. "I will need ink and paper and a courier."

"You'll find plenty of ink and paper on the table. I'll get the courier." He nodded and hurried quickly out of the room. He ran along the corridor, down the stairs, and through the great hall, where more uninvited guests were waiting for him. Finally, out in the courtyard, he whistled loudly.

"I'm behind you! There's no need to be noisy," said the voice of the bird-beast in his head. "I'm not a dog either," he said angrily.

"Ah, Shrike," Matrios said, surprised.

"What do you want?"

"We should go to the Republic." He outlined his plans, staying away from everyone so he would not be overheard.

"Why we?" the creature asked.

"We need a dwarf!" he snapped. "I need a Khaz'morun dwarf." He rubbed his eyebrows.

"And what do you need me for? Should I grab one in the market and fly it here?" Shrike said in a bored tone.

"Oh no!" Matrios held his head. "You'll have to take me to sign a contract with one."

"Good timing!"

"Why indeed?"

"I was getting tired of the pigeons here." Shrike sighed.

"What?"

"Well, I'm just a little blackbird. Even the doves aren't afraid of me when they outnumber me! So yesterday, I transformed not far from the village and ate a few."

"Did anyone see you?"

"You haven't been around lately, have you?"

"I haven't had time. Why?"

"There is a forty-gold wanted poster on my head." The bird-beast laughed.

"Great!" said Matrios.

"I didn't hurt anyone, but an old farmer saw me swallow a bird. After that, I disappeared behind his barn." The bird-beast spoke with glee.

"Don't make a fuss and keep quiet!" advised Matrios. "You don't want to get killed by some stray monster hunter, do you?"

"I wish." Shrike sputtered cynically. "When do we leave?"

"Just as evening falls, so there will be less chance of being seen."

"Then go to sleep! Your eyes are so baggy a foolish adventurer would pack them in!" said the creature. "If you fall from my back, I won't jump after you!"

"I'll take your advice," said the prince.

The weary man let the cynical bird-beast fly away. Then, with a weary posture, he made his way back to the castle where unwelcomed guests waited with questions and complaints. Matrios had no desire to engage in unnecessary arguments with the nobles and courtiers. He thought to himself, *Isn't Elizabeth supposed to handle these issues?* And so he grumbled to himself. But a lean, well-cut, and dashing young man, who was rather thin than muscular, stepped up beside him. Matrios looked at the tall fellow who matched him in height. His blue eyes flashed subtly in the torchlight; his clothes were reddish with some purple tints in the white stripes. The prince paused, resting his left hand on his hip while his right hand massaged his brow wearily. "What can I do for you?" he said wearily.

"The third heir to the throne of Hritandia, Prince Matrios, protector of the borders—"

"What do you want?" Matrios said, interrupting this pronouncement.

The man straightened up, his face flushed and terrified as his gaze shifted away from the prince's figure. Shame and desperation showed on his face, but he spoke to the nobleman again, unafraid. "My name is Elian. My father disowned me and banished me from my family for experimenting with strange things back home."

"Are you going to tell a nobleman that it's actually better to have your head on a spike?" Matrios looked at the boy contemptuously.

"Well, I am, actually—" the boy gasped in anguish.

"I won't have your head, don't worry." Matrios raised his hand, stopping the boy in his scattered thoughts. "What do you want from me, Elian the fatherless?" The prince smiled.

"I hear, my good lord, that Prince Matrios has invented white sugar!" The boy's eyes lit up.

"If you want to beg me for the method, I'll tell you that I've even refused the nobles." He sighed discourteously.

"I wanted to study alchemy, as I did at home!" The boy pulled a large book from his tattered pouch.

"Alchemy?" Matrios took the tattered grimoire. He flipped open the book, which contained various strange and odd diagrams. It seemed to him that the boy had dabbled a little in the science of chemistry, though as he read the notes it became obvious to him that he was more interested in the subject than knowledgeable. He closed the large grimoire and began to laugh.

What was left of the boy's confidence was gone with the thud of the heavy book cover, shattered in an instant with lost hope. With two hands, Elian grasped the spine of the book and tried to tear it from the nobleman's hand, but the prince held on tightly. The boy looked at Matrios, who was still smiling, but more determined than mocking.

Without the slightest trace of mockery on his face, Matrios looked down at the book and let it go, saying, "You have three days to make me something from sulphur, coal, and salt, then you won't have to spend any more nights outdoors, and I'll honour your skills!" He winked.

What am I supposed to do? Elian wondered.

Matrios, accompanied by Verilion, escorted Elian to the library, where he sat him down. He then began to explain to both men the necessary materials. "Begin with sulphur," he said. "The cleaner the better. There is a mine not far from here. And ask for coal, preferably clean, which must be crushed into dust. Finally, in the village storehouse, you will find a few handfuls of white salt crystals brought to the surface from the surrounding mines."

"Do I have to crush that too?" Elian asked, looking up as he took copious notes.

"Of course! Mix it up and try it out!"

"Try it out?" he asked.

"Yes!" snapped the prince.

"What should I get?" asked Elian sceptically.

"Where's the fun if I tell you everything?" Matrios smiled. "Even if I told you, the time limit would be in vain!" said the prince, standing up from his chair.

"What are the proportions?" said the boy.

"Oh!" said the prince with a snort, "I don't remember."

"Approximately?" the young man looked at the prince hopefully.

"More of one than the other two, perhaps?" he said without confidence. He turned to the knight. "Verilion, give him some bowls and two mortars, and any tools he may ask for and we have in our possession."

"Anything?"

"Don't use unnecessary things," Matrios said to Elian. "They'll only confuse your head. Prepare this for me, and then I will decide your fate."

"My fate?"

"Well, since you have experimented with things you should not have, I will simply throw you in prison if I see fit." Matrios looked at the boy with a serious face. Again, he addressed Verilion: "Take him to the cellar. There's a big table there where he can work."

"Prince Matrios!" Elian called after the man who was leaving.

"Yes?" said Matrios, looking back from around the corner.

"Thank you for not hanging me right away," said the boy shyly.

"Why should I have done that?"

"Experimenting with alchemy is a capital crime," said Elian.

Matrios took a step back and said without emotion, "Yes, like fornicating and all the other things that the priests forbid us to do."

"Yes, but please don't say such things about the Church." The young man waved him aside.

"Why did you come to me?" asked the prince.

"I hear my good lord doesn't despise uncommon things." Elian's palms and face were sweating as he answered the question, showing the pressure he felt but trying to hide.

"And where did you hear that?"

"The peasants were talking about my lord at an inn not far from here!" he said. "They told me all sorts of things about a destructive bow and how you could make sugar sweeter than honey with a devil's concoction."

"And that made you go to a completely unknown nobleman and risk rotting in prison?" He leaned against the wall.

"I confess I hadn't thought it through that far." Elian reflected on the prince's question.

"When you're in your laboratory, think it through better! If you fail, or are far from a solution when I return, I'll have you locked in the dungeon." Matrios spoke impassively.

A look of terror crossed the boy's face, but he already felt he had no chance of backing down, so he just nodded, accepting his fate and anticipating the rope around his neck.

Verilion showed him his new abode, which was damp and dark. It was a tiny room that looked like a storeroom. Three torches illuminated a table that was red with blood or wine, Elian couldn't decide which. He looked over the notes, which he had quickly compiled and sat on a small stool, thinking hard. What should he make with the stinkstone, wood-burned coal, and salt in the storeroom?

Soon a servant arrived with the requested tools. Along with the servant, a soldier arrived who would act as Elian's guardian as he sat in the cool cellar by the door. The thick choking feeling around Elian's throat only tightened. His heart leapt out of his chest, and he sat down on the bed the servant had made for him. It was uncomfortable, but better than the ground on which he had slept uncomfortably for days. Elian collapsed into himself and cried out to his mother in his thoughts. He was so far from his parents' home without anything to give him earthly comfort. He trusted only his own mind, but felt he was crumbling under the weight. He didn't want to go to prison, and yet he did. He burst into tears, after which the guard came up to the crying child. "What are you whining about?" he said sympathetically.

"No matter."

"You thought you were in prison or something?" The guard laughed.

"Well, am I not?" he snapped.

"Why should you be?"

"I have a prison guard, my bed is in my cell, and I'm in a dark corner."

I'm not your guard. I'm just looking after you."

"What?

"Lord Verilion told me that someone has to watch you in case you blow up the place!" The guard laughed.

"Blow up?"

"What do I know? I'm only glad to be here. Otherwise, I'd be walking around outside in the blazing sun." He sat back down by the door and left it open.

Elian got up from the bed and looked at the notes again, thinking quickly. Then he starting to look through his older notes, wondering if he had worked on something similar before.

Matrios. The evening came quickly for Matrios, who lay in bed snoring heavily, his tired body relaxing on the soft mattress. He was awakened by the bird-beast clinging to the foot of the bed singing a strange song. The song was in Matrios's head, and its lyrics somewhat indistinguishable. Shrike looked up at him, his eyes reflecting the light of the torches. Then he spread his wings as it saw the man awakening. "At last!" said Shrike. "I've been sitting here waiting for ten minutes."

"What was that strange song?"

I don't know. I heard it a long time ago when I flew over the mountain. A demon was singing it, and it stuck in my head."

"Anyway, I'll get up, and we'll be on our way soon. What time is it?" He sat up on the edge of the bed and yawned.

"I don't know, but the moon is high." Shrike turned to the window. "It's time to go."

Matrios got dressed, then slowly closed the door of his wardrobe, turned back to the bed where Elizabeth and the little girl were sleeping, facing the window. He smiled as he looked over the two fluttering, fragile creatures, then stepped to the fireplace. The flames were just dying down, so he placed a large piece of wood carefully on the red embers and then put on his coat, the furry interior of which warmed his body pleasantly in the cool interior of the castle. The bird-beast landed on his shoulder, and then said to the man, "The letter!"

"Yes!" Matrios took the paper from the table. He noticed a meal had been delivered and was covered with a cloth—two slices of bread, a small dried sausage, and a tomato. Matrios smiled and put the food in his bag. He feasted his eyes one last time on the beautiful woman's face and left the room. He walked down the corridor, his shoes tapping softly. Then he hurried down the stairs and met one of the soldiers on patrol in the great hall. The soldier merely bowed to the prince and made no inquiries, but Matrios felt the man's gaze on his back until he left the castle.

Outside, Matrios took a deep breath as the bird-beast dropped from his shoulder and quickly transformed, his eyes twinkling mischievously, as if he was planning something. But Matrios ignored it. In the crisp cool of the evening, he climbed onto Shrike's back and wrapped his arms around the thick neck once again. He took a deep breath, and when he felt the creature kick away, he steeled his soul and held his breath, bracing himself for the unpleasant, blood-curdling experience.

Shrike took to the skies in a leap, his huge wings beating against the air as he swooped towards the horizon as fast as a wild horse on the loose. He stopped when he reached the desired height and called to Matrios, "Don't be afraid! I'll fly straight to the city from now on!" He directed his heavy body with strong wing beats.

"Do you even know where it is?" asked the prince.

"Unlike you, I know the direction, and I'm not a fool!" Shrike chuckled.

The cold wind pinched the prince's face and turned his snow-white skin red and pink. He sat up on the creature's back when he felt the gusts of wind and believed that the creature's movements would not push him to certain death. He opened his eyes and stared into the dark sea that was the world. In the distance, tiny lights of villages flickered in the dark shadows. The moon lit the huge hemisphere of the sky, reflecting the sun's light into the sleepy night. Only the rustling of the wind could be heard high above, but the sight was stunning. Carefully, Matrios turned his head around and surveyed the black world, lights flickering like fireflies. Matrios tugged at the creature's left side. "Do you know where the city of Egerton is?"

"I've been near there lately, why?" asked the bird-beast.

"Can we fly there?"

"There's not much there," said the creature wearily.

"There's the city!"

"The shithole? What do you care about a disease-ridden shithole?" the bird-beast asked.

"Disease-ridden?"

"Even the animals are dying out there. The rabbits are thin and bony, and the rats—my God, how many of them there are!" Shrike said.

"Plague!" the man snapped.

"What?"

"A disease spread by rats because of their fleas!" explained the prince.

"The castle is probably half a week's walk from here for humans," said Shrike. "But for me," he added proudly, "it's less than an hour and a half."

"Just fly over it so I can see for myself!" ordered the prince.

"Then hang on!" said Shrike. He waited until the man tucked close to him again. Then he began to tumble. Soon after, flying in a different direction, the bird-beast spread its wide leathery wings and roared through the sleeping world. Indeed, the moon had travelled almost as far across the sky as Shrike had projected. And the silhouette of the city, dark with desolation, appeared before their eyes. As they flew overhead, the prince took out a parchment. Sitting on the bird-beast's back in the high wind, he tried to sketch the outline of what he saw below. The wind kept crumpling the sheet, and when he had finished, a great gust blew it out of his hands.

The bird-beast immediately began to fall, wings retracted. He caught the paper in his beak in mid-air as it swirled in the wind. Then Shrike spread its wings again, and the prince tumbled forward and fell over the neck of the creature. He gave a mighty cry, whereupon Shrike only gave a bored and frustrated snort and began to fall again.

He tucked his wings close to his body so that he could get under the man, and then slowly braked with them. Matrios clung to the neck of his rescuer. Slowly and gradually, Shrike slowed himself down, but they managed to stop well above the ground, and the bird-beast landed nearly two hundred metres from the walls. The prince tumbled onto the ground, landing on his back and panting wildly for air like a wild bull. Every bone in his body shook, and he felt his spirit leave him. He checked his body to see if all parts were intact. When he was sure he was in one piece, he sat up. "The drawing!" he cried.

"Here it is!" Shrike mumbled, spitting it out onto the ground.

"Ah great! Thank you" Matrios immediately grabbed the paper and hid it in the bottom of his bag. "Let's never do that again!" he said, laughing shakily.

"Tell me about it!" Shrike said. "You are the one who can't hold on!" he scolded.

"I know!" Matrios smiled. "Don't be angry, Shrike. Let's go!" Matrios crawled up onto the bird-beast's back with shaky legs.

"As you think—"

Chapter 11

The next morning, when Elizabeth woke up, she found her husband's bedside cold beside her. She looked around in the morning sunshine and discovered only her child resting on her chest in bed. She kissed the cheeky cheeks of the child and then pulled together her gown over her bosom and got out of bed. She noticed the empty plate lying on the table and the absence of the paper that had been beside it. She looked out the window and thought of her husband. She couldn't understand the feeling her heart was repeating. "Is it because I'm worried about him?" she asked herself.

As a noblewoman, she did not have time to dwell on such petty matters. In her husband's absence, she had to administer the region as a kind of deputy. Tibald knocked and entered at her word. He bowed as he did every morning. Then he let the maids in, who immediately stepped in and prepared Elizabeth's dress, hair, and necessary accessories for the day. Elizabeth soon forgot the fact of her husband's absence and chatted good-humouredly with the young girls, and when she was ready, she roused Linary from her sleep and helped her dress. Still holding the sleepy child, she hurried down to the dining room, where Verilion and a guest, a neighbouring nobleman, were waiting. They bowed deeply to her, and Tibald pulled out her chair and pushed her closer to the table when she was seated. Linary, awake but cranky, played with her food most childishly.

"I see the child is not yet a great student of table etiquette, or would she be a toddler?" said the nobleman with a haughty tone.

"No, sir, it's just that our family values a happy child more than an unhappy obedient one." She quoted her husband's words.

"Nonsense!" he snapped haughtily.

"How do you raise your children? If I know it well, you are now married to your third wife." She spoke with disgust in her voice.

"Me raise my children? Please! Raise them by myself? That's the job of the teacher and the priest!" he sputtered, insolently. "Too much love destroys children and makes them dull!" he said with conviction.

"Too little love castrates him." she murmured.

"Excuse me?"

"Ah, nothing ... I was just thinking out loud about today's business." She dismissed his suspicions.

"Will Lord Matrios not join us today?" asked the nobleman.

"He's been ordered to spend the day in bed. He's not feeling very well."

"The gods help him on his sickbed then."

Elizabeth couldn't decide whether this sentence was flattering or disapproving. She sighed and then started eating her own meal. She took turns taking delicate bites and wiping the sauce from her daughter's face. Meanwhile, Linary was giggling with her.

"Ah, chef!" Elizabeth said to the man who had just entered from the kitchen.

"What can I do for you, my lady?" asked the big man.

"Could you bring me some hot tea to go with my bread please?"

"Of course! Right away!" The man smiled, delighted.

"Tea?" the nobleman looked up.

"Our cook's speciality and his own creation," she boasted.

"Hey, you!" shouted the nobleman in the direction of the chef.

"Huh?" The big man looked over the noble.

"Get me a cup too, and quickly!" he said as if talking to a dog.

"As you wish," the chef replied unkindly, but with a posture befitting etiquette.

"How outrageous the behaviour of the staff!" the nobleman puffed.

"You know, my Lord Matrios is well disposed towards them, and they are not used to impersonal, disrespectful orders," Elizabeth explained.

"Then how do you order them?

"My lord … Let's say he is using magic," she whispered to the nobleman.

The air in the room froze. Even Verilion's hand stopped with his spoon halfway to his mouth as he looked at her in surprise.

"Magic?" asked the nobleman.

"Yes!" She smiled suggestively, as if she had been waiting for the question.

"What kind of magic?" He jumped up.

"He just calls it …." she mused, "please and thank you," she said with a penetrating look.

The nobleman sat back angrily, and Verilion looked at Elizabeth with a broad and kind smile. Tibald bowed humbly, and the cook stood with a cup in his hand. The servants felt simultaneously and unanimously honoured and blessed for having such a good master.

"Your heads will ache because of your servants if you give them too much freedom, I tell you!" the nobleman continued pompously.

"Perhaps." Elizabeth sighed and sipped her tea. She could taste the green flavour and the hint of the reddish berry as the hot drink warmed her body. Elizabeth sighed as she swallowed and gave herself over to the pleasure. She pulled the small pot of white sugar closer to her and added two spoonsful to her tea and began to stir it, immersed in her own thoughts. The metal spoon clinked rhythmically against the side of the glass as she fell back into thought. The nobleman didn't hesitate long either, sniffing the cup, a fruity aroma flooding his nose. He took a long pull on the hot drink, which burned his throat, causing him to cough violently. He began to choke as his tongue burned. "What the hell is this?" he snapped.

"Sir, be careful with that. It's hot!" Elizabeth said casually to her guest. She somehow felt a sense of satisfaction in herself as a small gloating smile appeared on her face. Verilion smiled under his moustache.

The nobleman looked impatiently at the two. The anticipation was wearing on his nerves. "I wish to speak to Prince Matrios!" He pushed himself away from the table.

"I cannot serve with my lord." She sipped her tea calmly.

"I will go up to him." He jumped up suddenly from his chair.

Verilion got up, overturning his chair. He looked at the nobleman with a bloody, deadly gaze. "Unfortunately, for the sake of my lord's quick recovery, I cannot allow anyone into his room."

"It would be unwise for you to go to him," Elizabeth continued the conversation. "For who knows? You may catch the disease yourself."

"Order your dog to stand down!" the nobleman shouted at her.

"He is only doing his duty," informed Elizabeth. "Don't worry, Verilion, the nobleman has come for nothing. My Lord Matrios does not wish to negotiate with him."

"What?" the fat nobleman shouted at her.

"I think you'd better leave as soon as possible," she said, giving him a bloodthirsty smile. "The roads can be dangerous in the night, and the next town is over a day's walk away."

"I … yes." The nobleman sucked his teeth angrily. He marched out of the room, slamming the huge door behind him.

Finally, Elizabeth could breathe a sigh of relief.

"Lady," said Verilion.

"It's okay," she reassured the knight. "I'm just getting tired of all the nobles coming and going."

"I can understand."

After they finished breakfast, she immediately set about her daily activities. She went out into the courtyard of the castle where she organised the work of the servants with Tibald's help. Verilion outlined the daily guard rota for her.

Meanwhile, Linary was picking flowers that grew in the tall grass and running among the soldiers. She enjoyed the way everyone she passed paid attention to her and bowed to her. She spent a lot of time outdoors, her curiosity about the world, even in such a small area, inexhaustible.

Gelborg appeared at the gate. Elizabeth called him to her, and they engaged in conversation about the morale of the people and the conditions of life. Oddly enough, he was much more reserved and better behaved in conversation with her than he had been with Matrios. She sent for the carriage, and after the stable master had prepared it, they set off at a slow trudge towards the ruined site on which the tiny village was being built. As soon as she alighted from the carriage, Verilion was waiting for her, looking after her as her bodyguard. "Verilion, why are you looking after me?" she asked quietly.

"I am the bodyguard of my Lord Matrios, but as he is away, I will help you and guard your safety and that of your child."

"You surely have better things to do."

"A knight has the greatest honour to guard his lord and his lady," he said without delay.

"I see."

Gelborg stepped forward on horseback and then jumped off and bowed. "Here we are." He pointed to the big house, its beams already leaning skywards. The old buildings beside the tiny artery in the background—huts of the deserted village—were crumbling, their roofs still patched, but they provided just enough shelter from the elements. "We're following the prince's instructions," Gelborg said directly.

"When will it be ready?"

He calculated in his head. "If we keep up the pace, we should be finished within a month."

"Can you count and calculate, Gelborg?" she asked curiously.

"I know the basics," he replied, surprised.

"Good." She nodded." Can you calculate the sufficient amount of required materials?" she asked.

"Not very accurately, but it's not the first house I've built, my lady."

Elizabeth did not question the man further, but simply stepped among the workers and looked at the building. The inside was covered from the ground with new planking. The beams of smoothly polished wood stretched skywards as if they were frames for a painting on each side. But there was no room for a window anywhere. Matrios had planned the house as a temporary dwelling for the villagers to live in so they would be sheltered from the rain and cold while the rest of the village was built around it. Later, this large building would be converted into a warehouse. The large building would be suitable for housing most of the people, albeit in cramped style, under one roof.

Even the crumbling barn was now filled with people, and after the sun came up, people usually took their breakfasts in the open air. They were mostly all in good moods, for life is happier for people who live with a purpose than it is for people who are just living without one. The prince had given them tools to work with and had set before them a plan, which they all had received with great joy. Even though there was much to be done, at the end of the day, they happily, if sleepily, returned to the crowded houses to sleep.

It had been Elizabeth's idea to order a few horses to aid in the construction, so that the work progress as quickly as possible. They were lucky that the wagons they arrived in had not yet been sold. They could have sold the sacks of sugar they were selling for the price of two wagons. The women who stayed behind and were unable to help with the building work soon found new work for themselves, mending clothes, tanning the hides the hunters brought, and working to keep the farm animals well. At the same time, the children were able to help with household chores.

Thanks to the ingenuity of Prince Matrios and the new land rotation and tools, people's lives improved rapidly. Now only a few people were needed to work the land, and everyone found employment in different areas of labour. But the immediate situation had not improved to the same extent as the long-term one, and that was the main cause of Elizabeth's headache. All the long-term improvements would be in vain if the people don't live long enough to see them come to fruition. A bag of sugar every day was worth little more than the value of the food they imported. What was needed was a source of quick income, even if it was not permanent.

When the peasants saw the lady who resembled a black rose, they were on pins and needles waiting for her to leave, but she had not come empty handed. Like a noblewoman, she walked over to the cook, who already had a meal roasting on the fire. She placed two small sacks into his hands on the table and looked up at him with a smile. "Soak this bag in a cauldron of boiling water and then flavour it with a bit of this!" she instructed.

The sweaty man said nothing. He just stared at the beautiful woman with a surprised look, mesmerized by her beauty. Carefully, he opened the two sacks and looked inside. When he saw the white sugar, he lifted his gaze again and stared deeply into Elizabeth's eyes in wonder, as if he had seen a nymph bathing in the stream. He put the small pouch down, releasing it from his clumsy iron hand, and knelt before her. Elizabeth smiled softly, and with slow steps walked back to the carriage with the knight at her side. With Verilion's help, she got into the carriage and left the clearing.

"Maybe that's why my lord likes them?" she wondered aloud.

The road dust kicked up behind them as the horse-drawn carriage rolled along the road. A brownish trail drifted behind them as if a comet were drifting sluggishly and lazily across the landscape. The Black Rose gazed out into a world of green and gold. The sky at the horizon was brilliant blue. The big knight interrupted her with a cough, the woman far away in her thoughts. "Has my lady heard about the newcomer in the cellar?" asked the knight.

She had, indeed, heard a bit of information. The strange guest who lived in the cellar like a well-dressed rat had caught her attention. Why would he want all those strange things—the coal that leaves a trail, the stinking stones used to clean barrels, and the salt that is sprinkled on the soil to make the crops bloom better. Nothing she had heard from the knights made any sense, but she hadn't had a chance ask her husband when they went to bed because he had fallen into a deep sleep as soon as he lowered his head to the pillow. She knew that she would never understand all that the prince had been creating lately, but it did not bother her a bit. It seemed to her that the things he created could make life better and simpler, and certainly no less amusing. "What do you know about him?" she asked.

"Not much. The prince has set the boy a challenge," the old knight said.

"A challenge? I suppose it has something to do with the strange items the boy asked for?" She raised an eyebrow suspiciously.

"It must have, since Lord Matrios listed the materials for him."

"I wonder what will come of this." She sighed worriedly.

"Why?"

"If it turns out that my husband is fiddling with alchemy, the Church will soon be on our backs, not to mention the fact that he took the priest from the church." She sighed again, even more devastated.

"I merely took the priest to the library, and strangely enough, he liked it there," said the knight with a chuckle.

"The little knight used his magic."

"You mean Picon?" asked the knight, blinking. "We couldn't help it. The prince cares for the life of that elf—and some others."

"A little too much," grumbled the woman.

"Don't worry, my lady. The prince hasn't been daring to approach women lately."

"Does he like men now?" Her eyes changed, now frozen with horror.

"I wouldn't say that." He choked back his laughter.

"Thank God! That is the last thing I need on my reputation." Elizabeth's face was once again troubled. She leaned on her elbow and thought of the events of the past weeks.

As they made her way to the castle, Verilion noticed the sweet and seductive smile on her lips. "What's so amusing, my lady?" asked the knight.

"Nothing important. I was just thinking how funny life is becoming." She looked out of the window where the cows were already working in the fields, pulling the ploughs.

"It's been a busy few weeks in the castle!" He ruffled his moustache.

"Doesn't the prince seem strange to you?" She looked up at him.

Of course!" He looked up.

"Doesn't it bother you?"

"Why should it bother me?" he asked, puzzled.

"Because he's so much different than he was before." She looked down at her hands.

"Do you prefer his old self, my lady?"

"Of course not!" she suddenly snapped, her voice high. "He's just so different, so unknown to me." She sighed and said, barely audible, "He frightens me a little from time to time."

"You are afraid of him? But a slap in the face made his ears and tail curl." The knight laughed.

Yes, that's what I'm afraid of!" she said. "What if it's only temporary?"

"We do better not to question the will of the gods," said the man. "Do as the knights do and enjoy it while the prince remains the way he is!" he advised kindly.

"I'm in a different situation, Verilion."

"Yes, my lady. But don't look so far ahead into the future. We never know what tomorrow will bring!"

"But—"

"With all due respect, you are still so young. You need not think so far ahead. You should be happy that the child has a good father at last."

"Have you known him for a long time?"

"Not very long. It was Tibald who was always with him. I only heard from him everything that happened to the prince."

"Yes, I heard the stories from Tibald too.

"Irrelevant. It doesn't make up for what his childhood was like in the eyes of the gods," he said. "But we have to let him have a chance to make up for what he did that was grievous in our eyes." He spoke thoughtfully."

"You speak ill of your lord!" she said angrily.

"And you seem to be going mad, my lady," said the knight.

"Even so, know your place, Verilion," she scolded him sadly, as if she did not want to be angry with him, and the Old Knight saw this and smiled kindly.

Slowly, the carriage rolled through the gate. A groom opened the door, and the beautiful woman stepped out. Elizabeth's mind was ablaze with ideas. She sighed heavily and looked wearily up at the castle battlements where the guards were striding tirelessly. Suddenly, they heard the muffled sound of a great explosion, and the earth began to shake. So strong and unexpected was the tremor that she fell to her knees in fright, and Verilion at once raised his arms and body to protect her.

"What was that?" he shouted.

"It came from the cellar!" cried one of the knights, pointing to the smoking castle windows.

"Linary!" Elizabeth screamed, and as her tearful eyes cleared, Picon rushed to her with the frightened little girl in his arms.

"Oh, my little girl!" she snatched the child from his hand.

"Find out what happened immediately!" cried Verilion in his husky voice.

"It sounded like a dragon!" said a knight, and they burst through the door of the great hall, swords drawn as they headed for the kitchen.

The cook was lying on a large sack, dazed and sweating, all the pots and pans scattered on the floor around him. The knights approached the door to the cellar, but its hinges had been torn from the doorjamb as if a giant iron fist had torn the door open in anger. From the rumbling darkness rose a thick and fetid smoke. The female knight in the back held her nose, and a look of disgust came over her face as she sniffed the air.

"I'm going first!" The one-eyed knight held his hand in front of his face as he plunged into the black mist.

Three warriors followed each other through the dense fog, finally finding the source of the blast. The soldier who had been charged with guarding the rat-man of the cellar lay unconscious on the floor. Behind him, as the smoke began to clear, the blackened source of the explosion became visible. The wooden-planked wall had been crumbled and torn as if it had been a flimsy string of sticks. A small body in the centre of the mess was writhing, burned and charred painfully on the cold floor.

The female knight ran to the injured person and immediately applied healing magic. One arm of the burnt husk had been cut off at the elbow. She looked around, but couldn't find the missing part of the man's appendage. They managed to stabilize his condition enough to keep him from drowning in his own blood. As they examined the area, they found a burnt grimoire beneath the table. But the top of the thick wooden table was almost completely burnt away. The one-eyed knight ran his finger over the charred layer and smelled the foul odour on it, the same odour he could smell in the smoke. Immediately, the knights grabbed the tortured body and began to carry it gently it up the stairs. There they laid him in one of the unused beds and immediately called for Picon.

As soon as the boy saw the burnt body, he began to pray to the gods as he invoked his magic to save the man's life, or rather what was left of it. Perhaps it was only thanks to the quick help or the prayer to the gods that Elian survived the encounter with the gunpowder. The cold healing water repaired the wounds on his body, but the magic could not help his hand, so it merely sealed off the elbow.

Elizabeth entered the room and found the young boy surrounded by soldiers and knights. "Who is that?" she asked, looking at the dying man.

"This is the boy Elian." Verilion came through the door behind her. "The rat of the cellar."

"How well do you know him?"

249

"I don't really know him except that he is a fatherless lad who experimented with unholy things." He scratched his head. "I know little of him."

"This is why you can't trust my husband!" she said, tense and irritated. "Look what's happened to this unfortunate boy!"

"My lady, I'm afraid he's been experimenting."

"I would not have guessed!" she said, reassuring the child. "Is there any other fool in the castle I should know about?" she asked cynically.

"None that I know of except the carpenter," he mused.

"The carpenter who made that ungodly contraption?" she asked, astonished.

"Yes!"

"What? Does he make a battering ram that bursts through the gate with an explosion?" She stepped out of the room, her head aflame with anger. "Do not let him die! I want to strangle him myself!" she called back imperiously.

The day passed slowly as one half of the knights supervised the care of the strange boy and the other half performed their duties as required. With the help of a few soldiers and peasants, men removed what remained of the contents of the smoky cellar and made sure the surviving structure was safe. They gave the burnt grimoire to Elizabeth, and she placed the blackened tome on her husband's desk.

She turned the pages of the strange book, looking at the ungodly texts of magic and alchemy. She leafed through it to the point where the writing had been crushed by the explosion and charred beyond reading. She felt she must finish off this heretic who had summoned such gross powers, and she was already heading for the door when she remembered Verilion's words.

She lowered the book and placed it back on the table. She smoothed the cover and left it there.

Chapter 12

The journey was long and exhausting, and although Shrike did not want to admit it to the prince, he was exhausted. They reached the city of consul on the east coast of the continent, which was the capital of the Republic. From high above, it seemed perhaps even larger and more alive than Brenera. The people swarmed like ants below, and the surrounding countryside was dotted with wheat fields and vineyards. The roads that led to the city from all over the state were paved with shining white stone. The city walls were strong and thick. The stone was painted in a red-and-gold pattern, and at least two flags of blue and gold waved in the salty south wind at every sentry post.

The famous and magnificent city of Pearl Bay was true to its name, and from above, they saw a network so magnificent and interconnected that Matrios could scarcely fail to admire it. But the bird-beast had to land. He flew rapidly towards the ground, falling almost impatiently, but he spread his huge leathery wings and stopped his gigantic body. Finally on the ground, Shrike collapsed and transformed. Matrios held the exhausted creature in his arms. Shrike had fallen asleep the moment his body shrank to blackbird size, now looking fragile and vulnerable. Matrios vowed to guard this creature.

After an hour's walk, Matrios finally cleared the dense forest, which was split by a thin path. Once he reached the gate, he noticed a serpentine line of people waiting to be taken in. He passed them, stepping to the front of the line. His unkind gesture was rewarded with two interlocking halberds in front of his face. Matrios, still holding the panting bird-beast, flinched and took a step back.

"What are you doing here?" one of the guards said to him.

"I'm going into the town," Matrios answered clearly.

"The end of the line is there!" said the guard, pointing to the long snake of humans.

"I've come with a letter of transit from Lady Elizabeth Silagi. I'm here on her behalf." He held up the sealed document. "Notice the seal of the Silagi manufactory." He looked at the guard."

"You can go!" The guard pulled away his halberd.

Matrios heaved a sigh of relief as he walked under the massive wall. As soon as he entered the city, a world hitherto unknown to him opened up before him. Hawkers were selling their wares under tarpaulins, sometimes on the ground, sometimes on tables. Taverns and brothels were lined up to receive guests hungry for various delicacies, but he saw no drunkards or naked women, the road was clear. The wheels of the carts knocked loudly, mingling with the other noises of the city. People of as many kinds as he could imagine were bustling everywhere, but he also spotted a few elves and even dwarves. He was amazed by the bustling life of the city, the beauty of the walls and facades, the progress of art and architecture, including columns, which, though unimportant in function, were unquestionable in beauty, towering above everywhere he looked. Suddenly, he heard a great shout of exultation. He looked over the arches of the tall buildings that towered above him. In the distance, the city's inhabitants and passing travellers were being entertained by expensive amusements in a huge coliseum. But he recovered from his astonishment when the wheel of a large cart jerked into his back.

"Watch where you're going!" shouted the carter rudely.

Matrios didn't linger on the street any longer. He soon found himself standing outside an inn. He liked the look of the place, so he pushed the flimsy door open, looked around at the good-humoured adventurers inside, smiled, and hurried to the bar. "God bless you, bartender."

"Which one, you boor?" the man asked back immediately.

"Both, but at the same time," he replied good-humouredly.

"What the hell got you into this tavern?" The bartender looked at the stranger as he wiped a cup.

"I was wondering if you had a tub where I could wash myself," Matrios said boorishly, even playing with the man a little.

"Yes, but it's not cheap!" said the bartender, snobbishly. "And there's only cold water! Ten silver coins!"

"Let's make it twenty—if you can provide hot water." He threw the coins down on the table.

"We'll manage." The man with the barrel body scarfed up the money. "You'll be called when it's ready, dear—"

"Let's stay you may call me Shrike."

"Are you a wandering dancer?"

"Why should I be?" he asked inquiringly.

"Because the name Shrike belonged to a famous dancer, a magical bard!" he told Matrios.

"I don't suppose he'll be coming to the inn today."

"It's not likely." The bald man laughed. "All right, Shrike! In the meantime, may I serve you something?"

"If you have some meat on the menu that isn't game, and perhaps a side dish, I'd be delighted."

"Of course. Fresh chicken today, meat off the bone, nice big servings too!" he said with a swollen chest.

"That sounds perfect!"

"Then I'll take three more coins. If you want a room, it will be nine coins for one night!" He slapped the counter.

"I don't want the room. I'm not planning to stay." Matrios dismissed the offer kindly.

"You know!" The bartender shrugged his shoulders. "Well, sit down somewhere."

Matrios walked over to a table that stood lonely in one corner. He sat down and put the bird down beside him, covering it with his own coat. He sighed tiredly, for he had not slept well in the last few days. He dined on two loaves of bread and meat, but hunger remained like acid inside him, and he could not sleep without food. Despite this, he was driven by curiosity, for his lady had written on the outside of the sealed letter the address where he was supposed to deliver it, and he was anxious to see where she was from. He glanced around the interior of the tavern taking in huge mounted heads—hunting trophies from both animal and monster confrontations. All peered back at him from the wall. The skull of some scaly wasteland critter dangled above the bar, twice the size of the deer head that hung across it. Above the bar, a flight of stairs led up to the rooms. Ladies wanting to sell their bodies writhed low over the railing. He yawned again and noticed a great thump. Across the room, gamblers who had been sitting at the card table began to brawl. Accusations and physical blows flew, and Matrios tried to keep himself as small as possible as the situation escalated. Finally, an even bigger thud rang in his ears. Someone had thrown a chair between the brawling parties, causing the attackers to scatter. The wooden chair shattered as it hit the ground, and finally the one who had thrown it appeared. It was a green-skinned creature Matrios had never seen before. The creature stepped closer to the battlefield and slammed his gigantic hammer against the stones. His face held a simple, brutish expression, and two fangs protruded from his mouth, one pierced by a golden metal ring. He grabbed one of the men by his shirt and lifted him off the ground with one hand, then pulled him closer to him.

"Gromgar wants to rest!" he said angrily. "This man too loud!" He threw the man onto the overturned table as simply as one would throw an apple.

All the patrons in the tavern gripped their weapons as the monster raised his hand to the man, but he only spat a substantial glob of spit onto the ground and spun the huge hammer, flashing his fangs ready to pounce. No one dared make the first move, and in the tense situation, the prince could only stealthily draw breath. A large boot flew towards the head of the walking mountain, and with a hard thud, the footwear fell lifeless to the ground.

"Morrigan!" cried the creature, turning around.

"Gromgar, behave!" said the woman, dizzy with pipe smoke.

"Ah, all right." Gromgar dropped his weapon and staggered back to his own table with slow, shamefaced steps.

"My boot, Gromgar!" said the woman.

"I not forgot, ma'am!" Gromgar angrily seized the bedraggled shoe and respectfully handed it to the woman.

Matrios looked at her. The woman's face was pretty, but it reflected her capricious manner. Her shoulders were broad, her chest no smaller. Her legs, though graceful, were strong. Her hair was black with a few red strands in it. She had tied it up in a ponytail. Her cheeks were red with scars, which gave a fearful glow to her seductive eyes. Around her, various creatures drank and ate. On her left sat a slight, frail elf. Matrios could not see his face for it was covered by a hood, but from the way the silk hung over its ears he knew he was not human. On the other side of her snored a dwarf, a cup of ale in his hand resting on his belly. The great beast sat down among his companions with his back to the prince, but still he did not obscure the formidable woman, who fixed her eyes on the eyes that scrutinized her.

Matrios's eyes met hers. Startled that she had caught his gaze, he turned his gaze back to his own table. But she was not to be denied. Picking up the discarded boots, she hauled them onto her feet, got up from her chair, and approached him with slow, devious steps, her pipe puffing out a thick smoke as she walked. Matrios made sure the sleeping Shrike at his side was still covered with his coat and perhaps tried to shrink himself even smaller. By the time she reached him, he was very nervous, even if he tried to hide it.

"I know you!" she said, towering over him.

Matrios didn't answer.

"You're the son of some nobleman, aren't you?" She put her hand on his shoulder.

"You've mistaken me for someone else," he pleaded. "I'm just a travelling chronicler," he replied in a weak voice.

"A travelling chronicler, you say?" She walked around him and then sat down. "And what would you say if I told you that you are lying?" she looked him in the eye with anger.

"Well, I should convince you otherwise," he said with a fake smile.

"And why don't you do it?" She opened her mouth in a grotesque grin.

"Why should I do it? We all believe in what we find shelter in." He leaned back in his chair in a gentlemanly manner.

"The man you resemble don't play with such wise words, only with other's bottoms." She leaned across the table to scrutinize him more closely. "There are so many similarities." She touched his chin.

"Maybe you've seen me preach somewhere." He pulled his head away.

"There you are, though it's been a long ago!" she snapped.

"Long ago?" He was confused.

"You're Matrios—the Vulture Prince, the Whoremonger!" she whispered as she leaned forward.

Matrios was simultaneously sweating and freezing. The hunger in his stomach had been replaced by a swirling pain of nervousness. He felt the swirling abyss consuming him. His face was flushed with sweat that ran down his forehead; his hands were cold and shaking. He was terrified, for he could think of nothing about who she was. He could only hope that she did not carry a grudge against his old self. He certainly didn't want her to take his head here and now. But she broke the silence between them as she sat back in the chair. "What the hell are you doing here, far from the capital?" She leaned back on the chair.

Matrios took a deep breath and felt that it would be pointless to lie. *Who knows?* he thought. *I just might anger this frightening woman!* "I'm just here on business," he informed her.

"Business? Are you going around the brothels?" She laughed.

"I wish I could, but I'm not." He smiled shyly.

"What would you say to a good round, then, if we met like this?" She slapped her hand on the table.

"I'm afraid I'm going to have to miss it!" he replied. "I'll be moving on soon. I just stopped in for a quick bite."

"Funny … there's something different about you." She studied his face.

"What do you mean?"

"You used to be so eager to sleep with someone like me, and now you refuse?" She smiled as she licked her mouth.

"Times have changed, and so have I." He shrugged. "I've been trying to be a good husband lately."

"You? A good husband?" The woman laughed. "The Whoremonger a good husband?" She slapped her knees. "Hey, boys, listen to this!" She leaned out and addressed the others. Her companions quickly approached and were already sizing Matrios up with their eyes, putting him under extreme pressure.

"Whose grief is this?" said the dwarf huskily.

It's the Whoremonger!" snapped the woman, introducing the prince.

"And who's that?" The elf shook his head.

"I've told stories of him, Faler! Have you not listened?" the woman said angrily. "We've had a few adventures and nights together." She licked her lips again as she looked at Matrios.

"Are you trying to make me jealous?" a huge man appeared from behind the company.

"Ah, Kerion." She groaned, startled.

"Who is this charmer?" He pointed his huge finger at the prince.

"Just an old friend," she replied, alarmed.

"Aha! And I suppose you didn't mean the nights in that way?" he asked rhetorically.

"Well!" the woman started to think.

"Gods forbid! I was about to leave anyway." Matrios jumped up from his chair, grabbing Shrike, who was startled by the quick movement.

"Stop right there, little man!" Kerion, the beastly man, gripped Matrios's thin shoulder. "Who the hell do you think you are, leaving like that?" He spun Matrios around and grabbed him by the throat.

"Kerion, I think—" the woman began.

"Shut your mouth!" he shouted at her.

"Kerion drink lot." Gromgar the orc sighed.

"Kerion, what will our employer say if you make a scene?" Faler tried to bring him to his senses with his monotone question.

"No scene, just a bloodbath!" Kerion lifted the prince and threw him through the thin door with a round-arched toss.

Matrios fell hard after his body broke through the wooden door, which was torn from the building. He slid down the porch and out to the middle of the road. Protecting the unsuspecting bird with his body, he finally got up on all fours and began coughing, trying not to vomit. Every inch of him ached as he moved, but he glanced up at the doorway. Between the broken pieces of the doorframe, the huge man approached. He took a last sip of his beer and tossed the cup aside. Shrike burst from Matrios's hands and, in a flash, the tiny blackbird transformed into a huge, hulking creature. Shrike caught the man's forearm with his beak and plunged his razor-sharp beak into the man's flesh. The gigantic man cried out and slammed his fist into the creature's serpentine eyes. Shrike released the bleeding limb. Spinning around, he struck the trouble maker in the stomach with his tail, sending him crashing through the porch railing and into the tavern wall. Matrios jumped up from the ground and ran to the bird-beast to calm him down. "I can't believe I haven't had a moment's peace!" he said.

"Calm down, Shrike!"

"What the hell were you doing here?" The bird-beast looked at him angrily.

"I didn't want to go in front of the father-in-law—"

"Go now!" Shrike ordered impatiently.

The city guard appeared around the corner. Matrios climbed quickly onto Shrike's back, and they immediately flew away from the scene. All the oncoming soldiers saw was something huge rising from the street.

The woman watched the entire episode, but she didn't have time to think because Kerion was bleeding profusely, so she had to see to him immediately.

A dwarf woman of small stature stepped out of the broken door of the inn. Her body was stocky, her legs were short, but her hair gleaming red in the sunlight, braided and tied behind her back. "What's going on here?" she said.

"There's been a bit of a fistfight," said Morrigan.

"It's got out of hand, hasn't it?" said the dwarf woman in a strange accent. "Let me do that!" she pushed Morrigan aside and took a strange instrument from her bag.

Matrios and the bird-beast landed in a small alley in the suburbs. Shrike changed back to a blackbird and began to fly around Matrios. "Why don't you have at least the brain of a mangy pigeon?" Shrike tweaked the man's hair.

"I was tired and worn out!" Matrios said by way of excuse.

"I don't care how you felt! You go where you need to go, do what you need to do. Then we'll go back home!"

"I wanted to take a bath while I still had the chance. "

"People bathe here once a week, you spoiled brat! I'm cleaner than all these peasants all together!" The creature kept on flying around.

Matrios left the argument to the bird and turned out into the street. He picked up the letter he'd dropped and looked at the address. It didn't tell him much, only that he had to go to the headquarters of the Silagi Trading Group. He began to ask passers-by in the town where he could find the place. The people there readily guided him from street to street, telling him where to go, as street signs were nowhere to be found.

However, after a long search, he finally reached the place he was looking for. He was amazed at the reliefs that lined the walls of the building, but he overcame his amazement and started up the steps. By the time he reached the top, he felt as if he'd been chased with a stick. He was tired and worn like an old rug. He pushed through the huge metal-reinforced wooden door, which creaked. To the left and to the right, people wandered in a great hall. Suddenly a man approached him from behind and addressed him. "Name and purpose of your visit?"

"Matrios Hritan!" he answered, startled and without thinking.

"I didn't ask for a joke. I asked for your name." The man cleared his throat.

"I am Matrios Hritan. I have come to see my father-in-law!" He handed the man the letter sealed with the family seal.

"Oh, I see! I apologise, good prince. I didn't recognise you. I'll tell a member of the board who can see you immediately. Please wait in the waiting room." The man bowed very low. Matrios didn't know anyone could bend his body so far. And then the strange man led him to a quiet place.

Matrios was unable to react to the rapid events and was already reclining on a comfortable half-bed in front of which a bowl of sweet-looking grapes rested on a beautifully polished stone plate. He took one grape and ate it. The sweet juice burst from the fruit with great force, and then he crunched the hard flesh of the grape, which separated sensuously from its skin. He tore off another grape. He had to wait a long time, and before he knew it, only the greenish stems of the grapes remained on the plate. When the fruit was gone, he leaned back, a little ashamed, and looked around. The waiting room was separated from the main hall by a thick door, and he was the only person there. Opposite him was a comfortable-looking sofa with beautiful gilt armrests. He wanted to take off his shoes so he wouldn't soil the bed on which he lay, but he felt it better not to after all this time. So he slid down, his head barely resting on the armrests, and looked up at the ceiling, which was also decorated with golden inlaid stones. Shrike flew round the room and stirred the stillness of the curtain, which swung slowly and lazily with the flapping of its wings.

"Do you want to sleep, or do you want to do something else when you've finished your plate?" asked the bird-beast.

"I can feel the tiredness, but I don't think it will overwhelm me. I'm too nervous for that."

"Would you at least open the window so I can have something to eat?" Shrike climbed back on the armrest.

"I don't want you to cause any trouble!"

"Like more trouble than you?" The bird-beast looked at him contemptuously.

"It wasn't my fault." He lowered his eyes.

"Yes, because you don't recognise everyone you've had dealings with."

"Let's get something straight!" Matrios sat up angrily on the bed. "I haven't had dealings with anyone, not even my own wife."

"Lame." The creature sucked its teeth." If not you, Matrios has had dealings with her before," Shrike explained.

"I hadn't noticed!" he said ironically. "She hadn't rubbed it in my face minutes before his colleague threw me through a door!" he said.

"Who are you angry at?"

"I'm just frustrated, that's all!" Matrios sighed and lay back on his side.

"Then be frustrated in the company of someone else," Shrike said in a bored manner.

"You're doing this just to get me to let you out?"

"Is it that obvious?" Shrike looked surprised.

Matrios stepped to the window and turned the latch. A cool sea breeze blew into the room and shook the curtains beside him. Shrike darted past his ear, and a few moments later, was a barely visible dot in the distance.

"I hope he comes back," Matrios said quietly and desperately.

The sun was low in the sky, and the prince was asleep on an armchair when the door creaked open. He jumped up from the armchair and looked startled at the source of the noise. A stout, short old man with a grey moustache stood at the door, his fat fingers gleaming with a cluster of gold and silver rings, his robes glistening with embroidered gems and lined with purple satin. His face was serious, and though his wrinkles were deep, his eyes retained the fire of a true warrior. On his head sat a small hat, also jewelled but of considerable weight. When he bowed, he lifted it from his bald head with his hand, and when he straightened up, he replaced it with a gentlemanly move. He stepped close to the servant standing behind him and, turning, slapped the man so hard that the servant slid across the granite floor.

"He's my son-in-law, you stupid bastard!" the newcomer burst out with the fury of a herd of wild stallions trampling the walls. He slammed the door behind him with such force that the gods themselves could hear. "I beg your pardon," the man said to Matrios. "I was not informed that a person of the first rank had sought my company. You may call me Janus Silagi."

"It's all right," said Matrios. "I needed a little time to get presentable after the long journey."

"I didn't have much time to talk to you during your wedding, but nothing is too late till we breathe our last breath!" Silagi clapped his hands together.

"I agree."

"What is your business here?"

"Elizabeth is well," said the prince.

"Oh, right!" her father snapped. "Well, since you're here, tell me about my eldest daughter." He nodded, unconcernedly.

"She's all right, and Lina—"

"What is it then?" The strange gentleman leaned forward, interrupting the prince. "Ah, the little girl?" he snapped." I heard about her four years ago. I hope Your Grace was pleased with the dowry," said Silagi.

Matrios swallowed his emotions and realised that he was not sitting with his father-in-law, but with a merchant. He adjusted his posture, which until now had been relaxed and comfortable. He tensed the muscles of his back and threw it rock-solid against the armchair. He rested his hand on the armrest and rested his left foot on his right knee. He supported his chin with his right hand and sat immaculately erect, exuding confidence and strength, but mostly emphasising his cunning, like a fox among rabbits.

The old man looked at Matrios and was surprised at his body language. Perhaps no one had ever been able to change so much in the blink of an eye with a mere change of position. The young prince's expression had also changed, which he did not like. The sweet childishness seemed to have been blown away and replaced by the outlines of an elegant smile, his eyes flashing like a vulture circling over a dying man. He had only heard news of the prince, which was not a tale of praiseworthy deeds, but this man felt quite different.

"I have come to ask a favour." Matrios put the letter on the table.

Silagi, with his big hand, picked up the envelope and opened it. He began to read the message slowly. His eyes ran from left to right over the writing and back to the beginning of the lines, and then he lowered his hand and looked up at the prince. "Are you mad, my dear boy?"

"What do you mean?" Matrios asked with unshakable confidence.

"Do you know how much a dwarf's week's wages are? Dwarves' time is as expensive as gold. Even more." The old man corrected the statement.

Matrios sighed, as if to condescend to the man sitting opposite, at which the old man's moustache twitched in annoyance. Matrios took the slightly crumpled parchment from his bag. The charcoal lines of the drawing gleamed as he unfolded the drawing on the table and showed it to the merchant.

Silagi leaned closer and, brushing his moustache with his fat fingers, looked it over. Then he sat back and thought quietly. "One hundred thousand Hritani gold coins," he announced, almost knocking the prince out of his character.

"What?" came the question after Matrios had collected his thoughts.

"I'll give you that much for that thing!" he said.

"Do you even know what it is?"

"No!" he said firmly. "But it's clearly a dwarven device!" he continued, just as determined.

Matrios stared at him with a curious look, a little confused, but then he understood. *For these people, everything I know is new, and everything that is a little more complicated is a dwarf device because they are the only ones they have seen with such things.* He thought to himself, "I just want to hire a dwarf to make these for me."

"And what's in it for me?" Silagi the merchant looked at his guest.

"I foolishly thought it would make my life easier to come here as your daughter's husband." Matrios sighed.

"There's always a warm meal and a soft bed waiting in my house while my daughter or her children breathe, but I'm a merchant more than a father." He continued to ruffle his moustache. "Would you like me to be a link between a dwarf and you?" he asked.

"Yes."

"Fine, but don't hope for much," warned Silagi. He stood up from the armchair and held out his hand. "There is a dwarf here now, but he is on duty, so I will not be able to introduce you. The other one is on a mission, though a job like this is not worth a mere coin's wages to this kind."

Matrios accepted the hand and shook it manfully. He found the old man's thoughts about the wages strange.

"Why?"

"She refuses to take simple jobs." He shrugged.

"I don't think this job would be easy even for a dwarf.

"Don't think so highly of your head." He put Matrios down. "You might abandon that contraption of yours if you saw mine," he boasted condescendingly.

"It is possible, but who knows if it is not my drawing that the dwarf is looking for." He smiled irritably, but he did not release the anger he was ready to destroy Silagi with, and he was careful not to unleash his magic.

"A female dwarf." He chuckled.

"Really?"

"Rare outside the islands. I've never seen one myself," he continued.

"It would be interesting to meet her," Matrios said. Could you show her in?"

"Of course. She's not much use to me anyway. She's just a headache, but she's not here yet." He sighed irritably.

"When will she arrive?"

"She was supposed to arrive today, but we haven't seen her yet."

"So she'll be here soon?"

"The next few days."

"Would you mind if I stay here for two days and wait her?"

"Okay. But don't cause any trouble, and I'll ask you to be considerate of me and not to visit any brothels in the meantime," Silagi said firmly.

"I've given that up." Matrios sighed with shame.

"I'll put you up in one of the rooms in my mansion, if that's all right," the man offered, extending his iron hand again.

"I would take it as an honour."

Matrios thus spent the rest of the day, which was but a short hour, at his father-in-law's side until a carriage, perhaps even more ornate and comfortable than his own, rolled up to the guild and took him and Silagi to the mansion of which the man had spoken. It was a large house, though by no means a mansion, but it occupied a vast piece of land. It was surrounded by gardens that were blooming with flowers and a lawn that was as green as emerald. The courtyard was well kept. Perhaps only the servants dressed as slaves marred the magnificent scene. They all had cropped ears and long eyebrows, like Adalanna. Matrios realized how it was, and, ashamed, took his eyes from the glassy-eyed workers "Those servants—" began the prince, disappointed,

"What? The elves?" Silagi said, recovering from his thoughts.

"Never mind."

A woman was waiting for them at the main entrance of the house. She was short and young, and her face was almost as beautiful as Elizabeth's. Matrios and Silagi stepped out of the carriage, and she bowed to them in a respectful manner.

"Father!"

"Margaret, this is your sister's husband."

"Which sister?"

"Elizabeth."

"I see." The edges of her face turned hostile, and her voice changed to a shrill ring. "Welcome to our humble abode," she said with careless elegance.

"Thank you for your hospitality," replied Matrios kindly.

They entered the house, which was as beautiful as the garden. The interior was old-fashioned. Wrought-iron torch stands held beautiful lanterns of wrought metal. The light from the lanterns flickered on the walls. Matrios noted the contrast to the burning ragged logs that illuminated his own castle. Beneath their feet was a carpet that covered the stone floor. The wooden walls were neatly planked, and paintings hung everywhere.

A servant led the prince to the bath, which he thought he had been missing from his life. There, at last, he was able to take off his clothes, which were dustier than he would have liked. He dipped himself into the pleasantly warm water, allowed the tension to drain from his body, and reflected on what had happened. He remembered the adventurer woman and how he hadn't even thanked Shrike for saving him, even if the bird-beast had scolded him for his foolishness.

After a nice warm bath, he fell into bed without supper, overcome by the fatigue that had been nagging him for two days. His dreams were bloody, and the noise of terrors rang in his head, filling his soul with an unpleasant uneasiness.

Chapter 13

The next morning, the world opened up brightly. The unfamiliar bed had been more comfortable and warmer than he was used to, but Matrios awoke from the night's terrible turmoil groggy and sweaty. He found himself breathing heavily, almost panting. His mind was tormented by the nightmare he had experienced—the streaming blood in the middle of the field; the trampled flowers beneath which the emaciated, mangled bodies of humans lay shattered in the tight grip of death; the hideous distant screams echoing in the skull that broke a man's spirit; the dramatic symphony of ear-piercing clashes as swords clashed; and the devilish sight of so much ruined flesh. He remembered only one thing that seemed to leave him frozen in blood as an unattainable goal on the porch of hell where the dogs' gnawing hunger was tearing him to shreds—a woman's figure as dark as night, and her eyes as white as newly heated steel, with their cold and piercing gaze that pierced his soul.

He wiped his unkempt face, feeling the rough stubble. He sat down on the edge of the bed and tried to control his heart, which was racing like a stallion, as fierce as the raging sea. When he finally managed to calm down, he got up and went to the basin of crystal-clear water. He thrust his head into the water and, holding his breath, plunged further into the shimmering ripples up to his ears. He lifted his face and reached for a towel. He wiped his dripping chin and looked out the window. He remembered his wife, the servant Adalanna, and Verilion, who had carried him through with faith and conviction.

But will it last forever? he thought. *Will not one of them betray me or lose faith enough to turn against me?*

The window looked out onto the front yard where a line of soldiers stood at attention, a few colourful figures waiting in line in front of them. Matrios recognized them—the muscular woman from the inn, the thin man, and the stocky dwarf. Someone was talking to the soldiers.

At that moment, the prince rushed past the bed and grabbed the clothes that had been laid out for him by a servant the night before. Dressing as he went, he ran down the corridors and stairs, which he'd seen only in the dark. Just inside the main entrance to the building, the young girl, Margaret, was arguing with the servants.

"I don't care who wanted to see them! They can't come in here! Not some dirty bandits!" Margaret yelled at an old man, apparently a servant.

"I understand, my lady, but the dwarf woman refuses to leave them outside." The servant bowed.

"I don't care!" She kicked the old man's shin, which made him fall to the ground.

Matrios stepped into the middle of the argument and looked at the girl with a disgust that was indescribable. Then he turned to the servant. "Are you all right?" It was then that he noticed that the man had extremely long eyebrows, and he realized that he was an elf. When the elven servant looked up at the prince, the elongated chin proved Matrios's assumption. And, when Matrios crouched down beside the old elf helpfully, the elf just raised his hands to protect his face.

"He's just a dirty elf!" Margaret spat, watching Matrios questioningly.

With a kind smile, Matrios held out his hand to help the elf servant, but he refused, and through gritted teeth, he rose on his own to his aching feet. "Excuse me, my lady. I'll inform the soldiers immediately." He bent, balancing on one leg, and limped out the door.

"What do you want here?" Margaret turned to Matrios.

"I now know where Elizabeth gets her hatred from." He looked at her with a fury that would have come from hell, and she was horrified by the look in his eyes that tore her soul apart. "Do what you want." She turned away, terrified, and left Matrios there.

"Is there no hierarchy in the Republic?" he muttered to himself.

Matrios watched with angry eyes as Margaret stepped outside through one of the massive front doors. Outside, the parties were almost jumping into each other as the soldiers held the dwarf back. The mercenaries suddenly drew their weapons, whereupon the soldiers pointed their spears forward and pushed the short woman with the scorched haired over, which only inflamed the anger of the woman and her companions.

"You're here at last!" Shrike, in blackbird form, landed on Matrios' shoulder as he stepped outside.

"Shrike!" said the man, surprised. "How did you find me?"

"It's not easy to get that stale smell out of my head after you let me to sleep in your coat," he said contemptuously. "I don't know if it's the tiredness or your smell that's got me down," he spat insultingly.

"What's going on?" Matrios asked, ignoring the bird-beast's insult.

"Some short, fat kid is here barking at the soldiers that the fat man himself sent him here to talk to you, but they won't let her through," he quickly explained.

"I see." Matrios quickly understood. "Would you do me a favour?"

"No."

"It would be fun." He smiled wryly.

"You son of a bitch! I'm in."

From Matrios's shoulder, the bird-beast flew high. When he reached about ten metres above the ground, he quickly transformed. Then he dove down, swooping between the two bickering sides with a deafening roar. The altercation had been slowly intensifying. At the sight of the huge bird-beast, the soldiers, clamouring for their mothers and throwing down their weapons, rushed past the prince, falling over each other, while the adventurers immediately leapt into attack formation, surrounding the dwarf woman and protecting her with their bodies.

"Wait!" ordered the woman in the dark clothes. "That same creature was at the inn!"

"Gods be good!" Matrios walked closer with a malicious smile. "I see you have recognized my little pet!"

"Your mother were a pet, you bastard!" Shrike said. Shrike stalked off, but Matrios ignored him and continued his role.

"You almost got our partner killed!" cried the dwarf warrior.

"I'm sorry to hear that." Matrios stopped about ten meters in front of them. Then Shrike, back in blackbird form, flew onto his shoulder.

"I'll have your head, you bastard!" cursed the dwarf.

"Get down, Magor!" said Morrigan, the human woman, putting away her weapon.

"Who the grief is this whoreson, Morrigan?" the dwarf asked.

"He would be Matrios Hritan, the third son of the Hritani king, the Vulture Prince, the Whoremonger, and I believe there are forty other names of such glory!" Morrigan laughed, resting her hands on the hilts of her knives, which she wore tucked into her leather belt.

"If we take his head, we shall have a great reward in the Pentrupun Empire," said the elf Faler, pointing his staff at the man.

"Be wise, Faler!" she smacked the elf on the head. "We are here to protect Olga," Morrigan said to the members, who lowered their weapons.

"Gromgar never see such creature," said the orc Gromgar.

"Gromgar has seen nothing but sand and shit!" Morrigan shushed the giant.

"All right, guys!" The dwarf woman pushed the others away. She turned to address Matrios. "If you're the one I need to talk to, then talk!" The stocky, red-haired woman wiped her heavily freckled nose, smiling while her eyes displayed mischief. Her shaggy hair was long, but she had tied it up on top of her massive head and secured it with an iron ring.

"That's a fat juicy dwarf!" said Shrike.

"I suppose you are the one my father-in-law did not wish to recommend." Matrios put his hands on his hips. "I would hire you to prepare something for me."

"And what would that be?"

Matrios hurried back into the house. When he returned, he was carrying his drawing. Meanwhile, the small group had been watching Shrike, who had merely been standing nearby in his blackbird form grooming his wing feathers.

"Little bird making mess at inn." The big orc Gromgar pointed at the creature.

"And you everywhere else!" Morrigan spat.

"Here it is!" Matrios handed over the paper to Olga as soon as he arrived.

The dwarf woman rolled her eyes as she opened the parchment. When she first understood what she is looking at, Matrios could see the shock on her face. Her hands trembled as she studied the parchment. Her legs bent as she ran her eyes over the lines. Her breathing quickened, and she looked up at the prince with a calm look. "How much?" she asked

"The drawing is not for sale."

"I'll beat you for it!" Olga said firmly.

"No need for that." Matrios raised his hand.

"This is clearly an old dwarven design!" exclaimed the woman. "If I don't take it from you, the dwarves of Khaz'morun will.

"I must spoil your mood."

"Why?"

"I'm flattered that you value my skills so highly, but I made the drawing myself."

She dropped the parchment and leapt forward. She punched the prince soundly in the stomach, causing him to immediately collapse onto the ground. "You liar!" she shouted. "Your kind can't even wipe their own arse properly, and you want me to believe that a whoreson like you drew such a miracle?" She continued her assault, but the others dragged the kick-slapping woman backwards.

Matrios's lungs were struggling. When he first fell to the ground, he had hit his forehead on a rather large stone. He now sported a rather large bruise, but as soon as he managed to pull himself together and regain his breath, he immediately called to Shrike. "Do nothing!" he warned the bird-beast.

"I wasn't going to," said the little creature in a bored tone.

"Who did you tell that to?" asked Morrigan the human woman.

Matrios pushed himself to all fours, then to one knee, and finally stood on his two feet again, panting. "I didn't lie about the drawing," he said.

"No shit! Here's a paper and charcoal!" Morrigan threw the tools on the ground at his feet.

"Draw here?" asked Matrios.

"If you can draw at least one straight line, I'll believe you!"

"That's it?" The prince snorted.

"Draw!" she snapped at him.

Matrios knelt down on the stones and spread the paper on the larger stone she headbutted. As he took up the writing instrument in his hand, he noticed that Olga seemed surprised at how easily and comfortably he grasped the thin tool.

"Nice pencil, though the carbon inlay is a bit thick," he commented.

"Draw!" she said in a quieter and more interested voice.

Matrios thought about what he could create to convince her, and then he realised that a simple drawing that he could quickly and easily put on paper would be the best choice. He pressed the magic wand to the page and then placed a series of short lines on the white background. It took a few minutes. The dwarf woman watched in awe as the chaos on the page slowly transformed into order. She watched the work in progress with a great sigh and a great hum. When he had finished, she took it from him and began to study it. It was not more than a minute before she lowered her hands and look up to the sky. "A human has outranked me," she said in a shaky voice that indicated she was close to tears.

The mercenaries froze for a moment as they watched their crushed companion childishly sobbing in the middle of the courtyard. Then Olga pulled herself together and stepped in front of Matrios. "Food and quarters!" she shouted at him without protest.

"What?" asked Matrios.

"Food and quarters. That's what I want for my pay!"

"Is this a joke?" he blurted out.

"And you must teach me to draw like this!" she added.

Matrios began to chuckle appreciatively. Then he got up from the ground, dusted off his trousers, and offered his hand. "I would be grateful for that!" He smiled kindly.

"I am honoured, master!" She shook his thin hand.

"Matrios will be enough." He laughed.

"Understood!" she replied, bowing.

"And less of that will be enough," Matrios said.

"But you're a prince." Olga smiled exaggeratedly.

"Did you have that in mind when you punched me in the stomach?" asked Matrios, raising an eyebrow.

"Did I?" She turned back to the others, who nodded in approval. "You see I didn't!" She looked back triumphantly.

"Whatever. We should sign a contract, I suppose." He rubbed his eyebrows.

"It's unnecessary. I'm fed up with humankind's papers," she sputtered. "You tell me where to go, and I'll be on my way." Her body language radiated wilfulness, and at that moment Matrios regretted having started talking to her.

"You're going alone?" he asked.

"Of course I'm not going alone! My friends are here!" She pointed to the people behind her.

"I don't think—" Faler the elf started.

I have no objection!" Morriganaised her hand.

"And where are we going?" Magor asked.

"To some hidden hole in the back of the gods, where nothing grows," the elf Faler whimpered.

"To the foot of the sleeping mountain," Matrios replied calmly.

"And my luck continues," said Faler in a monotone voice.

"If you don't want to come, you don't have to, Faler," said the dwarf woman Olga.

"It's not that I don't want to, but I know what will come out of it." The elf sighed.

"Don't whine!" said the dwarf Magor behind his back.

"How do you plan to get there?" Matrios asked.

"With a boat. I won't be walking all day!" said Olga. "By the way, my full name is Olga Thunderbrew."

"Thunderbrew?"

"An old name in Khaz'morun. My ancestors were brewers, but I'm more interested in my machines, much to my mother's chagrin."

"I guess that's why you're here and not there?" Matrios asked rhetorically.

"Maybe you're more than a Whoremonger. Perhaps you've got more intelligence in your head than in your cock?" Olga pointed to the prince's belt, chuckling.

"Most certainly, and I'll be waiting for you in a few days at the nearby harbour at the foot of Sleeping Mountain."

"Lest we arrive before you expect!" Olga said with a laugh.

Matrios addressed the others. "I suppose you won't be staying long."

"We are adventurers! We go where we please without boundaries, without worries." Morrigan smiled, as all her companions looked at her with approving glances. "As for our partner Kerion, we just met him, and I don't think you'd like a warrior beast any more than we would." She scratched the back of her head.

"Kerion is a real bull, but a good fighter!" Morrigan mused.

"It's your choice, but on my land the rules are strict." Matrios flaunted his principles

"Yes, for stealing an apple, they cut off not one but two of your fingers?" The elf showed his hands.

"If you steal out of hunger, it's forced labour." Matrios smiled.

"I'm starving, but you send me to work?" Faler said cynically.

"Starving with three meals a day? You must have a bird's stomach." Matrios observed.

"What?" Faler looked at the prince in wonder.

"I am a strict man, but I'm also forgiving and caring," Matrios said firmly.

"Caring, that's right! He always pays for his brothels!" Morrigan slapped her knee.

Just then, an ornate carriage rolled through the big gate. No sooner had the carriage stopped than the merchant Silagi jumped out and stepped in front of the group. He was surprised to see that nothing had come of the great fight he had been expecting, and he assumed the worst. "Where are my men?" he asked in a cold voice.

"They must be shivering somewhere in the shed," Matrios suggested.

"What have you done with them?" He turned to the adventurers.

"We? We did nothing!" announced Morrigan. "That strange beast that sits on the master's shoulder did it." She pointed at Shrike.

"Beast?" Silagi looked at the prince with surprise.

"You mean Shrike?" Matrios looked at the bird resting on his shoulder. "Yes, he jumped between the two parties to quell the fight that was breaking out."

"They're all such fools!" shouted the nobleman Silagi. Then he headed towards the house. "Shouldn't we start the discussion?" He smiled meekly back.

"We've already agreed," Matrios said with a smile.

"What?" The merchant was surprised.

"Right!" said Olga.

"We didn't agree on this!" Silagi grabbed the prince's shirt.

"We didn't agree on anything," explained Matrios. "My father-in-law just gave me a warm meal and a soft bed while his daughter and her children breathe." Matrios smiled.

Silagi sucked his teeth and released the prince, then looked up at him with a smile. "Well done." he said appreciatively. "You're smarter than I thought."

"Things have worked out in my favour!" Matrios said.

"What are you planning?" asked Olga.

"I think I'll head back to Brekan' Castle immediately," said Matrios. "I'd rather travel while it's still light and warm."

"Wait, my prince!" Silagi shouted impatiently.

"Yes?"

"I know you have something that would interest me." He twirled his moustache.

"I know what you mean." Matrios folded his arms in front of his chest. "You are well-informed. I suppose you were trying to extract this favour from me." Matrios smiled slyly.

"You know how it works. I thought that, since I am your father-in-law, perhaps I could use my connections and my knowledge to make a mutually beneficial arrangement."

"But you are more of a merchant than my wife's father," said Matrios.

"When life demands what life demands, you know how it goes." Silagi looked at the prince appreciatively.

"What is your offer?" Matrios lifted his chin.

"Sixty percent of foreign trade."

"Let's make it forty," Matrios said.

"Fifty, and I'll take over the domestic deliveries," the merchant retorted immediately.

"At a fixed price, by agreement." The prince smiled ominously.

"You want to fix the price of the product?"

"As long as I'm the only one who can produce it, I control the market."

"You should be called an empiremonger." Silagi sighed and then shook Matrios's hand in recognition.

"I roll the dice of the gods' lucky game." The prince slapped the merchant's iron palm.

"Then I'll have some company ready," said the old man.

"It's not important!" Matrios responded. "I meant I'm leaving right now."

"But you don't have a carriage!" Silagi looked at him curiously.

"I don't need one." Matrios pointed at the blackbird who still rested on his shoulder. "I have Shrike!"

The creature flopped sloppily off Matrios's shoulder and theatrically transformed into his huge beast form. The orc Gromgar roared in near ecstasy as the magic began to flow through the air. The others watched in amazement. Elizabeth's father fell back on his bottom as the hideous beast towered over him and he watched the prince clamber onto its back.

"See you in a few days!" Matrios said, and the giant creature squawked and began to rise, almost lazily, giving a noble dignity to the moment. Those who watched did so with open mouths and amazement.

"Don't fall off this time!" Shrike advised as Matrios balanced himself upright, trembling, on its back. Only when they were high enough to be barely visible did he lean down and grasp the beast's neck. Shrike scorched the air around them with a mighty whoosh and disappeared over the horizon leaving behind the astonished crowd who stood there, mouths agape, wondering.

Matrios and Shrike, quickly sailing through the morning wind, soon left the city walls behind. As they flew higher and higher, Matrios remembered that he had left his coat behind. "Shrike, can we fly lower?" he requested.

"For what?"

"I don't have my coat!"

"Your problem!" decided the creature

"I'll freeze here on your back!" shouted the prince.

"You sissy!" The creature tilted his body to the side and began to descend. Then he continued to soar in search of warm air currents.

For long hours, they sailed through the sky. To the freezing passenger, it must have seemed like much longer. In the evening, they stopped at an inn on the side of the road. Matrios dismounted the huge creature. Shrike turned wearily and then looked at the shivering man. He croaked contemptuously and looked at the rickety hut beside them. "Go inside and warm yourself by the fire," he suggested as he transformed and hopped wearily onto Matrios's shoulder.

"I had no idea it could be so cold in summer," Matrios said, shaking with cold. He hurried into the rustic bar with the bird on his shoulder and pushed open the door. All the field workers, who had planned to spend their last coins there, quickly surveyed the uninvited guest. Tattered clothes, dirty boots and wine-flowered faces greeted the prince, who was no better dressed himself. His own shirt had gained dirt stains when he rolled on the ground, his black trousers, perhaps the only fine acquisition in his costume, hung dusty and stained on him, while his tall boots were muddied up to his knees. He would have pulled the hood on his coat over his head, but it had been torn away. He just closed his eyes and strode to the bar. There the old peasant took a good, almost insultingly close and long look at him but just scowled and, instead of acknowledging him, drank the contents of his little mug, and then croaked sickly.

The barman turned to the newcomer. "What is it?" he asked politely.

"Do you have a room to let?" Matrios asked.

"The last little hole!" He held out his hand.

"How much?"

"A coin. If you want anything more, it's not in it, just so you know," he replied reluctantly

"It will do!" Matrios handed over the coin. "Can you give me something to eat?" he asked respectfully.

"There's sawdust bread and carrot soup!"

"What's in it?"

"I said carrot soup! It's got carrots!" The barman looked at Matrios as if he was a madman.

"Then I'll have two bowls and a plate of bread."

"Five coins!"

"It's a bit expensive," Matrios said.

"If you want to eat, that's the price. If you don't, then go away and leave it for someone else, you freeloader."

"Fine." Matrios sighed.

The innkeeper mumbled as he walked into the kitchen. Shortly, he returned with two bowls. They looked to be filled with water with a few carrot sticks floating around. The prince raised his eyebrows but said nothing. He took the spoon and looked at the "soup". He quickly finished the modest meal and pushed the second plate in front of Shrike. At least the bread seemed satisfying.

"Are you fucking with me?" the bird-beast looked up at him. "I'll have to have more than this," he said dismissively. Then he flew away through the glassless window.

Matrios was left alone. He spent a few minutes eating the second bowl of soup. It was only lukewarm, but it served to warm his chilled body.

He listened intently to the dozens of voices in the bar as conversation drifted among the peasants. They talked of all sorts of things, though they didn't seem friendly. Matrios thought to himself, *This is the best place to find out what the people really think, for a drunken man does not lie, and what is in his heart he will certainly tell his companions.* He ordered another pint of beer to make his sleep easier and to give him a reason to stay after he had received the key to the room.

"I tell you, there on the Sleeping Mountain is the prince himself!" said one of the peasants who sat not far from the bar. "And what can I do with that silver-spooned charlatan? I'm a day labourer in the field!" said another at the table.

"I say, let's go there!"

"What for, to kiss the prince's feet?"

"I heard from my nephew that, since the prince has been there, the place is as safe and fertile as a wild mare!" He struck the table.

"I heard it too, but it's the Vulture Prince, the Whoremonger there, and not the Wild Lion or the Golden Serpent!" This speaker waggled his moustache. "I think it's a lie!"

"I don't know which one he is."

"Believe me, my friend, you shouldn't go near that creature! It's not even that he despises men. He's so feverish they say his beast has turned him into a demon!" said the moustached man.

"Are you saying my nephew is lying?" retorted the previous speaker.

"The prince will starve to death soon," said another. "That place was last fertile when the Holy Mother walked the earth."

Matrios also eavesdropped on another conversation, which was taking place on the other side of the gamblers.

"What a big ass that woman has," cried a drunken bard. "She could fit an entire band on it, I tell you!"

"You're making it up." Another man nodded in agreement.

"I'll be a fly if I'm wrong!" The man spread his arms and spilled a considerable amount of beer out of his tankard onto the floor.

"What else was there?"

"I saw a large carriage with an escort and many small carriages rolling through the town right up to the gate," said the man, considering the diminished contents of his tankard.

"Perhaps the king found a new nobleman to trouble and wanted to chop off his head!" the bard guessed.

"We will attack the Brekan Castle," a rough voice rumbled through the ether.

Matrios lifted his head and slammed his tankard on the bar. He immediately turned his head towards the speakers and frantically searched for the source of the last ear-splitting comment. The patrons of the tavern didn't seem to hear his pounding, or they didn't care, as most of the people had drunk themselves nearly under the tables. Matrios decided he may only have misheard half a sentence. He looked back at his tankard, sighing.

"But isn't that where the Whoremonger is?" a drinker asked in a slurred voice.

The prince turned again, and this time he caught the owner of the voice with his eyes. A toothless and untidy large man sat at the table, surrounded by a few dark figures, a hood over his head. Matrios stood up and crept cautiously towards the drunk, hardly noticeable to those around him. When he got close to the table, he hid behind the thick beam, sitting down on the floor, playing drunk with his back against the beam.

"That's why we attack it!" said the hooded man.

"What good will that do you?" asked the merchant as he fished the carrots out of his soup.

"That's not your problem. You just take the grain to them! I believe you are delivering some already," the shady figure said angrily to the merchant.

"Aye, grain!" replied the man, a little offended. And then he slurped loudly from the hot soup.

"You'll take our grain to them too," he said.

"Is Parthonax helping the Crown nowadays?" the merchant looked up at the hooded man.

"He would like to support the prince's cause and make a sweet deal with him." He twinkled his suspicious eyes.

"How much do I get?" asked the merchant.

"You get three hundred now." He threw a purse on the table. "After we conquer the castle, you get twice as much."

"When?" The toothless man slapped down the money.

"Soon! We've got some inside men who can get us in.

"That'll do, then." The merchant rubbed his unshaven, unkempt chin.

"Deal?" the hooded man asked.

"I don't mind easy money." The merchant put the purse full of jingling coins away.

Matrios remained sitting on the floor after the hooded man had left the bar and the merchant had gone up to his room. He would remember that husky voice for the rest of his life, along with the merchant's face. Should he go after the man and kill him? It would be useless and would only give away the fact that he knew of their plan. Attack the merchant? Then those who might be following the wagon and watching to make sure it arrived in Brekan could report that the prince himself had taken care of the poisoned grain.

He sighed heavily as he thought about various scenarios despite the unquenchable rage that flamed in his heart. He rose, empty tankard in hand, and went up to his room. As he pushed open the creaking door, he saw the tiny room, almost a hole. It consisted of only a bed, tiny and uncomfortable, and a wall with the smallest of windows. Yet he felt good that the candle he had brought with him was not flickering on the floodplain of an unknown river. He was in a room where he could lay his head down to sleep. Though his thoughts wandered in his head, as soon as he blew out the flame, his eyes droped of their own accord, and sleep took him again, leading him to unknown lands.

Chapter 14

The next morning, the sun was already shining when Matrios got out of bed. He was surprised that he felt sufficiently rested and easy as he got out of his straw-stuffed bed. He stretched out, yawned, gathered his meagre possessions, opened the pitch-black door of the room, and ran down the stairs. He paused in front of the bar and beckoned in a kind way to the barman, who nodded his head wearily. Matrios pushed open the creaking wooden door and stepped painfully out from the darkness into the light. He raised his hand to his eyes as the sun's strong rays shone in his face, and when he got used to it, after a few long blinks, he finally sighed and whistled. Nothing stirred, not even the bushes on the other side of the road. Again he called and whistled, but still he could neither see nor hear anything. *Where in the world is that demon?* he asked himself.

"This is why you can't trust even one bird-beast!" He sighed as he started slowly walking down the road, having calculated his direction from the sun's position. The landscape had been inhospitable in the darkness, but the light showed a different face. Greenish meadows and swaying fields of yellow brought him pleasure as he trod the dust of the road. Above him, a mass of fat birds soared, singing their songs without a care or a flaw as they wound through the sky, sometimes chirping, sometimes descending, playing in the air. Every breath he took was full of the life of the surrounding forest, the sweet smell of its flowers, and the freshness of the wood. A few peasants were working in the fields, hoeing the soil and sometimes talking in the blazing sun, leaning on the handles of their tools. The prince stopped for a moment and looked at them. Two peasants turned to glance at the traveller. Matrios waved to them. After they waved back lazily, he continued on his merry way.

After perhaps a couple of hours of walking, Matrios spied a familiar small black shaped sitting on a low tree branch that overhung the road. When he got closer, he looked up at the sleeping bird-beast. He cleared his throat as the creature stirred and flapped its wings in fright. "What the hell?" croaked Shrike.

"Good morning," said the prince in an indifferent voice.

"Oh, you're here at last."

"I thought you were waiting at the inn."

"I was. But I saw a very beautiful fat fox, so I had to catch it." The creature pointed with its beak at the half-chewed carcass lying in the bush.

Matrios's stomach twisted as he looked at the mangled corpse, but he just looked away and sighed. "We must hurry back," said the prince impatiently.

"The dwarf woman won't be there for a few weeks, will she?" asked Shrike.

"I heard at the inn that someone is planning to attack the castle."

"Did you hear that right?"

"Yes."

"What luck," Shrike mused.

"Where are we, anyway?"

"Somewhere near the town we've been looking at."

"Near Egerton?"

"Yes, there." He flapped his wings.

"You brought me to the town that wants my head?" the prince snapped in annoyance.

"No. The city is about four hours away," said the creature calmly.

"And if bandits jump out of the bush?"

"You mean the ones lying in tatters about thirty yards from here?" Shrike looked at the man inquiringly.

"What?"

"I saw some armed men a little further on, so I had a little breakfast," he said calmly.

"You ate humans?"

"Same meat, only chewier," the bird-beast said thoughtfully. "It was just a couple of highwaymen. Life will be better without them." He spread his wings. "Save the wise words for yourself, body snatcher."

"Let's go." Matrios sighed angrily. "I've got a lot of work to do, and I haven't been home in four days."

The bird-beast just nodded triumphantly and flew off the branch. He had transformed before he landed on the ground and stood in front of the prince. Matrios climbed up onto the big back and wrapped his arms around the clumsy body. The creature spread its wings and lifted off the ground in a way that was now familiar to Matrios. He was now used to the fear that had always run through him upon lift-off. But now perhaps it could be said that he was less afraid each time he travelled on Shrike.

They flew low in the air, but still high enough that anyone looking up would have seen only a small unrecognizable speck soaring in the air like a strange eagle. After a few hours in the cold wind, however, the huge mountain, hitherto only a distant spectre, lonely and smoking in the middle of the great forest, seemed much closer. Matrios knew that home would soon appear on the horizon.

Matrios looked ahead, almost impatiently, his hands shading his eyes against the strong wind. Shrike began to descend, and soon he was whizzing along the road only a few feet from the ground where not a soul was to be seen. Shrike slowed, stirring up a huge cloud of dust with his wings. He finally landed on his feet on the wide gravel road, a short walk from the castle. The prince dismounted, stretched his limbs wearily, and began to walk slowly towards the castle.

"What happened?" Shrike flew up and landed on the man's shoulder.

"I was drinking when I heard someone say the name of the village."

"Is that all?"

"I moved a little closer and eavesdropped."

"Ah, I see!"

"A merchant will soon arrive at the castle with poisoned grain. The bandits hope we will eat it and become ill, which will weaken our defences," explained the prince.

"Well, if you're dying, you won't feel like fighting."

"Yes, and there's another problem."

"What's that?"

"There's someone inside who wants to help them. We need to find that someone!" said Matrios.

"Who could it be?"

"Anyone who works in the castle, except the old servant Tibald and the knights."

"You have any idea?"

"Not really. My first thought was the cook, but he seems too loyal, and he would have poisoned the entire castle long ago to make things easier for himself."

"Maybe. But what if that's plan B—if the poisoned grain doesn't work?"

"Could be, but I have a gut feeling about it," said Matrios.

"What about the maids?"

"I'd rather hide among them. They've got access to everything."

"How many are there? Ten?"

"Twelve."

"Station a knight among them so they can't send messages," suggested Shrike.

"I'm sure the spy will succeed even if she's under constant surveillance," said Matrios.

"How so?"

"A woman who fakes her life is always on alert, and humans are clever creatures."

"I think they are just delicious," commented Shrike.

"The 'inside person' must know the complete floor plan," mused Matrios.

"This will cast further suspicion on the servants."

"Yes, because the stable master is not allowed to enter the cellar and neither is anyone else," said Matrios. "So if it's not the cook, then it must be one the servants."

"We need to find out who the newest maid is. That should narrow it down," said Shrike.

"Then we'll need your help to follow her and find out if she is the spy or not."

"Follow?" said Shrike.

"If she leaves the castle, we need to know where she is, and it would be best to capture her and interrogate her before the attack. Who knows what she might know?"

"Why catch her? She's probably just some nobody that someone bribed," suggested Shrike.

"I don't think they'd trust such an important attack to an insignificant person who can't be trusted completely. They'd never know when she would to crack or fall out of character unless she's a trained actor. And she's probably not a highly trained strategist."

"I'd say I understand, but I'll leave it to you." The bird-beast sighed. "So, what do I do then? Attack her and carry her to you?"

"Not a chance!" snapped the prince. "Not too many knows that I can talk to you, and that's a huge advantage we can use as a weapon."

"So I should just spy for you?"

"Yes, in essence." The prince smiled.

"And what else do you want to do now?"

"You mean other than firming up this plan?"

"Yes."

"First, I need to find out how many crossbowmen we have, then how many bolts. Soon the Egerton army may move. We need to know how many men they have and how they are armed. Again, I need your help."

"We'll spy from above?" asked Shrike, getting excited.

"Yes. After we ascertain the size of their army, we'll have to hide the villagers so they don't get killed by the bandit army."

"It's strange that bandits do this," mused Shrike.

"I think they have someone backing them, but I'll talk to Verilion about that." The prince sighed.

The air was fresh and cool in the lush forest as the prince made his way to the castle. The offensive smell of the sulphur mine had not reached that location, and the chirping of birds filled the area with life. Rabbits and deer scampered across the road as he trudged along. He saw a dazzling world of green that he had never experienced in his previous life. He was lost in the moment just admiring the thousand colours of nature as he put one foot after the other. His worries faded away like a tuft of burnt wool. But as soon as he walked out of the forest, the sound of people replaced the nature's beautiful, sweet song. The sound of cows bellowing and the shouts of peasants filtered through the air. Matrios walked on calmly while the villagers looked at him questioningly. Why was the lord walking alone? He was a prince after all. And why was he wearing a white shirt? Several of the peasants did not recognise him at first. They thought he was a wanderer, and when they realised it was the prince tramping the road like a poor man, they were immediately startled and approached him.

"What is my grace doing here, my good sir?" asked an older peasant, taking off his hat.

"I'm just taking a breather," replied the prince.

"And the knights?" the peasant looked round.

"It's good to be alone, I suppose."

"Don't mind me wasting your time, but aren't you afraid? You are such a great man, and yet you are as alone as can be! If a bandit were to see you, who knows what inhuman things he would do to you, my good lord!"

"Don't worry about me. The bandits have been afraid to come near the territory for weeks!" The prince laughed.

"Not so, my dear sir!" said the man.

"What?"

"The other day, two adventurers caught a rascal!" said the man.

"Really?"

"I'll die if it isn't so!" swore the man.

"It will all change slowly." The prince smiled and looked down the road where two patrols marched at the bottom of the hill. When the two guards saw the prince, they were surprised. They approached with quick steps, and when they reached the prince, they knelt.

"Good sir!" said the taller of the two. "We will escort you back to the castle!"

"All right," said the prince appreciatively.

The peasant got back behind the plough, and the two guards took the prince in their protection and, without a word, accompanied Matrios who, like a fascinated child, feasted his eyes on the beauty of the surrounding fields and ploughs.

When they reached the castle, the sun was setting, and under red clouds, a cold rain was gathering. Matrios walked through the gate and into the wide courtyard, noting the tents that dotted the lawn. He looked around the courtyard, which was unchanged and still, and then he heard a loud shout above his head.

"Prince Matrios has come!" a soldier shouted, and the people of the castle began to stir.

Elizabeth came out of the door with Tibald and Verilion at her side and Adalanna behind her. Linary immediately untangled herself from her mother's arms and ran down the stairs, throwing herself into her father's arms.

Matrios was surprised at first, but with a sweet smile, he embraced the tiny body and felt he had come home. Verilion and Tibald bowed to him, as did the elf behind them. Matrios settled the little girl on his arm and greeted the assembled people. "I have arrived at home," he announced sentimentally.

"My lord, welcome home." Elizabeth curtsied in her beautiful dress. Matrios' face flushed red as he stared at the beautiful woman reverently.

"Was the wind good, sir?" Verilion asked.

"It was cold." The prince laughed.

"I'll have a bath prepared for you," said Tibald.

"I'd thank you for that, and something to eat, if you please."

"Of course, my lord!" The old man replied.

Matrios turned to Adalanna. "I see you can stand unaided now."

"Yes. I've been helping Lord Verilion with the patrols for days," said the elf.

"She has been a good help," praised the knight.

"Uhum." Elizabeth cleared her throat.

Matrios turned to the woman. "You look beautiful as always."

"Who is this Elian?" she asked, ignoring his flattery.

"A disowned son of a nobleman," explained Matrios.

"He blew up the entire cellar!" said the woman coolly.

"Oh my god!"

"Was it your idea?" asked Elizabeth angrily.

"Yes, but … is he all right?" Matrios asked weakly.

"The knights did their best, my good lord," reported Verilion.

"Did I … cause his death?" The strength drained from his legs, and he began to sway.

"He has lost only his left arm. He also received many burns all over his body," said the knight.

"He is alive?" Matrios looked up.

"Yes, but he is sleeping."

"Which room is he in?"

"The third room in the east wing," said the big knight.

Matrios transferred Linary to Elizabeth's arms and took off at a run for the castle. He went at such a pace that even Adalanna could not follow him. He leaped at the door, slamming it open with great force. He ran up the stairs, through the reddish corridors, and finally slammed open the door of the room.

The young boy was panting heavily as he lay under the quilts. Matrios stepped closer in disbelief, his feet almost skidding on the ground. He noticed the twisted healing skin where the bend of the elbow should have been. He was horrified and blamed himself. He clenched his fists and thought, *How could I have been so irresponsible?* He felt guilty for crippling an unfortunate boy with his own carelessness. Adalanna was the first to arrive after him, but she did not enter the room. She only stood outside the door and watched her master anxiously as he collapsed into himself.

Matrios had only self-critical thoughts. *How could I have put such a dangerous thing in the hands of such a young boy!*

"Lord … Mat … rios?" the boy spoke as his severed limb reached out to touch Matrios's hand.

Matrios looked from the burned stump to the boy's face. He was startled, and he wondered if Elian would scold him or blame him for the loss of his hand. But Elian only opened his eyes sleepily and gave him a veiled look.

"Seven times as much sulphur as salt and half as much coal as salt," the boy mumbled.

Matrios didn't understand what the boy was talking about at first, but when the meaning cut sharply through the black clouds in his mind, he just smiled in recognition. "Well done!" The prince leaned over the young man and patted his shoulder in acknowledgement.

Then the boy's smile changed. His face was as full of joy as the summer sun in a cloudless sky. Tears streamed down his scarred cheeks as the weight of the man's hand lifted the burden from his thin shoulders. "Is it true, sir?" asked the boy.

"What, Elian?"

"I have lost my left hand?" he asked, trying to overcome his crying.

Matrios couldn't answer. He put his hand to his face and covered his eyes in shame.

"I've been useful to someone at last." Elian smiled, and the prince looked at him in surprise. "My father always beat me when he saw a book in my hand instead of a sword," said the boy. "Now that I no longer have my hand, he can no longer force me to swing a sword!"

"Don't talk nonsense," said the prince.

"I will no longer be able to serve your lordship." Elian's face showed his disappointment. "At last, someone gave me a chance to prove myself, and then …" He lifted the stump and looked at the burnt limb. "I'm no good for anything now." He replaced the damaged arm onto the white sheet powerlessly.

"It's my fault," Matrios said. "It's my fault that this happened to you." He confessed his crime, humiliated.

"You told me not to produce too much, but I accidentally knocked over the candle on the table, and all the materials caught fire," explained Elain. "I won't be able to do much with one hand."

"What would you do?"

"I've become useless. I have no reason to live now." Elain sighed powerlessly.

"What if you could stay here?" offered the prince.

"I thank you for your pity, my good prince, but I still have a little self-respect." The boy smiled.

"I need someone to take notes, and your experiment has succeeded. That was our agreement!" said the prince determinedly.

"What?" the boy opened his eyes in surprise.

"If you succeed in your experiment, you will no longer have to spend your nights outdoors, and I will honour your skills," recalled the prince. "I remember saying that."

"But with this stump—"

"Even without your hand." Matrios smiled. "A promise is a promise."

Elian pressed his lips together, and hot tears streamed from his eyes. He tried to wipe his face with his hand, but only moved the stump, then cupped his other hand over his face and wept.

"Rest, Elian. You are not homeless from today," said the prince, repentant and kind.

Chapter 15

There were only five people in the great hall. Matrios sat at the head of the table with Verilion and Elizabeth beside him. Tibald and Adalanna stood behind him. In the late afternoon, the light of the torches played upon their faces. The prince seemed to be lulled into deep thought, and then the knight's deep breathing and loud sigh broke the music of the crackling fire.

"What shall we do with them?" asked Elizabeth.

"The Egerton troops will be here in four days or so, if they move," said the knight.

"But their informer inside our castle is a bigger problem," said Elizabeth. "As long as he can keep them informed, they will know everything we do."

"We need to find this informer." Verilion thumped his hand on the table.

"But we don't know who he is! It could be anybody," said Elizabeth.

"It can't be anybody!" Matrios said.

"What do you mean?"

"If it's all about me, then we have to go back only a few months and find out who the spy is."

"But there are many newcomers here," said Verilion. "We first took in the bandit army, then the wandering people."

"This person must know the castle and must be close to us!" the prince pointed out.

"Why couldn't he have been here before us?" Elizabeth asked.

"Because the news spread only a few days before we arrived, but it provided a good window of time for someone to arrive and do something."

"What do you mean by that?" she asked.

"Magic works only by working within the body and within reaching distance. Isn't that so?" Matrios asked.

"Until you renewed it," said Verilion.

"Then a Doppler is a possibility? " Matrios sighed.

A Doppler?" Verilion staggered back as he struggled to say the word.

"What is a Doppler?" asked Elizabeth.

"I'd be interested to know where you've heard of the best assassins, my good sir." Verilion looked at him.

"If you're a member of the royal family, you'll find unwanted information."

And here I thought there would be some strange creature that could take the form of others, Matrios thought to himself.

"The Dopplers are a notorious but little-known band of assassins who descend from Bretburg. They are half elf and half human, able to change their shapes and voices with magic. However, these changes require a great deal of their precious energy, and the process is dangerous."

"And you think, my Lord, that someone would employ such a man?" Elizabeth asked.

"It's obvious."

"They are extremely expensive!" said Verilion.

"Are they so expensive that you can get a prince's head as an investment?" Matrios looked at the knight. *If you say that way, then there is a chance*, he thought to himself. "We are looking for someone who has access to everything and knows the secret places and passages in the castle," he suggested.

"Whoever it is must be no other than one of the servants," said Tibald.

"Really?" asked Elizabeth.

"They are the only ones who can go anywhere, and would not seem strange if they were there," said the servant Tibald.

"But it could be you." Matrios raised his eyebrows.

"There are few people who know about my lord's birthmark," said Tibald, bowing.

"Then it can't be you," said the prince as Elizabeth looked at the two men strangely.

"Then we all agree it's another one of the servants," Matrios said.

"How can we interrogate them all?" Verilion asked.

"A good question. The easiest way would be to imprison them all and interrogate them one by one."

"That's not gonna happen!" Elizabeth raised her voice.

"It would be the last scenario I would want too," Matrios said.

"What about questioning them one by one without putting them all in the dungeon?" asked Tibald.

"Well, that's a possibility, but what questions should we ask them?" said Matrios. "They could have found out almost everything in the last few weeks."

"If he had to kill someone to assume her shape or capture her," thought Verilion aloud, "We just have to find the one she … But what if he's already buried her?"

Cross-examination time." Matrios smiled.

"Cross-examination?" Elizabeth looked confused. "What do you mean?"

"Has any of you observed anything out of place lately?" Matrios asked everyone in the room.

Everyone thought carefully.

"I don't have anyone in mind." Verilion scratched the back of his head in shame.

But then Tibald snapped his fingers. "There is a servant who often does not know her place," he said.

"Does not know her place?" Matrios asked.

"She does things that no one asks her to do, like bringing tea to the elf and speaking in front of your lordship as if she were just trying to get out of her ranks," he explained.

"Really?" Matrios raised his hand to his lips. "And who is this?"

"Does my Lord remember the girl who told you about the plant and the bathwater?" Tibald stepped closer.

"I know that one!" said Elizabeth. "She can't braid hair properly even though her own is almost always braided neatly."

"If she wouldn't I haven't tasted it!" Matrios froze for a moment. "The plant is poisonous if you don't boil the outer sap from it. She probably didn't know that. And she probably didn't cook it long enough, and she probably used too low a temperature. Her process was enough to harden the inside but not enough to make the outer layer splinter!" He slapped his palms together.

"My lord?" said Tibald in surprise.

"Get the knights, Verilion!" Matrios turned to the big knight.

"At once!"

Matrios turned to the servant. "Tibald, take some men to fetch the maid, and get her sister too. We don't know which one is the informer!"

"But it's not the one—"

"Bring them to me!" He said firmly, turning to Verilion. "Verilion, three knights go and fetch Linary immediately! I don't want to leave a target in case the spy escapes! Anyone who leaves the castle will be fired upon immediately."

"Understood!"

The great knight walked out of the building at a brisk pace and summoned the knights under the cover of night. They unobtrusively left their posts one by one or in pairs and gathered in the great hall. The soldiers, with their new crossbows in hand, had been waiting for the moment when they could use their new invention in the field.

Tibald had been sent with three knights to fetch the servants. They walked slowly and as silently as possible, torches in hand, through the corridors as if on patrol, and then entered the quarters of the female servants. Tibald knew from the soldiers that many servants received nightly guests, for some of them had husbands on duty in the castle, but this night was different. They stopped at the bedside of the girl with the short chestnut brown hair, who had been awakened by the ringing footsteps. The knights pushed the Doppler and her sister from their beds before they could react. The Doppler, however, was slippery as a fish. Sparing no effort, she freed her hand from the grip of one of the knights and drew her thigh-mounted knife. She sliced at his throat in an instant. The blade easily penetrated the wool-reinforced folds of the padded jacket he wore, but it could not pierce the chain mail to wound the man. He jumped and choked, the women screamed, and the other knight let go of the Doppler and grabbed his weapon, but it was a mistake because the darkness favoured the assassin, and the blade ran into his throat from the front, the sharp metal tip snapping on his spine. The Doppler leapt over Tibald, knocking him over, causing his head to strike the edge of one of the beds. In the commotion, she escaped from the room, but her pursuers could see that her arm was wounded as she slipped out of the grip of the knight.

The guards who were milling about outside heard the noise of the scuffle and quickly focused their attention on the building. Through the windows, they saw the Doppler rushing through the corridors in her scanty attire, knife in hand. She came across more knights—Picon, Dana, and another knight who were escorting the sleepy little princess through the corridors.

Dana immediately cast a great light into the surroundings, and Picon leapt backwards with the girl in hand. The Doppler held the knife in front of her, and her other hand seemed to be in a bad state, as it hung lifelessly by her body as she panted like a dog. Dana couldn't use her weapon in the corridor because the spear was too long. It was difficult to manoeuvre it in the cramped interior, so she raised her hands in front of her and muttered.

The Doppler's eyes went wide as the glint of light turned to a streak in an instant, and all she could do was react by throwing herself away, so the dangerous, hot streak of energy from Dana's hands merely struck her shoulder and tore off her broken arm. She was unable to get up from the ground because of the pain that was as searing as burning iron on skin. One of the knights stepped up to her, wearing his helmet, and grabbed the helpless girl by the hair, but she still had her knife, and she aimed it at his head. The blade sliced along the edge of his helmet leaving a long, sharp cut. The knight, in retaliation, struck a powerful blow to the attacker's head, stunning her. He straightened up and gasped loudly. Then he bent again and dragged her by the hair all the way to the great hall.

Meanwhile, Dana ran after the other assassin and finally met her face to face. Already armed and dressed in her battle garb, she rushed at the knight.

Dana remained calm, however, and knew that all she had to do was hold the assassin off until reinforcements arrived. She opened her arms wide as if in a friendly gesture to the assassin's blades, and then a blinding light appeared in front of her. The assassin missed her target with the thrust, and with a mighty kick, the knight pushed her, pinning her against the wall.

Dana was already panting and could feel the sweat soaking her clothes under the armour. She knew if she used her magical skill one more time, she would collapse from exhaustion. She pulled up her spear and pointed it at her opponent who was now heading for the exit having decided it would be a good idea to run away from the exhausted knight, for her priority now was to escape. She turned on her heel and started to run, but Dana threw the spear after her, and she dodged it. She stopped for a moment as the weapon whizzed over her with great force, but she continued to try to leave the castle as quickly as possible.

Around the corner, the injured helmeted knight waited as he heard the sound of approaching footsteps. He swung his war hammer at chest level, but even though the Doppler was surprised, she able to leap over the weapon while, at the same time, striking him down with the hilt of her knife.

Behind them, the other knights saw their companions crumple. Not one to let the fight end so easily, Verilion pushed one of the knights aside and unleashed the power of his own crossbow. The projectile was so fast that it whistled through the ether like an invisible snake. It bit painfully into the woman's thigh, breaking the bone. The woman fell to the ground with a mighty cry. The pain inflicted by the broken projectile was so terrible that, even if she had wanted to slit her own throat, she had no mental strength and her consciousness left the body almost immediately.

The knights took the two assassins down to the great hall, stripped them of their clothes so that they had no hidden weapons, healed their wounds so that pain would not cloud their minds, and then shackled each to a stake each, with chains.

Once the healing had taken effect, the hired assassins woke up and realised they had been beaten.

"Who hired you?" Matrios asked the naked women.

Neither of them replied. They didn't even raise their eyes to see what was around them.

"If you don't answer, we will torture you!"

"Go ahead!" retorted the one-armed spy haughtily.

"Ah, so you're the tougher one." The prince got up from his chair with a smile on his face. "You are the one who offered me the plant!"

"And what of it?"

"I should be grateful for that." The prince bowed. "However, a party from Egerton is on its way to my castle, and I don't feel like wasting my time."

"How?" She seemed surprised.

"Just luck? The point is, I know about the plan, so you might as well tell me more. If you do, I'll spare your life, yours and your friend's." He stepped to the other side of the table, just a few feet away from the two chained women.

The one-armed woman just spat on the ground and blinked her eyes angrily in the darkness, while the other one looked at her leg in a dazed and unconscious way because the torturous wound was fading away so quickly.

"What are their names?" he turned to Elizabeth.

"I remember the one-armed one as Gwendolyn," she said. "I don't think I ever heard the other's name."

At Elizabeth's words, Gwendolyn flinched and raised her eyes to the lady with murderous intent.

"I'm sure they didn't use their own names." Matrios sighed. "Where are the real servants?" he asked.

"You know that," said the doppler, smiling.

"Yes, I suspected as much." said the prince sadly. He turned to Picon. "Picon, take my little girl away from here," said the prince, and then he rolled up his sleeves.

The little knight said nothing, just bowed and stormed off with Linary, accompanied by two knights.

"What happened, Verilion?" the prince leaned against the table.

"We couldn't save one of our men—Robert," he outlined, never taking his angry eyes off Gwendolyn, the one-armed woman.

"I slit his throat!" she said gloriously. "Just like slaughtering a pig." She teased the knight with her ugly speech and seemed to have succeeded.

"Wait! Her first," said Matrios pointing to the silent girl. "Bring some water. Cool her off."

Dana went into the kitchen and returned with a full bucket. She splashed the ice-cold water over the naked girl, who screamed loudly.

"You fucker!" The half-armed doppler jumped up, but Verilion punched her in the face with his bare fist, causing her to fall back to the ground, powerless.

"Matilda!" cried the younger girl. Now they knew Gwendolyn's true name.

"She seems to be more talkative." Matrios sighed sadly.

Matilda winced at the pain throbbing from her broken cheekbone. She took a deep breath and leapt up agilely, despite the chains, apparently no longer clutching her only remaining limb, and leapt at Matrios, surprising Verilion, but Shrike was ready and the transformed creature pinned her down in one leap, grabbing her neck with its beak and slashing her belly with its claws.

Matrios felt his stomach churn at the horrendous sight of the girl drowning in her own blood. He swallowed hard in disgust and ordered the bird-beast to desist. He had been trying to tear the flesh from the helpless girl's head with another grip. Shrike backed off and resumed his blackbird form as the girl writhed powerlessly.

"Matilda!" the younger girl screamed as she tried to reach out to her sister, belligerent and helpless, held back by the loudly rattling chains.

Matrios faltered as he saw their helplessness, and this empathy mixed with pity overrode the fact that he knew these two had probably killed more men than his knights had in war. Verilion had lost a companion because of them, so he could not let them live no matter what, or the great knight's loyalty might falter.

"Tell us all you know, and we will save your friend," Matrios said to the younger girl.

"Sister!" she screamed, not hearing the prince's words, while the blood was already streaming from her wrist as she tried to reach the suffering body.

"Heal her! Gods damn it!" Matrios said irritably to one of the knights, who immediately applied his magic to her wounds and secured her back onto the stake.

"What happened?" Matilda looked up weakly, her eyes veiled.

"Matilda!" sobbed the younger.

"Seri—" said Matilda.

"I'm here." The younger drew as close as she could.

"I saw the tree." Matilda smiled, her body red with blood.

"We'll go back together," cried Seri. "We'll go back to the tree," she repeated, brokenly.

Verilion was about to interrupt them, but Matrios stepped in front of him and stopped the great knight.

"Do you remember the tree?" Matilda looked at Seri powerlessly.

"Yes I do. We were supposed to wintering over there together," Seri said through tears as she relaxed her tensed body.

"I want to go back there." The half-armed girl Matilda said as she looked up at the ceiling.

Matrios lowered his hand, and Verilion stepped up to Matilda. He lifted his huge hand and looked into her veiled eyes, which were still searching the ceiling powerlessly, then looked at the great knight and saw a pain that pierced even his armour. He clasped his palms together. Then he relaxed and murmured healing magic at the girl, who was barely younger than Dana.

"What happened?" Matilda cried out a moment later.

"Seri!" she shouted at her sister. "I knew you weren't ready!" She turned to her and scolded the girl.

"Verilion!" Matrios said firmly. "If we want to get anything out of them, you'll have to torture that one," said the prince, pointing to Matilda.

"I … understand, sir," said the knight bitterly.

"Go on!" shouted Matilda. "I'm not telling you anything anyway!"

"I know," he said. He pointed to Seri. "She will be the one who will sing like a bird."

"Don't worry, Seri, nothing will happen." Matilda looked over with a wicked smile. "I'll die before you get anything out of me!" she glared at Matrios.

"We've been hired by a lord in the Dukedom of Berolt!" said Seri suddenly.

"Seri!" cried Matilda.

"We've been hired to spy for them!" Seri continued.

"So you are not Dopplers?"

"We are—"

"Seri!" shouted Matilda.

Seri's hair turned red and her face changed shape. Her skin turned purple, and her height dropped considerably. She stood with her hands raised in the chains attached to the pole that towered above her.

"You fool!" Matilda squeezed the words between her teeth, and then she also changed, her hair lengthening and becoming a lighter shade.

Their legs were stouter, their heads larger in proportion to their bodies, but still they hid the features of young girls beneath their strange appearance.

"I'm sorry, sister, but they rule over death," Seri explained.

"Oh gods, what are you talking about?" Matilda looked at Seri, puzzled.

"Moments ago, that creature tore you apart," Seri said with tears in his eyes.

"What?" Matilda looked up at the bird perched on Matrios's shoulder.

"It's a monster we haven't met yet," Seri said in horror.

"What are you talking about? I'm here!" Matilda pointed to herself and then noticed her severed hand, the stump twisted at the shoulder as if it had been torn off. "What the ..." the words escaped her lungs as she looked at the stump.

"If they start to torture us, they won't let you die." Seri looked at Matrios.

"Indeed, I would like to avoid torturing young girls and anyone else." Matrios sighed in relief.

"I told you we were hired by the Duchy of Berolt. Now let us go!" Seri demanded.

"Why should I?" he asked, folding his arms across his chest. "What do you know about the army? The timing is too good," he continued.

"Sheri, no!" Matilda said pleadingly.

"I'll tell you when you give me your word that we can leave as soon as you know everything!" Seri said. Matrios nodded in agreement.

"Get them some clothes." Matrios covered his eyes.

The knights loosened the chains enough for the girls to sit on the cold stone. Then they folded a quilt around each of the girls to cover them and for them sit on as Matrios continued to question them.

"The Duchy of Berolt is funding bandits to attack the surrounding Hritani villages," Seri said.

"I already found that out by myself." The prince sighed.

"What?" Seri said.

"Why would a city in the middle of two nations be an island in the hands of neither of them unless someone was secretly funding it? So now I'm certain that it was the Duchy of Berolt." Matrios bit off the sentence, not wanting to give out his own information. "It just made my life harder."

"Our job was to observe, and when the army arrived, facilitate the capture of the castle," Seri said.

"Seri!" the older girl Matilda shouted angrily.

"I'm sick of the way we live," shouted Seri, "hiding in the shadows and hurting people so we can have a place in the world!"

"Seri, that's why the clan—"

"The clan this, the clan that!" Seri said. "They're just using us! What do you think they'll need you for with one arm?"

"That's our fam—" started Matilda.

"A family doesn't make you kill people!" Seri cried, sobbing. "I just want it to end," she whispered, barely audible through her tears.

"We're finished!" Matilda sighed. "Hey, you big brute! Cut my head in two while you have a chance to avenge your companion on me."

"I would, gods see my soul, but my desire for revenge will not bring him back." Verilion sighed in grief.

"Ha? Wilt thou not take my head?" teased Matilda.

"For what? You are young!" said Verilion. "If I had taken revenge on all those who have taken from me someone I loved, I would still be wandering the battlefields drenched in blood and guts. I'm pleased with the loss of your hand and with the knowledge that you will never be of use to anyone again. Atone for all the deaths you have done."

"What the hell? Is everyone here a fool?" Matilda asked in disbelief.

"He's just tired." replied Matrios.

"Don't mess with me!"

"Why would I do that? You came here, endangered my family, and never even once looked around."

"What?" Matilda was stunned.

"When was the last time you saw a happy peasant?" asked the prince with a gentle smile.

"I don't—"

"Any army defeated without blood?"

"I don't—"

"A leader who wasn't slaughtered?" Matrios asked. "War costs human lives, but a battle doesn't have to. The crops we planted on the land have begun to grow and improve in the last few months. The sprouted seeds are much greener than they ever were in the past. You may never have had the chance, with all the terrible things that have happened to you, to look at the little good that is around you, but it surrounds you no matter how much darkness there is." Matrios sat down on the floor opposite the girl.

"Oh, what do you know?" Matilda said in a scornful voice.

"You may think I was born with a silver spoon in my mouth, but there is something no one knows about me that is more terrible than anything else." He smiled bitterly as images of his own past flashed before his mind's eye. "Everyone has a terrible story to tell. I am no different."

Matilda couldn't say anything. She just looked down and tried to cover herself with her hands under the quilt.

"Verilion!"

"Yes, sir?"

"Get the two girls a cell without windows."

"Without windows?" murmured Seri.

"No hard feelings, but I don't want them to escape." Matrios stood up.

"If you let us live," said Matilda, "we'll have a fate worse than death!"

"And what if you die but live?" He turned back.

"What does that mean?"

"Verilion, a question!"

"Please, sir!"

"Is there any kind of contract that cannot be broken?"

"Only perhaps the slave contract, such as Adalanna carries," the knight mused. Then he turned to the elf. "Excuse me, my lady, she *did* carry!" he corrected himself.

"Isn't the elf a slave?" asked Matilda, surprised.

"Hmm?" Matrios looked puzzled, but he left the outburst at that. "Can I make a contract—a seal—with these two?" he asked Verilion.

"Certainly!"

"What does it entail?"

"A blood contract, really, whereby one party cannot harm the other. It is a magical seal that binds the inner magic of the two people," explained the knight.

"Take them to the dungeon. Let them think on their lives. If they join my side, they will receive a seal and from then on, they can live in peace on my land as my personal spies, whom I will honour and will not force.

Matilda tried to speak up and defy the prince, but Seri, whose chains were being unlocked from the stake, calmed her sister. The two girls embraced each other and were escorted by the knights to the dungeons where they were allowed to stay, dressed in new clothes and sleeping in comfortable beds, until the siege of the castle ended.

Chapter 16

After the capture of the spies, Matrios had to do all he could to fortify the castle for the siege to come. The stone walls, he believed, would hold for a long time, but the gate was a different matter. Behind the bridge of wooden pillars, the entrance, guarded by iron and strong timber could withstand the battle for a long time, but once it was torn down, they would be finished.

Even with fresh reinforcements, the garrison, originally consisting of barely seventy, had been increased only to slightly over two hundred, and even with that, there was not enough good-quality armour and weaponry for everyone.

Matrios' head was boiling from the sudden onslaught of trouble. He had ordered the villagers to flee as fast as they could to the mines to seek shelter in the tunnels, which extended far into the forest and out of the battle area.

The carpenters now carried all the timber they had cut to size to the castle and hoisted it over the walls. They were building a roof to protect those on the walls from the shower of arrows. They barricaded the entrance so that, even if the enemy broke through, it would be difficult to gain entrance.

A few days after the interrogation of the spies, a carriage rolled in under the gate driven by a toothless, big, fat, and sweaty peasant who snapped the reins. Verilion stood before the man as he dismounted with a loud grunt.

"Good day to you, my Lord." The bumpkin bowed.

"You carry grain?"

"I hear the prince buys food for a good price, so I brought my own to sell." He rubbed his hand.

"You did right. The prince was expecting fresh grain, but he prefers it a little roasted." Verilion snarled.

"Roasted?" The carter snapped his head up.

"Yes!" The knight laughed and turned to his soldiers. "Seize him!"

"What?" The toothless carter spat, but several large and menacing spears were aimed at his neck in an instant.

Verilion summoned additional knights. "Take the horses, remove the poisoned grain from the cart, and move it away," he ordered.

"Where d—" began the carter.

"Lord Matrios knows more than a dirty serf would think," said Verilion angrily, and he punched the man in the nose. The carter lay unconscious on the ground like a human skin rug.

The soldiers carried the food off the wagon, a little regretfully, as there was not much stocked in the warehouse, but the word *poisoned* meant that the oat grains were not to anyone's taste. When all the grain was in a huge pile on the ground, Verilion, with swift movements, doused it with oil and threw a flaming torch into it. The grain burned like dry chaff in a gale. The flames reached high, and in barely an hour, the bonfire had been reduced to just a grey pile of ash.

Later that day, the army moved out of the city. Shrike repeatedly rose to the skies and reported back to the prince the location and movements of the enemy. The defenders had to count on at least a thousand men. In the meantime, Elian had recovered and, even with only one arm, plunged into the reinvention of gunpowder. He and

Matrios put the potent mixture along with handfuls of small metal bits into several small, palm-sized cups made of clay. Due to its unsafe design, the resulting grenade was tested by one of the soldiers who threw it to the outer edge of the castle. As the powder exploded in the air, the deadly bits of shrapnel were thrown in all directions, leaving only a cloud of white smoke and a bang so loud that it caused a ringing in the ears even at a great distance.

A week later, however, as the preparations were slowly coming to an end in the setting sun, Matrios stood in the courtyard. From the ramparts, Verilion called to him. "My Lord Matrios! The village of Brekan is on fire!" Matrios ran up the wall and joined the knight. The flames coloured the evening sky red. Together they watched the enemy approaching carrying lit torches.

"They are here," Matrios said with deadly calm. With that, the battle of Brekan Castle had begun.

One by one, residents of the castle rushed up to watch the burning buildings and the oncoming army. Their anger was palpable. The soldiers were enraged. Matrios knew that all he had to do was to shout "Forward!" and they would take their revenge like beasts. But, instead he stood on the ramparts over the gate where everyone in the castle and in the courtyard could see him. Into the hush Matrios shouted, "Everybody in position! Let's give them what they deserve. If it worked there, it will work here!" He rubbed his palms together nervously. "Good people of Brekan and the veterans of the true army! You have seen the flames our enemy has set!" he cried.

"Let them burn!"

"Damn them!"

"Dirty worms!"

The curses rang out.

"I feel the same anger that you do," Matrios continued. "This great band of hoodlums has come to trample our land and frighten our children! Can we let them do this?

"No!"

"I'll kill them!"

"Burn them!"

"We'll show this rabble what those who attack us and burn our homes deserve!"

"Yes!"

"I'll kill them!"

Matrios spoke again. "With the weapon of the future at our backs, with the magic of the blessed knights behind us, we'll strike them so many times that they'll run all the way home!" He raised his hands. "Let us show them what the heroic people of Brekan are worth!" He drew his sword from its scabbard while the reddish light of the sun shone.

In the shadow of the castle walls, the attackers set up their camp, quickly erecting barricades about fifty metres from the castle using surrounding trees. When their structures were finished, they took cover behind them.

"What are they waiting for?" Verilion asked.

"I suppose they're waiting for the two prisoners to open the gate," Matrios answered

"They can wait for that."

"Aren't they preparing for a siege?" Matrios looked out into the darkness where a hundred torches lit the distant view. "I see they have a battering ram, but to use it they'll have to fill the dry trench that surrounds the castle."

"They may try ladders."

"If they do, they're fools." The prince pointed to the poles near the wall, which his soldiers would use to knock down any ladders the enemy have. "As defenders, we shouldn't be the ones to start the fight."

"Is that why you sent a good part of the people to bed?"

"No, I did that because I don't believe the enemy will attack until dawn." Matrios said calmly. "I want our men well rested."

"True, I would do the same," said the knight. "Go to sleep, my good sir, this is not your fight."

"True, but it's good for the soldiers to see me on the wall." Matrios smiled.

"It's true!" the big man slapped him on the back. "Tomorrow morning will be decisive. Not the first, but it could be the last," said the big knight with a smile.

"What?"

"It was the soldiers' custom in my previous order to say that before every battle."

"Not very positive."

"Yes, and that's why it's good. It keeps me on the ground," said the knight, pulling a necklace from under his armour.

"What is that?"

"It is the necklace that belonged to my daughter Lana." He showed it to Matrios. "When she was four years old, she saw it in a merchant's shop and wouldn't let me rest until I bought it for her." He spoke with a blessed smile on his face.

"Don't you have a wife, Verilion?"

"No, my Lord. I have only one daughter left."

"Childbed fever?"

"Yes," said the knight, sighing.

"Why should that be?" mused the prince.

"Don't let your mind be distracted by other things. Concentrate on the battle at hand." He gently nudged the prince.

"I'm going to sleep," said Matrios. "See to the changing of the guard."

"I will, sir!"

◆

The next day at dawn, when the sun was just peeking out from behind the forest canopy, the attackers' patience seemed to run out. Their troops were on their feet. Soldiers carrying shields were waiting behind barricades at the edge of the forest. Archers were positioned in the distance, and cavalry waited off to the left. A battering ram had been positioned between the warriors not far from the main gate. It was covered with a wooden roof. Past the troops strode a man in ornate armour and black clothing, sword drawn. With a booming voice, he opened the charge.

Matrios was already standing over the main gate in his armour. In one hand, he carried his own shield decorated with a raven. In the other hand, he carried his old comrade, the ornate sword. He lowered the grate and drew his blade.

"Do you want to be here, my good lord?"

"I can't be shivering in the castle. The men need me here," he said, panting.

"He's seen battle before. You shouldn't be afraid of the sight of a gut." The knight laughed.

"I'm not used to it, but I hope I can handle it." The prince sighed and pushed himself away from the wall and turned back to address his men. "Let's show the enemy what hospitality means to us!" he shouted, and the men below him cheered loudly. Matrios turned to Verilion. "I want that knight killed as soon as possible, no matter what!"

"I understand. But, sir, there is nothing noble in that." He expressed his concern.

"Was it not he who sent spies and burned our village?"

"It is true, sir! If it saves the lives of others, then I will do it."

"Let us leave that honour to others. Let us not waste our honour on mercenaries and bandits."

The first contingent of the mercenaries moved in, raising shields over their heads as they approached with ladders. From behind them, the arrow shower began. Each man raised his shield in front of him and was thus fully protected against the sharp projectiles. After the first barrage, they lowered their wooden shields, and Matrios shouted. "Fire!" An answering barrage of over fifty crossbows was launched at the enemy archers in the rear. They were surprised to find the defenders engaging them. They were even more surprised when, with great accuracy, the arrows from the crossbows decimated the archers standing a hundred yards away. The great power of the hand-held weapons enabled the arrows to fly straight, while the arrows from the enemy longbows flew at wide arcs with less accuracy.

The castle archers were reloading. Those on the ramparts who were not armed with the lethal crossbows raised their shields against the continuous arrow fire. They opened the defences and fired outwards, hitting one enemy soldier after another. The enemy archers, numbering about two hundred, quickly scattered when they saw the bone-crushing bolts penetrating the armour of their comrades or tearing their limbs into two.

The enemy ladder-bearing soldiers meanwhile arrived at the castle wall and set to work erecting ladders made of long slats. As soon as one ladder was set up and the soldiers started to climb, one of the youngsters on the ramparts would grab one of the long sticks and simply push the ladders away from the wall. The soldiers who had been trying to climb fell with huge thuds on the ground. However, on their third attempt, groups of soldiers held onto the bottoms of the ladders, and one man on the ramparts was not enough to push them away.

"Grenades!" shouted Matrios. The defenders grabbed the small clay pots, lit the fuses, which burned rapidly, and threw them down towards the bottom of the ladders. There, the bandits looked at one another as the bombs clattered onto the soft ground. They didn't know what these strange things were. But they learned when huge explosions shook the ground and the sharp shrapnel ripped through limbs and heads, leaving soldiers injured and dead.

The defenders cheered. By this time, the archers, after the enemy bowmen had retreated, were able to concentrate and destroy the enemy from above. Their vantage point helped them to find the weak points in the armour and chain mail. However, the tide seemed to turn, because instead of surrendering, the enemy archers ducked behind the barricades and fired at the wall from less than fifty metres.

Then big wooden sledge started its assault with more than eight people moving the wooden structure. It was slow, but the unpleasant outcome seemed unavoidable.

"Fire bottles here!" said Matrios as the battering ram got closer to its target. Verilion and some of the other soldiers picked up the prepared vodka bottles and lit the cloths that had been stuck into them. Then they threw the fire bottles at the battering ram. Some missed, but the ones that hit the wooden structure exploded apart. The alcohol seeped into the wooden planks, and the fire consumed them. The clothes of some of the men who had been pushing the structure also burst into flame, and the men ran, terrified by the fire.

The battle had only been underway for half an hour, and the defenders were already in a better position. The man in black reappeared on horseback from behind the trees followed by hundreds of soldiers who stormed the castle.

"Verilion!" cried the prince. The great knight raised his mighty crossbow, cocked it, and aimed. He drew his armoured hand along the sides of the deadly machine. Just as he was about to release the power that resided in the metal, an arrow struck him in the shoulder, causing him to close his eyes for a moment, just enough to ensure that his ferocious shot did not hit the rider in the chest, but only pierced his shoulder and knocked him from the saddle. The rush of enemy soldiers did not subside; they had no time to tend to the great fallen leader, who staggered to his feet and began to retreat.

Verilion rallied and pushed the prince aside. He pulled the heavy weapon up with one hand and lifted it up on the wall. Without magic, he released its wrath once more. "For the kingdom!" the big man shouted. The arrow flew towards the cowardly fleeing broken-armed man and skewered him in the back of the neck. He immediately collapsed like a house of cards.

As soon as Matrios saw the warrior fall, he cried out at the top of his lungs, "Their leader is dead!" His announcement roared through the battle, and the castle guards and knights drew swords and waited for their enemies with such determination that they did not know whether they were fighting men or frenzied demons.

The wooden protective covering over the ramparts left little room for attackers, who, after arriving at that height on their ladders, could barely squeeze their way between the stout boards.

Taking advantage of this, from behind, the defenders used the sticks they had been used to push ladders down, to push climbers to their stomachs and to push down those who couldn't hold on as well, or else the crossbowmen shot them down at close range.

Shrike flew over Matrios's head. "Let me play a bit. " The bird-beast's voice echoed in Matrios's head as the creature flew off to the distant riders, who were already thirsting for blood. He dove between them causing a great commotion. All that could be heard were the roars of the men, the frightened whinnies of the horses, and the loud, guttural roar of the bird-beast. Then Shrike flew up again and the horses, trampling each other and the fallen riders, fled as far as they could.

While Matrios watched Shrike's carnage, some of the stronger enemy soldiers threw themselves across the ditch and cut the chain that held the suspension bridge in place. This was a great loss. The battering ram arrived, its frame charred by the flames. The first blow shook the sturdy gate. Immediately several soldiers on the ramparts stepped back, confidently. Fuelled by adrenaline, they threw grenades down onto the attackers, killing the ringleader. However one of them threw his grenade wide, and the small clay missile bounced off the wooden roof structure. As it ignited, the blast killed two of the defenders, causing confusion in their ranks.

All the attackers needed was this one mistake. The commotion enabled two enemy soldiers to enter the castle. They were hardened and experienced mercenaries, and soon five more followed them into the courtyard. All the defenders were trying to repel the fierce fighters. Many were injured in the heavy melee as more enemy soldiers charged the crowded castle walls. The defending knights managed to push back a bit, but by this time more of the enemy had arrived on three ladders. There were more than ten of them, and they kept coming.

Matrios ordered: "Knights, hold those in the courtyard back! Soldiers, take care of the intruders on the ladders!"

From below, someone threw up a fire bottle. As it exploded, it set fire to the clothes of many of the enemy soldiers, who danced off the wall in terror, hoping to make it to the moat in time.

"Water-blade!" shouted Picon from below, as he tried to save a soldier. He sent a sharp, deadly thread of waterjet that passed through shields and armour like a knife through butter, severing limbs and heads from some of the attackers. A reddish mist splashed across the wooden roof, cutting some planks from it. This was enough to bolster the brave knights. Swinging their war hammers, lances, maces, and swords, they cast their magic into their weapons so they could beat those who tried to flee in confusion.

One armed, Verilion swung his mighty hammer. Every blow was as deadly as the claws of a beast. He swung the metal mace weapon, and with one blow, the helmeted head of a mercenary was crushed. The last of the enemy were pushed down from the wall, many of them suffering broken limbs. Those who dropped their swords in terror were captured and shackled. Those who resisted were sent to the afterlife by the thrust of a spear.

The enemy finally gave up the fight. As they ran back to their camp, the crossbowmen on the ramparts tried to hunt down as many of them as possible in the distance. The defenders erupted in a huge cheer, and then Shrike appeared on the castle wall again. "Can I play as well?"

"As long as you don't get yourself in trouble," advised Matrios.

"How many should I leave?"

"None!" Matrios said, raising the grill after looking at the number of people tied up inside the castle wall.

"Good answer!" said the bird-beast. Then he flew up and disappeared into the trees.

As the noise of the battle and the shouts of the defenders died down, the thundering voice of death and the terrible screams of the Demon could be heard shaking the forest. Birds flew up from the foliage, and the surrounding wildlife swooped through the clearing of the dead. Mercenaries, throwing down their weapons, burst out of the shelter of the trees, and crossbowmen were given the opportunity to practice their skills.

And Shrike swooped out behind them, feathers and skin dripping with blood. The defenders, who had been killing their enemies with great glee, stood with blood frozen in their veins, unable to move from what they saw as the bird-beast tore a man in two at the waist with its claws on his wings and then crushed another man's skull with its beak, all the while its blatant roar ringing deafeningly from its throat.

Verilion watched, motionless and frozen by fear at the destruction he had never seen before. This was no longer a battle; it was slaughter. There was no honour or chivalry, just destruction—a stomach-churning, hideous rampage of gore that could consume a man's sanity in an instant.

One of the defenders vomited as Shrike's claws slashed a fleeing man, tearing him apart and leaving him as shreds in the grass.

Matrios noticed the disgust on the faces of his companions and gave a loud whistle. The creature looked up and staggered to its hind legs, giving its last roar, declaring victory. But instead, he ignited fear in the defenders.

Shrike transformed and slowly, gingerly flew back to perch on Matrios's hand. He shook himself, droplets of blood flying from his feathers. "Your armour looks better this way!" he remarked after the human blood had splashed and started to run down Matrios's silver armour.

All those present were silent as they watched the prince and the bird-beast he commanded. Matrios sheathed his sword, released the bird, and turned to face them. He sighed heavily, then took off his helmet and raised his hands to the sky. "Victory!" was the cry from the man's throat, and the people in the courtyard gave a great shout of joy.

But those who had watched the bird-beast did not shout or cheer; they just watched the prince, silent and terrified. *What kind of man is he who commands such destructive power,* one asked themselves.

The devastation that covered the entire clearing would have made even the most experienced mercenary sick to his stomach. At least ten bonfires were burning as the bodies of the enemy were cremated and the priest prayed. But the bodies of the ten heroic castle defenders were to be buried with great respect by the prince. Matrios noticed that the gravedigger was strangely large and never spoke, and he was only ever referred to by all as the priest's father. In no time at all, he had dug the necessary graves, and the ten defenders were buried with honour.

Those of the enemy who had remained—spared by the beast or simply unnoticed—had been quickly thrown into the dungeon with the others. From there they had been assigned to the mines to perform forced labour until they served out their sentences.

The people returned to the village, which had been reduced to rubble, leaving the prince with much more to do after the battle than he would have liked.

The sowing had been done, so few people were drawn from the fields.

Matrios had to increase the amount of sugar he could produce even if it would later cause great political interfere. He sent a letter to his father-in-law, and within a week, the issue of selling sugar was settled between them. The entire accumulated stock of sugar was handed over to the trading company, which filled the prince's purse with a considerable fortune.

Matrios hired carpenters to speed up the rebuilding of the village, and he was now producing eight sacks of sugar a day, which kept the merchant's cart busy from day to day.

As life slowly began to return to normal, the dwarf engineer arrived and started ordering the things he wanted from the prince. The new forge was going to be expensive, but Matrios knew well that sacrifices must be made for progress, so he invested in the future without further ado.

It took only a few months for the people of the two villages to complete the first houses, which were spacious, beautiful, and sturdy. They were built of stones hewn and trees cut by the prisoners. The hired carpenters cut and shaped the wood beautiful beams and planks. The abundant rubber-like material, it turned out, would not permanently fray if melted over a flame and left to cool, so the builders used it to insulate around the windows and doors. Thatch rooves made the dwellings cosy. By the time autumn arrived, quite a few houses had been completed.

Matrios was pleased, but his greatest joy came when, in mid-autumn, just as the harvest festival was due, Olga Thunderbrew finished the final touches on the structure that had rested under the quilt. It was time to erect it beside the castle.

"Would you like to reveal it?" the dwarf asked Matrios.

"You built it. It's your child." The prince bowed.

"You are better than I thought!" she said appreciatively. She pulled off the cloth under which the rough lines of the structure had been hidden, and the huge metal structure appeared, with a tube a little over three metres long and legs that sank heavily into the ground.

"Beautiful!" Matrios said, amazed.

"Not as good as you asked for." The dwarf scratched her head. "I couldn't quite get the recoil mechanism right, but it can be loaded from the rear." She kicked the bottom of the cannon.

"Well done!" Matrios clapped his hands.

"Now, shall we make that rifle thing?" asked Olga, determined to move on to the next challenge.

"First …" Matrios smiled mischievously, "lock and load!"

Lightning Source UK Ltd.
Milton Keynes UK
UKHW010240090223
416650UK00001B/44